47 Houses
On The Long Journey Home

Lenore De Pree

D1478510

First published by Dog Ear Publishing
4010 W. 86th Street, Ste H
Indianapolis, IN 46268
www.dogearpublishing.net

ISBN: 978-1-4575-2218-5

This book is printed on acid-free paper.

ed in the United States of America

DEDICATION

To Gordon
who grew up dreaming he could fly,
        and our delightful kids
        who often did-

        and all the people who wondered why
        we moved so many times.

SECTION ONE

1957-1962

CHAPTER ONE

CHICAGO MIDWAY AIRPORT IN 1957 was not a remarkable place. Only decades before it had been carved out of the black muck of the city's truck farms, and up on the rooftop observation deck the faint ghost of onions still hovered.

But to me, that afternoon, it was the center of the universe. It was here, almost two years before, that my husband of only four months had disappeared. I had watched his plane heading into the sky bound for Korea's no dependents allowed DMZ—watched that pin-dot disappear into nothing, ripping from me the most important human being I had ever known in my troubled young life.

I thought I would die...

But here I was—scanning that same sky.

Today he was coming home.

I glanced at the tall, dark-haired woman beside me—Gordon's mom. Although a generation separated us, we had much in common. We were survivors; both daughters of restless Midwestern Dutchmen. Her father had left Michigan to claim a too-good-to-be-true land grant out west, raising his family in a sod house, and mine had left Chicago to settle in a one-room log cabin in the back hills of Kentucky, and ended up raising 90 homeless mountain children.

We had both worked our way back to our origins; she on an Eastern trek as a nanny to three children, and I as a refugee from my father's radical religious cult. We both knew that life could be hard, and that you could not believe everything you heard.

I scanned the sky above the airport, watching the planes landing...

What would it be like to actually feel his physical body, the long-legged, broad shouldered man I had married—to know that he was real and not something I had dreamed? Goodness knows we had written enough letters—at least one a day, letters as full of love as we could send with an airmail stamp, photos as daring as the corner drugstore would print. There were packages from him with jewelry and pieces of silk, and even a whole, colorful, traditional Korean outfit. I tried it on and sent him a snapshot—all except the shoes. Did human beings really have feet that tiny?

I baked cookies and packed them into the right-sized metal box to send through APO…

Those two years seemed endless, hollow. I had been busy, though, getting up at five o'clock to spend a few hours writing before a nine o'clock bakery job. The book was a not too cleverly disguised novel of what had happened in Kentucky. I could never write that real story… it was too terrible.

More planes landing. More flights called. Where was he? What if the long separation had changed him? Would he be the same, level-headed, feet-on-the-ground person I remembered? Had his experiences in Korea changed his view of the world? He had written about renovating a chapel, about finding a Korean pastor who had an orphanage, many of the children Korean/American mixtures. He'd collected money from the other soldiers for the kids.

Oh Lord, I hoped he was not getting interested in orphans. I'd had that up to the eyeballs.

But what about me? Was I still the same breathlessly in love girl that he had left behind two years ago? Life had not been a picnic for me. My mother had a studio apartment and a foldout couch we shared. I did not even have enough privacy to cry at night without going into the bathroom and turning all the faucets on. She and my father were in the process of a divorce, and she had a dim view of men in general.

Sometimes, to get away from the gloomy atmosphere in Chicago, I took a Greyhound bus to Michigan for a visit with Gordon's family. Mom De Pree and I worked and talked together in the kitchen.

Living in a dormitory with 22 girls as I grew up, I had never learned to cook. Gordon's mom was an excellent cook. She could make an apple pie to die for.

Apple pie…

My mom had never once made an apple pie, for the simple reason that she was terrified of making a piecrust. Somewhere, something had spooked her about making crusts. Had she tried once and failed? I grew up thinking that piecrusts were definitely dangerous. If it couldn't be dumped into a graham cracker crust, forget it.

But Mom De Pree threw caution to the winds and did it. She knew it would be good, and of course it was.

When Gordon got back safely I vowed I would make apple pies for him forever.

More planes coming in and taking off. So many people going places, doing things. What exactly were we going to do when he returned? Beyond a second honeymoon, I was uncertain. All I really wanted was a nice little house on a quiet street. I wanted to have his babies, kids who grew up to have bikes and roller skates—a peaceful, normal, American life. He had wanted that too, but had I sensed some change in his last few letters? Had he (jokingly of course) mentioned something about Hong Kong?

For a moment the awful thought crossed my mind:

KOREA.

A painful word that had nearly ripped my heart out... Surely he wouldn't be thinking of going back to Korea!

Gordon's mom was tugging at my arm.

"They're calling his flight!" she shouted above the noise. "We'd better get downstairs to meet our boy!"

I saw him coming down the corridor, tall, bag slung over his shoulder, his face lit with that smile of pure delight. We seemed to move toward each other in slow motion, colliding in midair. I felt his arms around me and his lips warm on mine. All the fear and anxiety and loneliness of time melted in that kiss, and I knew that I loved this man so deeply and terribly that I would follow him to the ends of the earth, and never be apart from him again.

CHAPTER TWO

CUMBERLAND FALLS STATE PARK WAS a popular and powerful Kentucky destination in the late 1950s. The governor often met there with his cronies, and the newly constructed DuPont Lodge was a fashionable place to stay.

But when Gordon made reservations for our "second honeymoon," he was not thinking of the lodge. There were tiny, one-room log cabins tucked away in the pine forest surrounding the falls, and that was where we settled in.

It had been a great day, hiking through the Appalachian Forest, swinging along the rutted paths, stealing quick kisses and running on. This was the forest of my childhood. Only twenty miles from here I had spent the first part of my life, but what a difference being here now!

We walked along the guard-railed paths near the falls. Holding hands like two adventurers in paradise, we followed the path and took the daring "PROCEED AT YOUR OWN RISK" narrow trail that led under the falls. We clasped each other tightly as the mighty river rolled over our heads, falling before our eyes with a tremendous roar to the chasm below. We clung to each other wordlessly, in awe of the powerful life force around us and within us.

This was what we would discover.

This was what we would live.

Then it was night, black as pitch, with only fireflies punctuating the darkness. We stood on the little porch of the cabin, leaning on the railing, looking out into the forest, watching the pinpoints of light. We were almost shy in the wonder of actually being so alone together. The whole world was ours. How should we celebrate it... what could we do that we had never done before?

Both of us had grown up in very conservative households where no one ever drank or smoked, or used a swear word. It would never have occurred to us to break out a bottle of wine, but with a little twitch of a mischievous smile Gordon reached into his pocket and brought out a pack of cigarettes. He lit one for me, then for himself.

I was shocked and fascinated.

"I didn't know you smoked," I said

"I don't," he answered. "Tonight is different."

We stood there, two red dots in the darkness, feeling like we were breaking the eleventh commandment. I watched his profile, slightly illuminated by the cigarette, and caught a strained look around his eyes. Suddenly, I could feel it. There was something unspoken between us.

"What...?" I said quietly.

He hesitated. "I wanted to wait for just the right moment to discuss this," he began.

My heart sank to some awful place.

"It was too hard to write about, because I didn't want to upset you..."

I stopped breathing. What was he saying?

"There's a possible job opening in Seoul for a couple to run a USO type facility for U.S. servicemen."

I breathed.

"A couple?"

"Of course! I'd never, ever, go there without you. You didn't think I'd do that, did you, sweetheart?"

I didn't know what I had thought, but it was there, even under the fierce love for him, that low flat-line dread that something bad could happen...that life was like that.

He put his arm around me and gave me a warm smoky kiss.

"You've got to learn to trust me," he said quietly.

"I do..." It was true. I did trust him more than anyone else in the world, which wasn't saying much.

"Promise?"

"Promise."

His mind was moving on to the next step.

"We'd have to take a trip to New York and meet these people. They'd have to look us over and see if they think we could do the job."

It was quiet except for the nighttime sounds of the forest and a little wind.

I could see it. The little house on a peaceful street, the bikes parked in the driveway, the neighborhood school for the kids to go to, a normal American life—the life I had dreamed of living with him—it was sliding away.

"How would you feel about it?" he was asking.

I looked at him, standing there tall and powerful with that strange incongruous cigarette in his hand. I took in a long breath, trying to show how brave I was, and suddenly felt like I was going to throw up.

Korea. I had thought of Korea as hell. Was I willing to go to hell with him?

He was still standing there, waiting for my answer. What if I said no? What if I refused to do something obviously important to him? Would it somehow harm us, and the excitement we felt about being together?

I saw him quietly taking the pack of cigarettes out of his pocket, crushing them up and throwing them over the railing into the black woods.

And sometime, in the middle of that warm and powerful night, I knew I would go wherever he went, and the little dream house on a quiet street could wait.

Someday...

CHAPTER THREE

143 CENTENNIAL STREET IN ZEELAND, Michigan was the quintessential American house of the 1950s. It had three bedrooms and one bath, with a living-dining room and a kitchen big enough for the whole family to congregate around the table. It was a cozy place to be that morning, and the aroma of perked coffee and hot bran muffins created an aura of solidarity.

Dad De Pree, the short intense man seated at the head of the table, stirred his coffee.

"So, Gord, what's this job they offered you in New York?"

Gordon glanced at his mom taking muffins from the oven.

"Well, it's not really a job. I guess it's just a pre-job arrangement."

"They going to pay you?"

"Sure..."

"How do you feel about working for Presbyterians?"

That was the sticking point. The De Prees had been Dutch Reformed since the seventeen hundreds. Working for Presbyterians had the taint of going over to the other side, like changing from Democrat to Republican. Of course, that could be done. Mom always voted Democrat and Dad voted Republican, effectively canceling each other out.

Mom was running a knife around the muffins, popping them out of their holes.

"That's no problem," she said. "It's not like they'd be working for Catholics or something. But what I can't understand is, why are they sending you to New Mexico to train you for going to Korea?"

"They let us choose where we wanted to go," Gordon said. "We could go anywhere we wanted to in the U.S. so they could evaluate our work before sending us overseas, since we're still in our twenties."

"But why Cuba, New Mexico?"

Gordon buttered his muffin.

"I guess it just appealed to us because we've never been there."

Mom poured coffee, a small knowing smile around her lips.

"I thought so," she said. "You really are like my pa. Same sand in your shoes."

The back door opened and another one of the four brothers came in.

"Gord," he said, nodding.

The brothers all used one-syllable names. Even the one sister, Lila, was shortened to Li. On Centennial Street in Zeeland, Michigan, no one wasted words. The worst name you could call a man was a "blowbag," someone who talked too much, especially about himself.

There were things to do before we left. At the Ford dealership in Zeeland we found a forlorn looking blue Nash Rambler trade-in, one of those funny new cars that looked the same coming or going. It was considered a real bomb, but it was cheap and had low mileage, so we bought it for the long haul west.

And Dad De Pree might not be too sure about this non-job we had taken, but one thing he knew: we would need furniture. He let us look through some "extra" pieces he had in the store: a table and four chairs, a bed, a sofa and an armchair, even a desk and a bookcase, and arranged for them to be delivered to that far distant dot on the map out West.

The last thing we did in Michigan was to drive to Grand Rapids and deliver the manuscript I had written while Gordon was gone, hoping it would be published. Sometimes I hoped it wouldn't. Would people who knew me be able to decode it?

Then we loaded up our suitcases and started out. Past Chicago, across the Mississippi, through endless cornfields and into Colorado, then south. What a beautiful country, this America! Endless variety; endless wonder. What a place! Why were we leaving it?

We would be back soon...

It was well into the third day of driving before we actually climbed the barren mountains beyond Albuquerque and drove into the little town of Cuba. There was one main street with a restaurant, motel, gas station, a trading post, a grocery store, and non-descript storefronts. The fragrance of pinion wood and mesquite mixed with the smoky aroma of dried chili peppers hung in the air. Horses and pickup trucks, Navajo Indians and Latinos in big hats and cowboy boots completed the look of a Wild West movie scene.

And down on the far end of Main Street was a huge sign in bold black and white letters, looking like it was announcing the end of the world:

CUBA PRESBYTERIAN CHURCH

Beside it sat a low, square, adobe house with weeds growing up to the windows. This was it.

It took almost a week for the furniture to arrive, and we spent the time meeting people, trying to remember who was Valdez and Martinez, who the Montoyas were related to, and who did what at the church. People helped us chop down the weeds and wash the windows. We inspected the inside of the adobe house. It had four newly whitewashed rooms and a bath, clean and bare and ready to move in. It wasn't too bad.

The church was a different story. The walls inside were yellow with age. The small bell tower had settled and hung at a rakish angle. Gordon scanned the place with a Dutch eye. It needed a good cleaning and a coat of paint...and that ghastly highway sign had to go.

While we waited we stayed at the motel, coming down to the café every morning to breathe in the aromas and chat with the owner, who filled us in on local lore and gossip.

"Yeah, we're just a little truck-stop town," she said, "but we got some real interesting folks here...a couple of doctors."

"Two doctors? In a little place like this?" Gordon asked.

She laughed, a deep husky laugh.

"Yeah, probably got kicked out of somewhere else," she joked.

I had my eye on the corner fireplace beside our table. It was deep, rich-blue tile, beautiful and simple.

"Could we build a corner fireplace like that in our house?" I whispered.

"We won't be here that long," Gordon said quietly. "We'll just do the best we can with what's here."

The furniture truck finally came and we settled in. We put the bookcase between the kitchen and living room to divide up the space, and the other pieces fell in place—just enough. Gordon set up the desk in a small study and the bed in the bedroom. We went down to the Indian Trading Post and bargained for a small Navajo rug, strung up some Indian corn and red chili peppers, and were ready to go.

The first Sunday was interesting to say the least. There was no choir, no pianist. One of the doctors' wives pounded out a few hymns. Gordon had a simple introductory homily, bracketed by the usual liturgy fill-ins of a traditional service. After the last Amen, he went to the back to shake hands.

They were friendly and kind. He kept glancing up at the open bell tower, wondering when the bell would fall on his head.

The next week he got to work on the church. Volunteers helped him wash down the walls and put on a clean coat of white paint. He inquired at Smeltzer's Café and got a local carpenter to come and look at the bell tower. The fellow rather nervously agreed that it should come down, and recommended that the top half be cut off at the roof and the hole sealed up. The bell came down and sat in the hallway, safe and silent. As a final touch, Gordon painted out the huge sign on the highway, then just decided to tear it down. He barely had time to prepare his sermon, but went to bed Saturday night feeling good.

When Sunday came, he was confronted by Martinez, Guterez, Montoya and company.

"Where is our bell tower?" they demanded.

"It wasn't safe," Gordon explained. "I had it taken down."

"Without consulting the session?" they asked. "You do not do anything without consulting the session!"

"I was afraid it would fall on someone's head!"

"That bell has hung there for seventy-five years, and it has never fallen on anyone's head yet."

When we were back in our little adobe house eating lunch, Gordon looked like the bell had actually done just that.

"This isn't going to look good in New York," he worried.

But the next Sunday, Martinez and company wore their usual smiles, only slightly strained.

"That's all right," one of them said. "I always say a preacher's not worth his salt until he's at least thirty!"

Gordon had just had his twenty-seventh birthday.

The fall weather was settling in over the Jemez Mountains, and our little adobe house looked so good we decided to do some entertaining.

Doctor Johnson and Mister Moore were an odd couple who attended the church sometimes. Partly out of curiosity, we invited them over for dinner. Doctor Johnson was a big, motherly-looking older woman, grey haired and low voiced. Jay Moore, a plumber, was a small young man with an odd conjugation to his verbs.

"It sure fruz bad last night," he said, coming in and rubbing his hands, "That was our first big frizz!"

I wished we had our blue fireplace.

"Jay, the proper word is froze," Doctor Johnson said disapprovingly.

Jay looked embarrassed.

I wondered how in the world they ever got teamed up. It must have been some mis-conjugation of verbs while Jay had his head under the sink.

Doctor Johnson looked around the house while I prepared dinner.

"How long have you been married?" she asked.

"A little over two years."

"You planning to have children?"

"We're working on it," I smiled, hands busy.

"It's a big commitment, having kids," she commented. "I waited too long, and now it's too late. Actually, I got married because I wanted to have a warm kitchen and bake bread."

I laughed, wanting to tell her how much I longed to have a baby...how much time we had wasted being apart...but this was my kitchen, not her office.

"If you need any advice, come and see me."

"I will, when I start baking bread," I joked.

But the next time I saw her, I was in her little makeshift office on a back street with my knees up and her hand probing my abdomen.

She rolled her large round eyes.

"Oh, my gracious yes, my dear, you are pregnant," she nodded. "When did you have your last period?"

I never could remember.

"Two or three months ago?" I guessed

"That's close enough. You're pregnant."

"Really? Oh, my God! Oh, my God!"

I had suspected as much. It was at one of those enchilada suppers the women of the church gave. No one had pancake breakfasts or potluck dinners—it was Enchilada suppers, piled high and hot and oily, prepared by the women of the church. The women actually ran the church. The men were there to make official Spanish Presbyterian noises and pass motions. The women fed.

I had felt sick when I got up that morning, and only went to the supper because I was expected to. After a few bites of the hot spicy food I knew it was not going to stay down.

Gordon had glanced at me.

"Are you okay?"

"I can't eat this," I whispered.

"Give it to me," he said. "We can't act like we don't like it."

I had covertly scooted my food to his plate, leaving a little on mine. He began to eat quickly and appreciatively, telling Mrs. Valdez how delicious it was. He was sweating profusely, beads of water falling down his face.

But now the truth was out.

When I told him, Gordon held me close, then brushed tears from his eyes, laughing and crying.

"Sweetheart," he whispered, "we're going to have a family!"

"Where?" I asked, mixing his tears with mine.

"Right here!"

But that was not exactly what happened. At a little over three months I started to bleed. Doctor Johnson ordered me to stay in bed.

Word had come from Michigan. Zondervan Publishing House was going to publish my book, *Line Tree*. We signed a contract, and long sheets of galleys came in the mail. I sat propped up in bed going through them. Writing a book was curiously like having a baby. I was going to do them both at once.

We told our moms. They were pleased, but apprehensive. How good was the medical care up there?

It was Christmas. My mom sent us a baby layette.

It was Easter. The bleeding had stopped, and I was getting as big as a house.

We decided to spruce up the church for Easter. I built a life-size paper mache and chicken wire garden scene with a tomb and a stone to roll away, and Gordon directed a play for the children of the church. I sewed up a big black maternity dress and hovered in the background like a stray cow.

Doctor Johnson checked me out. She thumped my protruding belly and frowned.

"You've got something strange going on here," she said. "I would love to have the honor of delivering this baby, but I think you might have some unusual complications. You would be wise to be near the hospital in Albuquerque where they have more equipment."

And that is more like what happened.

We had been driving the hundred plus miles to Albuquerque every two weeks to buy groceries, and now we included regular visits to a doctor's office. We also made inquiries at a Presbyterian church on Silver SE.

They were in need of a youth director, and there was an empty house across the street. Through all the proper Presbyterian channels, we were reassigned to Albuquerque.

We moved, furniture and all, into a little white adobe house with a red Spanish tile roof and a walled-in courtyard. I might have lifted a few too many heavy things when Gordon was not looking.

The week we moved, Mom De Pree flew out to help us settle in the house on Silver SE.

"How long before the baby is due?" she asked, eyeing my belly.

"About five weeks," I said. I could hardly wait. I could hardly breathe. I was miserable. It was horribly hot in Albuquerque, and the baby was restless.

"This thing must be an octopus!" I complained. "I can feel it kicking in eight places!"

"We all think we have it bad the first time," she smiled. "You'll be okay…"

That night a call came from Michigan that Mom De Pree's mother, she of the sod house fame, was seriously ill, probably dying. We were driving her to the airport when my pains started. We called the hospital and they said to pack a bag and come.

Bless Doctor Johnson's heart. We would all have died if I had stayed in the mountains…

July 21, 1958, was a wonderful and terrible night. Ultrasound was not yet invented, and we had no inkling of what was about to happen.

The doctor put me out, aware that this would be difficult. I heard him mutter something about twins, and wished these doctors would stop joking when I was in such terrible pain.

At some undetermined length of time later, I was in a hospital bed and Gordon was leaning over me. I felt vaguely guilty.

"What did we have?" I asked. "A boy or a girl?"

His face had a beautiful smile shadowed with worry.

"Both!" he said, as proud as if he'd done it all himself.

The babies were five weeks early, one breech and one transverse, and both had to go into special oxygen cribs called isolettes. The girl was five pounds, but the boy only four pounds and a few ounces, and more fragile.

We had thought of boys' names and girls' names, but not twin names.

"Why not something Southwestern?" Gordon suggested.

"We promised my mom we'd name a girl after her," I reminded him.

"How about Marita?" he said. "That's almost like Marguerite."

"Marita and…and Miguel?"

"Ooooph. That would be too much," Gordon said. "What if they think we named him after San Miguel beer?"

"Well, we could do Michael."

And so it was. Marita and Michael. We were so excited about finding twin names that we never even thought of middle names.

One week after the twins were born my mom flew out to help. Marita was home, and I was nursing her. She was pink-cheeked and blond, with blue eyes and long lashes. I watched her greedily sucking nourishment from my body and knew she would be a strong person, a woman after my own heart. Michael was still in the isolette, trying to gain up to five pounds. We visited the hospital every day, and I looked through the window at him, longing for him. He looked so lonely. Did he wonder where his mother was? Why no one was holding him? They fed and changed him, but my heart ached. Wouldn't it be better for him to have a few germs and some love?

When he finally came home I tried to nurse both of them. They had to eat every two hours around the clock. I was exhausted and afraid I was starving them. Gordon had to go to work.

My mom took a good look at me.

"Go to bed and get some sleep," she commanded. "I'm going to boil some bottles and fix up a formula."

She did. She knew how to do it. She had done it for at least a dozen babies in Kentucky.

When I woke up from a long sleep, I sat in a big armchair with one baby on my lap and the other alongside, feeding them both at once.

The day of my 25th birthday the doorbell rang at Silver SE. The first box of 24 books came from Michigan, and I opened them with a sense of triumph. I was 25 and had two babies and a book published. What did I care where we lived?

Mom was still there when the letter came from New York. The Korean slot had been given to someone else, someone older and wiser. When Gordon read the letter aloud, I was almost disappointed. I had dreaded going to Korea so much it was almost like a solid wall I'd pushed against, and now it was gone. I felt like I was going to fall flat on my face.

"Now what?" my mom asked. I knew she was secretly hoping we'd forget about going overseas.

Fortunately, the Dutch Reformed Church had not given up on us. The powers in New York were more in cahoots than any of us mere mortals suspected. All on the same floor at 475 Riverside Drive, they knew the whole story.

We had another letter from our own group, offering us a job in Hong Kong at a place called Fenwick Pier. Built on the waterfront, it was a USO type facility catering especially to the Seventh Fleet, and the job was for three years. Were we interested?

We looked at each other and smiled.

Yes. YES! We would simply load up the babies and be off for an adventure. We'd finish out the year in Albuquerque, and by that time they would be strong enough to travel…and by the time they were ready to go to school we'd be back in the US.

Living on Silver SE was actually quite pleasant. The babies grew and filled out, so different from the starved little mites they had been. We set up a playpen on the living room floor and they reached out to each other, touching fingers and sharing fascination with a spot of sunshine on a blanket or a toy. I read voraciously and played soundtracks from Rogers and Hammerstein, belting out the lyrics along with *Carousel* or *Oklahoma*. A woman from the church babysat for us, and we explored the shops and eating places of Old Town, La Placita and La Hacienda, giving us a taste of wonderful Spanish food. We might as well enjoy it—we had only a few months left before our contract in Albuquerque expired. We were bound for an exciting adventure. We were in a heady state of bliss…reveling in our life together.

Both of the babies were blond and blue-eyed. They looked so Dutch. What would it be like to take them to a city where all the children were dark-eyed and raven-haired?

Under the excitement I felt a little stab of apprehension.

But we would be doing it together.

It would be good.

It would be more than good. With a love like ours, it would be wonderful no matter where we lived.

———————

The twins were eleven months old when we took the train from Albuquerque to Michigan to attend a meeting in the East where we would lay plans for the trip to Hong Kong. For some mysterious reason the sound of the train wheels going around and the sway of the cars on the tracks made me deathly nauseated. I could not keep a thing down. I was thin and tired.

Gordon took me to a doctor as soon as we were settled in Zeeland. He examined me and announced that I was four months pregnant.

"But I thought…" I protested.

"Whatever you thought, it didn't work," he commented.

"Oh no!" I wailed. "I feel like shooting you!"

"I'm afraid you've got the wrong man," he smiled smugly.

When we told Mom and Dad De Pree, Mom smiled and shook her head, and Dad said only one word:

"Gord!"

Dad could pack volumes in that one word.

At the meeting in New York, a woman named Ruth Ransom was our personnel advisor. She was a short motherly woman with a bushel-basket bosom and an indulgent smile.

"That's all right now," she said, patting my shoulder. "When we send out young married couples we always budget for mistakes. The only difference it will make is that you'll have to leave sooner than expected. The airlines won't let you fly past the fifth month."

Sooner than expected—like now.

CHAPTER FOUR

IT WAS JULY, 1959.

The old Kai Tak Airport in Hong Kong was nestled in a densely crowded area of Kowloon. We barely missed the harbor and the crisscrossed clotheslines strung up over the rooftops before we touched down on the broiling runway. The plane door opened and a wall of stifling wet heat hit us.

We picked up the babies, one each, and collected our belongings. The trip had been a nightmare, up through Alaska, down to Tokyo, and on to Hong Kong, more than thirty hours of flying time...one of the last prop jets Northwest Orient used to fly the route.

The De Velders met us at the airport. They were the "old China hands" of our group, and had been in Hong Kong ever since the Americans were chased out of China in 1949. Walter was rotund and kindly, with a head of wavy silver hair and a hearty laugh, the very epitome of "avuncular." Harriet, although American, had been born in China and was as slender as an Asian. She even had the self-deprecating manner of an old-fashioned Chinese wife down to a T.

They whisked us off to our hotel, Harriet fussing over the babies. She gave me a quick once-over to see if the baby showed yet. Of course, they knew.

Harriet was a nurse; always a nurse.

"Let us take over when we get to the hotel," she offered. "You need to get some rest. I hope you don't mind, but we've gone ahead and picked out two amahs for you—a woman and her daughter. I hope you'll like them."

The Four Seas Hotel on Prince Edward Road looked more organically grown than constructed. Its four floors of slightly yellowed, pre-war colonial construction blended into the cracked moldy sidewalk, and the multiple

Banyan trees in front of and beside it grasped at the ground with roots like old gnarled hands. Colored tropical birds and flowers flashed through the green.

The air was thick with the scent of crowded humanity, of sweltering heat and poor sanitation.

They had reserved a small suite on the second floor with a separate room for the babies, and there we met Ah Gum and Ah Chung, the mother and daughter who would live in our home and work for us. Clad in a black pants and white top, Ah Gum had a round face with a wide smile showing her gold front teeth. Ah Chung was a silent whisper of a young girl, standing slightly behind her mother.

I was too tired to be horrified.

Servants?

They took the twins from me and put me to bed. I either slept or passed out. God only knows.

The next time I saw Marita and Michael they were ensconced in a twin stroller Gordon had purchased at Whiteaways, being pushed around by the amahs and happily sucking lollipops supplied by Aunt Harriet.

We stayed at the Four Seas Hotel for two weeks while Gordon and Walter checked out the job at Fenwick Pier and housing that would be appropriate for our family. Although the DeVelders lived in Kowloon near their work, they thought a place in Repulse Bay might be better for our young children. They found a little two-bedroom flat for us near the beach that would be vacated by the end of the month.

While staying at the hotel we went down to the dining room every morning for breakfast. We had to be careful not to come down too early or the waiters would still be asleep on the tables, their beds for the night.

Every breakfast was the same: a good English breakfast of strong tea, hot porridge, square thick slices of white bread toasted, and orange marmalade. Sometimes they scrambled a few eggs, but that was considered superfluous. We didn't dare mention that we preferred coffee. That was too American.

In 1959, Hong Kong was still very much a refugee city. People had escaped from terrible conditions in mainland China and were sleeping on the streets. Long lines of desperate people cued up for whole wheat crackers and milk provided by Church World Service. Chinese hated milk and would rather have had rice, but anything was better than starving. When we took walks near the hotel, the poverty was appalling. Children's faces were covered in sores, and I was afraid our babies would catch some disease.

Tuberculosis was rampant. Harriet had told us that we would have to have the children inoculated with something called BCG shots.

I was relieved when the day came to move to Repulse Bay, although the crossing of the harbor was something of a trauma…

We were passing through the ticket booth at the Star Ferry, and Gordon had handed both the twins to me while he got the tickets. Just inside the ferry concourse a short, stocky Chinese woman was giving me the eye…a baby on the right, a baby on the left, and a little bulge in between.

She accosted Gordon.

"Why you make you wife so bizz?" she demanded. "I give you my catt!"

He looked at the proffered square.

HOT PANTS MARY MALONE
Queen of Navy
We Give You Service

He handed it back.

"Thanks," he smiled. "I think we can manage."

I gritted my teeth, hating this filthy place.

Welcome to Hong Kong.

But Repulse Bay was another world. We took the number six bus over the winding narrow road overlooking the sea, and got off at a shady neighborhood of low-rise apartments interspersed with beautiful old flowering Jacaranda trees. It was clean here, with air blowing fresh off the South China Sea.

The second floor apartment was perfect for our little family. It had two bedrooms and two baths, a living-dining room with a balcony, a tiny kitchen, and servants' quarters.

I still could not get used to having servants. It seemed so un-American.

We had brought nothing along but out clothes, so we went shopping at Navy Purchasing for some simple furniture. A rattan couch with bright flowered cushions, a few chairs, some hanging round Japanese paper lanterns, a woven mat for the floor, some large tropical plants from the local gardener who watered the flowers every morning, a table, and of course, beds. Our bed, two cribs, two high chairs…we would soon need three of everything.

There was no air conditioning, but large ceiling fans suspended from high ceilings circulated the ocean air, and it was blessedly cool.

Two babies, one coming, and no washer or dryer. The wash was done in the bathtub, scrubbing and plopping it up and down, wringing it out by hand and going up to hang it on the roof.

But I didn't have to do it—the amahs did it.

Marita and Michael were over a year now, and I took them to the beach to play. The waves washed up on the shore of Repulse Bay and the clean wind blew gently through the tropical trees.

I could get used to this.

Gordon was getting established at Fenwick Pier. The catholic priest who was handing over the job to him filled him in on the duties.

"You'll be the administrator of the pier," Father McCahey told him. "Most of the sailors come here on R&R from the ships of the Seventh Fleet…"

Gordon was looking the place over. Simple, clean lines, functional…not much to change… He'd better listen.

"…a lot of the men simply use it as a passageway to get to the street, hell bent on getting what they're looking for ashore, but a lot of other guys want advice on where to eat and where to shop, what's to see and buy to send home…"

Gordon knew that drill, having been in Korea, but here there was a new element.

"Of course," McCahey was saying, "all the shops in Wanchai want to be recommended by *Servicemen's Guides at Fenwick Pier*," he grinned, "so you'll get lots of gifts. Every tailor will want to make you a new suit—free—for your recommendation."

"How do you handle that?" Gordon asked. All those free suits sounded good.

"Very carefully. Your honor is on the line here."

Gordon looked at the priest with his clerical collar.

"Do I have to wear one of those?"

"Afraid so. It's the uniform, the way guys identify you or else, especially at your age, you might just be taken for one of the blokes."

So Gordon went out to one of the tailors in Wanchai and had short-sleeved black shirts made to fit white clerical collars.

It was safe enough. Not many sailors would be wanting one.

On his hours off we went for long walks in Repulse Bay, pushing the twin stroller, or leaving the kids with the amahs and going shopping downtown in Hong Kong. The stores were delightful—the British department stores with everything imaginable, the Dairy Farm with food from England, the open markets with fresh produce from the New Territories, and most of all, Cat Street, better known as Thieves Alley. We picked up a couple of shiny brass pots made for boiling Chinese herbs and an assortment of used temple gods to adorn our little apartment. We especially loved the red and

gold character called a kitchen god—of course our kitchen was too small and
crowded to put it there, and Ah Gum, who had been (partially) converted to
Christianity, would have been scandalized, so we put it on a shelf in the living room. At Navy Purchasing we found a tall brass niche that could be
hung on the wall for burning a red candle, and a beautiful blue and white
Indonesian batik of a Buddha head. Bit by bit we were building an environment in which we felt comfortable—it was more than comfortable; it ventured beyond American into the beginnings of exotic.

One day we went for a ride in a rickshaw, one of the red wooden con-
veyances parked in a circle at the Star Ferry.

"Are you sure we should do this?" I asked, eyeing the half-starved rickshaw man, his muscles and veins standing out sharply against his bones.

"He needs the business," Gordon said. "You have to deal with reality."

We sat on the hard wooden seat, bumping over the pavement on our
way to a tailor shop to have a couple of maternity dresses made. (Not many
sailors would be wanting those either!) I wasn't very big this time, so I knew
I wasn't having twins, but my clothes were getting too small. We had registered with an English doctor on the Hong Kong side, approved of and paid
for by Walter DeVelder, so we felt secure.

We bought the third crib and got it ready. This baby was not going to
be one of Ruth Ransom's budgeting mistakes; it was going to be a celebration—our first Hong Kong baby!

December came and we put up a Christmas tree. They were available
in downtown Hong Kong. Ships came in the harbor, bringing everything
from everywhere. Ornaments, Santas, all the Ho, Ho, Ho of a big city, but
it was only on the main streets. In the little shops and alleyways it was rice
and peanut oil as usual. Christmas was a foreign holiday, a good way for the
locals to make extra Hong Kong dollars to spend at Chinese New Year, and
no more.

It was almost Christmas when baby Deidra came, a quiet little birth
with none of the hysterics and bloodletting of the twins' arrival. She was
born at Matilda Hospital, halfway up Victoria Peak, on December 17, at a
normal seven pounds, with dark eyes and dark hair, as though she realized
she would have to fit into this world of dark-eyed babies. Actually, she
looked like Gordon's mom—the French Huguenot bleeding through the
Dutchness—pink cheeked and dark haired, and beautiful.

The Sisters, as the nurses at Matilda Hospital were called, might have
inspired me to produce a dozen babies. They laid Dede in my arms to feed,
then took her away so I could sleep. They drew my bath in a big soaking tub

and pampered me—brought me afternoon tea and scones, and Ovaltine to put me to sleep at night. It was like vacationing in a spa.

Gordon brought Ah Gum and Ah Chung in with the twins to see the new baby. They were only eighteen months old, and not too impressed.

But I was. I snuggled the new one to my breast and fed her with a deep satisfied joy.

Gordon was having trouble with his clerical collar. I had asked him to go to Whiteaways and get me a nursing bra. He was never shy about such things. To him, everything in real life was natural and good.

"May I help you?" asked a young Chinese clerk with a British accent.

"Yes, please. I need to get a nursing bra."

She eyed his collar.

"Are you a father?" she asked.

"I surely am…"

"I mean, are you a real father?"

She had probably gone to a Catholic girls' school.

"Yes…"

"Then why are you having a baby?"

"I'm not. My wife is," he consulted the scrap of paper in his pocket, "and she needs a 36C."

"Your wife?" The girl looked at him askance.

These foreigners were always breaking their own rules.

When I got home after a glorious week at Matilda Hospital, I was anxious to reclaim my turf.

Ah Gum was busy getting the twins potty trained. I thought it was a little early, but didn't want to interfere. She was the one who had to wash the diapers.

Three potty chairs had joined the furniture in the children's room. It was starting to look like a Baptist Church nursery. Every morning after breakfast Ah Gum seated the twins on their thrones, and only after they had produced were they free to play. I let her do her thing, busy with the new baby.

Occasionally, I checked to see what was going on. One morning I happened to see Marita leaning over toward Michael's potty chair with a puzzled look on her face. She looked carefully, then looked back at her own equipment and realized something was missing. I was just starting to suppress a laugh when Ah Gum came cruising in to see how her trainees were doing. She checked.

"Miko, you velly laughty boyo," she scolded. "You no go poo-poo!"

Michael looked guilty and slid down in his chair.

Then Ah Gum came and checked on Marita. "You good gul. Velly good gul" she praised, smiling.

And then she picked my daughter up and wiped her bottom with her finger.

I nearly croaked.

When Gordon came home that evening I was livid.

"I'm not going to have that country bumpkin trying to train our kids to poop like a dog on a leash!" I fumed, "and teaching them all this awful Pidgin English. Who knows what kind of psychological damage she could do!"

He put his arm around me and pulled me close.

"Calm down, love," he said quietly. "I'm sure it's not that bad. She's basically a good person, and they'll be okay. You can't take care of all these kids alone."

"Yes I can, and I will. I took care of four kids when I was nine years old."

"And that probably wasn't a very good idea either," he said. "Try to be calm about it. You've just had a baby and you need to take time to get back to normal."

I was not in the mood for a lecture on female hormones. I tried to listen, but the guilty look on Mike's face haunted me. He was such a sweet little boy, and no one was going to do this to him.

That week I told Ah Gum that I was saving money so my mother could come and visit, and I would not be able to afford her help after the end of the month. She was a smart woman and knew I was lying to her. At thirty dollars Hong Kong a month she knew it would take me forever to save up enough money for one Hong Kong fare, but she smiled and said she understood. She left.

And then I was alone.

I was the one washing the diapers in the bathtub and hanging them on the roof. And I was boiling the water so the children would not get sick.

For six weeks I took care of the children by myself. I cooked our food and was relieved not to have so many people underfoot in the small apartment. Gordon helped as much as he could, but he had to go to work.

I felt glorious. The tropical spring weather was warm and the sun was wonderful. We bought a little inflatable pool to put in the front yard under a big tree, and the twins played in the water while baby Deidra lay on a blanket, blinking at her new world. I was tan and for the first time I could remember, looked good in short shorts. I weighed 110 pounds. At five-six I felt ethereal...detached from Earth.

And then one day, climbing the stairs to the second floor, I realized I couldn't make it. I sat down just in time to keep myself from fainting while carrying the baby.

That night I was curled up with a searing pain biting through my mid-section.

Gordon called Harriet, the nurse.

"You'd better get her to the doctor," Harriet said. "I'll be over to help."

Whether I really needed the gall bladder surgery or not, no one will ever know, but I was relieved when the surgeon said I did. Harriet took Dede and we got temporary help. I had to stop nursing the baby. Harriet put her on a bottle, and I had ten days of rest in that wonderful hospital, and a huge scar across my midriff.

"Having three babies that close together can really take it out of your body," Dr. Watson said. "Maybe you should take it easy for a while."

"I wish you'd tie my tubes," I said. "I've got enough children."

"You're a healthy young woman of twenty six," he said, "and there's no way I'm going to do that. You never know what life will bring. One of your children could die, or you could get divorced and want to remarry. Someday you may deeply want another child, and I'm not going to be guilty of making that impossible."

I would remember those words, and live to thank him.

Deidra was baptized in a Chinese church by Walter DeVelder. I missed my mom and wished she were there to see the baby. What is it about having a baby that makes one want to present it to one's mother…the continuation of life?

We did get another amah, Ah Yi, a quiet shy little person who took up less psychological space, and I took over the raising of the kids.

That summer we were thinking of things we wanted to do while we were in Hong Kong. Two more years and we would be headed back to the States.

"What would you think of having sailors over once a week or so for a nice, simple, home-cooked supper?" Gordon suggested. "I know when I was in Korea and Americans invited me over for a meal, I really…"

"I'd have to do the cooking," I hesitated.

"I'd love to have some of your cooking once a week," he said. "Shall we try it?"

"If you'll go to the market and buy the food," I agreed.

So we did it, on Tuesdays.

The men were young, our age and even much younger. We cooked simple food, baked potatoes and meat loaf with a few exotic vegetables from the market, and always an apple pie. They never seemed to get enough homemade apple pie! I began to suspect Gordon's motives. He could have been guilty of setting up this whole elaborate scheme just to get an apple pie.

I remembered the apple pie lessons at Mom De Pree's house when he was in Korea. How could I have ever guessed I'd be feeding apple pie to sailors?

One day Gordon had a surprise for me.

"Guess who just showed up at the pier?" he said over the phone.

"I haven't the faintest idea."

"Winston... Winston, one of your brothers from Kentucky!"

"Winston?" I shouted. "Oh my god, you mean my Winston? What's he doing here?"

"I'll let him tell you. Shall I bring him home with me? He has shore leave."

"Of course!"

He came home with Gordon that evening, all of eighteen years old, dressed in a sailor suit and looking just like he did as a little boy—same blue eyes and shy grin, with sandy blond hair cut short.

I rushed over to him and gave him a hug that nearly crushed the life out of him. We both cried—and laughed—and cried.

He stayed with us that night, sleeping on the couch, and we talked for long hours. My parents had taken him and his other three siblings in when he was less than two years old, and he became my responsibility...my little brother.

He was from a family of beautiful children. His sister, Maxine, became my best friend, my sister. We grew up together in that rather insane, beautiful place, sharing secrets, sustaining each other, trying to avoid the madness that was slowly destroying my father's life. Everyone thought he was a saint. They honored and revered him while he was slowly going mad. No one knew... And then one day it exploded. The authorities rushed in. I fled, escaping my father's wrath. I had done it. I had exposed him. He was ready to kill me.

It exploded, and children like Winston were thrown out like swimmers in a shipwreck, except not all of them knew how to swim.

Maxine came to live with me in Chicago.

Winston went to live with his mother, a mother who was too busy courting her third husband to take care of him. He was left to fend for himself. At 14 he was too young to get a job, so he lied about his age. He saved money to get a used bike and couldn't afford to buy a coat. The weather got cold in Michigan and he caught a cold, then got pneumonia. He went to an emergency room and they put him in a hospital. He had no insurance, so they gave him a choice. He could go to a reform school for boys, or sign up for a kiddie cruise with the Navy. He chose the Navy. He had been in for three years.

"I tried to live like they taught us to at the home," he said. "I even got down on my knees by my bunk at night and said my prayers. The other guys thought that was hilarious. They decided to play a joke on me. One night on shore leave in Japan they got me drunk. I woke up in bed with some woman, and all of them laughing their asses off. I didn't know what was going on..."

I had tears streaming down my face. Had I let him down? Had I been too busy surviving myself to care what had happened to him and the other eighty-some children who had been wounded by my father? Was it my fault?

No. I decided it was not my fault. If I lived one good life and took care of my own family, that was about all I could do to make this a better world.

Winston left in the morning. I wondered if I would ever see him again.

Deidra began walking at nine months, tripping over the floor like a little bird in flight. She had also tossed her bottle aside, wanting to drink out of a cup like everyone else. The traffic on the floor was getting thick.

With three highchairs, mealtime was a zoo, especially since Mike had decided the funniest thing in the world was to pick up his bowl of oatmeal and dump it over his head. The cozy little apartment was getting a bit too cozy.

Next door, a bigger flat with more floor space opened up, and Walter agreed that we did need more space. We picked up our belongings and carried them next door, and were ready to go the next day. A few more lamps and cushions, and that was it.

After the move Ah Yi packed up and decided, she said, to go back to China, or maybe we decided to send her there the night we came home after a party at a friend's house and couldn't find the children.

We went to their room to check on them and found their cribs empty. We stared at each other, shocked. They were not in their beds. We ran into our room to see if they were possibly there. Nothing. We looked out on the balcony, in the servant's room, everywhere. We began to panic... Should we call the police? Had someone kidnapped them for ransom?

Gordon was picking up the phone to call when I happened to glance under the dining room table. There they were, all three of them, draped over Ah Yi like kittens over a mother cat—all sound asleep.

"Babies cry," she explained, "I no know what to do."

Whatever she had decided to do, we didn't want it done again, bless her heart. I think we all mutually decided to part company.

Living as an expatriate in Hong Kong in the 1950s was a very isolated experience. The DeVelders were our expanded family, and we got to know a group of people in the foreign community, but it was a group so far removed from Chinese life that we actually did not have any Chinese friends. There was a couple from Shanghai, Charlie Low and his wife Catherine, who we came to know through Fenwick Pier. Charlie had a steakhouse and bar down on the Wanchai Waterfront called the Diamond Horseshoe. It catered to sailors mostly, but many Americans went there for a good steak. The Pier recommended the restaurant, so in a way we were more business associates than friends.

As a good businessman, Charlie took care of his contacts. At Easter, Charlie sent our kids enormous Easter baskets with chocolate bunnies big enough to sicken a fleet. Catherine came to visit us, dressed in her best Chinese cheongsam and high heels. When I complimented her on her shoes, she had her shoemaker copy them in a pair for me...of course a size too small. The Chinese could not comprehend Dutch feet.

Working at Fenwick Pier, Gordon had contact with many expat volunteers who came to spend time chatting with American servicemen. They were women from the mighty American Women's Club, and wealthy British-Chinese women who formed the charitable aristocracy of Hong Kong.

One of them was a high-ranking Chinese woman whose father had once been the Episcopal Bishop (Chinese) of Hong Kong. One day she told Gordon about Saint Christopher's orphanage, an institution out in the New Territories where homeless Chinese children were raised and educated in a British-Christian manner, including teaching them fluent English.

"There's a girl..." she said, "fourteen years old, an outstanding student. She's passed her English exams at the highest level. She's been at Saint Christopher's since she was five years old."

"What about her family?"

"Her mother was a bar girl—wanted a better life for her child. But she's graduated from the school now and has no place to go."

Gordon was silent, waiting to hear the rest of it.

"Would you possibly know anyone who could take her in—give her room and board, and some small wages?" she asked.

Gordon talked to me about it that night. Her name was Pang Sut Jing (fresh-fallen snow) and her English name was Gina.

Gina. Maybe this would be a good solution. Amahs were not really working out for us, but I could use some help around the house. Maybe we could give her a home for the year before we went back to the States. We could give it a try.

She came to visit us in Repulse Bay, a tall, gangly, fourteen-year-old kid with sparking dark eyes and a soup-bowl haircut. We decided to take her, for some reason never realizing that though she seemed excited to be at an American's house, she let her sponsor do all the talking. We settled her in the bigger servant's quarters of the new apartment with a bedroom, a bath, and a balcony of her own, and hoped she would work out.

When we went to bed that night, Gordon asked me, "Did she say anything to you?"

I thought a moment. She had seemed cheerful, but no, come to think of it, I hadn't heard her say a word.

"They said she spoke fluent English," I puzzled, "but no, she didn't say anything to me—just shook her head yes when I asked her if she wanted to live with us."

"Hmm…maybe the woman who brought her here talked so much she couldn't get a word in edgewise," he said.

But the next morning, Gina was up and in the kitchen. Her eyes were as big as saucers and she moved around like a quiet little mouse. She played well with the children that day and they responded well to her. They chatted with her, but she let them do the talking.

There was something definitely strange. She eagerly did everything I asked, understanding perfectly and working willingly.

"Do you speak English?" I finally asked her that night, trying not to sound exasperated.

She shook her head yes, and disappeared into her room.

I tried everything. I took her to the beach and she played beautifully with the children, making a creative sandcastle. I laid out some pieces of fabric and asked if she'd like me to make her a dress. She nodded yes.

I was just about to tell Gordon that this was not going to work…

Then one day, nearly a week into her stay with us, we were doing the wash, using an old Norge washing machine Gordon had acquired from some expat who was leaving Hong Kong. It had a big wringer, and a motor run by plugging it into a transformer by the wall, converting the 220 electricity to 110. The electric breaker was nearby to shut off the current in case of any difficulty.

The venerable old machine was chuffing and puffing, churning its usual load of too many diapers. I offered one gingerly to the wringer and instead of coming out the other side of the roller, it began wrapping around it. Larger and larger the wad got, pulling more and more current into the machine. The wringer gave a loud POP.

I screamed, frozen with fear.

Gina walked calmly over to the electric breaker and flipped it off. Then she looked at me and grinned.

29

"I didn't know you were afraid of anything," she said perfectly.

I looked at her, stunned. How had I never guessed? She was afraid of me. And now that I was afraid, we were even.

Gina stayed on, and that was the beginning of a friendship of equals.

During that last year, Gordon took the six to midnight shift at the pier. More men were coming ashore in the evenings, and Wanchai was hopping. He needed to be there.

We fed the kids early and put them to bed. Gordon left for work, and Gina and I spent the hours until midnight working on a special project. I had decided to paint a portrait of her... such an interesting face.

Painting was not new to me. I had actually painted in oils all my teenage years. It was the one thing that had kept me sane during those crazy years of my father's social experiment with the lives of ninety children in Kentucky, and the one skill I had taken from that traumatic experience.

But now, here in Hong Kong, I had the time and incentive to take it up again.

In his work at Fenwick Pier, Gordon met many fascinating people. Father Zeller, a Catholic priest/artist, was one of them. Assigned to a post in China just before the communist takeover, he had stayed a bit too long in 1949, and found himself in prison.

Father Zeller was a consummate artist who was suddenly separated from his art. He had no paints, no brushes, and no canvas. In prison he improvised, scrounging paints, bits of wood, and scraps of buffalo horn. He began to do palette knife paintings, using different shapes and sizes of buffalo horn.

When he was finally released to Hong Kong, he took the idea with him. Now with plenty of art supplies, he painted beautiful palette knife portraits of Chinese children—mothers with children—people in their daily lives. He became famous and did a fabulous mural in the lobby of the Hilton Hotel on Queens Road, of women burning incense at the temple in Chung Jau. He was the darling of the American Women's Club.

Because he had chatted with Gordon at the pier, Father Zeller kindly came to our flat in Repulse Bay one day and shared his technique, rubbing paints into the canvas to form a ground, and touching the surface with lighter paints to form a luminescent effect. He spread a newspaper over his knees and deftly showed me the technique. No brushes. I was fascinated.

And so, on the late night shift, I painted Gina's face, that impish child-about-to-become-a-woman's face, those dark eyes and that shock of blue-black hair lighting up the gold of her skin.

I realized she was beautiful.

Gordon came home late those nights, tired and yet sometimes unable to sleep. By the time the pier was cleared of men and locked up for the evening, it was often one o'clock before he made it over the long curving road to Repulse Bay.

One night he came in and pulled off his uniform shirt with the clerical collar, throwing it on a chair. He sat on the edge of the bed, elbows on his knees, thoughtful.

"I'll be glad when this is over," he said, sighing.

"Why, is something wrong?"

"Nothing unusual…I guess that's the problem. It's so usual. I was walking along the street tonight, checking things out, and I saw this kid lying on the sidewalk, dead drunk, looked like he'd been thrown out of a bar…probably robbed."

He paused and took a deep breath.

"The kid looked up and stretched out his hands to me, and he said, "Father, forgive me, for I have sinned.'"

He was quiet. I saw a tear sliding down his cheek and took his hand.

"It's the collar…" I said.

"I know…"

"The world's a mess," I said, thinking of Winston. Who would need to be forgiven for what had happened to him?

We had been in Hong Kong for almost three years and it was time to think seriously about returning to the States. After five years of marriage and three children, it was time to settle down.

I started dreaming again…a small town with sidewalks…a real washer and dryer…bikes for the kids, well, tricycles. Marita and Mike were almost four—sturdy, happy blond kids. They would easily get lost in a crowd of tow-heads in kindergarten, and Dede, at two and a half, was ready to take on the world.

When the job offer came from a college town in Northwest Iowa, it sounded perfect.

There was one thing, aside from the usual good-byes and promises to stay in touch that had to be done. Gina was 15, not quite ready to go out on her own to find a job, and needed a home. We wondered if Charlie and Catherine would have any ideas.

They came over for dinner, Charlie bringing his usual gifts (green glass pie plates this time) and his jolly self. Gina helped us cook and serve the dinner. I saw them watching her.

"She's a fine girl," Charlie said. "Just the same age as our Tina."

31

"We'd be happy to have her in our home," Catherine agreed. "We would treat her as our own daughter—let her go on to finish school and help a bit around the house."

It was almost too good to be true.

Charlie was a good Shanghai Baptist and had many friends among the Americans. How he reconciled that with having a thriving Wanchai Bar was considered a bit of a conundrum, but he seemed to find no conflict. It was a good restaurant, and if the sailors brought their girlfriends or whatever for dinner, it was no business of his. So Gina happily went to live with the Lows. She was a lucky girl.

When the time came to pack up our things there really was not much to pack. The furnishings we had acquired were so tropical that they would look silly in Northwest Iowa. We donated all the cribs, potty chairs, and high chairs to a local welfare center, tucked the blue and white batik Buddha and the assorted red Chinese gods into the brass herb pots and boxed them, packed our suitcases, and were ready to go.

As a last hurrah and farewell to Hong Kong, and all things nautical, we decided to take a boat across the Pacific, a big old Australian tub called the Himalaya, on its last voyage.

It was heavenly…

And then we were suddenly in a flesh and blood American Midwestern town—in Iowa.

CHAPTER FIVE

ORANGE CITY, IOWA OPENED ITS arms to us and treated us like ecclesiastical royalty. While we had not thought of ourselves as being extraordinarily holy during our three years overseas, to them we were pilgrims returning from a crusade against the forces of pagan darkness.

It was a bit overwhelming.

In response, and to show our solidarity, we bought a house.

We bought the Van Witchel house on Arizona Street, a structure built to last until the end of time. It was located in the middle of town, conveniently within walking distance of the college, the shopping district, and the church. It was a square solid bungalow with five bedrooms.

It would cost us all of eleven thousand dollars, an unimaginable sum of money, but the college paid well.

We had stopped by in Michigan long enough to let the folks and the grandkids get acquainted. Dad, of course, wanted to be sure we had furniture, so we had picked out a truckload of early American cherry and maple reproductions from the Quality Furniture Store in Zeeland that would look perfect in Iowa.

The people from the American Reformed Church, known to be suspiciously liberal, came over to help us paper and paint.

One evening we had a crowded roomful of people, paint rollers, meatballs, wallpaper paste and cookies mixed with stories as we told them about Hong Kong and they filled us in on their town. One man in particular, a lawyer named Earl Klay, was giving us an analytical eye. He and several other men were smoking up a storm. I caught a look in his blue eyes, screened with white smoke—I returned the look, wordless, comprehending...

...there is more to this scene than meets the eye...there is more about this town and these two young travelers that we want to explore...what exactly is it?

I saw Earl watching us, and wondered if he would be a friend and confidant, maybe someone who we could be honest with...maybe he could help us connect.

The house was an enormous project. We quickly bought local beds and lived in the middle of the mess, doing one room at a time, stripping down walls, papering, putting up curtains, getting ready for the load of furniture coming. It was almost easy to forget we had come here to do a job for the college.

But Pres Stegenga, the college president, smiled knowingly.

"Take your time to get settled in," he said quietly. "I know what you're going through. I was born in the middle east. My folks worked overseas. I know what you're feeling."

If he knew how we were feeling, he was doing better than I was.

Okay...we had the little town and the house on a quiet street, and there were sidewalks. And down in the basement stood a washer and dryer. The tricycles—maybe that was what was missing...

By October we were settled in. The house looked like an early American showroom (with a few Chinese gods and brass herb pots thrown in for accent pieces), and we were on our way to feeling permanent. We even had a beautiful blue braided rug, made by Gordon's mom from family coats and suits, gracing the living room.

The town hall sponsored a Halloween party with prizes for the best costumes. We unpacked the trusty Singer portable and sewed up three gray furry costumes with long tails and whiskers so our kids could go as "The Three Little Kittens who Lost Their Mittens." They won the prize, but were too shy to go up on the stage. They not only had lost their mittens, they'd never had any. It had been warm to hot in Hong Kong all year, and we had no winter clothes.

In mid-November the local newspaper called and asked if we would be their poster family for Thanksgiving. Why not? We were getting to be (very small town) celebrities.

We posed in our newly painted white wood paneled dining room with café curtains drawn just so. We were the quintessential American family with a boy, two girls, and mother and a father saying grace around a (desiccated looking) turkey supplied by the newspaper, with our eyes all properly closed in gratitude, except for Deidra, who broke the illusion by glaring indignantly at the photographer out of the corner of her eye.

We never knew what people were laughing about until we saw a copy of the paper. The photographer had taken multiple shots. Why had he chosen that one? Maybe Orange City had more of a sense of humor than we gave them credit for.

Heading for the holidays, the town snuggled in for the winter. The college put on a great choral performance, the churches rehearsed Christmas music, and the snow began to fall. The countryside, with cornfields laid out in brown and white stripes from last summer's harvested crops, made a charming grid-work of designs.

This was America, and like all 1960s America, it was deeply ethnic in its orientation. Orange City was not only Dutch, it was double-Dutch, evenly divided between the Reformed and the Christian Reformed churches who had some ancient squabble so deep they did not even buy their meat from the same butcher.

The snow fell, blending and blurring the sharp patterns.

In the renovated VanWitchell house on Arizona Street, we had only one sign of incipient rebellion. Upstairs in our very own hallowed space, we painted three bedroom walls Chinese red, and tacked up the blue and white batik Buddha on the remaining white wall. We even set the little kitchen god next to the alarm clock on the bedside stand just to remind us there was a world out there, a world we thought we couldn't wait to get away from, and now could not quite forget.

"The Dream of the Red Chamber," I said one night. "Isn't there some famous Chinese book or play about that?"

"I don't know," Gordon said. "I might have heard of it. What was it about?"

"I don't know either," I said, snuggling up beside him. "There's a lot about China I don't know. Why..."

"Maybe the library here would have a copy."

"I doubt it," I said, yawning. "How can you ask for something that you don't even know exists?"

Christmas was coming and the children, at four and a half and almost three, were excited. We put up a tree in the big bay window and decorated the mantle of the artificial fireplace with three stockings hung in a row. I didn't bother to tell the kids about Santa Claus—we surely didn't have a chimney for him to squeeze down. In fact, he might have run into the row of candles we were lighting in place of a fire. Frankly, I was afraid to lie to them about such things for fear they'd never believe me when it mattered.

The town was in full swing. The snow was deep and the decorated lampposts glowed like patterned halos along the street.

Dykema's Department Store was my taste of America. We bought little tights for the girls and little turtleneck sweaters. I sewed up red velvet jumpers for the girls and got Mike a bow tie. This would be their first American Christmas.

I hoped we could buy tricycles. Three would be a bit expensive. Maybe dolls and trucks would have to do it this year. It was something I had wanted for them. They hadn't even mentioned them.

My mom was coming. She would love it here. This was the life she had dreamed of for me, a real American life, and it was what I had wanted, too...

Mom was there for the Christmas program at the church. Our kids had been persuaded to join in the children's Sunday school choir for the special occasion.

They were all in rows with the smallest children in front. The church was decorated with candles and touches of red, with lovely Christmas organ music giving a sense of the Holy season.

The children were singing, all except for Deidra. She was nervously tugging at the bottom edge of her red velvet jumper. The more nervous she got, the farther up she pulled the jumper—up it came over her head, with her little black-tighted legs and bottom coming in sight. Up over her face came the last of the jumper until only the little black behind could be seen, wiggling back and forth to the music.

There were nervous titters from the congregation.

Up went the jumper, over her head, shutting them all out.

That got to be known as Deidra's striptease, and her parents had been missionaries....too yet.

Just before the holiday break, the president asked Gordon to come in for a chat.

"You're doing a great job of the chapel services," the president said. "The students love your approach. They feel that you've been very warm and sincere, and the fact that you've been overseas, as you know, that's greatly admired here."

"Maybe too much so," Gordon suggested.

Pres Stegenga nodded. "Of course," he added, "there are a few students who think you're too liberal."

"Why is that?"

The president chuckled. "You know how it is. There's a certain faction at this school that you could never be conservative enough to please.

They're not even conservative enough to please each other, so why pay attention to them?"

"But what do they object to?" Gordon asked.

Another one of those smiles.

"Have they given you the King James version test yet?"

Gordon was perturbed that night when we talked quietly in our room. Mom was across the hall and the kids were asleep. He told me about his visit with Pres Stegenga.

"I keep running into the same kind of wall," he began. "At the pier it was drunken sailors who thought I could forgive their sins, and here it's..."

"It's what?"

"I don't know how to describe it. You know me. You know how deeply I believe in God. I care about people. I want to make a contribution to the world by being an ordinary man, not some..."

"Some what?"

"Some pious stuffed shirt."

"Then why did you go to seminary?"

"I guess I thought...to tell you the truth, everyone expected me to."

"Expected?"

"Bruce was to be an accountant. Bill was the smart one, and he would go into politics. Lila was a girl, so she could be a nurse. Glen was the youngest, and he would take over in the furniture store...and I... I was a boy who loved to make speeches. I would stand on the gravestones in the cemetery and deliver loud sermons to the neighborhood kids, and I won all the medals for making speeches in high school, and during high school I went down to Kentucky to help in the Reformed Church's school there..."

"So?"

"So I was supposed to be a minister."

"Did you ever question that?"

"I did. The year I graduated from college I went down to Kentucky and taught for the summer. I loved the kids in the mountains so much that I didn't want to come back. I sent word that I wouldn't be starting seminary as planned, and got a letter back from the school strongly urging me to return to Michigan and start with my classes."

"Did you enjoy it once you started?"

"Some of it. We had some wonderful teachers—very scholarly. We had to study Greek and Hebrew, which I rather enjoyed. But when guys would sit up late at night arguing about shades of meaning in the original languages, or doctrines of the church, I..."

"You what?'

"I usually fell asleep."

I searched his face, knowing he would take what his family had given him and live it out in his own way; feet on the ground.

And he loved me.

How could I have been so lucky?

Not even Heaven could corrupt him.

My mom loved the house—loved it. We spent the days before Christmas baking cookies and getting ready for Christmas. The kids were curious about having a grandma. Aunt Harriet had almost filled that role, but she was an auntie.

"Are you my really truly Grandma?" Marita quizzed, licking cookie dough off her fingers.

I realized for the first time that Marita looked as much like my mom as Deidra looked like Gordon's. These life processes, passing characteristics from one generation to another, the true wonder of birth, the passing on of a nose or a personality from one human being to another…the miracle of a child's birth…somehow it all tied into Christmas.

There were no angels singing when my babies were born. It was more like the howls of hell. But when the blood was cleaned up and the child was put to my breast, it was always a miracle—a miracle wrought of love and pain, of joy and tears—the miracle of life. Who could ask for more?

And that was why it was so hard to tell my mom…

I, her only child.

It was another one of those quiet nights in the almost red chamber. We still had one white wall.

Walls.

Hitting walls.

Walls marked out territory.

Walls protected and encumbered.

Walls bloodied one's head when hit by said object—one's head.

Gordon was sitting on the edge of the bed again, and I knew something was about to be said. It was his agonized stance.

"Sometimes I don't think I can take it."

"Take what?"

"These definitions of what I am."

"Just be yourself."

"It's not only that…" he said slowly, looking at me. "Do you ever feel we missed some kind of huge opportunity in Hong Kong?"

"No, you finished your job there," I said cheerily.

"It's not about that. Sometimes I think we sort of slept through that whole three years' experience, unaware of so much of it."

"In what way?"

"We really didn't learn anything about the Chinese people. We didn't learn a language, or care about anything beyond our own survival in the American expat community."

Heck. I had thought just managing that was heroic, but I did know what he meant. I had been asked to speak at a ladies group at church and declined, saying I was busy, when the truth was I didn't know what to say. They wanted to know about the life of Chinese women, and I didn't have a clue. Should I have?

I felt my blood doing something crazy, flowing backward, or simply standing still.

"What are you saying?" I asked softly.

He leaned over and kissed me on the forehead.

"Should we try to go back?" he whispered.

And that was what I had to tell my mom. She looked the way I had felt when Gordon went to Korea.

"You can't do that!" she said, and started to cry. "When are you going to make him settle down?"

"I can't do that, Mom. I have to let him find his way. I can't kill his guts and have a dead man on my hands."

"Well, what about this house? What about the kids? What…"

I knew what she meant. What about me, your mother? Your father divorced me and I'm alone in this world…and now you are making it worse by going away again.

It was time to draw a line in the sand. We had always been close, but I did not want the tragedy of her life to leak over into mine.

"Mom," I said too quietly, "I'm married. This house can go to hell, and we'll take the kids along. And you will survive."

When Gordon told Stegenga, he was not shocked.

"You'll naturally have to work out the rest of the year, finish the semester, and I'll start looking for a new chaplain for next fall," he said.

Then he put his arm around Gordon's shoulders and said, "Bless you, man. I understand. But keep it quiet for now."

Quietly, Gordon contacted the people at 475 Riverside Drive, New York. They didn't seem surprised either. Yes, they knew Gordon. He was one of their own boys, and they had been watching him. Yes, this had happened before, but this time they were laying down the guidelines.

"There are openings," said the voice on the phone "but this assignment would not be short term. You would have to learn a language, have a long-term commitment, and be willing to go anywhere in the world we'd need you."

"What are the options?" Gordon asked.

"We do have one opening in the Philippines, one in the Virgin Islands, and yes, one in Hong Kong. There you would work with a united group of thirteen denominations, under Chinese leadership. You'd need total immersion in the culture and a fluent grasp of Chinese."

WOW.

With growing excitement, we discussed it at night in the red chamber. Were we brave enough? As scary as it seemed, was it better than where we were, where the growth potential would be zero to minus zero?

Gordon called New York and asked them to put us in the system as overseas candidates. They said we would have to report in August to a place called Stony Point, where we would be put through six months of intensive training in preparation for working outside the United States.

And yes, here was one place where the seminary degree would be essential. It would not limit our lives. It was our passport to adventure.

In a way it was a release. Once we knew we were not staying, we began to enjoy the house on Arizona Street.

We invited friends over for dinner, cooking up a storm. The Klays, the Kraiis, people from the church and the college—learning their stories, laughing at their jokes, and discovering that we really liked them.

But we kept quiet.

We drove around the countryside, discovering the farmlands, the wonderful industry and dedication to the land on the part of the people who lived there. The weather was cold, so the odors of pig raising were at a minimum, and the occasional stands of black trees stretched their branches in intricate lacework against the gray winter skies. It was a world in black and white, with an occasional red barn roof, sleeping, until the miracle of spring would come again.

Again the question...

America was such a beautiful place. Why were we leaving it?

The Klays invited us to their home, sensing some mystery about us. Barbara and Earl had three children, Rachel, a bouncy redhead of five, and two older children, Susan and Tim, in high school.

At five, Rachel was the perfect playmate for our three- and four-year-olds. Earl kept horses, and Rachel's version of horseback riding was to gallop her rocking horse recklessly in a corner of the kitchen, red hair flying.

We had breakfast at the Klays one morning. Earl was eyeing us through his usual curl of smoke. Earl looked so good smoking a cigarette he should have worked for a tobacco company. The curl of smoke seemed to give gravitas to everything he said.

Earl was also a big contributor to the college, and on the board, and a very close friend of Pres Stegenga. He probably knew. But he studied us with his knowing blue eyes, and smoked, and didn't mention it.

"Earl!" Barbara called from the stove where she was making pancakes, "you're probably asphyxiating those poor people. Put that darn cigarette away!"

He did, and he looked utterly naked.

Dykema's Department Store was endlessly fascinating to me. The winter clothes were on sale—such great bargains, but where would I wear them? Few places in the world that we might be assigned were as cold as Orange City, Iowa, and the few spring things were beautiful, but so expensive.

Maybe I should try to earn some extra money.

I was getting interested in painting again. The urge to paint and the need to earn some money conveniently came together.

Actually, I had gone on from painting the portrait of Gina in Hong Kong to try Father Zeller's buffalo horn technique on other subjects. They were the only other thing we had brought back here. There was a street scene with Chinese signs overhead and children playing kick-block with the light streaming down on them. There were boat scenes of Aberdeen Harbor, one of a woman rowing with a fishtail oar, and one close-up face of a fisherwoman with a big hat.

Earl found out about them. One day he came over to Arizona Street and asked to see them. They were still in the box upstairs. I had never unpacked them, thinking no one would be interested.

"These are great!" he said with his usual exuberance. "Would you consider selling them?"

"I guess so..." I said modestly, "but I wouldn't even know what to charge for them."

"How about a hundred bucks apiece?" he offered.

This was 1962, when a five-bedroom house could be bought for eleven thousand dollars.

"Sold!" I said.

I had four hundred dollars—enough to buy out Dykema's spring fashions—and four oil paintings were hung in Barbara and Earl Klay's home.

We had another interesting friend who we met at the church. Nelson DeJong and his wife, Ada, had a farm just outside of town. Nelson had a thing for people who had been to strange places and seen strange things. He loved to come calling, and I never knew when he would show up at the kitchen door. But one thing I could count on.

"I always whistle when I come calling," he explained. "I wouldn't want to come at the wrong time, so when you hear me whistle you'll know I'm there."

I never knew what to talk to him about, so I usually made him a cup of coffee and fed him cookies. We always had cookies.

"I hear you're a painter," he said one day. "How would you like to come out to our farm and paint my barn?"

It didn't sound terribly thrilling, but I agreed to do it. I hauled out the old tubes of oil paint and Father Zeller's precious pieces of buffalo horn and a palette, and was ready to go.

It was beginning to be spring, and the grass was greening, but it was still terribly cold. I set up an easel in the barnyard and started to work, but my fingers were shaking.

"You'd better go in the house and ask Ada for a pair of my long johns," he suggested. "I've got a real thick pair that I use when I feed the hogs."

I wasn't sure I wanted him to think of me in his long johns, but I was freezing.

Ada hauled out the long underwear and I put it on under my slacks. With a jacket, hat and scarf, I was warm enough to work.

I had just started getting into the job when a huge white sow and a litter of pigs came over to observe me. The sow grunted and sniffed at my palette, then decided she liked the buffalo horn. Before my horrified eyes, she decided to eat it.

Snarf.

There went my precious Father Zeller palette knife.

The sow half chewed it and swallowed. She began to squeal. It had stuck. Nelson DeJong came running, trying to stick his hand down the sow's throat. She was screaming. The piglets were flying around.

"My palette knife!" I yelled.

"Goddamn your palette knife," he yelled back. "That sow is worth money!"

I guess the palette knife finally went down and the sow didn't die, but I wasn't around to sort through the pig shit to see if it ever came out the other end. I finished the painting, but it was too cold to finish it that day. I returned the long johns and finished it at home in my warm kitchen.

The doctor's wife, Mrs. Grossman, heard about the painting and came over to see it. "Oh, I love it," she gushed, "but I just redecorated my living room and I've done it in hot pink, purple and green. This really wouldn't match!"

Well, that was a new wrinkle. Was I supposed to paint pink and purple barns? I had to decide if I was going to paint scenes to match people's sofas or just paint. I decided to pack away the paints. I had other things on my mind for now.

Earl Klay and Virg Rowenhorst decided to start an adult class at the church, a class that would probe into searching questions about early Christianity, its origins, and the history of its development. Being a lawyer and a banker, these two could bring up questions that would scare a theologian spitless.

We sat around in the class, spellbound, hearing men say aloud that Alexander the Great was also reported to have been born of a virgin, that this was the earmark of a significant person—it was quite the rage in the Greek and Roman world...and that Jesus Christ was only declared divine in 300 AD, not by church fathers, but by Constantine, who needed a deity for political purposes. These men had done a lot of studying, and the rest of us, brought up in conservative Christian families, sat around with our mouths open, glancing around nervously to see who else was there. This was dangerous stuff. And in Iowa? In this little pig-shit town?

These people not only had a sense of humor, they had a sense of reality. No wonder they were considered dangerous liberals. How could one ask these questions and still believe? Maybe people who dealt with the soil and the seasons hungered for something closer to the earth. It was the perfect launch for going to Stony Point, where everything and every assumption we had ever held would be put under the hot white light of inquiry.

It was time to put the big house on Arizona Street up for sale. At first it was a semi-secret, told only to one realtor. He quietly brought people by while Gordon finished up his term at the college.

People loved the house. They loved the perfect furniture, the five bedrooms, and the big farm kitchen. Would we sell the furniture? Sell it as it was, complete? Of course we would. What would we do with a truckload of early American furniture on our way to Timbuktu? Or anywhere? We needed to go lightly.

The people who finally bought the Van Witchel house were the ones who loved it all; but most of all they loved the red bedroom upstairs, our Red Chamber. That was the room that clinched the deal.

Sold.

They had two full-grown daughters, and we heard from the Klays later that the red bedroom had inspired the birth of their first son. That room could do it. But, fortunately, this time as we were contemplating leaving the country, I was not pregnant.

We spent the summer in Michigan, staying upstairs at Mom and Dad De Pree's house. The children had a chance to get acquainted with their cousins, Bruce's girls and Glen's boys. Lila was in California, and Bill was in Africa, working for the state department. They had never met his children. Then there was tiny 'little Grandma,' Gordon's grandmother, his aunts and cousins—relatives everywhere.

Mike, just turning five, was changing from the quiet little boy he had been into the boy with many questions. He had to know why this and why that, and how did that work and who said so.

We were on our way to Stony Point the day he asked the big question.

"Our cousins have lived in the same place ever since they were born. Why do we move so much?"

"We'll get settled soon," I promised him. "When we finish at Stony Point we'll know where we're going, and then we'll stay in that place for a long time."

"But why? Why can't we live in Zeeland like everybody else?"

Good question. How could I answer that so a five-year-old could understand it?

That day, August 1, was my birthday. I was thirty years old. We had been married for eight years, and I still didn't know why we were so restless. It wasn't just Gordon. I had caught it, too.

We were on the Garden State Parkway going up through New Jersey when Marita decided to answer Mike's question. She had been thinking about it. She stood up behind the front seat and said,

"Okay, everybody, be quiet now. I'm going to sing a song."

"I don't have to be quiet," Mike said.

"Oh, yes you do," I corrected him. "Let's listen to Marita's song."

She looked out the window at the passing scene and hummed to herself, and began a chant, clear and sweet.

She sang about the birds flying in the sky, flying through the clouds and looking down on all the people, the busy people working in their homes and walking in the towns...

She sang of the flowers, opening in the summer and fading in the cold, and of the trees turning green, and then shedding their leaves in the fall and standing bare in the cold winter...

I was in the front seat, breathless, wondering who this child was and where she gained such wisdom...barely daring to breathe...wishing I could record this. Gordon was driving, staring straight ahead, gripping the steering wheel, and Marita was still singing her chant-poem.

She was singing about mothers and fathers and children, going out into a new place to find out lots of new things, to find out where the monsters were and how not to be afraid of them...

I was sobbing. I couldn't listen to any more. I reached across the seat and hugged her.

"There aren't any monsters, Sweetie," I said. "Mommy and Daddy will always take care of you. You can count on that. If we ever find a monster I'll bite its head off and save you. I promise."

She hugged me back. "I know you will, Mom."

It was quiet in the car, too quiet. Mike broke the silence.

"That was a long song," he said, "but you still didn't tell me why we have to move so much."

"Because," Marita explained very patiently, "because sometimes questions don't have any answers the same size as them, and you need a song."

The camp at Stony Point was laid out like a large old motel, with central rooms for dining and meeting, and long corridors with rooms on each side.

Our kids spotted other children getting settled into their assigned rooms and struck up shy friendships. They were all going to be in Stony Point Elementary School for the September to December session—our twins entering kindergarten and Deidra assigned to a play group. The ordinary trauma of entering kindergarten was overshadowed by the overwhelming newness of everything else.

A wide variety of professionals were assembled. Doctors, nurses, teachers, school administrators, linguists, hospital administrators, psychologists... They were a well-educated lot, with little of the irrational fervor of some religious delegations. They were specialists, leaving the United States to make a contribution in some part of the world where their skills were needed.

We gathered in the dining room for the first evening meal. Families were encouraged to add a single person to their seating arrangement, and we included a young woman who was going to Liberia to work in a nursing school, training local Liberians to work in hospitals. Loretta was a big, dark-eyed, warmhearted woman, and the kids adopted her immediately.

The food was heavily vegetarian, teaching us all to get along with less meat. Rice...beans...lentils...spices, vegetables, breaking us out of our meat and potatoes palates.

The program started immediately. The children went to school or were assigned to play groups, and parents rarely saw them except for meals and evenings.

Some of the trainees knew where they were going—for others it was not yet decided. We were being broken away from certainty, made flexible, open-minded. Gordon and I had no idea if we would be learning Tagalog and going to the Philippines, or Cantonese and going to Hong Kong, or just speaking English in the Virgin Islands. We had to be selfless enough to accept whatever task we were assigned to.

Of the five months we spent at Stony Point much could be said, but one lasting impression was created. We were all going, wherever we were going, into a big and complex world. People would not be like us. They would not believe like us. There were Buddhists and Hindus, Muslims, Jews and Siks, every religion known to mankind. There were Communists and Socialists, Theocracies and military dictatorships, and tribal cultures. Did we understand what these people thought, and how it related to what we believed?

And did we…could we…believe in the exclusive claims of Christianity? Would that belief add to or hinder us in the work we would attempt to accomplish?

This was serious stuff.

Sometimes we needed a break; we needed to see life through the eyes of the children.

One day we could not locate Deidra. She had been in her play group, but no one could find her.

Then we spotted her. Off on the far side of the playground under a big red umbrella squatted two little figures, Deidra and Sarah, the daughter of a doctor going to Africa. They were blissfully playing, acting out some childhood drama without a stitch on.

"Well, you see," Deidra explained, as we rushed in to clothe her, "Sarah said in Africa some kids don't wear clothes, and we were playing Africa…"

Right in the middle of realizing that it was a big complex world, President John F. Kennedy was shot. Shot dead, in America. Did we have enough goodness in this country to bring it to others? We were a good country, but we were also a violent country. What did we have to say? Could we teach the world?

It was shocking—and sobering—and humbling.

The meat rule was broken for Thanksgiving and we had turkey. It tasted like something from another planet.

It was soon after Thanksgiving that we received definite word from 475. The Gordon De Pree family was going to Hong Kong. We would be assigned to the Hong Kong Council of the Church of Christ in China, hereafter designated as the HKCCC. Our first two years would be spent at New Asia College with no other assignment, so we could concentrate on becoming fluent in Cantonese. After two years of study we would be assigned either to a resettlement area in Kowloon, or to the building of a new high school on the Hong Kong side.

HURRAH! We were going to Hong Kong!

The twins remembered snatches of it—the big flowering trees by the nullah and the kiosk at the beach where they bought popsies—but Deidra, who hardly remembered anything, had a mission. She was going back to find her mountain, the place on Victoria Peak where she had been born.

She, of all of us, was a real Hong Kong citizen. She was going home.

Christmas was spent at Mom and Dad De Pree's house in Zeeland with piles of cousins and aunts, uncles and grandmothers. In the middle of all the confusion, Gordon's mom sewed doll clothes.

It was hard to say goodbye to my mom, but she had been working at it. She had decided to be proud of us. We made good bragging material. I promised to send lots of pictures and to write once a week.

Gordon and I decided to have a long goodbye America trip, and took the kids on the double-decker train from Chicago to San Francisco. Mom De Pree and a friend went with us. They would stay with Lila in San Francisco after we caught the flight to Hong Kong. It would be easy this time. No one was in diapers.

The long, lovely trip…across lofty mountains and deserts…

Sitting up in the observation car, holding hands and watching America go by again…it always seemed to be going by on the way to somewhere else. Would we ever live here?

Such a beautiful country.

Someday we would come back to stay.

SECTION TWO

1963–1967

CHAPTER SIX

NUMBER TEN CORNWALL STREET, KOWLOON, Hong Kong, British crown Colony.

Here we were, back in the place we had been so anxious to leave. The world inside our heads had gone through a radical change. We were ready to put America on the back burner and go plunging eagerly into discovering what we had missed the first time around.

The two-bedroom flat on Cornwall Street was one of sixteen in a square building at the foot of Lion Rock Mountain. The busses from the Star Ferry wheezed and plowed their way through the traffic of Kowloon, and in a cul-de-sac right in front of our apartment block they stopped and turned around, the drivers got out to stretch or smoke, and they headed back into the traffic. It was a good place to catch the bus downtown.

Getting started in a new place was getting to be a habit. We could do it in 48 hours or less. Beds, chairs, table, a couch...sew up a few curtains, hang a few Japanese paper lanterns, buy some large plants from a local gardener, lay out a few cherished items, and we were set to go. Décor? I started calling it decorating with shadows and purple onions.

But where we lived, or how, was beside the point. Our assignment for the next two years was to immerse ourselves in Chinese culture and language—mostly language. We were about to tackle one of the most difficult sets of sounds that English-speaking people could attempt.

I thought guiltily of my pidgin-English-speaking amahs. Would my Chinese sound like that to native Chinese speakers?

Chilling thought...

Gordon, I knew, was good at languages. If he could read Greek and Hebrew, Chinese should be a breeze. The only other language I knew was Kentucky mountain archaic English. But I would do it. We would do it.

The first priority was to get the twins settled in school. The only option was Kowloon Junior School, where all the DeVelder kids had gone. That meant little British school uniforms and backpacks. They had only been through the first half of kindergarten at Stony Point, and now would have to jump to the second half of grade one at KJS. That might be as hard as learning Chinese. They would have to adapt to a British accent, some of which was quite different from American English.

The first time we drove up to the gate at KJS and delivered our small uniformed American-cum-English school kids, my heart ached for them. We all had so much to learn.

We settled Miss Deidra (now four) in Mrs. Somebody's nursery school and left her to it. This, she reminded us, was where she was born.

New Asia College on Tin Gwong Road had the same tropical yellow peeling plaster and smell of mold as its neighbors on the busy Chinese street. The planes landing at Kai Tak Airport zoomed overhead, and next door at a primary school, Chinese students droned some incomprehensible sounds in unison as they had done for centuries.

But inside the rooms assigned to the language center there was a feeling of energy and high-powered tension. Newly arrived from her doctoral program in the States, Jenny Ling was in charge of the New Asia Yale in China program, an innovative method devised by Heyward Wong for teaching Westerners to speak Chinese fluently by translating Chinese characters into phonetic sounds. This was a fresh and experimental method, and we were the proving ground.

Jenny Ling was a professional. She was the size of a pea, but could strike pure terror in the heart of a two-hundred-pound man. Her special target was the quintessential American bigot, and she could smell one a mile off.

It was mid-morning tea break and we were standing around in the little break room on the roof of the school, getting acquainted. Such a motley group... Never mind language—some of us did not even inhabit the same psychological space within our own cultures. We were foreigners to each other. There were two catholic priests, a gaggle of Maryknoll Sisters, a swarthy Indian Army officer, American missionaries of all stripes and flavors, a doctor and his wife, and the two of us, however we defined ourselves. The only thing we had in common was the learning of this language—this

incomprehensible set of sounds that human beings actually used to communicate with each other...

We would all need to become as little children, learning to speak one
syllable at a time. It would be like re-entering the womb of the world and
being reborn.

For six weeks we did not learn a single Chinese word. We learned
sounds and tones, like music with no lyrics. Boo-Bah-Hai-Hah. Up and
down-tones. Up and down some invisible musical scale, swooping up and
falling down.

"But where's middle C?" some frustrated voice would wail.

"No middle C. You each have your own middle C."

Big help.

Men teachers and women teachers. Bright young Chinese with beautiful sculpted faces. Hour after hour; day after day. One sound in seven different tones made seven different words. Thousands of words

"This stuff is driving me nuts," I groaned

"You'll get it." Gordon teased, "You're no dumber than the average
Chinese three-year-old."

"I'm beginning to wonder," I moaned.

Marita and Michael were in first grade, where most of the other kids
had started to read. Being transferred in from kindergarten, they needed
help. We poured over Dick and Jane type books with them. Gordon got
phonics flash cards and drilled them. Sounds and tones in Chinese—English
in phonics. Crazy world. Who, where, why, and what were we?

We began to study actual meanings of the sounds we were making with
a textbook and tapes for practicing. The days were getting warmer and soon
the kids would be out of school. We studied mornings, and spent afternoons
out on the verandah, bent over the little tape player, checking our pronun-
ciation with the recordings.

There were other children in the building, British, Canadian, Australian, some from the Philippines and other Asian countries, and some
mixed marriages with interracial children. One day we were pouring over
the tricky sounds, ears to the machine. Marita came in with two of her play-
mates. She listened to the sounds for a few moments, then quickly went out
the door with her friends. That night she said, "Mommy, please don't speak
Chinese around my friends. Only coolies talk Chinese."

"What?" I said, newly shocked. Last year I would have agreed with her.

"My friend said anybody who knows anything speaks English. Only coolies speak Chinese."

"What's a coolie?" I tested her.

"I don't even know. Just don't do it when my friends are around, okay?"

They were picking up a British accent. "Mummy, you don't say basket; you have to say bah-sket." But they were learning to read well. Mike, especially, seemed to pick up reading almost magically. One day he couldn't read and the next he could.

We would have to go to school most of the summer, and the kids would be out. We would, to my horror, need to get an amah to help. On second thought, maybe she could help me learn to speak. What a novel idea!

I expected to learn Chinese in New Asia College, but if you had told me that Methodists would teach me to dance, I would have laughed. And laugh I did.

We had become a very sociable bunch, all sweating and groaning over the Chinese language, and the mutual suffering caused us to reach out across our intra-cultural barriers.

Getting to know the Maryknoll Sisters was a hoot. Sister Miriam John was one of the funniest women I have ever met, and Sister John Mark would waltz along the hallways jangling her keys (why did anyone need all those keys?) to some inner jazz rhythm...and the Methodist girls were a real eye-opener. They were mostly young short-termers, and had no visible pretensions of being serious.

One night they had a party up on the peak on the Hong Kong side. We left the kids with the new amah and decided to go out and have a good time. We sorely needed it.

I had never danced before. Whenever Gordon suggested dancing I told him I didn't know how. My father was such a super-religious person that dancing or taking a drink of wine was enough to send one straight to hell...even though he did things which were ten times worse. If you danced you were damned.

That night I must have been damned and never felt it, because I surely danced...and oh, my God, how I enjoyed it!

It was the 60s, and you didn't need to know how to dance; you simply got up and did it, joyful and free!

Gordon, being a normal American teenager, had always danced. His folks never minded, and Gordon, of course, never thought anything was wrong...innocent as the day he was born, yet somehow smart enough to keep out of trouble. That man was brought up right.

Learning to use Chinese with the new amah was a good idea, but it didn't work. She was from some country village in China that spoke a different dialect than the standard Cantonese we were learning, and as bad as her English was, our attempts at speaking Chinese to each other were worse.

The Indian Army officer at the language program always seemed to be a loner. He often stood by himself at the tea breaks, and since Gordon had a soft spot for any loner, we invited him over for dinner.

We were deep in the middle of cooking a roast beef dinner when the Indian fellow came to the door. I saw him wrinkle his nose, but paid little attention, introducing him to the family.

The roast beef was smelling quite odd. I excused myself and went out into the kitchen.

"What kind of spice are you using in the meat?" I asked the amah. "This smells funny for roast beef."

She looked at me, perplexed at my ignorance. "This no beefy," she explained. "This doi su."

"Doi su?" I said. "What's that?"

"You know, he come out, Mommy put in here." She patted her stomach.

I was horrified. Was this some sort of afterbirth, or God knows what? Gordon had bought it at the market for beef. Did he know the right word for beef?

"Doi Su," the amah said, putting her hands in front of her like paws and hopping around the kitchen on her bent legs. "He come out, Mommy put he in pocket..."

"Kangaroo?" I said, about to gag.

"Hiah. Kangaloo!" she laughed. "Pocket rat! You doo-no?"

The Indian fellow was at the kitchen door motioning to me.

"Ah...you know I'm Hindu and don't eat beef," he apologized. "Would you just have some scrambled eggs?"

"Sure thing," I said. "Sorry, I forgot."

"Never mind," he smiled. "Sorry to trouble you."

We all had scrambled eggs that night.

"Where's the beef?" Gordon asked.

"I...uh...it hopped away," I said, winking at him. I would explain later.

The perils of not knowing what we were buying at the market! Hopefully, as our Chinese increased, we would not be in danger of eating kangaroo, or having the amah hopping around the kitchen to tell me we had just bought one.

In the midst of all this linguistic and multi-cultural insanity, we needed to stabilize ourselves, to define who we really were…what we were becoming.

When our twins had been born almost six years before, we had to get up at six o'clock to feed them, so we got up at five o'clock to have some time for ourselves. We got a cup of coffee and thought over our day. If we were worried about anything, or annoyed about anybody, we talked about it. We read some bit of inspiration, maybe from Psalms in the Jerusalem bible, or the gospels. One of us read and the other listened, jotting down our thoughts. The only criteria was that it had to be a new thought, one we had never had before. We had come from backgrounds that were greatly different (although both Dutch), and we needed to find our own level of belief or disbelief, our own path to walk together.

For eight years we had been jotting these things down. Now, in the middle of this cultural maelstrom, I had an idea. "After we study Chinese in the afternoons," I suggested, "could I have an hour or two to start typing up some of our jottings? I feel so dumb in Chinese, but I did publish a book. Somewhere in the world I'm not a babbling illiterate!"

"That would be great!" Gordon agreed. "You have the publishing contacts—go for it."

"How about the kids?"

"While you type I'll take the kids," he offered. "We'll go to the park, or the market over near Lion Rock, or some days I could take them across the Star Ferry and poke around on Cat Street."

"They'd love that! Or some days you could just let them play down in the car park with the other kids, just so somebody's watching them."

"I could take them to the Y by the ferry and get swimming lessons in the pool," he suggested.

So while Gordon was being the good dad, I sorted through the jottings. What little righteous prigs we had been in the first writings, so obvious, such faithful repeaters of what we had been told. We would scrap those. As the writings went along, we had begun to ask more questions, deal with problems and complexity, even voice doubts. Where would this trajectory take us? As our concepts of God changed, would He be angry and strike back at us?

I flipped through the little tattered notebook pages and smiled to myself. Not likely. How important did we think we were?

In the meantime, we prayed to our growing god. Whether God heard it all or not, we surely heard each other. No pretense. No games. No hiding. Say it. Admit it. Search for it. Out loud. In front of each other. Wide open. Forgive…accept… Who needed a shrink?

I finished up typing the manuscript and sent it off to the publisher in Michigan, suspecting that by the time it saw the light of day (if it did) it would be a trifle irrelevant. These things had a way of morphing, and who knew what we would become?

As close as we had always been, we were becoming even closer, realizing that this experience would not only be a physical journey, but a journey of the spirit as well.

In our new identity we were given new names. Gordon was Ding (our new surname) Gwok Dong. I was Ding Guai Laan. Mike was Ding Wai Douh and the girls Ding Miu Chi and Ding Miu Kay. We had ivory chopsticks with our names engraved on them.

The whole first year in language school I was tongue-tied. Words went in, but they did not come out. I was like a one-to-twelve-months child, hearing but not speaking.

Then it was the second year. We went back to New Asia College and there was a whole new crop of people. They were dumber than I was. I started to speak out of sheer relief.

Gordon had been speaking all along. He was not afraid of mistakes. He made them and laughed at himself. When asked if he had any children, he informed them that his wife had given birth to two little horses (the sounds were off). They laughed with him, and told him that his face skin was much thicker than his wife's.

But the second year I started babbling like a toddler. The words came thick and fast. I felt them flowing from a new source somewhere in my brain, a total awakening, new pathways being forged. New thoughts that had not been there in my own language came with the new words. I was truly being reborn into this new world.

During that second year, Gordon was encouraged to form some alliances that would give him a chance to practice his Chinese. He chose a group of young boys being trained in a motor mechanics class. These young men talked him into buying a Vespa motor scooter, a means of transportation that could take him exploring the byways of Hong Kong. Mike was fascinated. He wanted a scooter like his dad's.

And Deidra was finally in "big school," togged in her KJS uniform and a proud first-grader. When we went for our first parent-teacher meeting, her teacher was all smiles.

"Deidra is doing fine," she said reassuringly, "but she's such a chatterbox!"

We took in one more family member, an exquisite young Siamese cat from the HKRSPCA. In Hong Kong, even the SPCA was royal. We named her Revlon, because her eyes were so beautiful it looked like she had spent hours on her makeup.

We were beginning to see our way toward becoming fluent in spoken Chinese. There was a fifteen-minute speech to prepare (no notes) and given as a final test. Then what?

Deidra was almost six. I started thinking. This had been a grueling, fracturing two years. I had chopped my long hair short, studied alongside Gordon like two classmates, and not dressed too carefully. I needed something to make me feel whole and truly feminine again.

Should we?

I discussed it with Gordon one night. I would really like to have one more child. Just one more. What did he think about it?

He took in a quick breath and enclosed me in a big warm hug. Children meant responsibility.

"Are you sure you can manage one more?"

"I'm sure I can. After the way I grew up with 90 kids, four is really quite a small family. And..."

"And what?"

"The other three came so fast. I'd like to have one more, in decency and in order."

"Wait a minute," he grinned. "That sounds Presbyterian."

"Okay," I grinned back, "then let's have it indecently and in disorder— however! I just want to have a baby!"

The day we took our final Chinese oral test I was so morning sick I thought I would disgrace myself.

"We'd better get you to the doctor for a checkup," Gordon insisted.

I had resisted going until this language hurdle was past.

The doctor, good Doctor Freddie Watson who had refused to tie my tubes, confirmed it. I was pregnant. He gave me a knowing smile.

Yahoo!

September. It would be born in the same month as Gordon, around the end of September. What if it (I kept thinking *he*) was born on Gordon's birthday?

...he would be dark-haired...another little Dutch French Huguenot to match Deidra... Two blonds and two dark-haired children, I told Gordon.

"Don't set yourself up to be disappointed," he warned. "You want to be able to welcome whatever comes."

When we told the kids they were excited.

"I sure hope it's a boy," Mike said. "If we get one more girl in this house, I'm leaving!"

"You are not," Marita countered. "Where do you think you would go?"

"Anywhere but here. I'm tired of being bossed around by you girls."

"Well, get ready for another one," Marita teased. "I think it's going to be a girl."

"It can't be!" Mike shouted. "The cat's a girl, too. You've already got three. It's not fair!"

We would see.

While we waited for the new baby, Gordon's official duties began. The overarching organization, the HK CCC, was the all-powerful local equal of 475 Riverside Drive in New York. The structure was mainly comprised of church leaders who had been ousted from China by Mao's government in 1949. It actually represented the Christian establishment in exile from China, settled in Hong Kong, holding on. The struggle it faced now was to throw off the domination of the foreign mission establishment and become totally Chinese in its power structure. The old China Hands who had never conceded that the Chinese were "ready" to take over the church organization, were still arm wrestling with upstart young Chinese who were proclaiming their independence from the West.

Independent in every regard, that was, except financially. The money from America was still welcome.

We, the DeVelders, and a new couple, the Poppens, were all RCA people funded by 475 in New York, but a canny young Chinese who had learned his lessons of power well from the Westerners, was now that power with an Asian face. A man named Peter Wong.

It was Wong and his council who decided what Gordon's work would be. First, he would form a relationship with a local Chinese church operating in one of the resettlement areas of Kowloon, focusing on the youth group. The second assignment would be to an Anglo Chinese high school on the Hong Kong side. The school was in the process of being constructed in Happy Valley, in the shadow of Tiger Balm Garden, a famous Chinese park.

It was in the youth group at Sum Oi Church that Gordon first met members of the Chey family. During our first stay in Hong Kong we never really had a Chinese family whom we considered real friends—business acquaintances, yes, but never real friends. The Cheys, Henry and Florence, and their seven sons and one daughter, became our friends.

They came over one day to the flat at number 10 Cornwall Street, and sat around the living room on brown folding chairs hastily borrowed from people across the hall. Not all seven sons came, only the ones who were not working that day.

Florence and Henry had been in China during World War II. They had owned and operated a small restaurant which catered to American soldiers stationed in China during the war, and had learned to like the foreigners. One of the uncles had actually married a Westerner, and the family considered themselves people with an international identity. Most of them spoke fluent English, but they were still beautifully Chinese.

Sitting around the circle, we were sizing each other up. We were actually using Chinese (with a few goofs, which they good-naturedly corrected).

Henry was a short, strongly-built fellow with a big smile and an outgoing personality. Florence, for all her seven sons and one daughter, barely weighed a hundred pounds. Perfectly coiffed, svelte in a cheongsam with size five expensive shoes, she was obviously the queen of the pack. Anyone with seven sons was assured of status in this life and the next. It was a benefit one would not lose even by converting to Christianity. Florence was set.

She reached out to me, a woman like herself.

"When will the baby come?" she whispered to me behind her tiny bejeweled hand.

"September."

"Ah, he will be born in the year of the horse—a very good year."

"He?"

She eyed my growing structure.

"Ah, yes. I think it will be a boy. I can tell by the shape of your belly."

She should know. She had done it seven times.

Henry had a moving business. He was chatting with Gordon, still sizing him up. "When you start working at the new school are you going to keep living here on Cornwall Street?"

"Probably not," Gordon answered. "It might be more practical to live on the Hong Kong side. Crossing the ferry every day might waste a lot of time."

"You get ready to move, just call me," Henry offered. "We've got lorries. You call Columbia Transport."

Gordon took Henry's card and stuck it in his wallet.

We had been thinking of moving to the Hong Kong side ever since the school assignment had come through officially. Then a very disturbing thing happened that pushed the consideration even further.

The kids had been playing in the parking area under the apartments that day. They had outgrown the mythical tricycles without even having one, but we had picked up a small bike which Mike claimed as his special right. His dad had a car and a motor scooter, and he, the boy, should have wheels, too.

A car had come toward him in the parking lot, and he turned sharply to avoid hitting it. The car and the handlebars of the bike collided, with Mike's fingers between the surfaces. By the time we heard him screaming and rushed downstairs, Mike's fingertip was hanging by a piece of skin, totally severed.

Gordon rushed him to the hospital down at the end of the street, and the doctor (the one from language school) was able to sew the fingertip back on.

Mike was restless that night, his hand throbbing. With a mother's ear, I was listening, even though fast asleep. I heard him cry out in the night and hopped out of bed to go and check on him. When I got to his bunk in the kids' room, he was sleeping, just crying out in his sleep, poor lamb. I put a quiet kiss on his forehead. I groggily got back in bed and knew nothing else until the next morning.

Gordon got up and reached for his trousers, always laid out on a chair. They were not there.

"What did you do with my pants?" he asked.

"I didn't have your pants," I said, going into the next room to check on Mike.

Something was wrong. The apartment felt strange. Then I saw Gordon's pants under the dining room table.

"Why did you throw your pants under the table?" I asked, puzzled.

"I wouldn't throw my pants under the table! What do you mean?"

"Well, here they are..."

Gordon claimed his trousers, suddenly checking the pockets. His watch and wallet were gone. We had been robbed!

I walked into the kitchen to put the kettle on. There the screen had been slashed by an obviously powerful knife, and the thief had hastily exited.

The pants under the table? The intruder had been startled by my sudden appearance in the middle of his operation and had hastily hidden under the table with the pants and the knife while I had stumbled past sleepily, inches from him.

The police came and checked the apartment, looking for clues. Out on the verandah the thief had scraped the putty from around a pane in the door and removed the glass to open the door latch.

We did not want to live in this apartment anymore. We had been violated. All things considered, Henry's moving lorry sounded good.

When Ah Whoever learned we were moving to the Hong Kong side, she simply vanished. We went back to look at her room and found it clean as a whistle. The amah next door told us she had gone back to China.

Maybe she missed speaking her village dialect.

CHAPTER SEVEN

THE PLACE WE CHOSE ON Macdonald Road was situated halfway up Victoria Peak. The mid-rise structure clung to the side of the mountain, street level in front, but plunging precipitously toward the back of the flat. The building had a rounded shape which gave it a pleasant look on the outside, but made for oddly shaped, rounded rooms internally.

I looked at the living room, puzzled. How did one put a straight couch against a curved wall? Had we thought of this?

I stepped out on the verandah, the ever-present verandah of Hong Kong life, and looked down at the concrete parking lot four floors below. The peak tram climbed silently up the leftside of our new flat, gliding on its cable. Presently its counterpart would descend on the opposite track as they pulled each other up and down the mountain

One street below on Kennedy Road was the school where our children would be going, starting again, like all of us.

Revlon the cat sniffed the place out, but withheld her opinion.

It was September, and the beginning of the school year at Kennedy Road Junior School. Each school had its own uniforms, so that meant a trip to the tailor down on Queen's Road for fittings. Three sets of skits, pants, blazers, shirts, and the all-important details like shoes. There were so many ways to look "right" and "wrong." Even within the dress code kids had subtle ways of being snobbish.

Marita was worried. "Mom, I need loafers, not those awful brown shoes with laces. Last year my shoes were wrong, and people looked at them."

"What did they say?"

"They didn't say anything. They just looked at them like I didn't know any better."

Most of the third graders at Kennedy Road Junior School were sons and daughters of British government employees and business people. Many of them also lived halfway up the peak. Our kids, being American, were in danger of wearing the wrong shoes and looking ridiculous.

But as the days went by, and we waited for the new baby, we began to appreciate the new school. Out in an open courtyard surrounded by classrooms the art teacher set up a field of easels. Once a week the students were provided with large sheets of paper, pots of paint and brushes, and encouraged to express themselves in color.

"We need paint smocks, Mom. You have to get them at the school. We have to have the right smocks."

The twins came home with their paintings. Mike had done a beautiful painting of blue water in the harbor, with small and large boats, and orange loading cranes topped by the mountain and sky. He proudly tacked it up on the wall in his bedroom.

Marita had chosen an entirely different theme: three girls in red dresses called "friends." The three figures were parted, two girls together, leaning their heads toward each other with the third girl standing alone, watching them. The drawings were childish, but profound. Mike was seeing his outer surroundings—Marita was turned inward, showing some pain under her outward bravado. It was so different from their outward demeanor where Marita was always the aggressive organizer and Mike the quiet one. What a tremendous responsibility it was to be aware not only of the outer needs of children, but also their inner development.

But I was pleased that the kids enjoyed painting. As a child, painting and writing poetry had helped me survive in a crazy adult world. Art protected one's soul.

The paintings were properly framed and hung in the living room.

The only art on my mind right now was the birth of our next child. What would he/she be, and what name would we choose?

We had not seriously discussed names.

"If it's a boy shall we name it after you?" I asked.

"No. People will call him Gord. I never liked being called Gord as a kid. What if it's a girl—shall we name it after you?"

"Heavens no. If she's my daughter she'll want her own name, not her mother's."

"We could use your name as a middle name for a boy," I suggested.

"Then what would we have for a first name?"

I pondered. A, B, C...C?

"The kids have been to see *Sound of Music* six times," I said, "and they all love *Winnie the Pooh* books."

63

So? This was getting nowhere. The new crib was standing in the corner of our bedroom, ready for the new child. It had a blanket and a Pooh Bear waiting.

Christopher Plummer—*Sound of Music.*

Christopher Robin—*Winnie the Pooh.*

"Christopher Gordon," I decided

"What if it's a girl?"

I couldn't think of any girl's names. I knew it was psychologically dangerous, but I simply couldn't.

Gordon's birthday, September 26, came and went. I baked him an apple pie and we waited. It wasn't going to be today.

September 27.

September 28.

September 29.

"Do you think we have the date wrong?"

"No, I think this child has a mind of its own and doesn't want to share a birthday with you," I teased.

"I'll take you for a rickshaw ride and shake things loose," he offered.

"Oh hush," I said miserably. I was ready to explode.

The morning of September 30 I packed a bag and we drove up to Matilda Hospital. The pains were coming.

This was our fourth baby. How would I handle the pain of childbirth this time? Was I afraid of it? Afraid it would kill me or split me open? No, I knew it would not do that. I had been here before, swollen, gross, in misery. Was there some way to grab the pain, command it, use it to bring this child into the world without fear?

Fear. It was the fear of the pain that made it so powerful. What would happen if I opened myself to it, embraced it, used it as mine?

I lay on the bed with Gordon holding my hand, silent as a cat giving birth to a kitten.

Pain? Yes.

Fear? No.

I breathed deeply, feeling the life force pulse through me.

I was standing under the waterfall while the river rolled over my head, crashing into the chasm below, caught up in the throes of creation…

Gordon leaned over me, touching his lips lightly to mine.

"Are you okay?" he whispered.

I looked at him, grateful. I was doing more than okay. I was giving birth to his child, our child, a child of the world.

The labor was relatively short this time. After a few hours of contractions the sister came in to check. She lifted the sheet and called for a gurney to be brought. The baby was already coming.

They wheeled me over to the delivery room. The sisters were prepping me and Doctor Freddie Watson was scrubbing his hands. He offered me some gas in a mask.

"Will it harm the baby?" I asked.

"Not really—just stun it a little."

He held the cone to my face. I breathed once and shoved it aside. Then I gave a mighty push and the baby was there. I heard a husky cry.

A buzz of voices...masked faces. I heard Doctor Watson, saw his smile. It was the I-told-you-so look on his face.

"Well, my dear, you have a handsome little boy—super little fellow!"

They laid the baby on my stomach, then held him up so I could see his face. We looked at each other, and I felt I had always known him. I had not shed a single tear during the whole delivery, but when I saw him I burst into tears—tears of joy.

"What's his name?" they asked.

"Christopher Gordon De Pree."

"In his father's honor?"

"His father and Winnie the Pooh!"

I luxuriated in the comforts of Matilda Hospital for almost a week, being pampered and spoiled. Chris' bassinette was beside my bed so I could nurse him, but the sisters took him away to bathe and change him. The sisters called him "Little Prince," the utmost compliment from people of a monarchy-based existence, and treated him like royalty. Chris weighed almost nine pounds at birth, and seemed totally content in his new world. He was dark haired and pink cheeked, just as I had imagined him.

This was my last child. I felt fulfilled, satisfied. We had, in royal terms, two heirs and two spares.

And... Mike had won! He had a brother!

They came to see us in the hospital every evening, and Mike was the proudest of them all. The girls would have to move over. There were two boys now.

"How are you managing without me?" I asked lazily, enjoying my hot baths and afternoon tea.

"Dad's a good cook!" Mike said. "He fries really good eggs, even better than you do, and he lets me do it sometimes."

I'd better get home soon. I was losing my clout.

Only one terrible thing happened while I was in the hospital. Revlon, the cat, was walking along the edge of the verandah railing when she lost her balance and fell four stories onto the concrete parking area below. Her front legs were broken and her head smashed.

They had taken her to the vet, who had set and splinted her legs and bandaged her head, saying it would heal.

I decided I had better get home. Now.

The cat was in a basket, splinted and bandaged—poor little beautiful Revlon. A warning bell buzzed somewhere inside me. Was this apartment, with it's terrible drop off the verandah, dangerous?

We settled Chris into his crib in the corner of our room. So much happiness, so much pride. As soon as I was firmly on my feet, I walked down Garden Road to Queens Road and hurried to Whiteaway's Department Store. I wanted to buy the most beautiful little boy outfit I could find, no matter what it cost.

The usual Chinese woman with a British accent looked at me over her glasses.

"We're all out of little newborn boy's outfits now," she said. "We'll have to wait for the next shipment from England."

"What?"

I had just had a baby boy. How could they possibly be out of newborn boy clothes?

"Sorry madam."

She began studying her long red nails.

I walked back up the hill to Macdonald Road. The world was not going to change...ships were not going to reschedule their arrival from England...and clerks at Whiteaway's were not going to give a damn, just because I had a beautiful baby boy.

But I was happy. Gordon was happy. The kids were pleased, and that was enough. I hoped poor little Revlon would survive.

A few weeks after Chris' birth there was a phone call from Doris Caldwell, a woman who was fast becoming a good friend. She had been in mainland China, in fact had gone there just as most people were leaving in the 1949 exodus. She had only begun her studies in Mandarin when the whole of China was plunged into war. She was warned to leave, but being very interested in what was happening, she decided to stay. She was arrested and put in jail.

"It was very complicated," she told me one day. "I saw a lot of what foreigners were doing in China and I didn't blame the Chinese for wanting to be rid of them. In prison I listened to the communist propaganda we were subjected to every day, and I have to admit..." She paused and smiled reflectively.

"Admit what?"

Another pause and a shy smile.

"I was more than a little pink! Maybe it was the Stockholm syndrome or whatever they call it, but I began to sympathize with what they were saying."

"Doris, how could you? Why are all these people refugees from China if it's so great?"

"Well, let me tell you the rest. I listened until I, and everyone else in prison, began to starve...and then I got sick. I changed my mind. China was a madhouse. I left."

"How did you get out?"

"There was a ship that took a whole group of us who'd stayed behind. I was taken home on that ship and hospitalized with TB."

Doris had regained her health, and, like some of us, wanted to come back, but not to China. She wanted to come to Hong Kong. She knew that there were many refugees from the mainland living in terrible conditions in Kowloon, and she wanted to help. It was the Presbyterians who had sent her back to the area of Kowloon she now served, Kwun Tong, home of many new factories. She and her group had established an organization, a family service center, which had multiple ways of helping the community. One of them was a group of women who had sewing skills but could not afford daycare for their children while they worked in the factories.

The center provided simple sewing machines for them and gave them a chance to work at home, bringing in their work and being paid by the piece.

Doris wanted me to come out and help her, maybe once a week.

"We could use a little design advice," she said. "The women know how to sew—they stitch well, but some of the designs they come up with are not, shall we say, not marketable."

"You're marketing them?"

"We could, if we had products good enough. The Welfare Handicraft Shop at the Star Ferry would handle our goods if they appealed to the tourists."

I hesitated. It would be a good chance to practice my Chinese. It could be fun..."

Give me a chance to think about it," I said, "I've got my hands full with the baby right now."

"Bring him along!" Doris laughed. "We've got plenty of babies out here!"

The Anglo-Chinese high school, Kung Lee, was going up. Gordon went down to Tai Hang Road daily and watched the great cranes swing back and forth, placing steel girders on the foundations that had been pounded into the rock layers of the mountain. Like everything else on Hong Kong Island, it was perched at a crazy angle on the hillside using every inch of expensive real estate.

The city was rising from its refugee squalor, and new structures were springing up overnight, some not so sturdy and some, like the new school, embedded in the rock.

Up behind the new school, Tiger Balm Garden spread its colorful maze of Chinese myths and legends depicted in gaudy fantasy figures. Farther up the hill squatter huts huddled together, so fragile that the tropical rains caused mudslides, washing the tar paper and stick shacks into the rain gutters and leaving people homeless.

It was a good place to build a new school. Out of poverty and ancient superstition a new thing could arise, a new generation.

There was much to be decided in preparation for the new school…
Uniforms.

The job, with all its style and color decisions, had been delegated to Gordon. They would have to be contracted for and made in advance of the school's opening in September.

Color was the essential decision. Every Hong Kong school wanted to have a distinctive uniform, one that could be instantly recognized as belonging to that school. The field was crowded. There were government schools, Anglican schools, Catholic schools, and private schools. Most of the schools wore navy blue or shades of gray, with a few venturing into dark greens.

I was going through a brown phase. All the new fashions from England down on Queens Road were brown. It was hot.

"How about brown?" I suggested. No one else had claimed that field.

"We'll get some fabric samples from the tailor downtown and see what the school group thinks."

We collected material swatches and poured over patterns for blazers, skirts, pants, all in shades of deep chocolate brown and tans with checkered shirts and blouses. Dark brown sweaters could be used in cooler months, and white shirts in summer. When Gordon showed them to his group, no one seemed too enthusiastic, but no one actually objected, and the order went ahead.

Brown it was. One would be able to spot Kung Lee students a mile off.

The school was nearly completed. The strong steel and concrete building stood out ruggedly against the hill, finished. Now the inner arrangements were being made, teachers hired, and textbooks bought. The office was set up to keep records in English and Chinese. Mr. Barton, an Englishman almost ready to retire, would serve as the headmaster.

As a church-funded school, Kung Lee would be subject to Hong Kong board of education scrutiny, but would not be government funded. The teachers would not be paid as much as those of similar education in competing government schools.

This was not a problem for foreigners, as they were funded by their own organizations, but for the Chinese teachers on the staff it could be a real issue. How could the school expect to hire and keep the best staff if they could leave and get better pay elsewhere?

Gordon worried about this in principle, but he was not the headmaster and had no say in the matter.

The English program was in splendid hands. Bernie Anderson, a Swarthmore graduate and Rhodes Scholar, was coming to give life to language and drama for the students. A young, blond, curly-haired American, he had met an English girl during his studies abroad and was thinking of getting married.

With his background in seminary, Gordon was put in charge of the BK program and student assemblies. BK, Biblical Knowledge, was an elective course which could be studied in preparation for the school Cert, the all-important exam at the end of secondary school, the passing of which was the key to any further advancement.

In the British school system the Bible was taught as Western literature. How could one hope to have an Anglo-Chinese education without knowledge of the basic book of Western civilization? There was not, overtly, any pressure to make Christian converts. The course was taught as the Chinese would teach Buddhism in America, to broaden one's horizons.

Many of the students would be from Buddhist families, or, following the trend of Hong Kong young people in the 1960s, of no religion at all. The lines would need to be carefully drawn between cultural information and the assumption of shared values. This was not Zeeland, Michigan or Orange City, Iowa.

The classrooms were filled, the books distributed, and the uniforms fitted. Gordon ran up and down the multiple floors of the building (no elevators) shedding twenty pounds. At 36, Gordon had long legs, broad shoulders, and an open face that broke easily into a warm smile. At six feet, two inches, he towered above most of the students, but he did not come across as foreign or condescending, or aloof. He was a warm, genuine, human being without a prejudiced bone in his body, and the students swarmed around him like bees, listening to his every word. Without knowing why, they loved him, and without any ulterior motives, he loved them back.

This was real. This was where he belonged, in teaching.

Although he was not teaching English as such, when it came to using the two languages he had genuine empathy with the students. They had the same difficultly pronouncing English words as he had experienced in learning Chinese—in reverse. They shared a bond.

Sometimes when we encountered Kung Lee students on the streets downtown we wondered about the brown uniforms. With the shades and varieties of Asian skin, brown had perhaps not been the wisest choice—the reason no one else used it. But if the truth be told, most of the young Chinese students were so good looking they would have looked fine in a paper bag.

Meanwhile, Gordon had the curious feeling that he was being watched. The man named Peter Wong had his eye on this popular young American.

Chapter Eight

MOM AND DAD DE PREE were coming to Hong Kong! We could not believe it! Dad had rarely been out of Michigan, except for a brief stint of duty stateside during World War I, and Mom had never been outside the United States. This was news!

There were dual reasons for the trip. Bill, the smart one in the family who had gone to Harvard and entered foreign service about the same time Gordon was in Korea, had been assigned to Ghana. Africa was his specialty. The folks had decided to make a world tour visiting both adventuresome sons.

We scrubbed and cleaned the apartment getting ready for their visit. The arrival at Kai Tak Airport with its heat and heavy smells of crowded humanity would be a shock, and we wanted the McDonald Road flat to be a refuge of Dutch cleanliness.

Practically speaking, it was undoubtedly the worst time in our Hong Kong years for them to come. The 99-year lease of the Crown Colony to the British as a result of the opium wars had 32 years before it was due to expire and return Hong Kong to mainland China, but the local communists were getting impatient. They wanted the agreement to end sooner, and were using every means to make it happen.

The Hong Kong governor's mansion up on Garden Road was only a few blocks from our flat on McDonald Road. Two weeks before, there had been a confrontation between rioting crowds and police with shields and tear gas. We could hear the roar from our balcony. Then one day on the way to a small grocery store on the hillside, our four children and I were caught up in a crowd of protesters shouting death to the foreigners.

It struck me as strange in that moment. Mobs and crowds take no notice of individuals. We were here to learn and understand, but to that crowd we were Westerners...a class of people they hated. If the mob turned violent, we could be killed. But we calmly made our way back to the apartment and life went on.

As soon as Gordon's parents came, we proudly showed them our adopted world. Downtown Queens Road and Devoe Road; Fenwick Pier where we had worked the first three years; the harbor and Star Ferry—all places we had written about in our weekly letters. They were anxious to see where Gordon worked now.

Kung Lee School was new and shiny. The students and staff surrounded the parents of their Ding Sinsang (teacher De Pree) with love and respect.

In front of the canteen where the students ate lunch, workers were scrubbing graffiti off the cement walls. Vandals had come during the night and scribbled "Death to the Foreigners" in large black characters on the crisp new walls. It was a dangerous time.

We took them to Repulse Bay where we had lived when the babies were small, and the Stanley Market, a fascinating Chinese village on the South China Sea. Then we settled in on McDonald Road to let them absorb the flavor of our family life.

The children had not seen their grandparents for almost four years. The twins were eight and a half, Deidra was seven, and Chris was one year. They were eager to get newly acquainted. Mom De Pree held Chris and pronounced him just like Gordon at that age.

The older kids were eager to show off. They took their grandparents out on the verandah and pointed out Kennedy Road Junior School far below, then up on the rooftop where the whole neighborhood could be surveyed—the Peak Tram wending its way up and down the mountain, and the harbor spread below with the ships and Chinese junks in full sail.

We were settled in our curiously round living room when the subject of Revlon the cat came up.

"We used to have a cat," Marita was explaining. "She was such a pretty cat. She was kind of like our baby before Chris was born."

"Yeah," Mike added, "she thought she was the baby, and then when Chris got born, she thought we didn't like her as much anymore. Whenever Mom fed Chris, she wanted to sit on Mom's lap too, and she wanted to crawl into Chris' crib and sleep right on top of him."

Mom De Pree's eyes were getting big. All the farm superstitions about cats smothering babies flashed across her face.

"Yeah," Deidra said, "the cat crawled right into Chris' crib!"

"Well, you did, too," Marita teased. "You still wanted to be the baby, too."

"I just wanted to see what it felt like again," Deidra defended. "I wasn't going to hurt him."

"What happened to the cat?" Grandma asked.

"She fell over the edge out on the verandah and almost got killed," they all answered.

"But she did get better, and we had to give her away because she didn't like Chris."

"She was jealous and swatted at his face, so some Chinese people took her—took Revlon to their house."

"The cat fell over the balcony?" Mom De Pree asked.

"Yeah, but she just got her legs broken and her head smashed."

Mom De Pree took in a deep breath and exchanged a glance with Dad De Pree. Nobody said anything.

They wanted a day at the beach, so on Saturday we packed a picnic and loaded the whole bunch up to drive to Big Wave Bay, an idyllic location on the south side of the island with gentle seas and a cool wind. We offered to get a white tent, knowing the ferocity of the tropical sun even under a seemingly cool breeze.

"No, "Mom insisted, "that's not necessary. I've worked on the farm in Nebraska. I tan, but never burn. I don't get sunburned," she insisted.

"But the sun is stronger here."

"The tent's not necessary—just a waste of money."

Dad rolled up his pant legs and sat in a chair at the edge of the water, letting the warm saltwater wash over his white feet. Mom rolled her skirt up to brown her thighs.

The next morning Dad's feet were so red and swollen he could not get his shoes on and had to wear bedroom slippers. Mom had blisters on her thighs the size of a laundry bag.

Dad doggedly put on his slippers. He still wanted to go to the tailor and see about being measured for a suit. It was raining (it rained almost every morning in Hong Kong) and he was standing under an awning in front of the tailor shop when the awning collapsed, sending a flood of water down his back.

About that time, Dad decided he hated Hong Kong. "I'm fiece of this filthy place," he sputtered, using a good Dutch expression of utter disgust.

Mom took Gordon aside for a good heart-to-heart talk.

"Gord..." she said, and he knew what was coming, "Chris is one year old. He's just starting to climb on everything. You used to climb on everything. I can just see him climbing up on that balcony...and..." She was crying quietly. "...and falling four stories like that poor cat did!"

He put his arm around his mom and promised.

"We'll move," he said.

"Go back to that nice place you used to live by the sea. It would be so much safer."

Just like that, we were going to move again.

We took Mom and Dad to the airport and as a final gesture of farewell, we were surrounded by a demonstrating mob on Nathan Road who shouted at us and tried to rock the car. The little Morris Mini nearly turned over.

The trip would be talked about for years, glamorized and softened, and edited in the retelling, but Dad never changed his mind. He preferred Zeeland, Michigan to that filthy city of Hong Kong. Much too dirty for a good Dutchman.

Word finally came down from China to the local communists. They were ordered to be patient, the lease would expire in time and they should not cause any more trouble.

The riots were over.

We had lived in number one and number two on Repulse Bay Road, and now we began to look for an empty apartment in number three. These were spacious, four-story dwellings, surrounded by flowering trees and fronted by a nullah (stream) that ran down to the beach. From the apartments one crossed a foot bridge, passed the kiosk where ice cream and drinks were purchased, and walked out onto a wide gentle beach. The water was safe for children, as the sand sloped gently under the waves for several hundred feet. Safety in the water was not really an issue, as all the kids except Chris were good swimmers due to Gordon's lessons at the YMCA.

Gordon's mom was right. We would be much safer here. The number six bus would take the children to school every morning, so they could continue to go to Kennedy Road School.

A new American school had opened in Repulse Bay, an international school spearheaded by the Lutherans, but for now we would let the kids finish out the year at Kennedy Road.

Florence and Henry came over to visit, and as we began to talk moving, Henry was the man. By the end of the month his crew had loaded up the open moving lorry and our goods were deposited in number three Repulse Bay Road.

Three bedrooms this time. Boys, girls and ours.

The second-story apartment had a large living room, separate dining room, three bedrooms, two baths, a sizeable kitchen, and a huge verandah that opened all across the front. This verandah had a sturdy cement balcony and a steel-screened guard rail high above it. Gordon checked it and breathed a sigh of relief. Chris could run and climb to his heart's content with no danger.

The older kids had weekly allowances and could buy treats at the kiosk. Mike, at eight and a half, was tan with a sun-bleached mop of thick golden hair. He loved to hang out at the kiosk. The Chinese boys who ran the kiosk called him gum-jai (little golden boy), and loved to touch his hair for good luck. Mike ate it up. Having a brother had done wonders for him, although sometimes when he thought about it, he was no longer the only boy, which had its problems. Now he had competition.

We had moved. The apartment and the neighborhood were beautiful. The breeze blew in from the sea, sweet and fresh, and the gardener kept the gardens impeccably. The kids were safe, but that year we felt oddly displaced. There was a sense of having stepped backward in our journey. We were in a good neighborhood, surrounded by the same expat community and rich Chinese as we had been, but it was not like before.

We were not the same.

We discussed this feeling late one night when the kids were asleep.

"Maybe you need to get more involved in things outside the house," Gordon suggested. "Have you thought any more about helping Doris Caldwell in Kwun Tong with her sewing women?"

"I'd have to get an amah, or some help on the day I'm away."

That still wasn't it.

"How about you?" I asked. "Are you still in touch with your motor mechanics boys?"

"Too busy for that."

"Well, you're up to your neck in Chinese students five days a week. What more do you need?"

"I don't really know," he paused. "Sometimes I feel the work I'm doing at the school is so one sided. I teach Western thought and beliefs to young people of this culture while I know so little of what my students' lives are about. What are the stories their mothers told them as young kids? What do they really think about life and the life hereafter? We teach them the stories of Easter and Christmas, but what do we know about their holidays and festivals, their legends and their classic myths? We've been taught Chinese words, but what do those words mean to them that they don't mean to us?"

I looked at him, puzzled. Gordon, like his folks, was a man of few words. He did things. He did not talk about it. Who, really, was this seemingly open yet complex, unconventional man I had married, and what did he want?

After twelve years, I still did not know. But one thing I did know. I loved him with a deep and fierce love, and would always be there for him, exploring with him...

I dreamed a strange haunting dream that night about Peter Wong, a man I barely knew. He was talking to one of his council, in Chinese.

'Watch him...' he was whispering, but it echoed eerily, like a voice in a cave, 'Find out what he wants...why he is here. Does he have dreams of making a name for himself in America? ...you can't control these foreigners unless you know what they want...mok dik...motives...'

I told Gordon about the dream over coffee the next morning. "Humph!" he said, and that was it.

Doris Caldwell from the Kwun Tong Family Service Center came over to visit in Repulse Bay, and we worked on ideas for her group of sewing women.

"How would it be to make a simple smock dress in different cotton ginghams and sew up a doll with a dress to match?" I suggested. "The doll would fit in the dress pocket."

"Where would we get the doll pattern?"

"I could make one—a simple cut-out with an embroidered face and yarn hair."

"If you can design it they can make it. They're really quite skilled."

That week I worked on a face for a Chinese doll. I still had trouble with the angle of Chinese eyes. The stereotype of little slanted slits certainly wasn't authentic. What was it that gave Oriental eyes that distinctive look within a range of so many different looks?

I remembered the painting of Gina, now hanging in Earl Klay's home in Orange City, Iowa. Gina's eyes were round and luminous, as well as exquisitely shaped.

I drew a pattern of eyes like Gina's, and wondered where she was now. She would be almost eighteen by this time. Had she ever finished school, as the Lows had promised?

I made a mental note to ask about her. How could I have forgotten her?

Gordon was home late one night. I knew he was going to take his scooter and drive out to Kowloon to visit the Motor Mechanics group he had mentored during language school. But as time went by and it was getting later, I started to worry. A storm had blown up with a fierce wind and sheets of rain. Where was he?

When he appeared at the door, I gasped. He was torn and bruised, with blood on his arms and face. He was soaked to the skin.

"What?" I croaked.

"I got caught in heavy traffic on Nathan Road—the reflections blinded me."

"Come on, let me help you get those clothes off. My God, man, what happened?"

"I lost control of the scooter...it slid from under me and I went down, right in the middle of the traffic."

I skinned his clothes off and drew a tub of hot water. He sank into the warmth, gratefully. I checked him over. No broken bones.

"You didn't get hurt?"

"Just a few scrapes and bruises."

I was like a mother, so glad her child has escaped danger she feels like killing him.

"You are going to get rid of that damned scooter," I scolded.

He didn't disagree. He might not come out alive next time. So, we advertised it at the bus stop, the route that came past Repulse Bay and terminated at Stanley Village.

MOTOR SCOOTER FOR SALE.

The two Chinese boys who came to ask about the scooter were familiar faces. We had seen them often when we took the bus to Stanley Village to buy fresh produce. Ng Wing Sung and Jerry Jau wanted the scooter. And that was the beginning of the rest of our lives...

We took the kids to Stanley on the number six bus that weekend, walking down the market street, poking around in the shops, savoring the aromas from the open air street stalls. The village was old, harking back to the days of piracy and smuggling. Its Chinese name was Chek Chu, or "the place of thieves." With only two main streets, it wound through rice shops and vegetable stalls, between alleys and down to the waterfront. Fishing boats tied up along the shore and huge old banyan trees shaded a crumbling wine factory—rice wine and its pungent aroma lay under all the other olfactory presences of the street: fish and rice wine and the smell of ginger and garlic.

"This place is pretty neat," Mike decided.

"It sort of stinks," Marita sniffed.

"It's not really a stink," Mike said, "it's just a different kind of smell."

That was the week it all came to the surface, the idea that Gordon had been thinking about and didn't dare mention.

77

"Did you see that little house across the street from the wine factory?" he asked one day.

"I didn't particularly notice it. Why?"

"An old English guy used to live there. He stayed in the village for a number of years researching Chinese creeds and customs. In fact, he has several books he wrote on the subject."

"You should get those. We could put them in the bookshelf with our language school textbooks and study them."

"But that wasn't what I was going to say. The old fellow died there not long ago, and nobody knew it until he'd been dead for over a week."

"Who found him?"

"People smelled something and called the landlord, and he opened the door and went in. The Chinese in the market were really spooked about it."

"Spooked?"

"The house has been vacant for several months. No one wants to rent it. A foreign devil died there, and they think that his ghost is wandering around...that the house is haunted."

"Stupid superstitions," I said, and then I began to think...

The Chinese were not the only superstitious people in the world. It seemed to be a part of the human mind, invented and named different things, but always there—sometimes dangerously, always illogically...

Gordon looked like he wanted to say something more, but he waited.

We went to Stanly Market again the next weekend. The house on the corner had a bold FOR RENT sign on the door. It was a strange little place, tall and narrow, three floors on top of each other with only two or three rooms on each floor. It had three wide curving tile steps leading straight off the street to a heavy door with a big brass handle and a high window. Windows ran around the sea side of the ground floor, and the third tier boasted a small balcony looking out over the boats and the water.

Gordon was looking at it. I looked at Gordon's face and was jealous. He was in love with it, this funny house on the sea.

That night he finally talked about it.

"What would it be like..." he began, "to spend some time there? We know the language. We're wasting it here in Repulse Bay where everyone speaks English. We could learn so much from boys like Jerry and Wai Sun, even more than that little Englishman knew. I read some of what he's written, and it's from such a colonial viewpoint. He almost speaks of Chinese as though they're specimens in a zoo or a scientific laboratory. There's not much life or sense of connection with fellow humans."

"Do you think they knew that?"

"No one seems to mind that he died."

Words...dangling in midair.

Words...not spoken.

I knew what he was thinking.

Then, one night, he finally said it.

"Would you...do you think you'd like to live in Stanley Village, just for a few years?"

I was back on the porch of the little log cabin at Cumberland Falls, and we were watching fireflies and smoking those absurd cigarettes...he was asking me again if I would do something that deeply terrified me.

I could see it.

Moving to Stanley Village to live on the market street would be like moving from Chicago to live in the back hills of Appalachian Kentucky. That miserable one-room cabin with no electricity and no running water. My mom had suffered from that life...I had suffered. Was I going to expose my children to a primitive neighborhood to somehow deepen our understanding of the world? Would Gordon recklessly endanger them like this?

I said NO.

For the first time in our marriage I said NO.

No way.

He looked wounded.

"All right," he said slowly. "You know I'd never do anything that you were deeply opposed to. That's the rule. If either one of us is really against it, we don't do it."

"I try never to take advantage of that," I said

"I know you do," he said, kissing me sadly.

I could not imagine my parents ever having that conversation. We were dealing with a different set of characters here, even though the story had similarities. It was not the house that had made her sad...

But Gordon did not bring it up again.

Every time we went to the market, I avoided looking at the house. It was still for rent. I felt like I was standing between Gordon and something he loved. Thank God it was not another woman. I knew what I would do about that, but how do you kill a house?

The kids were taking the city bus to school every day and they brought home extra reading books in their backpacks. One book that Deidra loved was called *The King's Stilts*. I read it with her. King Bertram was a strange but good king who ruled his kingdom very well. But after work each day he would go to a closet, take out a pair of red stilts, and race around his kingdom on them. The members of his ruling council were terribly embarrassed by this. They took his stilts and hid them, and the problem was solved, only it wasn't. Without his stilts, the king grew sad and let all his work go, and the kingdom was going to rack and ruin.

Gordon didn't say any more about the village, but he, too, was going to rack and ruin. I could sense it. The spark wasn't there. I was hiding his red stilts in the castle closet. Had I once told my mother that I would never kill his spirit, that I didn't want to kill his dreams and live with a dead man?

Okay. But what about the kids?

I had to admit it. This probably wasn't about the kids. It was about me, about old fears and miseries, and terrors they had never known. Was I projecting my own fears onto them?

So, for his birthday on September 26, I wrote him a card and cut out a pair of paper red stilts and put them in it...and said yes.

It was a decision I would never regret. Neither one of us knew where it would take us, but at least we would be on the same page.

There was peace in the house, and love.

But I would always be on my guard.

With finishing up the fall semester, it was several months before we actually moved. We reserved the little house by the sea, and Gordon plunged into the winter festivities at Kung Lee School.

There was a play directed by Bernie Anderson, and a dance. Gordon was in charge of the dance. The students decorated the canteen, and Bernie provided music for the disk jockey: Beatles music and other rock and roll. We danced with the Chinese students, sweet little Chinese boys and girls who were so eager to know all about the West, about America. As I danced with students who came up to my chin I realized they knew much more about American music and dance than I did. We had been gone too long.

Caught between cultures, I hoped we could learn as much about them as they were learning about us.

The word was getting out about our planned move to the village market. The CCC members were wondering why. What was this American trying to prove? What were his motives?

Barton, the present headmaster, was going to leave Kung Lee School at the end of the next school year. He was moving to Australia with a new young Chinese wife. He was seventy and retiring.

The CCC office called Gordon, and he had a meeting with Peter Wong. Would he consider being the new headmaster of Kung Lee?

Gordon was hesitant.

"I'm not qualified," he told Wong. "I don't have a Master's Degree in Education."

"We know that," Wong said, "and we've discussed it with your sponsor in New York. If you are willing to take this position, they will pay for you and your family to go to New York City and get your Education Administration Degree at Columbia University. It should take about a year and a half. Then you would return to Hong Kong and serve as headmaster.

"Why did you choose me?"

"Because we like your attitude. The students like you. If you continue to work well with us, you have a good future in Hong Kong education."

What could he say?

Of course!

This threw everything into a new light. Gordon would work until the end of May and we would be off to New York. We would still move to Stanley Village and live in the house until the end of the school year. The DeVelders, who, of course, had known about the upcoming assignment before we had been told, had one more element to add.

"We're letting our place go in Kowloon," they said. "How would you like for us to take the Stanley place and live in it while you're gone? We'd love some time in the village. It would remind us of our life in China."

Surprise, surprise...

So much excitement had hinged on turning a NO into a YES. I had never dreamed it; this whole chain of events cascading down in the wake of changing one word. I had chosen the path of honoring my commitment to Gordon instead of nailing down my safety.

Where would it all lead?

Henry Chey's moving lorry came huffing and puffing into Stanley Village, scattering chickens and stray dogs as it wound its way through the market stalls and stopped in front of the tall narrow house by the sea.

The lorry parked under the banyan tree, loaded to the top with our household goods. When and where had we accumulated so much?

A crowd gathered, curious.

The house had been painted inside and the warm white walls reflected cleanliness and good cheer. Hopefully the hungry ghost of the old Englishman would feel out of place and leave. Anyhow, ghosts didn't bother me.

The neighbors continued to gape as the contents of the lorry were carried out into the little house. Besides the beds, couches, tables, chairs and chests, there were boxes and boxes of that stuff that make boxes and boxes of stuff when one moves: clothing and pots and pans, and goodness knows what.

I could hear the buzz in the crowd.

"Wah...gam do yeh... So many things!"

81

It was embarrassing.

When the lorry lumbered back up the market street and left us to it, I looked around, dismayed. How could we fit a Repulse Bay household into a Stanley Market dwelling?

There was a storeroom on the second floor, halfway up the stairs. If need be we could put the overflow there.

The house was actually laid out in an interesting pattern. On the ground floor a fairly good-sized, L-shaped living/dining room took up most of the space, leaving a bath, tiny kitchen, and an enclosed courtyard overhung by a large banyan tree. A curved terrazzo stairway wound up to the second floor, which contained two bedrooms and a bath—perfect for the kids. On up the stairs was our perch—a bedroom, study, and a balcony over the street and the sea. There was plenty of room for our family, and whatever we had that did not fit here we would simply have to give away. By Stanley Village standards, we were living in a mansion.

We decorated the boys' room in red bedspreads from Whiteaway's, with navy accessories, and the girls' in soft blues and greens. Our bedroom was white, dappled by sun patterns reflected on the water.

Luxury of luxuries, we had a tiny Italian washing machine that took up most of the downstairs bath (one had to sit on the toilet slightly sideways). The wash would have to be hung on clotheslines up on the balcony, like everyone else in the village. We would be just fine.

I was hanging out the wash on the balcony that week when the old question arose, but in a different light. Should we have an amah? Would I be viewed as an American Imperialist if I hired someone from the village? I could use the help.

I had a mouthful of clothespins when I heard her across the street. The woman was hanging her clothes on top of the rice wine factory.

"Good morning! Have you eaten rice yet?"

"Good morning. I've eaten."

"Why are you doing your own wash? Why don't you have a servant?"

"Why don't you?" I retorted in Chinese.

"I am the servant."

"Oh…" That shot that.

"My boss is the wife of the man who makes the wine. She used to be his mistress, but the wife hanged herself when she found out about her husband and the other woman, so now she's the wife and I'm the servant."

"Oh, that's awful," I said. "Where did she hang herself?"

"Right here in the wine factory. Her ghost still lives here. You can see it at night in the corner. Some people say it's just the gas jets, but I know it's her."

Oh Lord, another ghost. They should have called this street Ghost Central.

"So…" the woman said, her voice blowing in the wind in the space between rooftops, "are you hiring a servant?"

"I'm not sure."

"You should. People need jobs. How can you live here as a rich American and not give a job to someone?"

Well, that was a new angle. Like it or not, I was obligated to have some woman underfoot 24 hours a day, seven days a week.

But when she came, she was quiet and kind, fortyish, with a shy smile and a glint of tough humor in her eyes. Ah Wai became a part of our family. She lived in one of the squatter shacks up on the hillside above the market. Her husband was a barber who gave haircuts on the street. She had four children, one only a few years older than Chris.

Chris, at one and a half, reached out to her with that instinct babies have, and I knew this amah would be different. We communicated totally in Chinese.

The children, wonderfully adaptable creatures that they were, caught the same number six bus at the Stanley terminal and continued at Kennedy Road Junior School. Walter DeVelder suggested we keep them there for the year. Entering the British school system as young as they had, they were all a year ahead of the American kids their age. The year in New York at Teacher's College Agnes Russell School could be a relaxed repeat year for them. When we returned to Hong Kong, they would go to the new International School and be just the right age.

We only had a few months to enjoy the village before leaving for New York, and the kids threw themselves into absorbing the street and the alleyways…the rice shop, with its peanut oil and soy sauce, the cloth shop, the fruit and vegetable stalls, the noodle stall, but most of all the Stanley Store, a flight of stairs up above the other humble businesses.

The Stanley Store was run by a Mister Hong, the acknowledged leader of the Communist cell in the village. On his shelves we could find almost everything we needed. He stocked American goods and British goods as one would sell drugs, because there was a market for them and the money was good.

Mister Hong smiled icily at us through his thick glasses as we opened an account at his store. He must have viewed us as Capitalist Imperialists, high-flying spenders. The truth was, we lived from paycheck to paycheck, and the account was a better way to survive when our check came late.

But the average people in the village were extremely friendly to us. As usual, people were wondering why we were doing what we were doing, and we had not a clue. We were doing it because it was interesting.

The Tin Hau Temple perched by the sea was farther on down the street where we lived. Tin Hau, the goddess of the sea, was the central figure of veneration for the fishing community. She, and she alone, had control of the winds and the waves that spelled life and death for the fisher folk; and she, along with Kwan Yin, the goddess of mercy, served together to be the caretakers of all family affairs. The candles and incense sticks were kept burning before the wooden statues of these goddesses night and day.

"Like Maliah," Ah Wai explained, "the Heaven-Lord Mary."

"Aren't there any he-gods?" I asked.

"Oh, there are some, but they take care of war and money," she explained. "They're not very important."

It was spring, and the village celebration of the annual festival of Tin Hau was in full swing. The village association roasted a large pig, painted red with an apple in its mouth, and the statues were paraded through the streets with loud gongs and drums.

Ng Wai Sun, who ran the local noodle stall, came to our door with pieces of roast pork to share with our family. We were being included in the village protection against unfriendly ghosts.

With our resident Englishman, maybe they figured we needed it.

We had our long-standing assortment of "used" Chinese gods purchased on Cat Street. In Iowa they had seemed amusing and a bit daring—certainly ornamental—but here they were real. Should we still put them up on the living room shelf?

Ah Wai was puzzled.

"Why do you have these?" she asked.

"Just because they're pretty, like pieces of art."

"Not here," she said warily. "I don't believe in any gods myself—they've never done me any good—but people coming in your house might wonder why you have them. You are Christ-followers. Those gods could bring you bad luck."

"Not if we don't believe in them," I said. "They're just pieces of wood."

"You never know," she shook her head.

She was trying to protect us. We were forming an easy bond and respected each other, although she warned me not to mistake a servant for a friend.

"Are you going to work for the DeVelders when we're in New York?" I asked.

"If they want me."

"I hope you'll be here when we come back."

Ah Wai was a great cook. She could take a tiny piece of meat and a handful of vegetables with a bit of fresh ginger and garlic, and make food to die for. Mike stood in the kitchen, watching. He loved to cook. He memorized what she was doing. And every morning she would boil Chris' egg just so—soft boiled and mashed, with a dab of butter.

"Ah Wai," he pointed to his egg one morning, "Ho sic. Ho sic, Ah wai." (tastes good)

Sitting in his high chair, speaking Chinese. Had we not noticed before? Would he be our first bilingual child?

Mike was learning language as well. On his wall he had pinned a vocabulary list. Each time he learned a new word on the street, he added it to his list. He had thirty words now.

He loved to stroll through the village with Chris on his shoulders, eating things like dried squid. The village kids followed him, calling out his name.

"Miko...Miko..."

Chris was "Teso...Teso."

Mike strolled down the street like a lord, with his brother waving to the crowd. He loved it. Golden blond hair falling over his eyes in a Dutch boy haircut; he was happy.

One place we never expected to visit was a family home up in the squatter shacks. Wai Suns's mother had a meat stall in the market, and Wai Sun himself stirred up the fragrant noodle dishes sold in the family's noodle stall, so they were perhaps better off than some of the market people who lived in packing crates behind their places of business.

Spring was coming, and the big Cantonese Opera was being set up down by the Tin Hau Temple. The whole town was celebrating.

Wai Sun's mother invited us over for dinner. We accepted, not knowing what to expect...

The hillside was a patchwork of shacks and pigpens, small vegetable gardens and chickens. Total disorder. But inside the door at Wai Sun's house, the rough wooden walls had been freshly whitewashed, and the sense of serenity surprised us. The main room was decorated with a large red and gold happiness character, and vases of golden yellow chrysanthemums in black pots completed the color scheme. A large round table and chairs were set up in the middle of the room.

They brought us tiny cups of warm, red rice wine. I was so impressed. Here, in the middle of all this confusion and obvious struggle to survive, there was good taste and graciousness, a sense of beauty. I felt humbled and honored, and decided to take a few decorating tips from this woman. Why not put up a big red happiness character in our living room?

The small kitchen had one rice pot and one wok over a fire...and the food was absolutely delicious. Four star.

The last event we witnessed in the fishing village before we left for New York left an indelible impression on us.

The town council put up a huge white tent down by the temple and opera singers came to entertain the villagers—not Germanic singers with beer bellies and horns on their heads, but small, graceful Chinese singers. Some of them were acknowledged heroin addicts, which was reputed to add to the beauty and fragility of their voices. They were robed in brilliantly colored silks, red and saffron yellow, shades of red and deep purples.

It was getting dark when we joined the crown by the sea. The space inside the tent was filled with people coming and going, chatting, eating, some paying no attention to the singers.

The gongs...the drums...the incense. I looked at Gordon. Remember this when we are in New York...

The older kids were somewhere in the crowd. We were not worried. Chris had fallen asleep in his dad's arms.

The other three had been invited backstage to watch the actors paint their faces, white and black and red, each color denoting the character of the actor.

We collected them up and headed back to our strange little house by the sea. The fishing boats bobbed out in the darkness, their flickering lights and the stars above running together at the horizon with no discernible line between heaven and earth.

The gongs and drums were pounding. The singer's voices soared.

This was what we would come back to.

This was what we would remember.

CHAPTER NINE

NEW YORK CITY LAGUARDIA AIRPORT was caught up in its stifling, late summer heat. Exhaust fumes hung over the street in front of the arrivals. A long taxi line snaked up ahead of us, people up front jumping into cabs and taking off. Planes rumbled overhead. Our turn, finally, was next.

Gordon tucked his family into the back seat and sat up front with the driver. We were headed for Claremont Avenue on the Upper West Side, near 475 Riverside Drive, Riverside Church, and Columbia University Teacher's College. In Presbyterian housing.

The driver was in a talkative mood. "Yeah, we're having a rough time in New York this summer," he said, almost proudly. "Just had that big sit-in at Columbia—doped-up kids flopped all over the place yelling: 'Give peace a chance.' Protestors, demonstrations, I'm tellin' you, man…"

"What are they protesting?" Gordon asked.

The cabbie gave him a look.

"The Viet Nam War, man. Where you been?"

Good question. Where had we been?

"You comin' here with a bunch of kids. I wouldn't take my kids any-where near Columbia University right now. Not on a bet. Damn dangerous place."

I was wishing he would (politely) shut up. The kids were all ears and eyes.

"I'm sure we'll survive," Gordon said calmly.

We pulled up in front of a solid looking red brick building, a mid-rise apartment between Broadway and Riverside Drive.

Our designated spot was up a few floors with an elevator. We dragged our luggage up and settled in. This would be our home for over a year. The pre-LaGuardia rooms were furnished with a futsy old New York charm—a living/dining room, a long narrow old-fashioned kitchen, two bedrooms, and a bath. The girls got the bedroom next to ours, and the servants' quarters off the kitchen would have to do for the boys.

I did a double take. Servants' quarters in America? Not the America I knew. When was this place built?

Everything was strange, unaccustomed. With gongs still ringing in our ears and fishing boats still dancing before our eyes, we adjusted to checking in at a front desk—corridors and hallways—elevators and big city traffic. The big concern of some residents was how the building had deteriorated since they lost the doorman. There was no uniformed guard to protect the dwellers of this building and give it dignity. We didn't think we would miss him.

This was the Presbyterian Mission House in New York. As usual, we were the Dutch cousins to the larger group. Some of them were from Hong Kong.

Down in the lounge on the main floor, important people came and went. The kids were fascinated by the television. We did not yet have TV in Hong Kong, only a few hours a day of something called Rediffusion.

But there were more important things to be done. Gordon registered the kids in their classes at Agnes Russell School, a branch of Teacher's College that had been the basis of educational experimentation and the writing of textbooks on education theory. Deidra, at eight, would go into third grade, and the twins, nearly ten, would repeat fifth grade. Fortunately, it would be a year of little academic stress and great exploration, preparing them for the International School experience when they returned to Hong Kong.

Some things, accidentally, worked out right.

With the three older children settled in their niches, Gordon enrolled in his program at Teacher's College. Having an undergraduate degree in English and a Masters in Divinity had seemed adequate at first, but a chance to branch out into Education Administration felt right. It was a new avenue to reach out and broaden his usefulness—and lessen his chances of ever being called "the reverend." Gordon had an absolute and deep-rooted aversion to being called 'the reverend,' even being cast in that category. He was a man, deeply and gloriously human, compassionate and warm, and being frozen into some ice-cake where he was robbed of his common humanity struck him as horrific. He was a man, made in the likeness of God, no more or no less reverend than any other man. He did not see himself as some demigod go-between.

Having a degree in Education Administration, as serendipitously as it had come about, seemed freeing.

Deidra, Mike and Marita loved their new school. Dede had become the quiet one of late. Chris had slipped in under and taken her place as the little one, and the twins were the "big kids." She was caught in the middle, and what she had to say was not so important.

But the third grade at Agnes Russell was her door to a magic world, a world where she could leave the family structure behind and be her own person.

At first it was the mouse committee. The teacher, Miss Opichi, noticed this little girl, small for her age, and felt, rightly, that the child was lost. She looked up Dede's record and found that she had been born in Hong Kong.

Someone had given the third grade a pet mouse. The mouse was in a cage, and the children learned to take care of it. The pet had to be fed and watered, and the cage had to be cleaned. To do these things properly a committee had to be formed.

Deidra was put on the mouse committee. She was not only put on the committee, she became the spokesperson for the committee. She was responsible for taking the mouse cage around to the other classrooms and talking to other classes about the care and maintenance of a mouse.

The old chatterbox Deidra came back to life.

Deidra loved that mouse with a passion. It became the symbol of her survival. I hoped nothing would ever happen to it.

Meanwhile, back at the apartment, Chris and I were on our own. Gordon was busy with his new studies, and I spent time with our youngest, reading to him, and taking long walks down Broadway pushing him in a stroller we had picked up in the basement store room of "things" people had used and left as they came and went to their various countries. I tried to keep up his Chinese vocabulary, the words I had heard him use so clearly with Ah Wai.

He looked at me and shook his head. "No, Mommy. No Chinese. You speak English to me. I talk Chinese with Ah Wai."

He was amazingly verbal for his age. Maybe that came from having older siblings, but he did not want to mix up his languages.

While Chris was napping in the afternoon, I tried to work on a book I was laboring to hammer out. It was not going well. I was trying to write about things I had not experienced. The jottings book we had done while we were in language school had eventually been published in Michigan, and had done very well—over a hundred thousand copies sold. It was a small book called *A Blade of Grass*, and was even being translated into Chinese by the CCLC in Hong Kong.

I thought about it nervously. Would I still like those writings? They had been written so simply, so much before we had started glimpsing the complexity of the world.

My mom came to New York to visit us. She was the one who had to sleep on my couch this time. I wanted so much to tell her about the village, but I was afraid it would conjure up images of Kentucky, and the differences would be incomprehensible to her. I did not want her in any way to compare Gordon to my father, and even though she had been wounded by some of the narrow thinking I was in the process of rejecting, I knew she was still very defensive of old "total depravity" doctrine and dogma. And, to tell the truth, I was only beginning to find new ways of thought, and did not want to expose my tender just-forming ideas to any kind of scorn. Maybe someday we could have these discussions, but not yet.

She took Chris for long walks down Broadway while I worked on the new book. It was tough work. I was trying to get inside the skin of an American-born Chinese who goes back to Hong Kong to find his identity. It was a good idea, but how did I know how a Chinese/American guy felt when he walked into a bar in Wanchai? I had neither the experience nor the hormones to have the slightest idea what he was thinking, but I kept working. Maybe somebody would like it.

Gordon was deeply involved in his classwork. A major test was coming up. A call came from a church in New Jersey asking him to come and speak about his work in Hong Kong.

"I can't possibly go," he said, stressed. "You'll have to take this for me."

"Are you kidding?" I said incredulously. "I've never made a public speech in my life. Sing—yes. Talking? No."

"Well, there's no reason why you can't," he said. "You're the word person in the family. You'd probably do a great job."

I went. Someone came in a car and took me to a meeting. I stood up behind a lectern, feeling like a total imposter, my knees turning to the proverbial jelly.

Looking at all those people and their upturned faces, ready to hear what I, the great intrepid traveler and explorer had to say, I almost laughed, except for the fact that my mouth would have been too frozen.

"I've never done this before," I began. "My husband is the speaker. I am seriously scared to death, and I'm going to need a lot of help from all of you."

I saw puzzled smiles, and a few people nodded uncertainly.

"Okay," I said, my heart hammering, "gather around. I'm going to tell you a story."

I told them stories about Hong Kong. They laughed. They cried. Afterward people came up and hugged me.

They told me what I said was beautiful. They loved me, and I was not afraid.

That was the beginning of being real with people about our adventures. Some people enjoyed it; some people were suspicious of it. Some did not want real; they wanted religious fantasy and reinforced stereotypes. But I was learning to be genuine.

I knew that what I was trying to write was not, but I kept doing it. Motion was better than inaction. Maybe I would have a breakthrough.

Deidra was writing a book, too. The third grade at Agnes Russell was taking students through the process of writing and binding a real book, with text and illustrations and a cover—a real cover with bound pages, done in a special machine.

Deidra was fascinated.

"Mom, I'm writing a book, like you!"

Her first book was like mine, writing about something she had never experienced. It was called *The Rotten Pumpkin*, and was not too convincing.

And then, the mouse died.

The third graders gave it a proper funeral on Broadway (in a little patch of grass on the median) and Deidra was inspired. She wrote about her mouse, and how much she loved it, and how sad she was when it died.

The book was illustrated and bound, and became her most prized possession.

"I'm going to be a writer like you, Mom," she said, hugging me.

I hoped she would be a better writer than me. I even hoped I would be a better writer than me, someday.

A magazine had heard about the talk I gave in New Jersey and asked me to write an article about life in Stanley Village. I did, and it was published.

Christmas was coming, Christmas in New York City—always fabulous, and almost too fabulous for us that year. The kids all wanted typewriters for Christmas. Gordon went to a used office machines store and found three old typewriters. They worked, at least somewhat. Our Christmas tree was a triangle of green scotch tape stuck on the wall with a small lamp table under it to hold the presents. The kids also wanted Beatles records. *Hey Jude* and *Lucy in the Sky with Diamonds*. Gordon scrounged up a small record player.

December was also Deidra's ninth birthday. For weeks she had been planning her birthday cake, an angel food with pink frosting and a ballerina on top. Then she changed her mind.

"No ballerina," she said, "just pink frosting."

And then she decided that she didn't even want to eat it. She was going to be a writer.

It was at a national meeting of the Reformed Church that we met the Peales—Doctor Norman Vincent Peale was without question the most famous member of the Reformed Church in America. His Marble Collegiate Church had long been a powerhouse in New York City, and his book, *The Power of Positive Thinking*, was known all over the world.

Doctor Peale was keenly interested in what we were doing in Hong Kong. Knowing of his publishing success, I asked him if he knew any channels through which I might submit a manuscript. He referred me to his editor, Myron Boardman.

Boardman referred me to a friend at Harper and Row, Tadishi Akaishi, who had become famous for his *Gospel According to Peanuts*.

I bravely submitted my misbegotten manuscript called *Green Mountain*, the story of the American-born Chinese, full of cultural insights—much too full.

There was a call from someone at Harper and Row. "This manuscript you submitted is not exactly what we're looking for," the man said, "but we have seen an article you wrote for the *Church Herald*, published in Michigan. We were very interested in that piece of writing. Do you think you might be able to write a book along those lines?"

I leaned against the wall, heart thudding.

Did I?

I certainly did!

So while Gordon went to class and did his statistics and graphs, and the kids went to Agnes Russell and got their imaginations opened up, and Chris kept us all laughing with the things he said (like trying to convince a Chinese visitor from the UN that his mom had BOOBS), I began to write. Chris was finally over two and could be sent to the nursery school at Riverside Church to play while I wrote mornings.

Now I was on the track.

I was writing what I knew. The sights and sounds and smells of Hong Kong, the pulse of life in that city that was becoming a part of my awakening as a human being. I knew I was writing for the religious department of Harper and Row, so I could not get too secular, but that was easy. At my core, I was still a deeply religious person, even though I hated some of the pretense and abuse of power I had seen. If I did not give a religious interpretation to my stories, I might wander into what I did not know again—into no-man's land. How did one continue to believe in God and become post-religious? It was not a problem I would solve in this book—perhaps the next one.

For six weeks I wrote like one possessed. It was almost like a long poem, a slightly-over-one-hundred-page-long, heavily italicized poem…in prose. It would probably be disdained by the non-religious as naïve and criticized by the religious as being too universalist. So be it. It was an honest statement of life as I understood it at that moment.

I dropped it on Eleanor Jordan's desk (the editor I would work with), and left it for them to read. I waited.

There were more calls from groups who wanted to hear about Hong Kong. Gordon was winding up his studies—tests and graphs and education theories, stuff almost as obtuse as theology.

I waited to hear from Harper and Row.

I went out to lunch with Eleanor Jordan at a little café near the publishing house. They were working on it, checking marketing.

I spoke to more groups. I was beginning to love it. My heart was in Hong Kong, in that mysterious little village on the South China Sea. It had become the whole focus of my life—our life—the place I had almost said NO to was becoming the reason for my being.

The mysterious, dangerous power of YES…

The call finally came from Harper and Row. Would I come in and meet with them…

I took the subway and got off at 33rd Street much too early. I sat in a coffee shop across the street, staring at a cup of coffee I was too nervous to swallow. At the appointed time, I went up to the religious department and sat down, waiting…

The editor motioned me in. We met.

They were going to publish my book. They were going to publish *The Spring Wind.*

THE SPRING WIND.

Gordon met me at our subway stop on Broadway. I came up the stairs and he was there, arms open. I flew into them and we twirled around, laughing and crying and doing a dance of joy.

It was another of those waterfall moments, caught up in the power of the life force…feeling it around us and within us…plunging us into that bottomless chasm of creation.

I forgot about the small sign by the railing that said: PROCEED AT YOUR OWN RISK.

The Spring Wind would be published in New York, by Harper and Row. A book club was ordering 35,000. Did life get any better than this?

Yes, it did.

We would be going back to Stanley Village, the source of our new inspiration, the place where we could dig even deeper into the mysteries of human existence.

I could already feel the next book. There was so much more to experience. We had barely scratched the surface.

Gordon finished up the requirements for the degree. We took a trip down to Canal Street in New York City and walked around through Chinatown, brushing up on our Cantonese and picking up a few items to take back.

At the airport we checked our twenty-one pieces of luggage and baggage, a Chinese Goddess of Mercy and a baseball bat (which seemed to fit in nowhere in the luggage), and boarded the big plane for Hong Kong.

All I wanted to do was to get home. Was Hong Kong going to be home with a capital H? Was Stanley Village the little town I had dreamed of? No, that was an American town. Stanley would be significant, but not home...would it?

Who really knew?

SECTION THREE

1969-1972

CHAPTER TEN

FOR A YEAR AND A half we had dreamed about the village, this enchanted spot on the South China Sea. We had spoken to American audiences about it, written a book which ended with our coming to the village market, and now we were here.

We woke up that first morning of the return with a complete sense of disorientation.

That had been the dream. This was the reality...

The sound of carts rumbling over the rough pavement...rattling the metal pails filled with swill from the rice-wine factory, going to feed the pigs up in the squatter shack area...the shrill call of voices as women exchanged morning greetings and earthy jokes...

Up on the ceiling, a small red lizard made its way across the water-marked plaster. I stared at the lizard, coming closer and closer to being directly over the bed, wondering if it would drop on our faces.

Gordon was still asleep. Should I wake him and tell him about the lizard, or hope it would go away? It seemed inconsequential with all we had to do. Let it crawl and drop where it would.

Downstairs, I heard Ah Wai banging pots and pans around in the kitchen. She had stayed, thank goodness. Practical, realistic, she would help us as we got our feet on the ground.

Around the breakfast table the kids looked as stunned as we felt. They would be going to the new International School this year for fifth and seventh grades, and felt apprehensive.

"We'll need new uniforms," Marita reminded us. "And shoes and..."

I knew. Be careful about the shoes. The right shoes. But who knew what the right shoes would be at HKIS? British shoe snobbery and American shoe snobbery might be different, especially in middle school. Oh well, play it by ear.

Gordon's thoughts were a million miles away, in a different direction.

"I'll have to meet with the CCC and check with them about their expectations for Kung Lee School this year, and my new job as…headmaster."

Headmaster. The new title sounded strange and uncertain, and as threatening as the wrong shoes.

Ah Wai came in with Chris' "soft egg," and placed it lovingly on his high chair tray. She waited, but he did not speak Chinese to her.

"Teso," she prompted. "Ho sic!"

He looked at her, uncomprehending.

He had forgotten his Chinese.

Ah well. He was only two and a half. He would pick it up again.

"Can we study Chinese at HKIS?" Mike asked.

I asked Gordon, but he was thinking about his meeting at the school.

There was a loud knock at the door facing the street. Jerry and Wai Sun were there with another boy named Jonathan Jeng.

"Foon Ying! Foon Ying!" they shouted merrily. "Welcome home!"

All of us became reoriented that week in our own way. Gordon went to Kung Lee School, going through the formalities of his new responsibilities and checking the teaching staff. We boarded the number six bus and went downtown to get the kids fitted for new uniforms at the tailor. An exclusive tailor had been selected for HKIS, and the uniforms were beautiful—a cool shade of blue, not too dark, not too light. They looked like airline uniforms. They were also very expensive.

I thought of the brown we had selected for Kung Lee and hoped the students didn't feel too hot and horrible in them. Actually, I didn't even like brown anymore, but how could a thousand students change their minds, or their identity, or their uniforms?

Decisions…consequences…

Since Ah Wai was there to do the cooking, cleaning and washing, I was gloriously free to walk through the village, sometimes with Chris, sometimes alone, soaking it up in a new way. This was now my village, no longer a thing I was doing to humor Gordon. It was the focus of my own fascination. I was probing it, uncovering its secrets, hearing its language and sensing its nuances, trying to captivate it, or was it captivating me?

They had explained to me at Harper and Row that a name became a property. Could a village become a property?

I walked the street along the sea, feeling it with new intensity. The rough-paved street, the maze of shops, ancient as China itself…the impromptu trees rising out of no place in particular—the whole composition of the village so organic—the ever-present sea sloshing against the back of the shops, creating its own sound track…a water music punctuated by the calls of the boat people.

Some families even lived on their boats. Small bandy-legged children with shiny eyes went to a special school in the village for the fisher folk. It was down in the market, next to the village latrine, which emitted a pungent odor. Stray dogs roamed the street, copulating at random. It all seemed to fit together, even the elements that might be shocking or odious somewhere else making for a harmonious wholeness.

The shops.
The Jeng's rice shop.
Round-faced Mrs. Jeng with her three sons and one daughter, and her somber husband. They sold rice and tea and peanut oil (bring your own bottle), and condiments like soy sauce and garlic and ginger. The boys all slept up the ladder in the loft overhead. Pearl, the teenaged daughter, slept downstairs in a tiny room all her own, next to her parents cubicle. The kitchen was a 3x6 slab of concrete with a gas plate, a wok and a rice cooker, standard equipment in the village.
The rice shop itself was their living room.

Jerry's mother, Mrs. Jau, was a chubby smiling presence on the corner across from the Stanley Store. Her story was totally different. She had three or four children (I never was quite sure), and an absent husband who visited occasionally. The packing crates stacked to form a solid mass in the center of the market mysteriously contained her dwelling. The youngest son was handicapped, and tenderly cared for by his family; but somehow, tending her vegetable stall and joking with her customers, Mrs. Jau looked well fed and happy. Was it possible?

Across the street, at Ng's noodle stall, Wai Sun stirred up fragrant noodles. After school Mike loved to spend his allowance there, perched on a stool, watching what Wai Sun threw into the wok to make such good flavors. We had seen the Ng's home, the "squatter shack" with the beautiful pots of yellow mums and the red happiness characters. No wonder Mrs. Ng looked so confident as she tended her butcher stall. The flies might be crawling over the meat carcasses as they hung in the tropical heat, and the rats scurrying along the open gutters avoiding the stray dogs, but Mrs. Ng's house up on the hill was hers—her own spot of private, simple beauty. She smiled confidently at her customers as she expertly cut chunks of meat and tied them with a long string for carrying.

Mrs. Ng also had two daughters, Wai Sun's sisters, Suk Yi and Suk Jing. They were our girls' ages, and came over to play with Marita and Deidra. At nine and eleven, our girls were halfway between Barbie dolls and Lucy in the Sky with Diamonds…

Thank goodness we didn't know what LSD was at that point, or what hidden messages there were in those good 60's songs like *Bridge Over Troubled Water*.

Who did?

Learning the culture of Stanley Village, we were also absorbing the shifts in our own culture, eager and innocent, and ever so vulnerable.

I watched the streets of the village and blindly loved it all, the fragrance and the stink, the kindness and the cruelties, and the wonderful banyan trees with their tangled roots above ground, often festooned with incense sticks and gifts of food to the gods, any god, just to keep peace with the universe.

The universe.

Space. This was the focus that summer. America landed the first man on the moon in 1969, and the world was stunned.

Half the village did not even believe it. How could they? The moon was a glowing orb that came up over the sea, a place where the rabbit sat under a tree, grinding powder that contained the secret of never dying—that had been stolen from the emperor by a clever concubine. The village people knew what the moon was.

How could Americans plant a flag on the moon? The moon belonged to the sky, and to all people. Who did the Americans think they were to put a flag on it?

But they smiled reassuringly at us and told us never mind; there were foolish people in all countries, even China.

How I loved the village, deeply, with a growing sense of questing awe. So primal, so archetypal, with roots going down below the conscious mind, so illogical, yet with its very illogic rooted in human fears and need and greed. It was the spinning of patently unbelievable tales to codify the mysterious forces of life. These were things that could be referred to with a knowing nod, and the listeners knew what it meant.

But the deepest and most unquestioned love was reserved for the man in my life. I listened and watched as he learned all the new ropes of leadership at Kung Lee School. The office force would remain the same, guarded by a smiling dragon lady named Mrs. Lee. The wonderful young students in their shades of brown would return one thousand strong for the fall semester. The teachers were shifting again, some of the best leaving to go to the government schools where the pay was better. A few new foreigners had joined the staff to strengthen the English department. Bernie Anderson's girlfriend was now in Hong Kong and they were talking about getting married. One of the DeVelders' sons had graduated from college and would be teaching at Kung Lee—and Gordon would be the new headmaster. The Hau Jung—a very respected position in Hong Kong.

He was thirty-nine, a man with a future. Tall and handsome with his Dutch/French Huguenot features, open minded, and thoroughly admired in New York and Hong Kong as the man who would lead. He was cherished at home by his four kids who adored him, and his wife who was deeply in love with him.

He was a lucky man, and not a little apprehensive about it all. Exactly what did Peter Wong want from him?

The little study up on the third floor of the Stanley house was set up with a table and chair, and a manual portable typewriter. In a notebook beside it I kept notes on the village.

The Spring Wind was published in New York. I was too far away to go on speaking tours or help promote it. The publishers had needed a publicity shot and Gordon had taken it, out on the balcony overlooking the sea and the boats. I looked intriguingly young and thin. With my hair cropped short in the bathroom mirror... I looked hungry and vulnerable and hopeful.

HKIS opened for the 1969 school year. The three older kids boarded the number six bus every morning, walking through the village market clad in their classy, new blue uniforms, bound for Repulse Bay. Together, they were a force. We never worried about them boarding public busses, even though they were young. They were together, and anyhow, who would hurt American kids?

They were on the side of the winners. And their shoes were okay.

This was the year I would at last be free to observe a full fall to spring spread of festivities in the village. For years we had lived in Western areas of Hong Kong, knowing that the Chinese were observing such things as the Moon Festival, the Ghost Festival, the rituals of Chinese New Year, but these had been observed by our family as outsiders (the heathen are burning boats on the curb). Now, residing in a Chinese village where the old customs of China would be the main event, we would be drawn in as participants.

The Moon Festival, in the eighth month of the Chinese calendar, was fast approaching. Because of the moon landing in July, we'd had a preview of the myths and legends surrounding this festival, but now we would see it in action.

100

Moon cakes were stacking up at the Stanley Store. Businesses were gifting each other with the small round cakes packed with sweet dark bean paste, the yellow yoke of an egg set squarely in the middle. When the slices were cut they resembled a dark sky with a sliver of moon, or a full moon if cut through the middle.

All the shops on the market street were festooned with moon lanterns for sale—paper rabbits, round moon shapes, even a few daring and heretical planes and paper astronauts. They lined the winding street, fluttering in the sea breeze, their colors bright to gaudy.

Our American children chose their favorite shapes, eager to light them and take part in the children's lantern parade by the sea.

The Chinese teenagers were ready to give us the real insider information about the festival.

"It's most important for the girls," Jerry confided. "The moon is the power for the female part of the human race as the sun is for the male. At the Moon Festival, the girls and women use their power. To persuade men...

"Persuade them to do what?"
"Oh, to marry them, of course!"
"Do you have a girlfriend?"
"Yes, well maybe, but not yet."
Jonathan Jeng pushed him.
"He likes my sister Pearl," Jonathan said.
"Does she like you?" Gordon asked.
"Maybe," Jerry admitted.
"My mother doesn't like you...yet. You don't have enough money," Jonathan teased.

The festival consisted of three days: Welcome the Moon, Enjoy the Moon, and Chase the Moon. It had a bit of a Sadie Hawkins or Leap Year connotation, with tacit permission for girls to be more aggressive than usual.

People sat on rooftops or up on the hillside to get a better view, but on the main night of the festival the most amazing place in the village to observe the moonrise was along the seashore, where the reflections in the water added to its power.

Out in the enclosed courtyard under the banyan tree at the house on the corner, our kids excitedly lit the little candles in their lanterns. Mike had chosen an airplane, Chris a rabbit, and the girls round moon shapes.

Jerry and Wai Sun went with the older three as they joined the children walking along the sea. The moon was huge, golden, touching the dark water with horizontal waves of brightness. The line of children stretched from our house on the corner down to the Tin Hau Temple—beautiful, gentle, light and darkness.

We stood at the doorway with Chris, waving his lighted rabbit at the moon.

The laughter of children on the night breeze.

So peaceful, so beautiful.

The lapping of soft ripples on the shore…

There would be special incense burned at the temple that night. Mothers would pray to the goddess for good husbands for their daughters, and the girls would work to make their mothers' prayers come true.

We were back at the house, tasting moon cake and getting ready for bed, when Mike asked, a bit worried, "Did you see the American flag on the moon?"

"No, you silly twit," Marita scolded, "it wouldn't show!"

"Well, I was just wondering," Mike said slowly. "That moon was pretty big…"

The quiet gentleness of the Moon Festival in no way prepared us for the fevered intensity of the Devil-Ghost Festival. For weeks ahead of time we could feel the anticipation building up in the village, beating under the surface like a submerged heart, stirring up emotions under the calm of the streets. There were things to be dealt with.

In the flat grassy area between the temple and the sea, construction began. Bit by bit it took shape, a huge image nearly twenty feet high. The materials used were all combustible: wood, paper, ropes, paper mache, string and fine wire. As a crowning touch, a fierce head was molded out of plaster-like material, with a gaping mouth and glaring red eyes.

"It will have red light bulbs plugged in the night of the festival," Jerry promised, "so it looks really scary."

"Why?" I hardly knew what questions to ask about such a repulsive-looking creature. "Why does it have to look so terrible?"

"Because life is terrible for so many people," he said patiently. "If we have an awful-looking image to help us picture evil, we can be reminded to…"

"To what?"

"To destroy it," Wai Sun said. "It makes it easier to do what we should to forgive…"

"No, that's not the only reason," Jonathan Jeng said quietly. "You know the thing about tradition and young people. Young people have very clear minds, and they want to throw off the old fears and superstitions they see around them, but the older people are confused by life, and they want to keep the superstitions to comfort them, to make them feel safe."

"Who's doing it this year?" Jerry asked.

"My brother and me," Jonathan said.

"Doing what?" I asked.

"You'll see," they promised.

The night of the actual festival the streets of Stanley Village were alive with a curious fever. At the doorway of every shop, pots of incense glowed and dishes of food were set out. The hungry ghosts would come down the street and no one wanted to risk forgetting to feed them. Women scattered handfuls of coins along the street, immediately followed by a troupe of eager children who scooped them up.

"Can we pick up some money, too?" our children asked.

I asked Mrs. Ng, who laughed.

"Who do you expect to pick it them up?" she said merrily, "the ghosts?"

Obviously, the rules were tricky.

Down by the temple the area facing the sea was festooned with hundreds of small lights. Fires were lit and the smell of roasted meat floated on the sea breeze. Drums beat a soft undercurrent with the occasional burst of gongs.

Tables spread with layers of buns were positioned in rows, making a veritable field of food. Between the sound of gongs, Buddhist priests read from ancient scriptures, their voices blending with the drums in a singsong pattern.

The eyes of the King of the Underworld made more terrible by electricity glared out, red and angry and fierce.

People milled about, listening, waiting. Overhead, lines were strung between poles with hundreds of strips of paper attached to them, fluttering in the sea breeze.

"What are those?" I asked.

"The people have done things that are wrong," Jerry explained, "and if they write them on paper, they will be forgiven. Also, some of these are forgiving the ghosts that come back. Then the ghosts can go away and not return."

"When are we going to eat?" Mike whispered. "I'm starving..."

"Shhh," Gordon said. "Not yet."

We hungrily eyed the tables groaning with food. Rows and rows of buns stuffed with spiced meat lined the tables.

"What are those gloves doing on the table?" Marita asked. "Do people wear gloves when they eat the buns?"

"No," Jerry explained, "those are the hands the ghosts use when they eat the food. Ghost have no hands."

Marita looked at me. That was an answer?

"And you see the toilets?" Wai Sun pointed out. "One for the men ghosts and one for the women ghosts. No one wants the spirits to be uncomfortable because they have to pee."

There was a burst of activity. Two figures rushed to the foot of the evil image and stuck a lighted torch to its base. A flash of fire flared up the paper structure.

Equally quickly, two older men raced in with cloths to beat the flames out. The boys relit the fire. A "battle" ensued between the fire starters and the fire fighters.

"It's like a drama," Jerry whispered. "The old ones want to keep the old ways, and the young question traditions. We want to throw them off, but the old people want to keep them."

"Who wins?" Gordon asked.

"We always burn the image," Jerry said, smiling, "but then the next year they build another one. Then we burn it again. This has been going on for hundreds, maybe thousands of years."

The constant sound of the soft rolling drums...

The gongs, announcing another reading...

The droning voice of the Buddhist priest...

The burning image...

Someone had pulled the plug, and the eyes no longer glared red. The King of the Underworld was dying, being forced back into his nether domain.

The kids were yawning.

The food would not be eaten until midnight, until all the hungry ghosts had sated themselves.

"Let's go home," Gordon whispered.

Long after the children were asleep that night we could still hear the distant beating of the drums and the clanging gongs. There was a mighty roar as the King of the Underworld finally collapsed into smoldering ashes. Evil was vanquished, and the ghosts of the past would be placated. The buns would be consumed, and the wrongs written on the pieces of paper would fly away and be lost in the sea.

"I wonder what sort of things people write on those scraps of paper," I mused. "What sort of things people here do, that they need forgiveness for?"

"People are people," he said.

I wondered what kind of things I would write on those papers. There were things I would never be able to forgive, or forget, no matter how many pieces of paper they were written on. Some things were unforgivable.

It was hard to fall asleep that night with the wind sounds blowing up from the sea. People were streaming past our house, finally going home.

I hoped all the hungry ghosts had eaten their fill of buns and would cause us no mischief. Where was the line between fantasy and reality on a night like this?

Such ludicrous stuff. Ghosts (who have no bellies) needing gloves to eat food because they have no hands? Huh? This was as crazy as some of the stuff I was brought up to believe…

I struggled to clear my mind, to shut it down…to forget.

The wind blew. There was a banging noise downstairs. Gordon had fallen asleep. It sounded like one of the shutters in the living room. Maybe I had forgotten to close the window.

I felt my way down the terrazzo stairs. It was dark with only the street-light on the corner casting ghostly shadows.

Pitch black inside the house…

I was afraid of the dark. Thirty-five years old and married, with four kids, and terrified of the dark.

I fastened the loose shutter and started back up the stairs. I felt it, that terror, that awareness of something in the darkness. It was in the corner of the living room glowing pale green.

I ran to the stairs and tried to climb them, then sat down, frozen with fear. It came closer and I could see my father's face—the glaring eyes, cursing me. The eyes came close to my face. I would not run…I could not run, so frozen with fear.

Let it come!

Then I felt the green face pass into me. It passed through me and on up the stairs. It was gone.

I took a deep breath. I was still alive.

And suddenly I realized I was not afraid, not even afraid of the dark.

I sat for a moment, wondering how I could tell Gordon about this. Would he think I was losing it?

Maybe I had fallen asleep and dreamed the whole thing. That's what it had been—a bad dream.

I climbed back into bed and snuggled close to his sleeping form.

My rock.

105

Chapter Eleven

AFTER A WILD NIGHT OF burning the devil and encountering a ghost, it was time for a little solidarity with our own culture.

Well, not exactly our own, but something closer to it than Stanley Village.

The Church of All Nations, which served as the chapel for the Hong Kong International School, was basically Lutheran, and Lutherans were German, not Dutch. To the average Chinese, we were all foreign devils, but we did have our fine-line distinctions. Many Chinese asked if there were so many different ways to be Christian how did anyone know which way was the right way?

Of course. We all knew that we were right, and the rest of them were...suspect.

So, on Sunday morning we loaded up our family of six in the green Morris Oxford and drove slowly through the still sleeping village market to go to Repulse Bay

The school was familiar territory to our kids by now, as they attended classes there five days a week, and many of the Church of All Nations members were their teachers and classmates. We adults were the outsiders.

The inside of the chapel was beautifully constructed. The end of the sixties and the beginning of the seventies was a wild time for America, and the expat community was no exception. Church architecture was up for grabs, along with skirt lengths and drug use.

But the most striking feature in this chapel was the round platform at the front, a circle with a completely round altar rail. The podium stood in the center. Above it, bright, stained glass windows let in colored light, and in the very center of the light hung a large cross casting a shadow. When communicants went up for the communion service, they knelt in the shadow of that cross, passing a large brass chalice which everyone drank from. The symbolism was beautiful for the believers. It was art built on theology.

I watched the service, clutching Gordon's hand on one side and Deidra's on the other.

Believers...

Was I still a total believer in all of this, or was I beginning to question some things? Would I ever be a total, unequivocal believer in anyone's programmed system of belief, or would I be one of those who rather painfully reserved judgment until I could assess what effect beliefs had on one's life? I had been brainwashed once...

But I had to admit it. The service was beautiful, and a little less exotic than burning the devil at midnight. I listened to the words of the rituals. The Lutherans were big on rituals.

Maybe rituals were good.

Did rituals comfort?

Did they numb the mind?

Did these people know what they were saying, or had they said it so often it rolled off their tongues without ever touching the heart or mind?

Chris was downstairs in the nursery school.

I wondered what he was being taught.

Deidra was examining my nail polish.

Gordon squeezed my hand.

We had to write letters to our folks this afternoon, as always...

I hesitated, coming to a startling thought. The problem with the Lutherans was not so much that they were different from us—the problem was how much alike we all were—that solid wall of Christian exclusiveness.

We were the adopted children of a placated God, going to heaven because of our belief. We were saved and were going to heaven while the rest of the great unwashed of humanity was going to hell.

I sat, sad and detached, knowing I could not teach this to my children. There must be some way to believe in God that was not so fracturing to the whole concept of what it meant to be human.

We joined the church and the kids sang in the HKIS choir. They wore their uniforms and the right accessories, and we were welcomed, except for one very strict family who were afraid they might be damned for kneeling next to us at the communion rail because we were not Lutheran.

But the service was beautiful.

Did anyone hear the words?

The Church of All Nations…

There were truly people from all nations there. A colorful delegation from Tanzania, sitting up on the front row, head dresses and colorful robes of striking shades, beautiful tones. They came and knelt at the round alter and drank from the common chalice—until we heard about the AIDS epidemic in their country, then we only dipped our wafers in the chalice.

One had to adapt.

Times were changing. But were they really? Hang onto the traditions. We humans all do it—fearful of what would happen if we do not.

Meanwhile, back at Stanley Village, life went on as usual. Mr. Hong, the communist, watched our every move. Why were we there, living on a village street in substandard housing when we could afford to live in Repulse Bay like decent foreigners? Were we spies? Were we CIA? We needed to be carefully watched.

Such good intentions, such different worlds…

At Thanksgiving time the church took up a food collection for the poor villagers of Stanley Market. They collected canned beans and pumpkin, cranberry sauce, canned peas, and corn. Someone brought the boxes of canned goods to the village and deposited them in front of Mrs. Ng's meat stall.

The villagers thanked them kindly and took the food up on the hillside to feed to the pigs. Who could eat such dead food? At least the pigs would turn it into fresh pork.

The Catholic Sisters up on the other side of town came into the market to buy, their long robes swinging in the dust. Word had gone out that the sisters could wear civilian clothes, but most of them preferred to stay covered. The habits were a comforting belief.

Ah Wai's older son had gone to a Catholic school. Now her second son was studying at the same school

"They're good people," she told me. "My son is getting a good education, but I hope they don't expect me to believe their religion…"

In spite of her warning about friends and servants, Ah Wai and I were truly becoming friends. We chatted endless hours in Chinese as we went about our daily existence. She taught me the secrets of Chinese cooking—how to use a cleaver to chop—how to lay out a piece of chicken and see where the muscles ran in order to cut across them for tenderness. I watched her and listened to her story.

She had stayed in Mao's China long after her husband had come to Hong Kong with the two older boys. Ah Wai's marriage had been arranged.

She was basically sold to the highest bidder when she was fifteen. It was not a good marriage. Her husband left China and she lived in a commune, trained as a midwife, and assisted in the birth of commune babies.

"I loved doing that," she said. "I loved helping babies come into the world."

"To be born Communists?" I asked.

"Ah, that didn't bother me. Everybody has to be something. You Westerners are so worried about what you believe. I don't believe anything, besides being Chinese."

"Do you have some kind of belief in the life after this one?" I asked curiously.

She laughed, covering her mouth in good Chinese fashion, and shook her head.

"Why the devil would I want another life? If I get through this one, that's going to be enough for me!"

Ah Wai lived up in the squatter shacks. She worked six days a week for us. Her husband cut hair in an old barber chair out on the street and gambled away everything he earned. She had two young children and two older ones.

I could see her point. Maybe one life was enough for anybody, if one really lived it. But how could we live in such a fractured world?

Christmas was coming-
The war in Viet Nam was getting worse.
Young Americans were being slaughtered.
For what?
No one could quite remember...
Something about dominoes.

Drugs were rampant at HKIS.
The teachers shook their heads.
This was a new age.
A new generation.
A new level of awareness.
The kids knew what they were doing.
Seeking unity in a broken world...

A student died of a drug overdose
Died, at sixteen, of drugs.
NOBODY KNEW WHAT THEY WERE DOING!

Winter, for all it was worth in Hong Kong, was coming. The weather was cooler in the market and there were not as many flies swarming on the meat hanging in the stalls. People wore light sweaters, and the pots at the street noodle stall sent up white steam.

The Stanley Store stocked goods with a Christmas motif: Santas and oranges, nuts and chocolates, and mincemeat for pies. If it was a good seller, Mister Hong would sell it. He would never think of eating any of it.

Jerry Jau, Ng Wai Sun, Jonathan Jeng and his sister, Pearl, were becoming our friends. Henry and Florence Chey and their sons, Danny and Nelson, were becoming part of our family, and we of theirs. Nelson was attending Kung Lee School, getting ready for the all-important school cert.

Most of our friends were Chinese. Our world had changed.

We spoke Chinese. We ate Chinese. We had begun to think, even to dream in Chinese. There were new pathways in our brains.

Our kids did not speak Chinese. The class had been dropped at HKIS because some students did poorly and it caused their GPAs to drop. These were kids going places, and did not want a bad mark on their records for an inconsequential language.

One evening Jerry and Wai Sun dropped in to talk to us.

"We've shown you two of our Chinese festivals," they said. "Now Christmas is coming. This is your big festival. Could you help us celebrate it?"

"Why?"

"Well, we know all about Christmas on the outside, the Santas and the trees and the presents."

"And the Mary and Joseph, but..."

"But what?"

"We would like to know how you feel at Christmas—what it feels like to celebrate Christmas as an American. Can you show us?"

They knew it all. What was left for us to show?

"We'll try," we promised.

That was the week it happened, the day that would stand out forever as the beginning of the rest of my awareness, my conscious life...

Gordon had taken the three older kids to church. I stayed home with Chris who, thankfully, had a slight cold. I might have stayed home even if he hadn't. I needed to be quiet. It was Ah Wai's day off.

"You take the kids," I bargained, "and I'll cook dinner, a real American Sunday dinner, and I'll make you an apple pie."

I knew he would sell his soul for an apple pie...

They were gone, in the big dark green Morris Oxford, down the market street and out of sight. I grabbed a light sweater for me and one for Chris, and went out the door with him perched on my hip. I headed for the Stanley Store to pick up some cinnamon, and green apples in the market.

I was just outside the front door, coming down the terrazzo steps with Chris in my arms, when the sensation began. I looked up. A young Chinese woman was coming toward me with a child in her arms. I looked directly into her face.

There was a light coming from her eyes, a flash of light that entered my eyes and bounced back to hers.

Shared.

Was it a minute? A second? An hour? I did not feel time…I was somewhere outside time…

There was a circle of light around her head, dancing and shimmering…the circle spread out to include her whole body with the child in her arms…the radiant edges expanded the circle to include the stones of the street, the market stalls, the rice wine factory…the banyan tree…light, radiating, expanding, taking in the sea and boats, the sky…radiant, shimmering, pulsing, moving…

I felt a rush of joy, a deep comprehension of oneness, the rightness of all things, the sacredness of all life. Nothing disparate, nothing left out…it all belonged…it was…

Was there a name?

No. A presence.

The presence of the Creative Power…

Everywhere…

In everything…

Life…un-named…un-captured…

I turned around and fled back into the house, closing the door behind me.

What was that? Where did it come from?

And what was I going to do with it?

And what did it have to do with Christmas?

Wherever it had come from, I felt a curious peace, a deep unnamed understanding.

I felt like celebrating…

Chris looked at me curiously. I must have looked awestruck.

"Are we going to get apples, Mommy?" he reminded me.

"You bet we are, buddy. Let's make Daddy a pie!"

And that was how we started to celebrate.

Celebrate!

What a wonderful time to be asked to celebrate Christmas in a fishing village on the South China Sea, on the opposite side of the world and the other side of the moon.

Ah hah! Maybe that's why Mike couldn't see the American flag; it had been planted on the American side of the moon.

Nonsense, of course—it was all one world.

So how should we celebrate Christmas here in a way that transcended cultures?

Our Christmas stories would not have offended anyone. They were used to heavenly concubines and cowherds in the sky, but they knew all our stories, thanks to BK, and wanted something more.

The feeling of Christmas…

Where would we start?

We began with a single red candle planted in the brass niche and set in the window that faced the street.

Just a simple, lighted red candle.

Jerry, Wai Sun and Jonathan came to our house and we discussed it.

Gifts? No. No one had any money.

A tree?

They would find one on the hillside—actually, have to steal it at night, as cutting a tree down was illegal.

A party?

A party! Yes, a party would be wonderful!

Who would we invite?

"We could invite everyone we know in the village," I suggested.

"And family," Jerry added. "Everyone in the village is related some-how—uncles, cousins, grandparents—so you would be inviting the whole village."

"Is our house too small?"

Jerry looked around the living room. His family lived in the tangle of packing crates in the market.

"Not too small."

"But everybody?" I doubted. "Would it ruin it for the people who are invited if they knew just anybody could come?"

"No," Jerry insisted. "This is the way to do it. Then if they don't come they can't blame you."

Could we do it?

"Let's do it!"

The boys helped us find the proper paper for the invitations, and wrote them out in careful Chinese characters. Each shopkeeper, each market stall owner, everybody in the village we knew, or the boys suggested we invite, was included. After each name they added Tong Ga (and family). We even invited Mr. Hong, the communist from the Stanley Store, doubting that he would come.

The boys delivered each invitation and we began to get ready for the big party. A village party... Now that was Christmas!

Up and down the market street and around the bend to the Jeng's rice shop, people got their personal invitation to a party at the Americans' house.

On Ah Wai's day off we began to bake cookies. Mike wanted to help me make a fruit cake, so he greased the papers to line the loaf pans while I stirred up a dishpan full of fruit cake dough. It would hardly have time to mellow, but it would still be good, like moon cake. The girls cut out sugar cookies, and stamped out gingerbread men and decorated them. The kitchen looked like a typhoon had hit it. Chris licked spoons.

Jerry and Wai Sun helped.

"We'll be here the night of the party," they promised. "We'll boil up lots of water for tea. Everyone will want tea."

As good as their word, they came in one night with a Christmas tree. It made the proverbial Charlie Brown tree look practically lush. One side had grown against the hill and was essentially bare. We put that side to the wall and decorated the front.

"The policeman nearly caught us!" Wai Sun said, laughing.

"Well, invite him, too!" we said merrily.

It was going to be the party of the year. Gordon had consulted with Bernie Anderson at the school about some good music, and had it on hand for the young people if they wanted to dance. There was plenty of room out in the courtyard. "Rudolph the Red Nosed Reindeer" and "Jingle Bell Rock..."

Everything was set.

Then the mail came, delivered with a swish and a plop through the front door slot.

Life magazine.

Full pictures.

The cover story...

The Mai Lai massacre. A young American, Lt. Calley, and his men, had gone on a rampage in Viet Nam and killed a whole village of Asian men, women and children. The pictures of their broken, bullet-riddled bodies were spread over the pages, red with blood.

When I saw it, a mighty wail rose up from my belly like a wounded thing.

No! No! An Asian village like ours.

Bodies!

Why? Why now? Why ever?

Try as we might to hold the world together, it was hopelessly, horribly broken.

Americans had done this. We were American.

The boys heard the news and came over. Gordon and the older children came home. We were all in shock.

"Never mind," Jerry said. "People won't blame you. We'll be here to help you."

"But... A party?" we said.

This was to be the Festival of Peace, of Peace on Earth and Goodwill to men—to men, women and children who had been shot to ribbons...

What was left to celebrate?

"Maybe we need a party more than ever," the boys said, "because people are sad."

So we went ahead. When one red candle burned out in the window, we replaced it with another...and another...

The day of the party-

Those last frantic hours before a party.

Women are notorious for getting unreasonable, rattled, even cross, and I was doing it. The kids, who had been such a help, seemed to be underfoot.

"Shall I take Chris out for a walk?" Mike suggested. "And could we have a dollar to spend at the store?"

I shelled out a Hong Kong dollar and told them to go out and have fun in the shops—good riddance.

"Don't get popsicles," I instructed Mike. "That orange dye gets all over Chris' face, and I don't have time to give him a bath before tonight."

"Okay," Mike agreed.

Mike said okay so much that the village kids had started calling him "Miko-okay."

They were out of the house. I looked around checking the table in the dining room and the lighted tree. The table was piled high with real American goodies, but I knew some of the villagers would not eat sweets. They had strange beliefs about the effects of certain foods on the body, and sugar gave people "Hot airs," some obscure Chinese term. But for those we had bowls of peanuts and platters of little sausages.

There were candles to light.

The music was set up.

And there was the terrible underlying worry. Would anyone really come? What if nobody came?

What if…

The door burst open and Mike came in with Chris on his shoulders. Chris had a big orange stain from one side of his face to the other.

"Mike!" I scolded. "What did I say about popsicles?"

Mike started to open his mouth, then stopped. He slid Chris down off his shoulders, then went up to his room and slammed the door.

I was too busy to catch what was going on.

It was six o'clock. Time for the party. Gordon was home. The kids were clean and the table was loaded. The boys were in the kitchen, tending the pots of tea.

It was quiet on the street.

Where was everyone?

"Don't worry," Jerry said. "You know it's six o'clock until it's seven o'clock. No one wants to be impolite and come early."

Then there was a timid knock at the door. Wai Sun's two sisters came in bringing a bag of oranges.

One by one.

Two by two, then a stream of people were coming down the market street, coming in the door. We greeted them with a mixture of joy and sheer relief. They had come! Joy to the world; they had come in spite of every-thing!

They came in, smiling, people we saw every day, but this was different. The house filled up. We were elbow to elbow; no room for anyone to sit. Talking, laughing, sampling the strange, sweet foreign food and taking refuge in the tea and peanuts…celebrating the foreign holiday as nervously as we had celebrated the Ghost Festival.

The older people had done their thing and were beginning to leave when the boys asked if we could dance. We put on some Christmas rock music and the young people, including our kids, began to dance out in the courtyard under the banyan tree.

Joy to the world.
Dance!
Dance to peace in the teeth of war.
Dance to joy in the threat of horror
And darkness.
Dance with the stars and the angels.
Nobody knows the words.
Dance with the flow of the music.
Wordless, coming through the body
Of the world
Dance!

The night was getting chilly and we came in the house. The phone was ringing. Mr. Hong, the Communist, was on the line.

"I'm so sorry I didn't get there tonight," came the unexpected voice. "I had a meeting, and then got caught in traffic."

"Oh, uh, that's all right."

"No, I was really coming. But come to the store tomorrow. I have something for you...a small gift."

"Oh, that's not..."

"Yes, you come." The voice was decisive.

I put the phone down. Had he really been going to come?"

The young people were filling the floor space in the living room. Someone had picked up a mouth organ, one of the kids' toys. Playing a tune on it.

"It came upon a midnight clear..."

I heard the music, shocked, surprised.

"Do you know that?"

"Oh, of course," Jonathan said, laughing. "We know all your Christmas songs. We learn them at school. Could we sing them with you?"

We sat in a circle on the floor and began to sing. The red candle in the window flickered, casting shadows. We sang and sang. They knew all the Christmas carols. They sang in Chinese and we in English, but the music was the same.

I looked at Gordon. We both had tears in our eyes.

We were celebrating.

When they had all gone home that night and the kids were upstairs asleep, we took what was left of the last candle and made our way upstairs to the little white room that was our own.

It was quiet down over the street, with the twinkling lights of the fishing boats bobbing in the darkness.

We blew out the candle and turned to each other, breathing deeply of the bittersweet smoke, feeling that pounding force of the power of love...for each other, and our children, and the world we were discovering.

Such power.

Would it bless?

Would it burn?

The next morning I went to the Stanley Store to see Mr. Hong. He had a large basket filled with foreign Christmas foods, English tea biscuits and chocolates, and a bottle of imported wine with fresh oranges.

"A gift for your family," he smiled.

"Oh, Mr. Wong, we didn't expect gifts last night."

"I know. But I want to give you this gift. I..."

He hesitated.

"I'm interested in your family," he began. "Yesterday your older son was here with his little brother. They came in with a whole crowd of children from the street. They were calling his name."

"Mike?"

"They call him Miko. He was going to buy two ice cream cones from the freezer, and then he saw the other children standing there. Instead of buying two cones he bought ten popsicles, and shared them with the other children."

Oh, my God. And I had scolded him.

"Did you teach him that?" he asked.

I could not answer without disgracing myself.

By the time we got around to Christmas day that year it was almost redundant, so much had already happened. We did manage to get Chris a tricycle (down payment on the mythical bikes), and the top few items on the other kids lists. We even exchanged a gift with each other, but they seemed trivial compared to the gifts we had already received.

But with the gifts of love and openness came other worries. The kids were beginning to make friends at HKIS. Deidra's friend, Nancy Wingo, was the daughter of an American who worked for *Life* magazine. In fact, he was on the team that had written the *Life* magazine report of the Mai Lai massacre.

Deidra and Nancy were in the Christmas pageant at the church program, trying to keep a straight face under the costumes and not burst into nervous giggles. Deidra wanted Nancy to come to our house for a sleepover.

"No way," Nancy said. "It's interesting down there, but I'd never sleep at your house. I'd be scared!"

Scared?

Marita's friend, Mona Brower, was the daughter of a Dutch business-man and a highly sophisticated Thai woman. They lived in Repulse Bay in a palatial apartment.

Marita was invited for an overnight.

"Oh Mom!" she said when she came home the next day, "they have everything! Even the floors have big soft carpets, and they have thick purple towels in the bathroom. I would never invite her here!"

I looked around our house. It certainly would not be classified as "rich," but it was charming...unique. It had character—it was interesting.

But if the kids were becoming embarrassed to live here in the village, how important was it for us to continue to live here—and for how long?

It had been Gordon's idea to come here. I had opposed it, sensing that these dangers might arise. Now, I loved it. I was deeply emotionally involved in the village.

The thought flickered through my mind, totally unbidden and most unwelcome. Was I getting sucked into a cause? A good cause that might hurt the people I loved most?

I brushed it aside. We would see.

CHAPTER TWELVE

IT WAS CHINESE NEW YEAR…

In the house on the corner by the sea, we were almost as excited about the coming festival as if we were Chinese. In thanks for her extra month's wages and week off, Ah Wai had bought a Kumquat tree as a gift, and it sat in the entryway, splendid and golden on a painted blue chest. Gordon had brought home bags of dried fruits, candied carrots and melons, shaved sweet coconut, peanut brittle and watermelon seeds to serve with tea to callers during the holidays.

The night before New Year's we went to the flower market by the Star Ferry to buy a blooming peach tree for the living room. We carefully filled red lucky packets with money for the children and the unmarried. Like every other household on the street, we were prepared.

All Chinese children grow an inch a year, and can see it happen if they stay awake all night. But who can stay awake all night to find out?

Jerry had told us the story of Jo Gwan, the Kitchen God. It was his duty to observe the doings of the family for a year, and on this night he would rise up to heaven and give a report. In order to insure a good report, his lips were rubbed with honey, making sure only sweet words were conveyed.

"That's so silly," Marita said. "How could a little wooden carving float up in the sky?"

"Well, how could a big fat man float down from the sky at Christmas?" Mike argued. "A lot of things that people think are silly, but they still believe them…sort of."

The day dawned bright and clear, bringing in the Year of the Dog. The street was quiet and the shops were closed while everyone slept off the Nin Sa'man feast of the night before. On the edge of the beach, all twenty-one fishing boats were anchored. They bobbed lazily on the blue morning sea, their dark grey timbers aflutter with red strips of paper announcing good luck and prosperity for the new year.

In the house on the corner we missed the rattle of pig carts. It was so quiet it was almost impossible to sleep.

Gordon rolled over and gave me a sleepy grin.

"Aren't you supposed to get up and serve me tea this morning like a good obedient wife?"

"Only if you drink tea."

"I'd prefer coffee."

"That changes the rules."

We laughed, awash in this intercultural no-man's land.

We were hardly up before Jerry was at the door.

"Gung Hey fat choi! Congratulations and prosperity!" he called happily, clasping his hands and bowing slightly.

"Gung Hey fat choi!" we all answered, and Gordon reached for the two red packets to place in his hands, since he was still unmarried.

Chris ran around in circles.

"Gung Hey fat choi!" he echoed. "Where's my money?"

Jerry caught him up and hoisted him to his shoulders, prancing around the room with the little boy.

"Why are you congratulating us?" Mike had to know.

"Because you are alive! And may your life be successful!"

There was another knock and Wing Sung was at the door.

"The Dragon Dance is coming in a few minutes," he said excitedly. "My brother will be dancing the lead part this morning!"

We heard the beating of the gongs and the shouting of a crowd, and ran out the door. The main dancer was dressed in black pants and a white shirt. He held the creature's gaudily painted head, leaping, bending, jumping, and shaking to the rhythm of the drums. Other dancers carried the tail, and a tambourine player baited the creature along.

The gongs pounded wildly, and the creature leapt in the air and came down with the agility of a big cat.

Is it really a lion, or a dragon?" I shouted to Jerry above the noise.

"It doesn't matter," he said, shrugging his shoulders happily. "It's a kei-lun in Chinese, but there is no such animal, so you can call it whatever you like."

"Then it isn't a dragon?"

"We don't know," he said. "No one's ever seen a real dragon."

The street was packed with people who seemed to have materialized out of the silence of a short time before. Everyone was dressed in bright new clothes; men in blue padded silk jackets or Western suits, and women in colorful padded silk jackets and black pants. The children were rosy cheeked and laughing, decked out in bright red jackets with pink or orange ribbons in the girls' black hair. Everyone was smiling and calling out greetings to someone.

The jostling crowd engulfed us and swept us into the street. It took us past the boarded up market stalls and down the far end of the wine factory street to the Jeng's rice shop. They came out smiling and calling greetings, and joined the crowd. There was a press of bodies, a movement as of one living organism, and no one apologized for having touched another.

The lion-dragon led the crowd on, dancing and leaping, bowing and shaking, low and high, up and down. I watched this celebration of life, this welcome to a new year of being that would follow its patterns of height and depth, complexities and joys.

I looked up and saw we were near the lion-dragon. The face of Wing Sung's brother peered out of the mask.

"Gung Hey fat choi!" said the lion-dragon. "I'll be at your house to drink tea this afternoon."

It was the first time a kei-lun had ever spoken to me.

At the other end of the street tiny children were imitating the dance. A small dragon only about two feet tall was jumping and shaking its tail while a miniature tambourine player hopped about. The tradition was being passed on.

Each day had its own special designation…

On the fifth day of the New Year the Jeng boys came to our house.

"Our mother wants to invite you for dinner tonight," they said. "If she invites you, will you come?"

"We would be honored."

The boys went to tell their mother and came back in less than half an hour.

"She invites you to come," they said politely.

"At what time?"

"Around six."

At a little before six we made our way down the wine factory street, between the high stone walls, past the noodle shop and down to the rice shop. Most of the places of business were still closed for the New Year festival. Even at the Jengs the iron grating was pulled over the wooden shutters, and we had to knock to enter.

The boys welcomed us through a section of grating just wide enough to squeeze in one person at a time. We filed past the covered barrels and on to the back of the store where burlap sacks of rice were stacked to the ceiling.

It was dark inside the shop, with one light bulb hanging from the ceiling shaded by a newspaper. The old wood of the beams was dark and ancient, and the smell of burlap and salt water filled the air.

One folding table was set up in the middle of the floor, and I began to wonder how all fourteen of us would sit at one small card table.

Jeng Tai came out of the kitchen, her face red and shiny from bending over the fire. She was beaming and ordering everyone around.

"Pearl, pour some tea. Welcome, welcome! My husband is still at a mahjong game he's been playing all day. You have to let these men gamble a little money at New Year's time… He hasn't come back yet. Ah yah, sit down and drink some tea. Eldest son, get some ho-lok—some Coke for the children…"

She hurried back into the kitchen where the rich aroma of garlic and ginger mixed with soy sauce and rice wine smelled incredible. The dishes began to arrive on the table, but Mr. Jeng was not home yet, so no one sat down. We stood talking to the Jeng boys while Pearl and her mother produced one dish after another, and deposited them on the table. I watched the chicken with mushroom soup, the sautéed prawns, the steamed fish, thinking how nervous I would be if I were putting all this on the table when my husband had not appeared, but Mrs. Jeng seemed cheerful as if nothing were happening. The Jeng boys kept slipping out the door one by one to remind their father to come, but he was busy with his game and in no hurry.

In the center of the bamboo shoots and mushrooms, the fried bean curd and steamed fish, there appeared a platter of French fries and a bottle of ketchup.

"We didn't know what your children would like," Pearl explained. "We thought they might like these."

"Oh, our children eat anything," I said confidently, since we had just had that discussion before we left the house.

Mr. Jeng was still out playing mahjong, and we all stood awkwardly around the table letting the food get cold.

The boys stood and talked with us, patient for hungry boys.

To pass the time, Gordon asked questions. Gordon could always think of a question to ask. He amazed me.

"Is this a New Year saying?" Gordon asked, pointing to a wooden plaque on a wall post facing the street.

"No," said Jonathan. "That's a good luck writing. When my father bought the shop many years ago, he had a wise man come and tell him if the location was good, if it lay right with the wind and the water, the Fung Sui. The man said it was all fine except for this post, because it cuts right in the middle of the shop facing us, so he wrote these words on the wall to correct the problem."

"And now it's all right?"

Jonathan looked at Gordon and smiled, scraping his toe across the floor shyly.

"Of course, I don't believe this," he said quietly. "We younger people have been educated. You'll have to excuse my parents. They are uneducated country people."

More questions from Gordon...

He was more questions than answers. Sometimes I wondered if he even remembered the answers; he preferred the questions.

"But you must have heard many legends and stories as a child," I asked. "Did you think of them as being real when you heard them?"

He looked at me, wondering why I wanted to know.

"Of course. All children accept things as true when they first hear them, because children are innocent and trusting; and then one day you understand that these things cannot be true, because the world is not that way. Then as you grow up, you know that they are true in a different way. The stories and legends say something about life. They are not true or untrue in the usual sense, but they contain something true."

"What would be an example of that?" I asked, looking at him so he would know I really wanted to hear the answer.

"It's like the belief that the goddess Tin Hau protects all the sea people. In olden times they thought it was dangerous to rescue people drowning in the sea. Even if a child fell in, no one would rescue him, because it was believed if someone fell they had somehow angered the goddess, and the life of the one who rescued him would be demanded as a payment. But now this idea is going away. Modern lifeguards are coming to the beaches and they take the name of Tin Hau to save life. There is even a Tin Hau temple that is considered the special temple of the lifeguards who work at beaches. People try to change the old superstitions into something useful as they become educated."

Mrs. Jeng was bustling about, calling us to the table, finally deciding to eat without Mr. Jeng. She scolded the ginger-striped cat and the two dogs, said her house was old, ugly and dusty, and there was nothing on the table to eat, then over assurances that it was beautiful house, very well-kept, and we had never seen so much delicious food, she settled us on the stools.

As the guests of honor, our family was seated first, then all the various sizes of Jengs formed a second outer ring around the table, reaching their chopsticks between our shoulders. It was the first time I had ever seen fifteen people seated around one small card table, but it worked, knee-to-knee and shoulder-to-shoulder. It was even a good way to keep warm.

M. Jeng finally came, looking like a tall, hollow-cheeked Abraham Lincoln, and was absorbed into the group with greetings and murmurs from the boys as a token of respect.

"Ah Pa—eat rice."

He was a proud man. Surrounded by sturdy sons, a beautiful daughter, a good business and an obedient wife, who could blame him?

With the arrival of the man of the house, Mrs. Jeng brought out a shiny new bottle of brandy. She poured it straight into tall water glasses with a glug-glug sound and set one at each adult's place.

Gordon looked at me and I looked at him. Neither of us dared to tackle a whole water tumbler full of straight brandy.

"Come on, Dad," Deidra reminded us, sensing the hesitation, "you said to eat what's put in front of you."

The Jeng boys understood English and looked at us, and Mrs. Jeng glanced at them for an explanation.

"Is something wrong with the drink?" she asked, sniffing the bottle. "It cost over ten dollars. I'll take it back if it's bad and get another one. The store is open."

"No, no!" Gordon said. "This drink is fine! There's no problem—we just don't know if we can drink so much of it. You're too generous."

"Ah, you're so polite. Drink! Drink all of it. This is a celebration and you have given me much face by eating in our humble home tonight. Drink!"

We sipped it, warm and strong and bitter, and she beamed and bustled around the table. Chris chased the ginger-cat through the burlap sacks while the older children ate bean curd and abalone and seaweed, and we all stepped into never-land in the rice shop with the rough beams and the sea at the back door.

I began to feel the dragon dancing in my head and knew that unquestioned acceptance, like straight brandy, could warm the heart and blur the judgment.

Gordon could not finish his drink. At some point Mr. Jeng reached over, took Gordon's drink, and drank it straight down.

I don't know what happened to mine.

Did I drink it?

On the sixth day of the New Year, wide-eyed students from Gordon's school came to pay their respects. They sat for hours talking to Gordon while they ate watermelon seeds and dropped the husks on the floor. The depth of their respect seemed to be measured by the length of time they sat.

Dark-haired boys and shy little girls with soup-bowl haircuts who sat and giggled and carefully covered their teeth...beautiful in their brown uniforms...

On the seventh day it was everyone's birthday.

Ah Wai made wonderful Gok-jai for us—small round circles of pastry filled with chopped peanuts, coconut and brown sugar, folded in half and crimped around the edges, and deep fried.

Mike wanted to know how to make them.

I looked at Marita. This year she would be twelve, and was growing into a pretty, blue-eyed, blond, about-to-be-woman.

And Mike was growing taller, still with that mop of golden Dutch hair.

Deidra would be ten; still so little for her age she was like a small dark-haired doll.

And Chris would be three.

He had his tricycle and was zooming around the courtyard with it, talking a blue streak. He had been unusually verbal since eighteen months. Now he had decided he needed to learn how to write his name.

And we...we would turn thirty-seven and forty in this new year.

Everyone's birthday.

Was it good for us to stay here?

In the end, the decision was taken out of our hands, unless we had decided to go really over the edge.

I was busy writing notes about Chinese New Year in my notebook that morning. A flock of village children was gathered on our front steps eating and chattering like small birds. I heard a commotion, and then the sound of pounding on the front door.

I ran quickly down the stairs and opened the door. A young man was nailing something to the heavy wood.

You are to evict these premises by April 1

By order of

P.T. Yu, solicitor for Y.W. Zee

A strange mixture of emotions raced through me—shock...relief... loss...sudden unsought freedom...

"But why? What have we done wrong?"

The young man answered like a robot.

"The landlord says his mother needs this house."

"Is that the real reason?"

"I'm only the employee."

125

"But do you know the real reason?"

"I...you know the rents are going up everywhere, and I suppose it could be for a rent increase. He must legally evict you before he can ask you to sign for a higher price."

"Then this is not a real eviction notice. The man would talk price?"

"I suspect so."

"How much would the rent increase?"

"Um, perhaps thirty percent."

I was so startled I shut the door in his face, and he left.

Thirty percent? I reopened the door and ripped the notice in half, and threw it in the open gutter. Then I picked it up and threw it in the garbage. Then, just to be safe, I shredded it into tiny bits and flushed it down the toilet.

EVICTION NOTICE.

That would be village gossip fast enough without having it plastered on our door.

I called Gordon at the school office.

"Evicted? You're joking."

"I wish I were. They want to raise the rent. I think this is just a legal game."

"But we're not going to..."

"Unless you think we should."

"I don't know. Think it over. I've got a meeting right now; see you later, love. Don't worry about it. We'll work it out."

That evening Jerry and Wai Sun and the Jeng boys came over. Of course, they knew all about it. Everyone in the village was talking. The Americans were being evicted.

"Should we pay the extra money and stay, or leave?" Gordon asked our 'advisors.'

"How much?"

"Thirty percent."

"People in the village will know," Jerry said. "Everybody knows everything you do."

"And they'll laugh, and say you've been taken for a fool," Wai Sun added.

Jonathan, the studious one, said quietly, "I think most important is, people will wonder why you stay. If you can pay such a high rent, why do you live in a poor neighborhood like ours? You must have some strange reason, they will say, and everyone will begin to guess why."

"Perhaps the Kai Fong will think you are Communists, come to stir up social discontent."

126

"And the Communists will think you are agents, working for the CIA…"

"And other Americans will think you are trying to shame them by living more simply, to show they do not need so many things…"

"Or Chinese will think you are here because you feel sorry for them."

We listened to the swirl of voices in the room. Not a one of these reasons was true. But how could we describe what our reasons were when we did not even know them ourselves?

Had we ever had reasons?

No, they had been more like longings.

That night we asked our children.

"Would you rather live here in Stanley or move back to Repulse Bay?"

There was a disbelieving croak from Marita.

"Do we really have a choice?" she asked guardedly.

"Hey!" Mike said cautiously. "Ummm…"

"What do you mean?" Deidra asked.

Marita, as usual, took charge.

"Well, if you really want to know, it's hard for us here. We don't speak Chinese like you do, but we know you guys really love it here, and… I guess we'll do whatever you decide."

"It's okay," Mike said. "I really don't mind it."

Some warning buzz in my belly…some memory from the past…told me this was a crisis point for our children. If we did not listen we could damage them, all for a perfectly good cause, or no cause at all.

Parents did that to their kids. I knew… I had been forced to live out my parents' beliefs, even when it threatened to ruin my life, and I had rebelled. I did not want our children to have to rebel against us, silently or otherwise. They were our most priceless treasure.

We contacted P.T. Yu and told him to tell Y.W. Zee that his mother could have the house, and we hoped she would enjoy it.

April one.

Somewhere in the rusty recesses of my unused Western mind, I realized that would be April Fool's Day. Had we been foolish to move to the village?

No. It had been a great, transformative experience, one we would never forget and never cease to be influenced by.

But suddenly, it was over.

The Chinese boys who had befriended us promised to visit us in Repulse Bay.

We would still come back to the market on Saturdays, but it would be different.

Thank you, Y.W. Zee.

Back in Repulse Bay, on the same street where we had lived in three other houses, there was a beautiful old duplex on a corner lot, a two-story stucco with a wide verandah on the ground floor leading into well-kept gardens. Two huge red-flowering Jacaranda trees spread their branches over the green lawn. The nullah ran past it and on down to the Repulse Bay beach. The beloved nullah...

It was available April one.

Upstairs lived an American family, an ABC reporter named Steve Bell, his wife Joyce, and their two children.

Walter DeVelder came over and inspected the apartment, and approved. The cost would be covered. It was one block from HKIS. The kids could walk to school.

So, we bound up our slightly wounded hearts and called Henry Chey.

The moving lorry came huffing and chuffing along the village market street and stopped in front of the rice wine factory. People stopped and gawked while we loaded up our goods, looking forlorn and naked on the open truck.

We moved back to Repulse Bay.

Ah Wai would continue to live with her family on the hillside and take the bus to Repulse Bay to work.

"Only one stop," she smiled. "I'll come with you."

Only one stop, but a world away.

The new house was a delight. The kids ran excitedly through the rooms, claiming their spaces. The broad, covered, terrazzo veranda space and gardens...large living / dining room...bedrooms...baths. The girls claimed the big front bedroom. Ours was the master suite. Because Ah Wai would not be a "live in" amah, the boys had the servants' quarters, two separate rooms with a half-bath and space for a TV. We would have TV! (for a few hours a day). The kids could watch *Hawaii Five-0* like their other classmates!

Chris had his own little room, close to Mike's, where he could park his tricycle.

Everyone was excited.

Gordon and I had our "first," an air conditioner. In all the years in Hong Kong we had never had one...and venetian blinds.

I sewed new curtains for the other rooms.

We bought rugs, and had the old couches recovered.

Décor- early corduroy.

We bought a beautiful, big, monkey-wood dining room table for family meals and company. We even bought new soft towels for Marita, even though I couldn't find purple ones.

We would take all the experience we had gained and live like real Americans again—almost.

But the best part of the whole arrangement was our upstairs neighbors. Steve was an ABC reporter assigned to cover the war in Viet Nam, and was gone six weeks at a time. Joyce, a pretty young brunette, and her two girls, Allison and Hillary, became part of our family when Steve was gone. When he came home we shut the door between the apartments and let them be.

Joyce and I spent days at the beach with our kids. I had an American friend, and between us, we were "Mom" to most of the kids on the beach.

I needed to laugh, to be young once more. Joyce loved to laugh. I let my hair grow. We shopped for clothes. She was a godsend.

We were in our thirties, and both felt gorgeous.

Of course we were!

At least our husbands thought we were, and a few stray men on the beach who tried to pick us up did as well, until they realized that six kids were calling us "Mom."

The kids played in the yard. We had a swing set. The kids put on music, and danced. Hillary, at less than two years old, loved to dance in her diaper with her mother's purse on her arm.

They did dramas. Chris was always the "Prince," dragging his royal (bath) robes behind him. We even had a garage.

But we had not forgotten. Our house was the meeting place for young people from the village and Kung Lee School. We roasted hot dogs out in the yard, and pulled out the guitar bought long ago at Navy Purchasing (that other life). We sat out on the verandah steps and sang seventies songs like *We Shall Overcome* and *Kum Ba Yah*, blending worlds on our own turf. We had left the village, but it would always be alive in us.

In the kitchen I painted the wall in broad swirling colors, and wrote in big letters a verse by Joseph Pintauro…

> To believe in God is to drink wine,
> It is to eat bread,
> Not by yourself,
> But by some other magic.

Then Steve was captured by the Viet Cong. For days, we sat with Joyce until we heard he had escaped. He was coming home.

It was good.

There was a poetry contest announced by the *South China Morning Post*.

I entered it. So did hundreds of other expats.

I won it.

With a poem ending with the words:

"...for beauty that I could not use

nor bear to lose."

We lived in that magical house for almost two years. We found a pre-school teacher for Chris over across the nullah, and at four he not only knew how to write his name, he could read. He could read the *South China Morning Post*, and his favorite Rudyard Kipling book, about Mowgli, the Jungle Boy.

"But I still like you to read it to me, Mom."

We made bows and arrows from the bamboo growing in our yard, and the kids loved the beach, the warm ripples of water washing in over the white sand. They were all excellent swimmers, totally at home in the water, with wonderful tans. The girls posed in their bikinis for Japanese tourists, for a dollar. I even had an orange bikini that I loved, but Gordon, in a rare display of conservatism, thought it scandalous, so I tossed it out.

Keep the peace...

Chris wanted to know all about God. Every impressive building or new Hong Kong skyscraper he saw going up, he would ask, "Mom, is God bigger than that?"

"Yes."

"And even bigger than that one?"

"Yes."

"Then how come God can be small enough to live inside us?"

"Because God is the biggest and the smallest of everything. Bigger than big, and smaller than small."

He pondered that for a moment.

"Oh, that's good," he said, as though he had solved something.

How did I know that someday he would need to know that?

I didn't.

By the Spring of 1971, Gordon began to feel serious problems developing in his job as Headmaster at Kung Lee School. More teachers were giving their notice, moving over to the government schools for the fall semester. The teacher drain was making it hard for the school to come up to standard, and the low standards made it impossible to be accredited. Until the school was accredited, it would not receive government subsidy.

It was a Catch-22 situation.

Gordon went to the CCC office to talk with Peter Wong. He had a simple plan.

Pay the teachers the same as government schools paid. Teachers paid well would stay. Teachers who stayed would get the school's grades up. With grades higher, the school would be accredited. With accreditation would come government subsidy.

It would be a wise investment.

Peter Wong was not about to be told what to do by an American. He had seen enough of that in China.

"I appreciate all you've done for Kung Lee," Wong said, "but I do not like the fact that you are meddling in money matters. Your job is to educate; mine is to manage the funds."

"But I can't run a good school when the teachers keep leaving. All we get is inexperienced teachers who are learning on our students and moving on..."

"The money is no concern of yours."

"The money is teachers' salaries—teacher's lives—these people have families."

"I will not pay the higher wages."

"And I will not continue to see the school struggle."

"The money is not your decision."

Gordon seldom lost his temper. He managed to hold his tongue—barely. But this problem had to be solved.

Peter Wong, like the rest of the human race, was a product of his experiences...and Gordon did not intend to be a victim of those experiences.

He talked to Walter DeVelder about the situation. Walter wrote to New York and they sent a human resources man out to look at the problem.

The young HR man listened to Wong, and listened to Gordon, then he came out to have dinner with us in Repulse Bay.

"Peter Wong is really ticked at you," he said. "He always considered you to be a very agreeable, not to say pliable, fellow...not like the old China hands. How come you two are butting heads?"

"It's a matter of principle."

131

"Do you really care about those teachers' wages? Can't you wait for him to operate the system his way, and pay the better wages when government funding comes through?"

"It won't come through his way."

"So you're going to hold out?"

"I am."

"And what if he doesn't agree to the pay raise?"

"Then he can find another headmaster."

"You're really going to tell Peter Wong to piss off?"

"You said that, I didn't. But yes."

That spring, Gordon made it official. After two years, he was resigning as Headmaster of Kung Lee School. He was not going to waste his life in a political battle.

A new person was found. Hudson Soo, Hong Kong born Chinese, educated in the U.S., was coming to be the new headmaster.

They had a farewell program for Gordon at the close of school that year. Bernie Anderson had the students sing a special song to Gordon.

I sat in the audience, hearing the words and music of *To Sir With Love*, and cried. The Chinese students had really loved Gordon, and he had returned their love. He had loved the teachers too, and that was why he was leaving. Maybe if he left it would no longer be a matter of saving face and Peter Wong could afford to give in. He simply could not bear to let Gordon, an American, win.

Hudson Soo was Chinese.

Gordon had a hunch that the teachers would get their raise…next year.

It was time for a vacation to the U.S., to touch base and see our parents. We took an American President lines ship from the pier in Hong Kong. It was a hot, steamy, early summer night, and nearly one thousand students from Kung Lee crowded the pier for our leaving. We felt honored and loved and sad, and deeply touched.

To Sir, with love…

He knew how to take all that love,

And not get all mixed up.

I wanted everybody to love him.

But most of all,

We loved each other.

We would go on.

We spent the summer in Zeeland, staying with Gordon's parents. It was good to feel their strong comforting presence after all the cultural and emotional battles we had been through.

Deidra scrounged up a bike from a neighbor and was off to see Zeeland. She remembered how to ride from the Cornwall Street days.

"I can't believe there are so many De Prees here!" she laughed. "Even the cemetery is full of them!"

In Hong Kong, we had been the only De Prees in the phone book.

Mike wanted to help Grandpa in the store. He rode along in the delivery truck.

Marita had bought a pretty new long dress when we stopped in Hawaii on the way back to the U.S., and wore it everywhere. The girls had cousins—cousins' clothes and gadgets to discover. It reminded me of when I used to go from Kentucky back to Chicago to connect with my family. I had been as much a novelty to them as our kids were in Zeeland.

I seemed to be living the same life I grew up with, but with such a difference! This time there was love, real, true, solid love. Not an abstract love of God that pushed us into a cause, come hell or high water, but real, true, human love. The real stuff.

We sat around the kitchen table, that high court of family justice, and Mom De Pree listened as we talked. We told her about our new discoveries, about our new ideas and expanded views of the world.

"Yeah, I'm just an old-fashioned woman," she said, "but it all sounds good to me. Could be true, you know."

My mother had a job in Grand Rapids now, so the distances were not as far as when she lived in Chicago. When the two of us went shopping together, and I shared some of our insights with her, she was not so sure.

"I don't really understand what you're getting at," she said, "but I guess I'll still see you in heaven, won't I?"

I didn't dare answer her.

Heaven?

"Mom, heaven is like a Chinese dragon. Nobody has ever seen it, and everybody knows exactly what it looks like."

She looked frightened.

My mother had been frightened all her life, a frightened, obedient, religious woman.

"You should come to Hong Kong and visit us," I suggested. "Come fly out and spend some time with us on the beach."

Mom loved beaches, and water and swimming. She decided to take me up on the invitation. She would come out for the twins' thirteenth birthday.

Dad De Pree. as usual, was worried about the job.

"Are you going back there?" he asked.

We have one more year in Hong Kong to decide if we want another job there."

"You won't work for that stubborn Chinese fellow?"

"I think not. There's an opening at the International School, tenth-grade English. I can do that while the kids finish up eighth grade."

"Those kids will be ready for high school," Mom De Pree said with a worried edge in her voice. "You be sure you'll be where they can get a good education!"

Mom was still sore about having to leave school after the eighth grade, and work. All her kids had graduated from college. She did not want her grandchildren to be compromised.

"Don't worry, Mom," Gordon assured her.

For the De Pree family, education was the eleventh commandment. How thankful I was for that.

Then we flew back to Hong Kong. As we touched down on that elusive, almost-not-there runway at Kai Tak Airport, I still had that quickened heartbeat, that love of this Asian city. This place had taught me so much, so much that I might not have learned elsewhere. Just a month of being back in the U.S. had reminded me of the old structures, the smallness of some thinking that would have kept me chasing my tail in circles that I could not break out of, in anger over the past, and the remembrance of things I could not forget or forgive.

But we were back—back in Repulse Bay to finish up our time here.

The kids geared up for their last year at HKIS. They would be in seventh and eighth grades, and their dad would be a teacher!

Chris was the most excited. He was finally going to kindergarten. He dressed in his uniform the first day, so eager to be a real school kid.

When he came home that afternoon he seemed almost sad.

"How'd it go, Chris? Did you have fun?"

"Not really."

"Why? What was the matter?"

He looked up at me, puzzled.

"Those kids don't even know how to read!"

I thought he was going to burst into tears. Instead, he said, "They're just dumb!"

"Woah, buddy," I said, hugging him, "they're not dumb. You're just ahead of yourself... They'll all learn to read soon. Everybody does, sooner or later. But you must promise me something."

"What?"

"Don't ever think of other people as being dumb. Maybe they're smarter than you are in some way. See what you can learn from them, and if somebody needs help reading, maybe you can help them."

"I promise," he said, hugging me.

After that, Chris loved school.

My mom did come that summer, in July. We walked the beach and talked, but out conversations were for the most part superficial. I could not tell her in depth what had happened to us, or to our thinking. We swam and sunned, we went shopping together. She took us to the Hilton to celebrate the twins' birthday, and she bought two hand-carved chests in Wanchai to ship back home.

She had a good job in Grand Rapids, and I was happy for her. I knew she loved me dearly, but she did not understand where I was coming from. She still clung tightly to the ideas that had wounded her. What could I say?

Perhaps I would still be like her if I had never dared to immerse myself in another world.

Overall, 1971-1972 was the year of the great abstraction, in Hong Kong and in the world. In the Hilton Hotel on Queens Road Central, Father Zeller's huge mural of women lighting incense in a temple had come down, and in its stead appeared an equally huge abstract by Douglas Bland, husband of Deidra's first-grade teacher.

Reality was gauche.

Abstraction was in.

Father Zeller tried to go with the flow. He painted geometric abstracts. Nobody liked them. He was lost.

Gordon reported for school at HKIS that September, ready for teaching tenth graders whose first language was English. He had a list of interesting books he wanted to explore, the latest recommended by Bernie Anderson. It would be exciting.

He was greeted by a classroom full of American kids, and very rich Chinese kids, some of whom looked at him blankly through drugged eyes. Although there was a solid core of students with good values, a number of the students were from families with more money than family life—big companies—banks—booming industry start-ups in Hong Kong. The kids had limitless money and little supervision.

Drugs were very in…

Bob Christian, the Lutheran head of KHIS, did his best, but he was one voice in a storm of confusion.

There was a streaker at the Star Ferry protesting god knows what. The police called the school and asked if he was an KHIS student.

Bob Christian answered, , tongue in cheek, that he could not accept responsibility, since the person in question was not in uniform at the time.

The Hong Kong China Watchers had their ears pricked. Things were stirring in Beijing. There were rumors that Nixon might be coming to China. The China watchers were saying, "Beware the sleeping dragon."

The China watchers were like the old China hands, but smarter , and graduates of more prestigious universities. They had their fingers to the wind, fresh with spit.

The Whiteheads were China watchers. We were invited to their home in Kowloon to hear the soundtrack of *Jesus Christ Superstar*. Churches were up in arms over it. It was depicting Jesus Christ as an ordinary man, caught in the traditional religious and political battles of his time.

We went to the Whitehead's house and had a glass of wine, then sat with a crowd of foreigners (mostly hired by churches) on the floor and listened.

Gordon and I sat there on the floor, holding hands, listening to the music and the words.

My heart was pounding madly. I had tears streaming down my face. Somebody was saying something real. They were tying religion into life, God into man. Not your usual incarnation theory, but something more.

I could not stop crying, and I could not say a word.

...He's just a man...just a man...

What was so downgraded about being a man...or a woman...those containers of the mighty spirit of life itself?

God knows I had been hanging onto traditional Christianity by my toenails... This was deeply stirring.

And, of course, a lot of people hated it.

Our house at Repulse Bay was just down the road from HKIS. We met our kids' teachers, and some of them began to hang around the house by the nullah, chatting. The teachers from Kung Lee stopped by occasionally, too.

Bernie Anderson and his girlfriend Linda were getting married. They asked Gordon to perform the ceremony. The wedding was on the Kowloon side in the Kowloon Union Church.

Being gifted writers, they wrote their own vows. The vows were so amended and restated that no one knew at exactly what point they became man and wife. But married they were, traditional or not.

The Bells were leaving. Because of his outstanding reporting of the Viet Nam War, Steve was being assigned to Washington D.C. He was being considered for the post of ABC's anchor on *Good Morning America*.

Joyce was out of her wits with delight. We would miss them, like family.

A guy named Don Emory moved in upstairs. He worked for Winston Cigarettes. By his own definition, "a dirty old man who sells cigarettes to innocent little kids." He was anything but an old man. He was a beautiful, charming and handsome young man, and we all adored him. But we did not exactly approve of him.

Was that necessary?

The girls fell in love with him.

The boys adored him. And we all enclosed him in a kind of family love that was complex and peculiar. He adored us back.

What if he did bring a new bar girl home every weekend, and turn the music up loud enough to shake the floor upstairs? We loved Don Emory, in spite of ourselves, and he loved us back.

With our boxy green Morris Oxford parked in the driveway next to his yellow MG convertible, we would have gladly swapped.

But with four kids?

Some things were not possible, even in 1971.

In December, the Church of All Nations asked me to write a short skit to put on in the chapel, instead of the traditional manger scene. Being in high gear and fine fettle, I composed a short skit so "relevant" and so obtuse that no one got the point.

Maybe there wasn't one.

Oh well, it was 1971. The whole world was going to hell in a hand basket. What did we expect?

One thing we certainly did not expect was the sudden rediscovery of Gina.

One day there was a knock at the back door. I went to see if someone was making a delivery.

Catherine Low was standing there, red faced and angry. I invited her in, but she would not sit down.

"You and your do-gooder husband,!" she shouted, "should be careful of the way you meddle in other people's lives. I took that young slut, that child of a whore, into my family as a daughter, and what has she done? She's ruined our family—she's stolen my husband!"

"Catherine, please, let's sit down and talk about this..."

"There's nothing to talk about. He's keeping her in a hotel; he won't let me see her, he..."

I tried to console her. I had seen this story before.

A few days later there was a call from Gina. I recognized her voice, soft and quiet.

"I'm sorry Catherine bothered you," she apologized.

I asked her if the Lows had ever sent her to school.

"No, they kept me as a servant. Catherine was always gone, playing mahjong and gambling away Charlie's money. Then he got sick—some back trouble—and I had to take care of him."

I could see what had happened.

"He's been very kind to me. Don't worry about me. I'll be all right."

This was older than 1971. This was the human story, even older than China…

Ah Wai came every day to our Repulse Bay house. She cooked and cleaned, careful not to disturb me when she swept around my desk in our bedroom. I was writing again.

Every day while the kids were in school, I sat at my desk with the little portable manual typewriter and wrote.

I had been in touch with the editor at Harper and Row, and he was interested to see what I was coming up with.

Actually, I was reaching backward. There were holes in my thinking. I was stuck on what happened in Kentucky, the horror and pathos of that whole thing. I could not get beyond it. Even with the huge experience of awareness in Stanley Village, I was still blocked somewhere deep inside.

But I could not write about THAT. I would take the emotions and the horrors of that experience and transform them into a novel. All the characters would be fictitious. Emotions would be re-channeled. It would be called *Walking Barefoot*, and set in Appalachian Kentucky.

I wrote and worked. I knew the writing was worthless. I tried to make it real…more explicit…sexier…more degraded. Didn't people love dirty, degraded stories?

I tore it up; ashamed of the crap I was writing.

What about the next Stanley Village story I had notes for?

Not enough distance.

I needed distance and perspective…

Honesty. Who gave a fig about my honesty?

I needed to write the real story, the one that was blocking everything else….my father would kill me. He had hired a bodyguard. I would not put it past him to hunt me down if I ever told that story.

We were due back in New York next summer. I would stop in and have a meeting with the editor.

Because of the poem published in the *South China Morning Post*, and an article in the fashion page about the China Doll fashions from Kwun Tong (they were doing very well), the paper sent a reporter to Repulse Bay to interview me. They wrote a long and detailed profile of me with a huge photo that made me look like the goddess of mercy. Gordon had talked me into putting my hair up on top of my head in a tight topknot, so slicked down and pulled up it actually slanted my eyes.

The goddess of mercy?

Or a missionary in a bun?

In penance, he bought me a big, black leather hat, which I wished I had worn for the photo. Down over my face.

Too many identities.

The Cheys came to visit us.

"When are you moving again?" Henry joked.

"No more moves," Gordon said. "Next time it will probably be a move back to America."

Florence picked up on that quickly.

"I'll send my tailor over," she promised. "You have to have some pretty silk cheongsams to take back to America."

Actually, they had come to ask a favor of Gordon. He had helped their son Danny find a place in the college in Orange City, Iowa, and they were pleased. But now they were worried about Nelson. He had failed his school cert for the second time, and he was depressed, wondering what his life would mean.

We knew Nelson well. He often baby-sat our kids when we lived in Stanley Village. He was like a big kid, laughing and playing with them. He was like a big brother to them. But now he was in trouble. Every year too many young Chinese students in Hong Kong committed suicide because of the shame of failure…

Gordon promised to spend time with him.

Henry patted Gordon's shoulder in thanks.

Florence invited us over for dinner, for the family feast before Chinese New Year, the Nin S'aman, the New Year's Eve feast.

It was an honor.

On Chinese New Year's Eve we took the Star Ferry over to number ten Playing Field Road where the Chey family lived. They were all there, except for Danny; six sons and one daughter, our six, and various relatives and amahs.

The foods were traditional that night, each dish having a meaning. We laughed and chatted, in English and Chinese, surrounded by the warmth and love of a Chinese family.

So many dishes, so many flavors. Gordon loved them all, except for the dried Chinese mushrooms in the chicken soup, and the long, fatty, spicy pork sausages. Actually, he could not stand either of them, but as soon as he safely devoured them, Florence kept piling them on his plate. He should not have pretended. When we left that night Florence saw to it that he was loaded down with a bag of dried mushrooms and a box of sausages.

The first of many...for years to come, until we finally confessed.

Gordon made work of looking after Nelson. The Cheys joked that Gordon had adopted him. He was our Kai-ji, our adopted boy. Gordon took Nelson to the airport, and encouraged him to apply to Japan Airlines for a job. Reach out...forget about the school cert... There was a whole big world out there.

Nelson was successful. He began a long career with JAL.

And Danny was doing very well at the college in Orange City, Iowa.

We would not need Henry Chey's moving lorry again, but our families were inter-connected.

We would sell everything when we left Hong Kong, and keep the money for one last, long trip.

Doris Caldwell and a friend (and her little dog Tittles) offered to come and stay with our kids while the two of us spent a weekend in Macao. Doris managed the large and famous Family Service Center in Kwun Tong, and we had no doubt that she could manage our motley crew for a few days.

We took the Hydrofoil to the former Portuguese province of Macao, now with partial communist "protection" since the Hong Kong riots. We had been there before, but this time we decided to stay at the Lisboa, the famous casino with its bright dancing lights and gambling tables.

We watched the money being lost and gained, the gamblers seemingly heedless of the money they were risking. We had never gambled a dollar in our lives—had probably not had a dollar to spare, and felt no compulsion to join in these games. But in some ways, we were gambling our own future—where we were going and what we were doing.

What would it mean if we returned to the States and terminated any chance of continuing to live in Hong Kong?

We stopped at a little wine shop in the hotel and bought a bottle of Portuguese Mateuse, and went to our room to talk.

"Have we thought this through?" Gordon asked. "What are we really doing?"

We poured little bathroom cups of the sweet wine and toasted each other. We had come a long way from Cumberland Falls.

"Okay," I began, "are you finished with what you wanted to do here in Hong Kong?"

"I think so. By standing up to Peter Wong, I pretty well cut off my ability to work here. The RCA and the CCC are committed to each other."

"But you still have good ties with the RCA in the States?"

"Right."

"Do you think you could…"

We were sipping the wine, trying to get to the real issues.

"The Reformed Church has been nothing but good to us," he said. "I still feel a great deal of loyalty to them."

"But…how did you feel last summer when we were back in Michigan, and…"

"I know."

It was quiet. We sipped the wine. It was not particularly good, but it was beginning to give us a buzz.

Some things were so hard to say. There were not words for them, not easy words.

"We've changed," I said. "We've not changed in our deep belief in God, but we are…"

"I know," he said.

"Do you ever…wish…you could find a kind of work where your paycheck was not tied to your beliefs?"

It was quiet.

"I…guess I do…" he admitted.

There were tears in our eyes as we shared a deep kiss. The sweet Portuguese wine was on our lips, and the gambling was going on downstairs.

Gambling?

We were taking the biggest gamble of all, and we pledged our love to each other deeply and totally, whatever happened.

We would start over again.

SECTION FOUR

1972-1978

Chapter Thirteen

WE WERE BACK IN IOWA.

It had been a long and exciting trip, our last fling, we thought, before settling down in America...

We had gone from Hong Kong to Bangkok, where we stayed courtesy of the airlines in a hotel where baby elephants opened the door for us. The Dusitani had thick, soft, purple towels, like Mona's mother.

Marita almost wanted to stay.

Gordon wanted to go to Russia, but we had not been able to get visas in Hong Kong. Someone suggested we could get them in Thailand. A taxi took us far out from the city to a Russian outpost in some godforsaken field. The man looked us over and decided we looked innocent enough with our four kids, and gave us visas to go to Russia.

We stopped in New Delhi, where there was a power outage on the runway, and we never got off the plane, and then on to Jerusalem. Chris came down with a fever and I had to stay in the King David Hotel with him while Gordon took a tour with the rest of the kids. They ended up being invited to a Palestinian wedding by the taxi driver. On to Greece—Athens—which none of us ever wanted to leave. We stayed in a terrible hotel, with the doorknobs falling off and cockroaches everywhere, but we were no wimps. We had seen it all.

In Russia the bathtubs had been disconnected and were sitting out in the hallway, but we saw the Bolshoi Ballet, and Lenin lying in state. Chris was only five, getting his first around-the-world trip.

And then, suddenly, we were in Iowa.

Orange City, Iowa.

The Klays took us in for a few days until we could get our bearings. Their whole bottom floor was occupied by De Prees. I had forgotten about

144

the paintings… Gina… The Boat Woman…the children playing in the Hong Kong streets. I had been so possessed with writing, that painting had been far from my thoughts.

They seemed shocking…

Earl took Gordon around town, showing him the changes. A new furniture store was going up.

"What are your plans?" he asked Gordon.

Gordon had to admit he was not sure.

"Well, you stay here until you get things sorted out," Earl advised him. "You're welcome to stay in the mission house, free of charge, until you get your feet on the ground."

The people at the church were almost politely uncomfortable with having us back. Hadn't we been sent overseas to work? What were we doing back in Iowa?

The mission halfway house was completely furnished and we settled in uneasily.

It was August, and still very hot in Iowa. Our old friend, Nelson DeJong, of the long underwear, came by with a basketful of tomatoes and corn, whistling, of course.

The hot weather was stirring up the rank smell of the pig farms. People who had always lived here never even smelled them.

We had to find some kind of temporary job. The furniture store was putting up cement block walls. They could use another man on the crew to carry cement.

With two Masters degrees and four kids, Gordon started carrying "mud" for sixty-five cents an hour. Everyone in town was deeply embarrassed.

"If he's a preacher, why ain't he preaching?" was the whisper. "What's the matter with him?"

The other workers on the building were not quite sure how to relate to him. Was he a reverend? What the hell was he doing carrying cement?

I tried to make the temporary house feel like home. The kids were wondering what the new school would be like. We had two in high school, ninth grade, one in junior high, and one in elementary, first grade. Chris had just turned six.

I had a budget of thirty-three dollars a week to feed six people. We clipped coupons first and made up the menus with what we could afford. Fortunately, growing up I had learned to live on nothing. Thirty-three dollars a week was better than that. We did not go hungry. A big pot of stew went a long way, and Chinese cooking had showed me how to make a large dish of delicious food with two little pieces of chicken and a lot of vegetables.

It would be our twins' first high school experience—in a new town. Rachel Klay, the same age as Marita, tried valiantly to help our kids "break in." They were the only kids who had not been in the class since kindergarten.

School started. No uniforms this time.

Clothes. We managed with what we brought along, and a brief shopping trip, and Goodwill.

But...

Marita saw a copy of *Seventeen* magazine. On the cover were beautiful wool pants and a top for fall. The outfit cost twenty-five dollars—red pants and a plaid shirt-jacket.

"She wants that so much..." I said to Gordon.

"But we can't afford it."

I stopped in at the local drapery shop and asked if they could use an extra seamstress. Goodness knows, I had made enough curtains in my life.

They were sorry, but it was a family business and they never hired outside help.

I was so ashamed, I nearly died.

But from somewhere, some leftover or hidden pocket, we found that twenty-five dollars. They carried the outfit at Dykema's Department Store, and I got it for her.

She was so thrilled.

Marita wore it to school the next day. The weather was still too warm for wool, but she couldn't wait. She felt so beautiful

On the way home, they met some kids from school.

A boy in her class said to her, "Those red pants sure make you look fat!"

She came home and cried, and never wore the pants again.

Deidra wanted to be part of the junior high marching band. She had never played any kind of musical instrument.

"I'd love to play a flute," she begged. "Do you think I could get one?"

We found a place where we could rent a flute, and Deidra started to learn to play. The band would be marching in a few weeks and they would be playing "The Washington-Lee Swing."

Nobody knows how Deidra managed it, but she practiced until her fingers were sore. When the band marched, there was Deidra, playing "The Washington Lee Swing."

"I'd like a flute for Christmas," she suggested.

Mike tried out for football. Being an American kid who had grown up in British-Chinese territory, he did not know one end of a football field from the other. He had not even watched sports on TV. But they took him and he tried. He even scored a point once, accidentally, and had his name called out over the loudspeaker.

Coats and boots for everyone.

One present each for Christmas.

How we managed those four months we'll never know. Perhaps we managed because we had seen people who had so much less.

Florence and Henry Chey came from Hong Kong (bringing dried mushrooms and sausages for Gordon) to check on their son Danny at the college. He was doing wonderfully well—top of his class.

They wanted Gordon to show them around, so he took them out to a pig farm. They had to wear plastic bags on their feet. Tiny little Florence with her size five feet and a Chinese dress…

How would we ever put our worlds back together again?

Then Gordon got a bright, and desperate, idea. Doctor Norman Vincent Peale had expressed interest in us. Part of Gordon's education had been made possible with a Peale grant. Would it be a good idea to contact the Peales and see if their foundation had a job opening?

It was a long shot, but what did we have to lose? Gordon wrote a letter, asking, and we waited.

Earl Klay tried his best to find a job for us. How about opening a youth center, or working with the parole board?

A letter came from the Peales. They were pleased to hear where we were. And, our letter had come at a very opportune time. They had been searching for a person with Gordon's background to assist at the Foundation for Christian Living at their headquarters in Pawling, New York. Would we be interested in coming for an interview?

Would we!

Maybe Doctor Peale would be open- minded enough to suit our taste. He seemed to be able to extract the goodness from Christianity without getting bogged down in the theology.

In fact, I smiled inwardly.

My father, in his avid fundamentalism, had chosen three men, Franklin D. Roosevelt, Harry Emerson Fosdick and Norman Vincent Peale, as candidates for being the Anti-Christ.

This was funny.

He would do.

So halfway through the school year we said goodbye to Iowa and headed east. We had a job and a good salary, and the kids could go to school in the Northeast. Things were looking up.

We found a house on Quaker Hill, a semi-posh settlement up above the town of Pawling. It was a bedroom community of the famous and formerly famous who related to New York City, sixty-five miles up the Hudson River on a commuter line. Our neighbors were Norman Vincent Peale, Lowell Thomas, Sargent Shriver, and John Allen, an editor for *Reader's Digest*.

The place we bought had been a carriage house of a larger estate. It cost all of thirty thousand dollars, and as we sat around the table in the lawyer's office signing the mortgage, it seemed a solemn occasion. But, of course, now we had a good salary: $25,000 a year. We were in clover.

The house was ours. We could do as we pleased with it. We papered and painted, and scrubbed and fixed it up, a bedroom for each of the kids and an extra bathroom downstairs. Seventies orange shag carpets to go with the avocado green kitchen appliances. It was the time of long sideburns and gold neck chains, and afro hairdos. The sky was the limit. Flame-glo orange red shag carpet, no less. Gordon reported for his job. He liked the people he worked with. They were friendly.

The kids settled into Pawling High School for the last half of the year. Deidra was still in junior high. Chris was finishing up first grade. I was so glad he had learned to read early. He was ahead in his class.

We bought clothes. We made friends. We settled into the little Quaker Hill Church down the road (quasi Presbyterian) and we were happy.

I had a direct 65-mile train line to downtown New York and the publishing world.

Was this the little town I had always dreamed of? Would this be it?

The kids all had bikes.

The girls were cheerleaders.

Mike went out for track (forget football).

Dad De Pree had supplied us with a truck-load of furniture, and we were comfortable. Chris had a best friend and started taking piano lessons. We got two Siamese cats, named Simon and Samantha.

We were real Americans, finally.

Weren't we?

I often thought of Hong Kong...

I remembered one day crossing on the Star Ferry, going to help Doris and her women out in Kwun Tong. I was watching the people on the ferry and dreaming idly...wondering...what that moment in Stanley Village had meant to me...that wonderful epiphany on the street with the woman and the child...

That feeling of the all-pervasiveness of the Creative Power...that radiant circle of expanding light...encompassing all...proclaiming the holiness of all things...the feeling of nothing left out...

Suddenly the idea was sharp and clear in my mind. The unseeable, indefinable power did not have one face, one likeness. These...these many beings in their coming and going, these were the faces of God.

This was the idea for a new book: *Faces of God.*

I took the train to New York and went to see Eleanor Jordan at Harper and Row. She listened to my ideas for a few minutes, then took me into the senior editor's office.

"Listen to this..." she smiled.

Clayton Carlton listened. His face lit up.

"I like it!" he said enthusiastically. "Write it and let me see it. This could be big... *Faces of God!*"

I went back to Pawling and started to write. These writings would be adapted from the next batch of 'jottings' we had been collecting for several years. We would be co-authors, since we had both recorded them.

One hundred and twenty explorations into life and people—one writing to a page. About people, wherever life found them, and seeing them for what they really were, expressions of the Creative Power.

I actually wished I could call the book something else and have it mean the same thing...

God, the English name, had such bad press. It evoked so many different things for so many different people.

And some people, I knew, didn't want to think of it at all.

The village of Pawling was a quintessential East Coast town, strung out along the railroad track. The original inhabitants had been Irish Catholics, and the Catholic Church still had the biggest crowds on Sunday.

But the socio-religious lines did not seem to be so tightly drawn as they were in the Midwest. Many of the people who worked at the Peale Foundation were Catholic, and nobody seemed to make a big fuss about it. The whole attitude toward life was just a little more relaxed in the Northeast.

Sometimes a little too relaxed...

The first time our teenagers came home and told us there was an after-game party where they—cheerleaders and football players—had been drinking, we went to the school principal and asked questions.

"Can't we do something about this? Can't we get the parents together and agree on some rules?"

"You can try, if you want to," chuckled the school principal, "but if you call them on a Saturday night, nobody will be home. They'd all be out having a drink themselves."

So much for that.

We would have to have our own rules. The kids were indignant.

"Mom, you want us to try to fit in," Marita argued. "You like for us to be cheerleaders. What are we supposed to do when the others all start drinking?"

"There must be something else to drink."

"Mom!"

"What do they drink...mostly?"

"Beer."

"Well. Take a can of beer and pretend you're drinking. I don't want you to feel left out, but if you ever come home drunk, don't expect me to appreciate it."

Was that the right thing to tell them? Decisions...decisions... It was like Stanley Village. How much adaptation was good? And then there were drugs. Not as bad as at HKIS, because the kids were less wealthy. But drugs.

The school, generally, was good. Dealing with too much openness was easier than being frozen out, like in Iowa, wasn't it?

But no drugs.

Lordy me, even being a parent in the good old USA wasn't a bed of roses.

Gordon's work at the Foundation mainly consisted of reading the hundreds of letters that came to Dr. Peale each week. People had read his books and were writing to the famous wise man about their personal problems, and asking how his insights could apply to their lives. Gordon had to put himself inside the mindset of Dr. Peale and draft letters in reply. These needed to be edited by Foundation writers, mostly a woman called Carol Porter, to check that they 'sounded' like Dr. Peale and were genuinely helpful. People who needed serious psychological counseling were referred on to professionals.

Then the letters were signed by an autopen, like letters from the President of the United States.

At first Gordon felt strange. Having people receive a letter that they thought was from Dr. Peale personally was somehow daunting, and then he realized that as long as the approach was the same, the same positive uplift to people's lives, this was a real service he could do, both for the Peales and for the people who followed them. It was all the same message of hope.

The Peales had an apartment in New York City and a highly influential circle of friends. We were, I suppose, aware of the social and political power they wielded, but being young and basically optimistic, we plunged right in. We enjoyed the whole atmosphere. What was wrong with power? We were grateful to have a share in its shadow for a change.

I cooked a Chinese meal (remembering all of Ah Wai's instructions in my head in Chinese), and entertained the Peales, the Boardmans (Dr. Peale's editor), and the Porters. If I had stopped to think what I was doing, I would have been petrified. These people had dined in the great restaurants of New York City and Europe, and here they were, seated around our dining room table, eating my Stanley Village Chinese food.

Just down the road from our house, the Peale's daughter, Liz, and her husband, John Allen, lived on a gentleman's farm. John was a senior editor at *Reader's Digest*. Our girls babysat their children.

Quaker Hill was riddled with the famous and the had-been famous. Lowell Thomas lived on down the road and attended Quaker Hill Church. He liked the brownies I brought to the coffee hour at church, so I baked a dozen and brought them to his house. I remembered hearing his voice on 'Cinerama' in Chicago.

There were actors and ex-actors, a fashion page artist for the *New York Times*, a federal judge and big bankers. Everybody was famous, or once had been.

The kids survived their first year of Pawling High School and began to feel at home. Deidra was actually growing tall, shooting up. Both of the girls were popular (enough) at school. Mike was running cross-country, and enjoying it, without having to know the intricacies of American sports.

We sat watching the school football game with our girls cheerleading in their little short skirts, loving being Americans, and felt like this town was just what they had needed.

We had been in the house on Quaker Hill for almost two years when Gordon began to notice the foundation under the old carriage house was crumbling. He began to worry about the soundness of the structure. We called Eddie Cook, a local builder, and asked him to take a look. He told us the old rock foundation, over a hundred years old, would have to be replaced.

"How much would that cost?"

"Oh, I'd say at least twenty thousand…"

"Could you do it?"

"Not by myself. We might have to jack the house up to get a new foundation under it."

"Would you recommend that?"

Eddie took his builder's hat off and scratched his head, thoughtfully.

"I don't know what to say."

"Should we keep the place?"

"You might just fix it up a little, and then sell it. I've got a place down on the edge of town that I've just bought, and we're going to renovate it. You could be in on the ground floor, help me design it the way you'd like it, and then you could live there. Wouldn't cost you much more than fixing up this old place, and you'd be closer to town."

We talked about it that night.

"Gordon, we cannot move."

"Why not?"

"Don't you remember when we moved here and fixed up the kids' rooms we promised them we would live here all during their high school years? Don't you remember?"

We had. Mike, in particular, had been so excited about fixing up his room. He had a large attic space at the head of the stairs, full of his personal treasures and posters—his lair. No one else was allowed in without his permission.

"He probably wouldn't mind," Gordon said. "He's sixteen now, and I've been thinking of getting him a motor scooter."

"A what?"

"We were looking at a motor scooter he'd really like to have."

Well. You never knew what these men were thinking. "The men" in the family had succeeded in staying fairly close together, but this time Gordon had misjudged the situation.

When Mike heard that we might move, he stood at the door of his room, feet spread apart and arms crossed over his chest. His face was red with suppressed angry tears.

"You said…" he began, "you said we would stay here! You promised, and I believed you! I'm never going to believe you again, not ever! Never!"

Mike had decided to get his blond hair permed in an afro. He had earned the money house painting and paid for the "do" himself. He was getting tall, and with the blond Afro and newly acquired teen pimples, I looked at him and wondered who he was. Was this my Mike? No. It wasn't.

And who had moved into the attic in his place, I wasn't quite sure.

Gordon worked on the house down in the village with Eddie Cook. I went with him one day, just to see it.

The weathered, grey wooden house sat back from the road in a dismal place called 'the swamp'. It was two- storied with a front porch and a stone fireplace. Inside it had a fairly large living room with a low ceiling (beams could be exposed to heighten it), a dining room and a kitchen, a master bedroom and bath, and four bedrooms upstairs.

The house wasn't bad. It actually had a kind of woe-begotten charm.

But that swamp…

"I don't know…" I said. "Are there snakes here?"

"Snakes?" Gordon asked. "Eddie didn't say anything about snakes."

I had grown up in the woods. Gordon was a city boy. I could smell snakes before I could see them.

Then we went down in the basement where there was just a cement slab and four walls of crumbly dirt. The washer and dryer were down there.

"Yuck," I shivered. "What if they come crawling out of that dirt while I'm putting the wash in?"

Gordon laughed and gave me a hug.

"You and your snakes!"

We sold the house on Quaker Hill to a family from Long Island. He had just retired and didn't mind putting in a new foundation. He needed a project to keep himself busy.

Before we moved from Quaker Hill, Deidra had one more thing she wanted to do: go horseback riding with her friend Cathy. Deidra had never ridden a horse, but she had never done many things. She figured she could do anything, regardless of the fact that she had never done it before. That worked well, most of the time.

The day they went horseback riding, the girls decided to ride bareback. They raced the horses across a large pasture, hanging on to the horses' manes while their own long hair flew in the wind.

Suddenly, they came to a stone fence. The horse stopped abruptly. Deidra flew over the horse's head and onto the stone wall.

When they brought her home she seemed to be unhurt. We took her to the local doctor who checked her over and told her to take it easy…rest. She was probably a bit in shock.

Deidra lay on the couch for most of the two days while we moved. She was strangely quiet.

We moved the rest of our goods into the swamp house, closed the door on the Quaker Hill house, and began a new stage of our lives.

In more ways than we knew.

The first week in the swamp house, we were all in our rooms and asleep. It was a Saturday morning and no one had to rush to school or work.

153

Suddenly, there was the most terrifying scream I ever heard in my life. Everyone came pouring out of their rooms. The scream had come from Deidra's room.

She was lying on the floor in the middle of a grand mal seizure.

Mike had taken CPR in school and was trying to help her.

"No-no-don't," I said. "Don't touch her…"

Gordon called emergency and they were there in moments, heading for the Danbury Hospital.

The call went out over the Pawling Police radio (which everyone in town listened to): "De Pree female, 14. Suspected OD."

There was a doctor on duty at the Danbury Hospital who specialized in neurosurgery. He was from the Philippines and had been working on new methods of dealing with brain injuries. He prescribed large doses of Pheno-barbital.

Deidra had to go back to school, but she was stunned. She fell asleep in class. She began to gain weight. Word circulated around the school that she was on drugs. They had heard it on the radio.

I was taking the train into the city to meet with the people at Harper and Row. The writings for *Faces of God* were finished.

On the train I sat next to a man—one of those random conversations with a stranger—and we talked of our families. His daughter, 16, had just died while having a grand mal seizure.

I stared out the window of the train thinking of the day Deidra was born, my Hong Kong baby who was now a beautiful young girl. Could I ever bear it if I had to give her up?

I sat in the clanking train, swaying with the other passengers, trying to be thankful for every year she had lived, and tried not to demand any more…tried…

By the time the train had reached the city I had found a kind of calm. This great gift of life, so powerful, so mysterious, and also so fragile. Never assured, for any of us. A gift, one day at a time. I would take what I was given.

The new headquarters of Harper and Row at 10 East 53rd Street were awe-inspiring. I took the elevator up to the Religion department and left the manuscript with Clayton Carlton, and took the train back to Pawling…and waited.

It was only two weeks before the call came.

"This is outstanding…" he was saying. "This will be great. This will be up there with *Are You Running with Me Jesus!*"

154

I had never heard of it. I hoped somebody had.

"We'll get a contract off to you...we're thinking of a first printing of 25,000."

At least something was going right.

An artist was going to work on a cover, composed of many faces that would, at first glance, look like the face of Christ. (Salman's?)

No...no! Don't use a traditional concept. This has to stay clean. People's faces, no religious iconic portraits!

They ended up with starbursts, and a major problem. The top salesman took a copy of the galleys to the Methodist Press—Cokesbury—pointing out to them the one reading they might object to, a reading about being able to see God even in the face of a person drunk and asleep in the gutter.

That was too much.

They blackballed the book, and the first printing was cut down to five thousand.

Sorry, Jesus. You'll have to go running without me.

Life and the shadow of death.
Success and disappointment.
Oh my god...
Even being an American wasn't easy...

The church on Quaker Hill was a powerhouse of notable people. A simple colonial-looking structure with a lovable, retired Presbyterian minister named Ralph Lankler, it attracted a remarkable group of worshippers.

For years the Reynolds people from Winston-Salem, NC had "summered" on Quaker Hill. Before cars were in use, they had come up from North Carolina in their grand horse-drawn carriage. When the Reynolds swept into town, the summer was officially started. Even in the seventies, the current matriarch still had her spot in the front row wearing a large broad-brimmed hat.

The Brachs, the candy people.

The Wangemans, who managed the Waldorf Towers in NYC for their friends, the Conrad Hiltons.

And Judge Peck, the father of Scott Peck. He was publishing *The Road Less Traveled* at Harper and Row at the same time we were publishing *Faces of God*. We met at the Porters and exchanged books.

We settled in with all these people, singing in the choir. Our kids were in the confirmation class. We went to church suppers and fairs, acting as though we had been tamed all our lives. We almost looked civilized.

At Christmas we had a big party at the swamp house. The ceiling had been lifted and the exposed beams were charming. A crackling fire burned in the stone fireplace. We invited people from all walks of life, and had a wonderful party. It helped that there was snow on the ground and the house looked rustic, not shabby, covered in a beautiful blanket of snow.

Marita had a boyfriend, Jon. His parents ran the YMCA in Pawling, a favorite spot for New Yorkers to come for conferences and group meetings. The Peales held conferences there.

Marita got a job at the Y, serving in the dining room. She also was becoming quite an artist. She and her friend Mary did a mural at the Y—a bright, lovely design of parrots in a jungle. The high school art teacher, Mr. Greene, took a special interest in Marita, and she adored him—had a huge crush on him—and he carefully led her into realizing how much talent she had. She began assembling a portfolio of watercolors. Maybe she would go to art school in New York.

Gordon could not get Hong Kong out of his mind. A woman who had worked at the Deep Love Church in Hong Kong had moved her family to Chinatown, New York City, and invited him to come for a visit. He ended up being a regular visitor to Canal Street, relating to a group of young Chinese who were immigrating to the U.S., trying to become Americans. He felt a great kinship with them and they sensed it. Speaking both Chinese and English, he was a welcome part of their group. Sometimes he even gave talks in Chinese.

I watched him, feeling him teeter between worlds. Chinese young people had become a part of his heart.

Spring came. The twins would be seniors next year. They began to think of college. Deidra was still in her medicated fog. What would her future be?

Mike was off in another world, discovering girls. He was a top student, popular, the afro had gone...we stared at each other across the breakfast table like strangers.

There was something about Mike that troubled me...something about him that stirred up anxiety, and that reminded me of somebody...

Was it my father?

Oh no! I hoped not. The very idea struck terror to my heart.

Could such things be inherited?

I pushed the disturbing thought out of my mind. Oh God, don't let me pass on these chains of anger and fear; don't let me project my wounds onto this innocent boy. Can he help it if he looks like his grandfather?

His grandfather!

I had never thought of him in those terms. He was a ghost I had, more or less, dealt with. The problem was...he was not really dead. He was very much alive, and he had never seen his grandchildren.

Did I want him to?

In order to remind myself of what a super kid Mike really was, I wrote the story of our Christmas in Stanley Village, of Mike and the dollar and the ten popsicles at the Stanley Store. I gave it to John Allen to see if *Reader's Digest* would be interested in it as a true-life story. I titled it, "A Dollar's Worth of Peace on Earth."

I had almost given up hearing about it when John Allen drove up to the yard at the swamp house and handed me a bag with ten orange popsicles in it, and a check for two thousand dollars.

Reader's Digest had bought the story!

That was the good news.

The bad news was that Lila Wallace had a thing about Communists. She did not like the fact that Mr. Hong, the Stanley storekeeper, had been pictured as a basically decent human being.

Reader's Digest could not publish the story, but I could keep the two thousand dollars.

We decided to put it in a special fund to help with Mike's education.

Guideposts Magazine would use the story.

American was terribly complex.

Then one day, with the blue Loostrife blooming in the swamp, we turned up the driveway and saw them, two very boldly marked copperheads, crawling across the driveway and slithering into the swamp. They were probably mating and would hatch dozens more.

Eddie had asked us to make up our minds. He needed to sell the house, and we could have it for fifty thousand dollars.

We said no.

No thanks.

We wanted to leave it, and all the bad memories, behind.

Maybe moving would help.

On Dutcher Avenue, the parsonage of the Methodist Church in downtown Pawling was for sale. It was a well-constructed, three-story house, built in the early nineteen hundreds by a Mr. Donaldson, who was a consummate craftsman.

The ceilings were high, the woodwork was beautiful.

Sliding wood-paneled doors separated the two parlors, and an exquisitely carved stairway circled up to the second floor. The windows were tall. The plaster had been done by a generation who knew their plaster.

But the house was gloomy, dark and dingy. The windows were covered with thick, dark maroon, velvet drapes. The fireplace was boarded up. The whole place was hopelessly outdated. Nothing but a light bulb had been changed since the 1920s. (Was Mr. Donaldson, by chance, a Methodist?) Although the place had been willed to them, they did not want to spend the money to renovate it.

So it was on the market. Thirty thousand dollars.

What a steal!

Gordon checked the foundation this time. It was solid.

Five bedrooms. Big old-fashioned kitchen. Butler's pantry with leaded glass windows. A master bedroom with a bathroom big enough to have a party in. A real 1920's mansion.

There was only one problem

Rats.

The basement had a large wooden platform floor built up over damp clay, with just enough space under the wood to harbor rats. Scores of them.

We had lived in houses with ghosts and snakes, so why not rats?

We bought it.

Of course, the first thing we did was to exterminate the rats. Gordon hired men to do the job. They poisoned the rats, and then began to shovel them out. Piles of them. They counted over a hundred, curled up and dead, and hauled them off.

The whole basement was torn out, hosed out, disinfected. The whole house was searched until not a hair of a rat survived, and then we began to remodel.

We lived, cautiously, in Eddie's house for two months while we tore the Donaldson house apart. Down came the maroon velvet drapes. We opened up the fireplace and had someone pull out the dead squirrels that had clogged it up. The thin wallpaper was steamed off and the beautiful plaster painted white. The woodwork was scrubbed until it was spotless, and refinished.

The wood floors were resurfaced, and the butler's pantry made into a galley kitchen with the big kitchen turned into a family room. There was a formal dining room that we would redecorate later. The master bedroom was actually two small bedrooms combined. Along one whole wall I painted an eight-foot high mural of black and white winter trees. We bought a large piece of brown, black and white faux fur for our bedspread, and slung it over the low Hollywood bed. It looked incriminating without even having anyone in the bed.

The kids had room, room, and more room. Chris had such a big bedroom he could put up his train tracks and leave them up. Marita and Mike had large roomy places on the third floor.

But Deidra wanted the smallest bedroom in the house. It made her feel safe and cozy. She was feeling lost enough.

Deidra was not improving. Even with the heavy medication, she was having a grand mal seizure at least once a month. She was heavy and puffy.

We spoke to a doctor who went to Quaker Hill Church. He suggested we change physicians, and gave us the name of a neurologist friend of his.

In talking to the new doctor we became aware of what we were dealing with.

"This is not just the result of an injury," he said. "It may have been dormant and triggered by trauma, but Deidra has epilepsy. The electrical currents of her brain are not firing properly. She will need to be on medication for the rest of her life."

He saw the stricken look on our faces.

"But people learn to live with this condition. We have to get her off the meds she's on. There are much more efficient drugs now, and hopefully she'll be able to control the seizures."

We were so grateful something could be done.

In a week, Deidra was more alert.

In six weeks, she had lost twenty-five pounds of puff and fluid, and she was not falling asleep in class.

She was becoming our Deidra again.

The dreaded regular seizures stopped, with only an occasional lapse. What a wonderful gift to have her back!

Deidra made up her mind, at fifteen.

"Okay, Mom. I have epilepsy, but I'm not going to let this disease define me. I'm going to live a normal life."

And then she added, "So back off, Mom…don't over-protect me."

Deidra came back to life, but life in Pawling High School never came back to her. It was still rumored that she had overdosed on drugs, and nearly died.

Now that we had the big house in town on Dutcher Avenue, our teenagers wanted to have a party—a real party. They had never given one.

"What's your definition of a real party?" we asked.

"Well," Marita outlined, "we'd need to use the family room-kitchen area, and have lots of good food…and…"

"And what?"

"Beer?"

"Are you kidding? You're all under-aged for drinking," Gordon reminded her.

"But Dad, can you imagine going to a party and having soda pop? I would die..."

This was going to be a problem.

We compromised. Should we have?

There would be plenty of other drinks, and one gallon jug of wine. The kids could use it wisely. Nobody would get drunk.

"And of course, you'll have to be gone," Marita said. "You can't be any-where around."

Thanks.

We let them choose the foods, and the drinks.

On the Saturday night of the party we had a job to do. Our formal din-ing room had never been papered, and we could do this with the door shut to the back part of the house. The kids could have their thing, and we would wallpaper the dining room and chaperone—in absentia.

We cut and pasted and hung sheets of paper. We could hear the kids coming and going through the back kitchen door. There were lots of cars, music and laughter. Everybody seemed to be having a great time. More cars. We cut and pasted and papered. About two o'clock in the morning we fin-ished and went to bed. The party was winding down.

The next morning I glanced out the upstairs window and could not believe what I saw. The lawn between our house and the Methodist Church was ankle-deep in beer cans.

I must admit it. I laughed out loud.

What sweet revenge!

In a few hours the bell would ring and people would be coming to the church. We threw on our clothes, grabbed a stack of black plastic garbage bags, and woke up the kids.

"Come on! Get up! Help us pick up these beer cans. Hurry!"

Marita sleepily explained what had happened.

"We're real sorry, Mom and Dad. It was okay at first, and then word got around that there was a party here, and all kinds of kids crashed it, and brought six-packs. We couldn't stop them—we didn't even know some of them..."

Had we dreamed of a quiet little town with a house on a quiet street, with...

Was this it?

Since we had the dining room so nicely decorated, we decided to entertain. Gordon had found a beautiful walnut table, long and narrow, with a dozen hand-tooled, leather-backed chairs to set off the new chandelier and wall paper. It practically cried out for company.

We invited the Peales, the Porters and the Boardmans to come over and see the "new" house. It was finished now, and we could settle in for the duration.

We carefully planned and cooked the meal. The dishes turned out well, and the wine was chilled. We even had warm apple pie and ice cream.

We had been with the Peales almost three years, and the relationship had been comfortable. We respected their lifestyle and they treated us well. Dr. Peale was especially interested in my writing.

"You working with Harper and Row?" he inquired. "Good idea! Stay with the big presses. Don't get identified with these little religious publishers. You can never get conservative enough to please some people."

I knew what he meant. I was even having difficulty with the religious section of big presses.

We were peacefully having coffee when the bomb dropped.

"You've got such a nice place here, I hesitate to mention this," Dr. Peale said in a thoughtful tone, "but we've got a situation on our hands. *Guideposts Magazine*, as you know, has been incorporated on a non-profit basis, and, darn it, that little magazine is making too much money..."

He stirred his coffee. It was quiet.

"We've been thinking about an outreach project, some way to invest the profits in a creative way without throwing ourselves into a new tax bracket. I've got a friend, John Gailbreath, who leases land in Kowloon, Hong Kong, and they're putting up some high-rise apartment buildings on the land that used to be used by Mobil Oil..."

We listened carefully. Where was this going?

"The long and short of it is," Dr. Peale continued, " in one of these high-rises he would rent us the whole first floor to start some kind of school, or preschool facility for the new community. *Guideposts Magazine* would like to fund this as an outreach."

He was looking at Gordon with that keen businessman-cum-minister look he had.

"...and Gordon, as the only Chinese-speaking American on our staff, would you be interested in going back to Hong Kong to form, staff and operate a school for *Guideposts Magazine*?"

Gordon and I exchanged glances.

"That sounds very interesting," Gordon said slowly. "Maybe we'd like to have some time to think about it. There are a lot of people and angles to be considered."

They loved the house...the dinner...and they were gone.

161

And our whole world tilted a hundred and eighty degrees.

We went upstairs when the dishes were done and tried to get some sleep.

Gordon was quiet. His eyes were big, and I knew his heart was pounding. I laid my head on his chest. I could feel it, that big, warm heart.

Hong Kong.

It was in the room. We could see it, hear it, smell it.

Both of us still loved it. We had left the island thinking we would never go back. But this was different.

It would be an American company, working for a famous American. No connection with a Chinese church organization and all its bittersweet memories of China missions.

The job would be to take over a huge raw area of real estate and make it into a pre-school, to serve a community.

Dr. Peale, with his more practical interpretation of the gospel, was not so theologically bound. We could follow the deepest truths of our hearts and they would not be tied to our paycheck. All we had to do was to start and operate a top-grade facility.

In our bedroom with the black and white tree mural, and the faux fur bedspread, we probed our thoughts and our futures, and our hearts.

We did not sleep that night.

The next few days we discussed the possibility with our family.

Marita and Michael were graduating from high school and would be going off to college.

Deidra and Chris had been born in Hong Kong, and to them it was home. They would go along with us.

And we...we still had a tremendous soft spot in our hearts for that Asian city. Perhaps we still had unfinished business there. The departure had been so abrupt, so traumatic. Would going back help us to resolve things in our own way and time?

We told the Peales—Yes. We would take the new assignment. Gordon not only had the language; he had the credentials to start a new school—a degree in Education Administration from Columbia University in New York.

Of course they had looked into that. Credentials were important to the Peales. They were professionals. We would be dealing with a new set of rules.

The twins graduated from Pawling High School . Mike was president of the senior class. He had applied to Grinnell College in Iowa, and was accepted.

Marita went to New York City with her boyfriend of three years. They went out to dinner at a lovely restaurant (Jon had such good taste), and he told her he was gay. She had wondered why they never made out like the other kids in high school. She thought something was wrong with her. She was almost relieved.

She decided not to go to the School of Design in New York if we would not be there. She applied to Grinnell, and they would go to the same school together.

They were not very much alike, and would probably not see much of each other on campus, but at least they would be there as security for each other.

My mom was getting remarried. After twenty years of being single, she, at 62, was marrying a man of 79. He was Dutch, and kindly, and I hoped she would be happy.

She came to Pawling to visit, and I took her shopping to help her find a suit to get married in—a pale blue linen suit that made her look pretty.

I held her hand while she got her ears pierced. At 62, maybe she was finally growing up.

"Do you think you'll ever see your father again?" she asked me.

"I don't know."

"He's never seen any of his grandchildren."

"I know. Do you think he really cares?"

She sighed. I knew she still loved him.

"Maybe, deep down somewhere, but he'd never admit it, or maybe he doesn't know how to care."

"I've been thinking…since we're going away, do you…should I invite him…give him a chance to meet them?"

"Could you handle it?"

That was the question.

I wrote him a letter at his Florida address, and invited him to come up and see us before we left for Hong Kong. It was a weird other-worldly feeling, like addressing a letter to someone who was dead.

He wrote back and said he would come if he could bring his third wife, Nellie, along. I could see myself introducing my ghost father and his third wife, and trying to explain them to my children.

I wrote back and said that unless he came alone, it might be difficult…

He wrote back and said that he was very busy…that God had important work for him to do, and that he would not be able to come.

I tore the letter up and thought, *Okay. God can have you. I'm done with you.*

The kids never met him.

There were so many things to be done. We put the house on the market and had a garage sale.

I still had the sequel to *The Spring Wind* in my writing materials. It was titled, *Festival,* and was an account, in story form, of the year we had spent in Stanley Village celebrating the traditional legends. I took it to Clayton Carlson, who sent it on to the trade books division of Harper and Row.

"You're writing yourself out of religious stuff," he told me. "I've sent your work to a new editor, Frances Lindley. She's a hard little nut to crack, but she's very, very good—edited *The Gulag Archipelago*…

Frances Lindley was a thin, fifty-ish woman with straight, steel grey hair brushed behind one ear—very New Yorkish, deep voiced, brusque, with occasional flashes of unanticipated warmth.

"This is a charming story," she began, "and who knows, we may publish it someday. But first, tell me something…"

She looked at me keenly, her blue eyes squinted. "Who are you, and where do you come from? And why are you writing this unusual type of thing? There's something unexplained here. What is your personal story?"

I told her.

She sat listening, smoking.

I told her about my Chicago Dutch parents who had gone down to the Appalachian Mountains of Kentucky and moved into a one-room log cabin, and who had raised ninety mountain children while I was growing up, and how beautiful it had been, and how it had all gone so horribly wrong.

"Oh my gawd!" she said, taking a huge drag on her cigarette. "That's the story you should write!"

"But I can't!"

"Why not?"

"I…my dad…it's dangerous."

"I know. Your dad would kill you," she chuckled. "I feel like killing my own kids sometimes, too."

She really didn't know. But she knew what she wanted.

"I'll tell you what. Let me hold onto *Festival,* and you write the Kentucky story first. Then we'll see."

"I'm going to be leaving soon," I told her. "We'll be living in Hong Kong."

She was busy taking notes and smoking, squinting her eyes against the smoke.

"We'll then, write it there," she said brusquely, "as soon as you're settled."

I had my orders. Who was I to disobey Frances Lindley, editor at Harper and Row, and editor of *The Gulag Archipelago*?

It had been taken out of my hands.
I would be writing for trade books.
A new path opened in my brain.

It was settled. We were going to Hong Kong.
For everyone concerned, it was good. Deidra, especially, needed a different place to finish high school. She would be going back to join her own classmates at HKIS. Chris, too, would be joining the kids he started kindergarten with. At fifth grade, they would all be good readers now.

Gordon and I had a twentieth wedding anniversary coming. We would actually be celebrating it in flight.
How fitting.
We were sorting out stuff to sell. One thing in particular I couldn't find. On our honeymoon we had picked up lake pebbles, smooth, dark brown rocks, and had fashioned a lamp out of driftwood and stones. It had survived all our moves. Sometimes it had even been stored in Mom and Dad De Pree's attic with our other treasures.
But it was gone.
"Did you see our driftwood lamp?" I asked.
"Not really," he said evasively. "It was getting a little shabby anyhow."
"What do you mean, shabby? Did you throw it out?"
He got a silly grin on his face.
"Well, actually I was going to surprise you," he said, taking out a little drawstring bag.
There was a hand-wrought silver ring with a large, brown stone set skillfully—a stone from our driftwood lamp.
"I thought maybe this would be easier to pack," he said, slipping it on my finger.
We were on the move again, taking our warm hearts along. He hadn't forgotten.

I wrote a story for John Allen, called: "A Pebble is Forever."
He loved it, but said the *Digest* couldn't use it. DeBeers Diamonds advertised with them, and they might not like it. I doubted that lake stones would replace diamonds (for most people) anytime in the near future.

The house on Dutcher Avenue was bought by a Catholic family with twelve children of their own, and a few adopted extras. It seemed right.

The day we left Pawling was like the day we left Kung Lee School. Friends from Quaker Hill Church, from the town of Pawling, from the

Foundation, from the high school, all came to the train station to see us off. The train was moving slowly. We were waving. The years in Pawling had been good. We knew it was right to go, but we were glad we had come.

I looked out and saw Nancy Tanner, my friend from the Book Cove, Pawling's bookstore. I would miss her.

Chris looked out the window, waving at his classmates.

"If everybody loves us so much, why are we leaving?" he asked, brushing away a stray tear.

Chris was almost ten.

The year was 1976, the 200th birthday of the United States of America. New York City was in a festive mood. The tall boats were anchored in the harbor.

Frank Wangeman from Quaker Hill, and the manager of the Waldorf Towers in Manhattan, put us up for the week of our departure in the Presidential Suite of the Towers. We went to see *A Chorus Line* and met Mrs. Douglas McArthur in the elevator. We hoped the kids wouldn't break anything. The suite was crammed with gifts from Kings and Queens from around the world. It was the perfect end to our Pawling days.

Marita and Michael took a flight to Iowa. The rest of us hopped a plane for Hawaii and on to Hong Kong.

We stopped in Hawaii for an overnight, because it was the date of our twentieth anniversary. Deidra and Chris slipped out early and brought back a bottle of Blue Nun wine and some crackers and cheese to celebrate our anniversary breakfast on a balcony overlooking Waikiki Beach. We were on our way again.

The first twenty years had passed.

What would the next twenty bring?

Somehow...the dream of a little American town with a house on a quiet street seemed dim. Was that what we had found in Pawling? Not really. With its undercurrent of New York power, it had been exciting, but not the dream. The only thing that had happened was the kids finally had bikes, I had permission...no, a command, from a trade publisher to write what I had always feared to write...and Gordon could start his own school.

And the best part was that Doctor Peale (although converted from Methodism) was with the Dutch Reformed Church. We were back in the fold—more or less.

CHAPTER FOURTEEN

THE TWO-STORY HOUSE ON Cambridge Road in the heart of Kowloon was in a neighborhood popular with expats. It had the British colonial pre-war tropical look that was treasured in the seventies.

We had not brought any furnishings, just suitcases and a few boxes with necessities like a sewing machine and a portable typewriter. Chris had his treasured GI Joes and his piano music. Deidra had her flute.

We would have to find another piano.

The usual décor...rattan furniture, big tropical plants, hanging Japanese white paper lanterns, hemp floor mats, a few tailored cushions in bright colors... Decorating with "shadows and purple onions" again.

Kids' HKIS uniforms...we knew the drill.

There was another American family upstairs with a boy named Stephen, Chris' age. The kids could take the bus to school.

With all that settled, we went out to Mei Foo Sun Chuen (beautiful and prosperous new village, with shades of hope) to look at the neighborhood where Guideposts Kindergarten would be built.

We took the ferry out to Mei Foo and climbed up onto the new area where the high-rises were being constructed. Blocks of sixteen-story buildings were grouped into small neighborhoods, each with its own shopping center, car park, and open garden areas. It was new and exciting.

The area that Guideposts was renting from the construction people was up one floor leaving the ground floor for shopping and parking.

We took the elevator up and stood on the first floor. It was a raw open space, all dusty concrete and steel girders with a few walls, but studded with building supports for the floors above.

It was huge...wide open and challenging. This was where Gordon would build a school.

167

We took the bus back to Cambridge Road, heads whirling with plans.

First, the floor plan would have to be drawn: classrooms, teachers rooms, bathrooms, the office, a large place in the center of the cluster for assemblies, and some kind of indoor play area. These would be three- to five-year-olds. It would require books, play equipment, teachers, uniforms—a whole program for a beginning enrollment of 500 children.

Where to start?

We would have the winter to accomplish all of this and the next summer to publicize it, enroll students from the Mei Foo community, and start the school in the fall of 1977.

The all-important school uniforms would have to be designed...

This time we did not try to invent the wheel. We played it safe with navy, red and white—500 little children with shiny black hair and eyes would look astounding in red blazers and navy skirts or pants with red and white checked accessories. Yes!

Most Hong Kong preschools at the time had interiors that were shades of hospital green. Gordon decided on pure white walls and red carpets, with panels of rich blue or golden yellow—vivid, exciting shades and shapes.

Gordon rounded up carpenters and plumbers, and rug and tile layers. He advertised for teachers, and began to build. We had a generous budget and *Guideposts* would pay for the whole set-up. In the middle of the play area he had workers build a life-size, wooden, Hong Kong bus, red, of course, that the kids could climb into and slide out of.

With Gordon's project safely launched, I took out the trusty portable typewriter and went to work on the book Frances Lindley was excited about.

Did I really want to write it?

Did I dare?

Could I do it?

It had been twenty years since Gordon and I fell in love and I ran away. Could I even remember it all when I had tried so hard to forget?

It was quiet at the Kowloon flat.

I sat at the table, notebook full of pages, a pen, and closed my eyes. I sat still until I was almost asleep, peering into a place in my mind that I did not even know existed. I began to feel things. The cold wind coming in the cracks between the logs, the smell of potatoes frying in an iron skillet, men sawing through huge trees and letting them crash in the forest. The sound of hammers...

I began to write. I wrote from a place deep inside me, a frightened wounded place where a small child crouched, afraid of the dark.

I wrote with tears streaming down my face, unconscious of the words. It all came pouring out onto the paper.

Oh yes, this was the book I should write, the book that had been blocking all the others.

I would not be polite. I would not cover things. This book would tell the truth down to the bare bones.

I would do it if it killed me.

The Peales flew to Hong Kong to see how we were doing. They looked over the wasteland of the open space to become a school and wished us well, then came to Cambridge Road to see our apartment.

It certainly was not the house on Dutcher Avenue, Pawling, but it was cheerful, tropical and colorful. It even had a bit of pizazz. Our rattan sofa had tailor-made cushions that looked soft, but had somehow turned out to be like bricks. Dr. Peale sat down hard and looked rather startled, but quickly regained his dignity.

"Let us know if you need anything," he said kindly, and then he was gone. The Mobil Oil people were taking him back to the airport.

We had been working so intently that one day we decided we needed a break. We took the Star Ferry across to Hong Kong side and walked along the waterfront in Wanchai, Gordon's old stomping grounds.

The Royal Hong Kong Yacht Club perched above the harbor, with beautiful boats anchored along the shore. A long stone breakwater reached out a protective arm between the open harbor and the boat area, creating a typhoon shelter where the fishing boats could take refuge from the frequent storms in Hong Kong.

We strolled along, hand-in-hand, feeling the cooling sea breeze and watching the boats.

Then we saw it.

A stunning teak and white ocean-going junk that had been turned into a houseboat. Its hull gleamed white with teakwood decks. It was at least sixty feet long, and there was a sign on the side.

FOR SALE

"Must be nice," I sighed, "for some people..."

But Gordon was star struck.

"Would you like to go out and see it," he asked. "Just for fun?"

Before I knew what we were doing, we were in a wallah-wallah, putting out to the big boat. We climbed up the ship's ladder and knocked at the door.

We had knocked a few times and were about to leave when a lovely blond woman came to the door wrapped in a huge, golden bath towel.

"Oh, come in!" she smiled.

We did.

Bea Lane excused herself to get dressed while we sat in the galley kitchen of the boat. Gorgeous. Golden yellow and white with wide designer stripes, a full kitchen with a long, narrow, teak table and booths, all gas appliances, stove, refrigerator, freezer, and all teak floor and walls surrounded by windows looking out over the water.

Bea was back, dressed.

"Come on, I'll show you around."

We saw it all, the wheelhouse lounge with royal blue and white wide striped sofas, a TV, glass coffee table, and big bar stocked with wines. The pilot wheel, the ship's own generator, the master bedroom and bath with tub and shower, and a huge king-sized bed with portholes looking out over the sea, walk-in closet, three other bedrooms, and a second bath and shower. There was also a washer and dryer, and down in the hold were two powerful Gardener engines to take it out to sea.

Open decks on the bow.

Covered decks in the stern, with outdoor tables for dining…

This baby must cost a cool million.

"We were just curious," Gordon said apologetically. "I'm sure this is out of our range."

It was such an understatement I almost laughed.

Bob Lane appeared up the side of the boat. He was a Pan Am pilot, and this was his Hong Kong pad.

We spent the afternoon on the boat. The kids had keys and could get in the apartment.

Over a glass of wine, Bob laid it out.

"We have to sell because Pan Am is pulling its people out of Hong Kong, and we've got to get rid of this boat."

"But we're not even serious," Gordon told him.

Bob kept on.

"We're going to lose a ton of money, but we've put it on the market for forty thousand," he said.

Forty thousand? For us, it might as well be forty million. We lived from paycheck to paycheck, and had kids in college.

"Sorry…it's beautiful, but there's no way we can even think of it," Gordon insisted.

"Here's my number," Bob said. "Let me know if you change your mind."

"It's not…"

"Now, look," Bob smiled, "I could hold the mortgage. You pay me once a month. How much allowance does your company give you for housing per month?"

Gordon told him.

"Give it to me instead of paying for an apartment, and we're in business. Pay a couple thousand down, and pay the rest like rent."

It sounded good-too good to be true.

"I really appreciate it," Gordon told him. "I'm sure we can't do it, but we'll think about it."

They shook hands and we got back in the wallah-wallah, and went home.

Beautiful, but no way.

Deidra came home from her day at HKIS.

"Oh, Mom and Dad, it's so great to be back here! Lots of kids from my old class are here, and we're going to put on a big school play, a musical. We're going to do *Guys and Dolls*, and I'm going to be one of the hotbox dancers. I've got to get some dance shoes made in Wanchai…"

I looked at her, so healthy and happy. She was suddenly taller than I was, slim and beautiful. So different from the over -drugged invalid she had been just a year ago. Thank goodness she had a new school to go to.

She was blossoming!

Chris had met a German boy his age. They were going to play GI Joes together. Could Karl come and stay overnight? Of course!

It was another one of those nights.

I was half asleep—half dreaming—half awake.

The boat was riding into the waves. I was standing in the bow, the wind on my face, hair streaming behind me…

Gordon turned over.

"Are you asleep?" he asked.

"No, not really."

"What are you thinking about?"

"I'm not really thinking."

Back on the other side.

Almost asleep.

"Are you asleep?"

"No. Why?"

"I keep thinking about the boat."

"Are you crazy?"

"Probably."

After half an hour he sat up in bed.

"Shall we go back and talk to him? The way he laid it out, we could probably do it."

171

That was another night we did not sleep. Possessed with the power of adventure, of experiencing the sea, of that big king-sized bed in the state-room— the royal blue and white striped bedspread, the big golden yellow towels…the thrill of it all. It burned in our bellies like pure hot lust.

We went back the next day to talk with Bob Lane and decided.

Come hell or high water, we agreed to buy it.

CONCERTO

A sixty-five-foot ocean-going junk was ours!

It would be a secret. We would tell all the kids at Christmas when Marita and Mike came home from college.

Home?

It would be redefined again.

This time it would be a boat.

Gordon went to work each day, smug with his secret. He put carpenters and painters and tile craftsmen to work, carving out a stunningly designed school for five hundred small beautiful Chinese children.

I drew designs for the children's uniforms and took them to the designated tailor, who would sew them up in winter and summer fabrics.

We designed a red, yellow and blue logo, with two children (in uniform) and a street sign. Gia Bow (*Guideposts*) in Chinese meant a street sign, or showing the way. It translated well.

We wrote words for a school song.

Whatever needed doing…

But most of all, I wrote my story. It poured out. I laughed and cried, writing in pen and later typing it. Sometimes when I typed the handwriting I was surprised, not knowing consciously what I had written.

I had stopped caring what the result would be. This story had to be written.

Then one day, in a sequence that would have seemed contrived if it were a novel, there was a messenger at the door on Cambridge Road. A Western Union uniform. A motorcycle. A young man handed me a telegram. It was from Ruth, one of the Kentucky sisters that my parents had raised.

I stared at the telegram, not able to comprehend its words.

"DADDY VOGEL PASSED AWAY. MASSIVE CEREBRAL HEM-MORAGE.IN FLORIDA.

I read and re-read the message, unable to absorb it.

Then I was shocked.

My first conscious reaction was that I had done it. I had killed him by writing this book.

No...I couldn't have killed him. He had been dead for a long time, hadn't he?

I would not take the blame. He had died to me years ago. I was relieved that it was finally official.

I could not even cry.

It was the week for earth-shattering telegrams. There was one from the Peales.

DO NOT PURCHASE BOAT.

We telegraphed them back.

SORRY—PURCHASE FINALIZED.

They were not happy. They wrote a letter back saying this was a serious lapse in judgment, and they hoped they had not misplaced their good faith in us.

We responded that we would continue to perform our duties with the utmost dedication, but that we felt the choice of living quarters was up to us.

It was the beginning of an uneasy relationship with a threat of being terminated after the three years hanging over our heads.

We had thought of the Peales as liberal, open minded...they had thought we were responsible, reliable. We were both disappointed.

If we proved to them that we were the right people to establish Guideposts Kindergarten would the situation right itself?

We hoped so...and doubled our efforts.

The first two chapters of the Kentucky Story (working title) were finished. I packed them up and sent them to Frances Lindley at Harper and Row. A letter came back saying she would definitely be publishing the story, and a contract, with an advance, was in the works.

WOW!

I wrote back, telling her how pleased and empowered I was, and mentioning my father's death.

She replied, quickly.

"This may sound strange to you, but thank goodness! We hesitated to publish this story as a novel, as novels have to be logical (pass the believability test). This story is so far into the realm of unreality that it must be published as a true story..."

True story?

Yes, now it could be a true story.

That it was, and so much stranger than fiction.

The college kids were home for Christmas, and the apartment on Cambridge Road was filled to capacity. We decorated the tree, baked holiday goodies, and put four little model junks with red sails (from the Communist store) under the tree with the other gifts. When the kids opened the "toy" junks, a note said:

"Surprise! We're going to live on a boat! Mom and Dad."

Deidra and Chris laughed.

"We thought something was funny. You guys have been acting weird!"

Marita and Mike did not react as strongly—they would be in college anyhow. Then they realized they would be home for the summer, a summer in Hong Kong with four kids on a boat!

Everyone wanted to go out and see it.

Merry Christmas!

We would move aboard in January.

Happy 1977!

There were so many things to think of living on a boat. Because of its sixty-five-foot length, we needed to rent two mooring spaces.

In order to really enjoy the experience, we needed a "boat boy," someone who could steer this monster safely through the typhoon shelter filled with sampans and out to the outlying islands, someone who had a pilot's license.

And, we needed to belong to the Royal Hong Kong Yacht Club. We were not really Yacht Club people, but we would need the swimming pool and showers when all the kids were home. The showers on the boat would run out of water quickly with so many people aboard.

So we had to apply for membership.

Somebody sponsored us.

We had to go to a party at the club and 'mingle,' to let people look us over and give approval.

We were given an application form.

What boating experience did we have?

There were boxes to be checked. What had we done? Sailing or rowing?

Sailing? No, never.

"We did some rowing at the Y in Pawling," Gordon said.

"Oh, for heaven's sake, don't mention that!" I said. "They don't mean paddle boats at the Y! They mean like Oxford or Cambridge...you know, real rowing-rowing..."

We were self-confessed landlubbers, out of our depth, but we joined. They figured we were uncultured Americans. We needed showers, and the club dining room was a nice touch.

We even found our boat boy. Ju Gwong came aboard one day, a pleasant-looking fellow in his early twenties. He had been born on a boat in Aberdeen Harbor, and lived his whole life on the water. He had a pilot's license, and would be our general boat boy, taking care of the vessel as well as piloting. He lived at home in Aberdeen, and would only come on weekends or when we needed him.

There was only one thing we had to do ourselves: turn the generator on in the morning to recharge the batteries in the hold. It meant pressing a big button on the wheelhouse instrument panel just the right amount of time to get the water flowing out the pipe on the side of the boat, and letting it go. If we did it wrong, the whole thing choked and shuddered to a stop.

It scared me to death, but I did it. Gordon refused. It was good to know even he was scared of something.

We settled into life on the boat as if we had always lived in a typhoon shelter. The twins went back to college, and Deidra and Chris went back to HKIS to finish out the year. We had moved Chris's piano on board the boat (quite an operation by sampan) and his Kowloon teacher agreed to come once a week to give him lessons. Was it unusual to see a ten-year-old boy playing the piano in the wheelhouse of an ocean-going junk? We never thought of it.

The rooms at the kindergarten were taking shape, and Marita had promised to do a mural on the wall when they came back for the summer.

With everyone settled again, I began to work on the remaining chapters of the book. It was a perfect work environment, all set up at the long teak table in the galley, comfortable in the padded booths, the swaying motions of the boat gently rocking in the current.

As I delved deeper into the story I began to feel a great sadness for my father, not for his death, but for his life. He had been such a talented man, so charismatic. People loved him and trusted him. He had brilliant ideas, and was so clever. He wanted to do something extraordinary with his life, to accomplish something outstanding...to validate himself.

Validate himself...

Wasn't he valid, as a human being?

Maybe not.

He needed layers and layers of religious terms to justify himself—religious terms that might have been harmless to a person with a more balanced mind, but somehow he slipped over the edge and into a world of hallucinations and miracles…

…and demanded that we live out his hallucinations, his unusual world.

Fourteen miles back in the country. Virtual prisoners.

No social services supervision.

He needed help, counseling, perhaps medication.

In the forties and fifties, anyone who went to seek mental health help was…it was the kiss of death. He would be finished.

And so we lived out his divided mind, the mind of an apparent saint who underneath was a dangerous predator.

He must have had moments of terrible awareness, when the good side of him glimpsed the evil side.

Were those the times I saw him weeping bitterly?

What terrible guilt he must have suffered, what terror of being discovered.

I wrote, telling of the fourteen-year-old girl he seduced, telling her she was giving herself to God…and as I wrote, I found the fear and anger I felt toward him fading into a terrible pity. I pitied him, so divided, so tormented, so confused…once he had broken the taboo he repeated it, time after time…unable to stop himself…

As I wrote of his tragic life and the havoc he wreaked, I thought of the Ghost Festival in Stanley, of the Hungry Ghosts that came back year after year if they were not forgiven of their wrongs. Now that he was a true ghost, I could forgive him…

I would forgive him, but not for his sake alone. I would forgive him because then he would leave me, would not cause me to fear that my children would inherit any part of him. I would see them for the beautiful young people they were, and not project those fears on them. I would decide to love them, especially Mike, who had some of his physical characteristics, as gifts of God, vessels of the Creative Power, untainted by what they had not experienced… untainted by what I had experienced…

The Hungry Ghosts of Stanley Village…

Yes, ghost. You are forgiven. Now go, and do not trouble me any longer. I do not need you in my life.

Go…you are forgiven.

The kindergarten was taking shape.

The next item on the agenda was to go to the education department on the Hong Kong side to register the school with the government.

The education department of the Hong Kong government was a busy place. Hong Kong was growing, and schools were popping up all over the city to educate the booming population of young people.

The woman behind the desk was friendly and courteous. She took Gordon's information as to the location, size, sponsor, funding…all duly recorded.

"And who would be the head of the school?" she asked. "Would that be you?"

"We thought we perhaps should have a Chinese woman," Gordon began, "with Chinese mothers to deal with and understand the cultural things…"

"Ah ha! Very wise," she nodded, continuing to make notes. "And do you have someone in mind?"

"We interviewed one person, but no decision has been made."

The woman smiled slowly.

"If you're still looking, I have a suggestion to make."

"Please!"

"There is a very excellent Chinese woman, now working at an Anglican school, but thinking of making a change. She is from China, has done some outstanding kindergarten work there, and of late has been very interested in using the Montessori method of learning. You're acquainted with this?"

"I know of it."

"This woman's name is Maggie Tam. She will be looking for a position this fall. Would you like to have her contact information?"

"I certainly would."

"You would have no trouble getting your school registered with her as headmistress. Our entire department knows and respects her."

Gordon contacted Maggie.

She came out to visit the kindergarten at Mei Foo, and a great bond was formed. A Dutch American from Michigan and a Hong Kong Chinese woman from Canton met and began planning the program for the school. They clicked.

"She's a great find," Gordon told me. "Very open minded. She doesn't want three- to five-year-olds sitting still in class, learning by rote. She loves a hands-on approach, letting the children learn by doing."

"And what does she think of your color scheme?"

"Loves it. She is going to make this school a success."

"Is she Anglican?"

"You know, I didn't ask her. Many of the children will be from traditional Chinese backgrounds, so she'll have to be judicious how she handles the religious thing."

Maggie Tam was a godsend, religious or not.

She also knew many good teachers in the field. With teachers who answered the *Guideposts* ads in the Chinese newspaper, and friends of Maggie, the school was staffed with top grade educators.

Things were shaping up for fall.

The drama at HKIS was coming up. Deidra needed to go to Wanchai and get fitted for her shoes as one of the hotbox dancers. She was excited.

The small shoemaker had her put her foot up to be measured.

"Wah!" he said, incredulously.

He went to the workshop at the back of the shop and brought out his entire workforce. Deidra put her foot up to be measured again. They had not believed him.

"Wah!" he smiled triumphantly. "Da king-size feet!"

Of course, everyone laughed. Size ten feet on a girl always blew Chinese people away. It was like having two heads.

When De went to pick up her shoes the day of the dance, they were size eight. That was the biggest last they had. She had to dance in shoes two sizes too small.

But she danced beautifully.

She would make it.

With eight blistered toes.

CHAPER FIFTEEN

WE BEGAN TO ENJOY LIVING on the boat. Sixty-five feet long and twenty-two feet wide, the Concerto became our new definition of home. Every morning Chris and Dede put on their sky blue KHIS school uniforms, caught a sampan to go ashore, and boarded the old familiar number six bus to Repulse Bay. Gordon caught a bus going the other direction to take the Mei Foo Ferry, and I set up the galley table to write. Page by page it was being written.

The big boat rocked gently in the morning tide and currents, creating a fluid pattern, a pattern new to our own accustomed Hong Kong lives.

On weekends Ju Gwong came to take us out of the typhoon shelter. We cruised out to the outlying islands, exploring the sea around Hong Kong. The younger kids were both excellent swimmers, and had no hesitation in diving off the boat into the sea when we anchored at a far-off beach. The dive from the boat was nearly twenty feet, but they loved it. They grew brown and strong, young sea-creatures.

Deidra had completely grown out of her doped and swollen look. She was a different person, tall and lean and long legged, with dark eyes and a long dark mane of hair down her back. At seventeen, Deidra was a striking beauty.

Some Saturday mornings she loved to sit in the lobby of the Mandarin Hotel, enjoying her queendom and watching the world go by…and, unbeknown to her parents, smoking cigarettes. At first I thought she was just picking up second-hand smoke at the hotel, and then I asked her.

"De, are you smoking?"

"Uh-sometimes…" she admitted.

"De, you know… You have to think carefully about this. You know it's dangerous to do anything that will narrow your arteries and decrease the blood flow to your brain. The doctor said…"

I saw her close her eyes and squeeze them shut to close me out.

"Mom," she began, slowly and patiently, "please don't overprotect me. I need to do some things that make me feel normal at school, and believe me, smoking is the least of them."

"I don't want you to smoke."

"I won't do it on the boat."

"I don't want you to do it anywhere."

"Mom, are you trying to make me afraid of life?" There were tears in her voice.

"No, I'm just trying to keep you alive."

"Okay..."

Okay what?

One Saturday when we were being lazy and staying on the boat, the phone rang. It was De, calling from the Mandarin Hotel.

"Mom, I was sitting here watching people this morning...and Mom, I saw this guy. They kept coming up to him, the hotel staff, and calling him prince this and prince that. Then he came over and sat next to me, and I said, 'Hey, are you a real prince?' And he said, yes, he was a real prince from Saudi Arabia. And Mom, he wants me to go shopping with him. He said he's going down the street to pick up a dozen pairs of shoes he had made, and he wants to buy some shoes for me."

"De..."

"I know, Mom. Don't worry. This is the first real prince I ever met, so do you think I'm going to tell him I wear size ten shoes? You always told us our vanity would keep us out of more trouble than our virtue would..."

"De..."

"So I told him no thanks, and he said okay, he'll give me money to go shopping for anything I want."

"De, don't take any money from him!"

"But Mom, I need new underwear..."

"I'll buy you new underwear."

"Okay, Mom, remember you said that."

She was gone. My beautiful seventeen-year-old adrift in downtown Hong Kong, learning to survive and enjoy life in a way I could never have imagined.

We were learning to live in our water neighborhood, so different from anywhere we had ever lived, both more posh and snobbish (the club), and more earthy- verging on the rough side.

The fishing junk moored next to us was approximately the same size as ours. The Lee family had lived on it for years, and had numerous children.

We saw them every day, hanging out their wash or cooking on the deck. We waved and called greetings in Chinese. Of course, being able to say 'good morning' in Chinese was not considered 'speaking.' The common saying was that every foreigner knew how to say 'good morning' and 'garbage.'

Mr. Lee sometimes took out a small fishing boat to catch shrimp. When he came in with the fresh shrimp, still alive, and we bought a bucket of them from him, they were the sweetest, most delicious shrimp we had ever tasted.

One day when we were doing our fresh shrimp purchase, Mr. Lee asked if he could come on our boat.

"I've seen people living here," he said, "but I've never seen inside."

"Welcome," I said. "You can look around anytime."

Our house in Stanley had always been open. We seldom even locked the door, unless we were going somewhere. Why not do the same here?

He came up the ladder one day when I was alone. I wasn't sure that was such a good idea, but I didn't want to be unfriendly. He looked around the galley, so different from his boat where they cooked in a wok over an open - flame.

"You show me around?" he asked, looking sly.

I was peeling apples in the sink. "You can just go look," I said.

"Where's the bedroom?" he asked.

I felt warning bells.

"That way, right down the steps."

"You show me?"

"No, you can go look by yourself."

"I see you and your husband down there at night," he said insinuatingly.

Remind me to check the blinds…

He grasped my arm above the elbow.

"Your flesh is still very firm," he said. "I know all about you Americans. I watch American movies—American women are very wild."

My heart was racing. What if this man attacked me?

"I think Mrs. Lee is calling you," I said, glancing out the window. "She's wondering where you are."

He dropped my arm and left.

I would have to find the right degree of friendliness in the typhoon shelter.

In all our years in Hong Kong, I had never had anyone harm me. I was not going to take this too seriously. I probably wouldn't even mention it to Gordon. I didn't want him to worry.

Besides, Lee was just a little shrimp himself. I could probably beat him up.

Hong Kong's brief cool spell that passed for winter was over, and the thick sweltering heat had set in again. The winds over the sea began their yearly disturbances and we knew the typhoon weather was coming up.

We had lived through many typhoons in Hong Kong, but this season would be different. We would be on the water.

One morning we awoke, aware of a new pressure in the air. I went up to press the button and start the generator, and saw them streaming in from the open harbor, fishing boats of all shapes and sizes, motoring into the typhoon shelter and beginning to jockey for the best mooring spaces to shelter from the storm.

They kept coming in and crowding, one beside the other. I saw someone jump up on our bow with a rope in his hand, and called to Gordon to come up to the galley.

Gordon went out on the deck.

"Excuse me," he said in Chinese, "but what are you doing?"

"Don't you know?" the man smiled. "We have to tie all the boats together with ropes to steady them. If we have a solid wall of boats, the water won't throw them all around."

Gordon helped the man secure the heavy ropes and we became a part of the great typhoon flotilla.

The winds began at number one typhoon signal, a red flag flying at the Star Ferry, and progressed to number ten. Ten meant we were right in the eye of the storm.

We all stayed on the boat that day as the heavy rains began to slash across the water. The wind increased, picking up everything in its way. Bamboo scaffolds surrounding the new buildings were particularly dangerous— a flying pole of bamboo could kill a person. The whole city battened down to wait out the storm.

On board the Concerto, we were snug and dry. We turned on the TV and popped corn while the storm raged around us. Our boat, tied to all the other boats, barely moved on the troubled dark water of the sea.

...and if someone walked across the bow of our boat, we knew we were a part of the pathway to the shore. We were a water community, tied together.

Some things were a little too 'together'.

The day after the typhoon hit was the worst. Women aboard the fishing boats had been busy making shrimp paste, and the concoction was spread out on the decks to dry in the sun. The stink was overwhelming. It reminded me of a description I had read of a bait shed that smelled 'like the unwashed ass-end of some giant creature.'

The shrimp paste would ferment and be used as a condiment. The boat people laughed when we complained, and said it was their strong cheese. The Chinese word for cheese was pig shit- a foreign food that no one would eat,

'Oh would some power the giftee gi us
To smell ourselves as others smell us'
Was that Robert Burns, loosely translated?

Gordon bought a little dingy boat so the kids could paddle around inside the breakwater, or go ashore when the sampans were not available. One thing they learned, the hard way, was never to row under the back deck of a fishing junk, the part that jutted out over the water. It was called the poop deck, and for good reason.

That spring we sat up on the bow after work, looking up at the sky above us, watching the cloud formations and seeing patterns in them…watching a dog turn into a dragon, or a horse into an angel…all a matter of interpretation, and changing before any points could be won.

After dark we sat on the deck and watched the dinner boats float by. The typhoon shelter was famous for its evening sampans that could be rented, manned by seafood chefs who cooked live sea creatures on the boats for tourists and adventurers. We saw a heavy steel cleaver come down and cut a live red crab in half, and hands tossing it into a vat of boiling water…people eating and laughing.

Some said the dinner boats also provided other services behind the draped awnings. The harbor was a beautiful, tough, earthy environment. Had the Peales thought we would be drawn into its revelry?

Not much chance.

We were hopelessly innocent.

They were coming in the fall for the grand opening of Guideposts Kindergarten. We knew they would be pleasantly surprised.

The twins were home for the summer of their eighteenth birthday. The boat was our house. Spaces were adjusted. The girls shared a room, Mike had his space, and Chris claimed the little bed up in the very tip of the bow.

One morning Chris came running down the stairs to our bedroom with a horrified look on his face.

"Mom! Dad! I woke up and I couldn't see out of one eye! And when I touched my face there was this huge cockroach covering my whole eye. I thought I was going blind!"

The boat was not infested with roaches, but a kind of flying insect was the problem. They were huge—some three inches long. Fortunately, they usually flew on and did not stay.

Chris, being seven years younger than the rest, was worried because he was not growing fast enough. Everyone else in the family was tall, taller and tallest. Mike was over six feet. Chris was barely up to my chin, and was getting that pre-pubescent chub.

Deidra was worried that her boobs weren't big enough.

Chris was worried that his were too big. He was sure he would be the midget in the family.

Worries…worries. We might as well be in that little house in suburbia—the worries would all be the same. Life on the boat wasn't as different as it seemed.

De was keeping up her cheerleading skills. When the boat rocked, she would lose it and have to start over again.

"Look Dad, look…no wait." She would go lurching across the galley, starting the cheer over again.

Marita bought paints and brushes, and caught the ferry to Mei Foo with Gordon in the mornings. She was drawing and painting a large mural of children on the wall of Guideposts Kindergarten. She had been studying art at Grinnell. In some ways I was sorry she had not gone to the school of design she had planned to go to in New York, because we were not there. I asked her how she felt about it.

"No, don't worry about it," she said. "When I went to the art school for my interview, I decided I didn't want to go there anyhow."

"How come?"

"I dated a gay guy for three years in high school. That was enough!" she laughed.

"That's too bad."

"No, Jon's still a good friend, but I'd like to find someone who's more than a friend at college; someone who's happy I'm a woman."

Had I known any gays in college? They must have all been in hiding. The world was changing.

Wherever she had learned it, the mural at the school was amazing. It was simple black lines of children in activities, on a white wall. Very sophisticated. She worked on it, day after day, one more beautiful thing to show the Peales when they came.

Mike and De found jobs at McDonalds for the summer.

In 1977, McDonalds was something completely new in Hong Kong. If proper market research had been done, there would never have been a McDonalds in the whole crown colony. The Chinese hated milk, white bread, fried potatoes…almost everything McDonalds had to sell. But they loved McDonalds. One shop had opened on the Hong Kong side near Kung

Lee School, and in a year's time there were thirteen McDonalds. Chinese kids loved hamburgers. Their parents and grandparents took the kids as an excuse, and became addicts themselves.

Hom-Bou-Bow became a craze.

Mike was hired as a burger flipper and pot washer. Deidra took orders at the counter. She had to learn the Chinese names for things. She managed until a girl from India came in and ordered, in perfect English, a meatless hamburger.

What was that?

Crazy mixed-up world.

With six people of all different ages on the boat it was hard to coordinate our schedules, but one thing we agreed on: we wanted to take the boat out and anchor off a beach overnight.

Did we pick the date at random, or did we know that the weekend was the Dragon Boat Festival? We had once set our calendar by Chinese festivals when we lived in Stanley Village, but at this stage of our lives they had blurred into the background of our whole concept of life—there, formative, wonderful, but no longer central. In an unintended imagery, we would observe the festival at a distance, from our boat, anchored off the Repulse Bay Beach.

But when the older kids heard which day we were going out, there was a huge cry.

"Not that weekend! There's going to be a party of kids who went to HKIS when we did—college kids home for the summer. It's a big deal and we really want to go."

"All my best friends are going, too," De chimed in. "We'll all be seniors in the fall."

My mind did a quick calculation. Dragon Boat Festival would be a great time to be on the water. The party was, obviously, a necessity.

"That would work," I said. "We'll anchor out from the Repulse Bay Beach, and you can come out to the boat after the party."

"What time would we have to come home?"

"Oh, you can stay, as long as you're home by twelve o'clock."

"What if the party's not over?"

"Then you can sleep on the beach. We can't stay up all night."

"I'm not sleeping on that beach if it's crowded with people," Marita said.

"Then you better meet your dad at the pier by twelve."

Ju Gwong came that Saturday afternoon, the first day of the Dragon Boat Festival, and we packed enough food on the boat for the weekend. By four o'clock we were all assembled, the mooring lines untied, and we were chugging around the back side of the island toward Repulse Bay.

The western side of the island had built up in the past few years, and where just a few years before thousands had lived on boats, there now stood tall new apartment buildings and housing estates. The crowded boat community at the heart of Aberdeen still stood, and Gordon pointed it out.

"There's where we'll go to have the boat slipped and painted in August," he said. "That should be interesting. We'll be right in the shipyard, up on a dry dock, for three or four days while they scrape off the barnacles and repaint it."

"Out of the water?"

"Yep."

"How can we use the generator?"

"We can't. It will be candlelight and stars for a few nights."

That sounded good to me. No roaring generator.

Up ahead the long sandy stretch of Repulse Bay Beach swung into sight. For all the days I had spent on that beach when Marita, Mike and Deidra were toddlers, I had never seen the beach from the sea. It was like seeing the world inside out. The whole background of the past was the foreground of the present. I was where the horizon used to be, far and drawn out against the sky, and the people on the beach were like little ants, crawling over the sand. It felt godlike, giddy, to be dancing on the horizon with the past pasted against the shore...

I had been a mother ant with three little ants on that sand, thinking they would always stay as they were—Mike who walked straight into the sea until it came over his head, Marita who always had some scheme going, and De who was determined to run around naked. Maybe they had stayed as they were, only grown up.

We anchored the boat, ate a hasty supper, and the older kids got ready for the party. Ju Gwong rowed the boat to shore.

It was almost nine before the sky began to get dark. The sun dropped, huge and red behind the scattered islands, sending fiery ripples across the waves. The beach, usually deserted by five or six, was as crowded as ever. All along the shore charcoal fires blazed up in the twilight, and the aroma of meat marinated in soy sauce and ginger drifted in the evening breeze coming down over the water. The junk bobbed and swayed gently on its anchor, a big white bird on a red sea.

Ju Gwong, Gordon, Chris and I sat out on the aft deck watching the sunset and the fires along the shore.

"Why are there so many people on the beach tonight?" Gordon asked Ju Gwong.

186

"Special holiday—double fifth."

"I know, but isn't that Monday?"

"People come early. They sleep on the beach all night and cook outdoors tonight and tomorrow, and then the dragon boats race on Monday."

We had seen them for two weeks in the harbor, training the Causeway Bay team for the big day. The boats were long and narrow, around one hundred feet long and only five feet wide, so they took skill and practice to handle. Every afternoon around four o'clock we had watched the crew, carved dragon head high in the bow and red flag flying at the tail, racing through the water from the noon gun to the open water beyond the breakwater. A drummer sat mid-ship pounding his slow deep drum while the bronzed young men raised and lowered their paddles in rhythm. Out in the harbor the long narrow craft swung around and came back past our junk, the drummer beating faster and faster on the last stretch until we could barely see the paddles fly.

It was one of those Chinese festivals that could be celebrated at whatever level a person chose to celebrate it. For the philosophical it was the remembering of a poet who died to uphold the standards of the country against an evil ruler. For the hungry it was a feast of sweet rice cakes wrapped in bamboo leaves. For the young and strong it was a celebration of muscle and skill—all in honor of the poet Wat Yuhn.

It was completely dark over the water now, and the fires along the beach stood out like glowing red flowers against the black mountain.

"Do you want to go ashore tonight?" Gordon asked the boat boy.

"Not necessary. I'll be here to sleep on the deck and watch the boat. If the wind comes up it could pull the anchor out, and we could drift aground, or out to sea. Never worry; I'll watch for you tonight."

A swimmer came through the water and we looked down to see his form, green and phosphorescent against the deep black water.

"Very dangerous," Ju Gwong commented. "Maybe a shark might eat you if you swim at night."

The swimmer went past the boat, casting his strange green light into the darkness,

At twelve o'clock Gordon rowed ashore to meet the kids at the pier. Only Marita and Deidra came back with him.

"Where did Mike go?" I asked.

"He decided to stay. Mike hates to leave a party early," De said.

"Where will he sleep?"

"Oh, don't worry about him," Marita said. "He'll find a place to sleep."

It was eight the next morning before we awoke. The crowd on the shore was thicker than ever. A dull roar of voices could be heard across the lapping waves, like a hive of swarming bees.

I was just putting the coffee on when there was a thud on the ladder side of the junk, and some wet bedraggled creature pulled itself aboard. For a moment I thought it was a tired swimmer, or someone trespassing, and then I looked again. It was Mike. He was fully clothed, jeans and sneakers, and drenched from head to toe.

"Where were you?" I said sleepily.

He sat at the galley table and told me his story. It wasn't cold and he didn't mind being wet.

When he left the party that night it was around two o'clock. There was nowhere to go, and since the dingy had left at twelve, he decided he would sleep on the beach. But when he actually got to the beach, he decided that for one young, blond, foreign devil to sleep alone on the sand might not be such as wise idea. Besides, there was hardly a spot long enough for him to stretch out, the place was so crowded. What should he do?

"I thought about it," he said, "and I remembered that temple to the Sea Goddess we used to play in when we were kids, the one with the big turtle out in front? Well, I went in there, and there was this big image of the Sea Goddess resting on a lotus blossom. It was dark in there, so I felt around and there was a smooth cool place of cement down inside the lotus blossom. I was so tired, I didn't care where I slept by then, so I just crawled in the big flower and went to sleep.

"And then this morning I woke up and the place was crowded with people. I peeked out and saw all these women burning joss sticks and stuff, so I thought I'd better think of a good excuse for being there. I slowly rose up and came walking out like I was in a trance, looking straight ahead. Everyone just stared at me and fell back to let me through. I walked straight to the edge of the pier without turning around, and fell like a log into the sea, and swam out here in all my clothes…"

I poured him a cup of coffee and we sat at the galley table, laughing.

I could hear it. It would become a part of the legend of the temple, how on this one Dragon Boat Festival, a young golden-haired god had arisen out of the lotus blossom and fallen into the sea…all in honor of the poet, Wat Yuen.

The Fourth of July was always celebrated by the American community in Hong Kong, even though the holiday itself was a bit of a touchy subject. After all, The Fourth was a day when America celebrated its independence from England, and celebrating it on British territory was at best, uncomfortable.

But the American consulate always made a big deal of it. Hot dogs and Cokes(or was it Pepsi?) were served free, and wealthy Chinese women came in their fur coats in July—in sweltering Hong Kong—to add to the surreal nature of the day. Most normal Chinese ignored it.

We observed the day on the boat. We had been going to ask Ju Gwong to pilot us out to some island for a picnic, but our three older kids had a different idea.

All of their growing-up years they had heard about Wanchai's bar area. Gordon had worked at Fenwick Pier. We had driven past the lurid bar fronts, the flickering neon lights of the Pussycat Bar, the Lock and Key. Charlie Low's Diamond Horseshoe Restaurant, teetering on the edge of respectability, was a place that fascinated them. Marita and Deidra, as little girls, would go into the ladies room, an all powder-puff pink place, and watch the bar girls put one more layer of kohl around their eyes...

This Fourth of July the three older kids wanted to go through Wanchai to see behind those doors.

We figured that after a year at college in the States, there would not be much that shocked them, and let them go.

Chris stayed on the boat with us.

Shore leave had been curtailed that night for the sailors on U.S. ships because of the nature of the holiday. Drunk Brits and American sailors might be drawn into a reenactment of 1776 with a fist fight or two, so the Suzy Wong area was not as populated as usual.

But the famous Hong Kong flesh trade kept busy—always busy—and there were some Americans sailors.

The kids started out at the Yacht Club. A bunch of students from HKIS whose parents also belonged to the club, went to the shower rooms at the pool and changed into costume for the night. White shorts, red and white striped socks, blue T-shirts, red hats—anything red, white and blue. They cheekily stopped by at the Yacht Club bar to wish all the Brits a happy Fourth of July, then went out to see what was on the other side of those dark doors behind the neon lights.

Marita told us about it when they came back the next morning.

"Don't worry, Mom. We didn't have enough money to do any serious damage. We just looked. We did collect enough change among us to buy a few boxes of gummed red stars, and every time we saw an American sailor, we stuck a red star on him and gave him a kiss—old patriotic spirit, you know."

"Rita...in Wanchai?"

"Mom, prostitutes don't earn their living by sticking red stars on sailors. I think they understood. And then...oh yeah, I nearly forgot to tell you the main thing. Our stars were all gone, and we only had a little money left, when we walked past this bar where a funny old man with no teeth was standing outside. He nodded and smiled at us, and said, 'Come in! Come in!'

"We told him we didn't have any money, but he just laughed and said, 'Never mind. I got no money, too! I give you flee dinks! Happy American seven moon four day!'

"I guess he was used to having sailors celebrate the 4th of July, but this was really neat. We went into this creepy big bar, and there was nobody inside. It looked like it used to be nice, with red and gold dragons carved on the walls, when there were more sailors here during the middle of the war, but now it was all dusty and deserted. There were a couple of girls behind the bar, and the old man told them to give us free Cokes. Then he put money in the juke box and asked us if we'd like to dance."

"Nobody wanted to at first, and then Mike and Dede started doing the hustle, you know, that brother and sister thing they do, and everybody started joining in. The girls came from behind the bar and wanted us to teach them the new dance steps...and before I knew it, I was doing the bump with this cute little Chinese girl. She was just about my age, maybe younger, and all of a sudden we bumped, and I realized this kid I was dancing with was a prostitute—a real Wanchai whore, and I felt so weird. I wondered what it would be like if she were me...going to college...and I were her, doing what she does to live...

"Mom, do you know how weird that made me feel?"

There were tears in Marita's eyes.

I did.

I never asked Mike what he felt about that night. Boys seldom discuss such things with their moms, but Mike and I were on better terms than we used to be. It had been good for me to finally dare to write the Kentucky book, to let all the ghosts and dragons of the past go. I did not need to hover over him, afraid. Mike would be a good man, very much his own person and not the shadow of somebody else.

I was glad that all our kids were growing up to be strong compassionate people. So many children of expats lost their way in drugs and too much money. I was grateful that the path of our journey had led us back to the U.S. for their high school education. God knows, Pawling High School was not heaven on earth, but it gave them a good place to see what it meant to be Americans—an identity no better and no worse than any other identity, but, thankfully, their own.

There was a letter in the mail from Harper and Row. As usual, my heart skipped a beat, hoping everything was still on schedule.

Frances Lindley needed legal permission from me for a section of the Kentucky story that included Harlan Sanders, better known to the world as Colonel Sanders, the Kentucky Fried Chicken king. Sanders lived in Corbin, the town in Kentucky where we had gone to buy our supplies. He and my father had been quite good friends. At Christmas, Sanders himself shut down his restaurant and cooked a chicken dinner for our whole group of 120 children and adults. If Sanders thought we needed a better road out to the children's home, he would go straight to the governor and petition our cause. Several times I was one of "the girls" with my father and Sanders as he zipped along at one hundred miles an hour on the road from Lexington to Frankfort, hell bent on some agenda. The first piece of art I ever sold was to Mr. Sanders, for ten dollars.

Now I needed to contact him, but how?

I was living on a boat in China.

He was living in Shelbyville, Kentucky.

I had no address, no phone number, so we reserved a three-minute international call at Cable and Wireless down at the Ocean Terminal. I called Shelbyville, Kentucky, asking the operator for Harlan Sanders' number. Luckily, he was famous. She put me through to him and before I knew it, I was talking to Sanders.

When I told him who I was, he said,

"Well I'll be damned. I was wondering what happened to you. Where are you?"

"In Hong Kong, Mr. Sanders. I need you to help me."

"What's the problem?"

"No problem. You see, I'm writing a book about our life in Kentucky, and there's no way I can write it without telling about you. You did so much for us there."

"So what do you need from me? Money? Everybody needs money from me now..."

"No, all I need is permission to use your name. You're a famous man now."

"Yeah, for whatever that's worth. I'll tell you what. You send me a piece of paper and I'll sign my name, if I can get around all these damned lawyers. You can write whatever you want, sweetheart. You take care of yourself now..."

The phone clicked off, the three minutes gone. Bless his heart. I could see him so clearly: big, warmhearted, sweaty, complex man, equal parts of saint and sinner...

It was no wonder he and my father got along so well. It was framed and on the wall in his restaurant…

There is so much good in the worst of us,
And so much bad in the best of us,
That it little behooves any of us,
To say aught about the rest of us.

The summer passed so quickly—swimming in the pool, going out to sea, diving from the boat into water so blue it seemed unreal, snorkeling, building fires on the beach, building memories for a lifetime.

We took the boat to Aberdeen Harbor to have it slipped, an awesome process. The sixth-five foot junk was put on skids and pulled up out of the water on ropes with pulleys, getting it into position far up on a rack where the whole hull was exposed.

It was towering, enormous. In the water it was a big boat—up in the air with the whole hull exposed it looked like Noah's ark.

Colonies of sea creatures had attached themselves to the wooden structure. They had to be scraped. The hull had to be tested for weak spots in the Yucca wood. It had to be repainted white.

For four days we lived on the boat, suspended in space. The older kids came and went, catching the Aberdeen bus to the downtown. Ju Gwong's family lived in Aberdeen, so he was never far away. At night the teeming mass of Aberdeen boat dwellers moved slowly, lights on the many sampans and the quiet hum of families doing what families do everywhere: eating, sleeping, living.

Gordon and the older kids came and went each day, climbing up a huge ladder to get into the boat. It was an out-of-the-water boat experience. Every day small men scraped and painted, tapping and testing the hull, and seeing if we were sound. Chris and I watched.

The last day on the dry dock in Aberdeen, we awoke in the morning feeling there was something different in the air. The sky was still deceptively calm, but it had rained during the night and the sea was perturbed. Long, white-fringed waves reached up on the beach, then scuttled back to churn with the rest in an angry swirling huddle.

There was a feeling of enchantment in the wind as Chris and I headed for the beach. Gordon had gone to work at Mei Foo, and just the two of us were out exploring. The sand was warm and wet under our bare feet, and the cool wind tore at our hair. We scrambled over rocks that jutted out to the sea, calling to each other to witness some new treasure, some miraculous find. During the night someone had built a fire on the ragged rocks and roasted sea urchins, and we poked at the bone-like spines and precise flower-like shells, charred to a lifeless grey in the ashes.

We scrambled over the rocks, jeans rolled up and sweatshirts flapping in the wind. It was a magic morning, a morning suspended in time when a mother and her son were the same age, when time and age within a few short decades were of no consequence, where both of us felt equally wise and infinitely small.

We jumped down from the rocks and ran along the far beach, racing each other and the wind, collapsing on the sand, careless of the dampness. The waves had come up in the night and the beach was strewn with lovely white shells. It was an unusual sight, not there the night before; a field of treasures like one would dream of finding and then awake with empty hands, but they were there, dreamlike, yet real, bony-beige white shells with glowing pink translucent tints.

We ran here and there, shouting above the wind, delirious with the wonder of them.

"Look at this one, Mom!'

"Oh, and this one, Chris!"

"Oh, Mom, this one is so beautiful…look!"

I glanced at his young child's face, exquisite summer tan with a ruddy translucent glow, like a treasure from the sea. Everything about his face was lovely, and at ten, so searingly transient. He was like a beach before a storm, with all of the wild beauty and none of the danger…

I took the shell carefully from his hands, huge and white and tinted pink, and felt my throat tighten.

"May I keep it?" I asked.

"Forever," he said solemnly.

"I think we've got enough now," I said. "Why don't we leave them here and walk to the end of the beach."

"Will they be safe?"

"Safe as can be. There's nobody here but you and me."

We walked wobble-legged down the sandy stretch, my arm around his shoulder and his arm around my waist, stamping heel prints into the sand. The waves were getting stronger, surging up in sheets of foam and gliding back into their dark swirls. Up and down, come and go, reach and run. There was something deeply moving in the rhythm of the sea, like love-making or the contractions of childbirth—a wild joyous ecstasy that bordered on pain.

I gave Chris an impulsive hug.

"I'm so glad you were born."

"I'm glad I was, too. What was it like when I was born?"

"Happy. A lot of pain and a lot of struggle, and then you were there, a beautiful little man who looked at me in a puzzled way, like you wondered what was going on."

"What did I look like?"

"You were wet and slippery, like you'd just had a long swim, and the doctor laid you on my tummy, like the biggest present in the world…and I was so excited all I could say was thank you, oh thank you!"

"But didn't I look funny?"

"Oh no, you looked at me, solemn as an owl, and I felt like I'd always known you and we'd always be friends."

Chris's small arm tightened around my waist, and he looked up, his face glowing from the wind.

"I was so silly when I was a little kid," he smiled. "I used to want to marry you when I grew up."

"Lots of little boys feel that way. It's all a part of learning to sort out the different ways you love people. Do you remember what I told you when you were a little kid?"

"I do, because I was worried. I couldn't marry you because you were already married to Dad, and I thought if I had another girlfriend your feelings would be hurt."

"I knew you felt that way."

"And then you told me that every man gets to have two special women in his life: a mother and a wife. The mother is there when he gets born…"

"And she'll be there, no matter what," I prompted. "And he doesn't have to worry about losing her—she'll always love him."

"And then he gets to choose the other special person himself," Chris said. "And he takes a new person into the family."

"And that's good!" I said.

"And that's good!" he sang. "I'm happy that everything is good."

I caught him up in both arms, and we twirled and danced in the wind and the sand…

The shells were waiting in a pile on the beach, and we gathered as many as our hands and pockets could hold. It was beginning to rain, big wet splashing drops, driven by the wind. There was a shout from the direction of the junk, and Ju Gwong was waving. He thrust his hand in the air and held up three fingers.

"Oh, we'd better run," I called to Chris. "It looks like typhoon number three is up!"

If Gordon had known the storm would come up so fast he would never have left the boat that morning. There had been only a stand-by signal at seven o'clock, and after a summer of waiting out stand-by signals, no one had worried. But now the storm was coming, and to leave the big junk up on the slipway, exposed to the wild winds, was to invite disaster. The only choice left was to lower it into the stormy water and try to head for the typhoon shelter.

Ju Gwong found two boat builders who could help him get back to the typhoon shelter, and Chris and I stood helplessly by while they quickly made preparations for letting the boat down. The steel cables on the power-driven winches relaxed to let the big junk drop back into the water, inch by inch. When the junk was afloat and towed far enough away from the shore to avoid jamming the propellers, the motors began throbbing and we were on the way.

The trip back to the shelter was not as wild as we had feared. The swells were heavy, and we had to tuck away everything moveable to keep it from flying across the decks. I checked to see where the life jackets were— stored inside the bar. We plowed ahead through the grey churning water. The sea was warm if we did have to don the life jackets… It took almost two hours to go the short distance between Aberdeen and Causeway Bay, the engines laboring against the heavy seas. The western end of the harbor was battened down against the storm. Debris and bits of trees were flying through the air.

The brownstone breakwater looked like the gates of heaven when we rounded its edges and headed for the shelter. The water inside the sea wall was solid with boats.

We nosed through the waterway and up ahead saw a welcome sight. Our two moorings were open.

Ju Gwong guided the junk into our spot. In a few moments we were tied and moored, and all hands on deck were lashing us firmly to the next junk. Mr. Lee was helping, tying us to his boat. We were solid and snug against the storm, part of the giant flotilla of storm fighters.

I put the kettle on and made tea for everybody.

By the time Gordon and the rest of the family reached the junk, the signal was up to number eight out of a possible ten. The city had come to a halt, and everyone was running for cover. The sea was so choppy that sampans were suicide, and the last three members of the family came home hopping over the bows of the five junks wedged between us and the shore.

On land, the signs flopped and rattled in the wind, and the bamboo poles from construction sites hurled through the air like deadly javelin. Windows shattered and storm swept across the city with violent gale force.

But on the junk, snug among all the other boats, we hardly moved at all. The lounge was cozy with the rain beating down on the covered deck. The kids watched *The Pink Panther* and made their favorite popcorn on the galley stove.

Chris got out the shells we had collected that morning and sorted them in rows for everyone to admire.

"I kind of like storms," he grinned. "If it hadn't come, we wouldn't have all these good shells, would we, Mom?"

I glanced at the shells, and at him, hoping I could remember him always the way he had looked that morning—a joyful child, open-armed, exulting in the wind, singing a song of life and freedom...

And I hoped the woman he chose someday would love him as much as the woman he was born to.

The kids were working on knockout tans to go back to school.

One day there was a thump on the side of the boat and someone came climbing up the ladder. It was a day when we were all on the boat, greased to the gills and lying out on the deck sunbathing.

He came up past the galley to the bow, extending his hand.

"Hi, I'm Mark Gabor, from Random House in New York. Do you mind if I chat with you for a moment?"

We all scrambled for our towels and tried to wipe off at least a little of the oil.

"Hello Mark," Gordon said. "What can we do for you?"

He was small and dark and wiry, a very New York looking guy.

"I'm on a round-the-world tour to photograph houseboats for Random House. I'm doing a coffee table book on people who live on the water around the world. I saw your beautiful junk from the shore and came out. Do you mind if I get some shots?"

We all scrambled around this unusual and unexpected creature.

"Make yourself at home," Gordon invited. "Take any shots you like."

The kids were fascinated. Marita brought him a cold drink. Chris followed around in his footsteps.

Mark stayed with us for the afternoon, photographing every angle of the boat. We invited him to stay for dinner, but he said he had to meet someone.

All four kids were listening to his every word. Random House—*Houseboats Around the World*.

We would be in a book!

"I'll bring all the photos to New York," Mark explained. "I can't guarantee which boats they'll choose for the final cut, but I'm pretty sure yours will make it. This is beautiful!"

Mark came back the next day and asked us if we could tell him how to get to Macao. He had four ready guides. They took him on the hydrofoil, stayed the day with him, showed him around Macao, and came home, sunburned and excited.

"I'll be in touch…" he promised. "As soon as I know, I'll send you a letter."

It was months before we heard, but when the letter came he had included a copy.

Houseboats Around the World.

We were the only foreign family written about in Hong Kong, and there was our Concerto, inside and out, with Mr. Lee's boat on the next page. We had made it.

Mark wrote on the first page: *Cheers! Stop and visit me when you come to New York.*

The summer was over. The twins were back in their second year in college. De was a high school senior, and Chris was entering sixth grade. We had run into trouble with his piano lessons—the woman who was teaching him was forbidden by her husband to come out to the boat. We were in a "bad" neighborhood.

A bad neighborhood?

Maybe the Peales were right…

It was wonderful to hear Chris play his music on the boat. Could we find another teacher willing to take a sampan out to a junk and teach one small boy?

We found one man who taught at his music shop in Causeway Bay, but Chris told us he leaned over him and had bad breath. Could he please forget lessons for a while?

Guideposts Kindergarten had opened the beginning of September. The sparkling white walls and red carpets were balanced with royal blue and yellow panels for displays. The Montessori books and methods had been taught to the teachers by Maggie Tam during the summer. The children's warm weather uniforms were adorable: little blue jumper skirts or short pants buttoned at the shoulders, tiny red and white checkered shirts. The winter uniforms were posted in a window display downstairs on the shopping level to give the parents a taste of things to come.

But most important of all, hundreds of beautiful small Chinese children assembled in the rooms. They were being taught to sing and dance as well as read and write in two languages.

The big red Hong Kong bus in the open play area and the child figures of Marita's mural added more interest. The school was a reality!

The *Guideposts* logo had been carved into a sign. The children were learning the school song, getting ready for the grand opening.

The Peales were coming.

The last time they had seen the space at Mei Foo it was a dusty, wasteland construction site. Now it was a vibrant, beautiful school, with teachers and music, and books and color, and hundreds of lovely children.

We were excited, and a little apprehensive. They had not communicated with us much since what they considered the "boat fiasco." Arthur Gordon, the editor of *Guideposts* magazine, and his wife Pam, were coming with them. They were all staying in the Mandarin Hotel.

The day of the open house, the Peales were truly impressed, and, I thought, almost chagrinned. The school was open. It was licensed with the Hong Kong government. It would be a credit to *Guideposts* magazine.

They were especially impressed with Maggie Tam. Where had Gordon found her? What were her ties? Anglican Church?

Then the hundreds of little children sang for them, the school song. They had printed copies of the words handed to them.

Little children all are we,
Learning every day to be,
Kind and loving, strong and free,
Building our society.
Yes, we are learning,
Yes we are growing,
Yes we are learning,
God's children all to be.

There was nothing pressured or doctrinaire about it. It was the simple acknowledgement of a fact. These Chinese children, whatever their background, were all God's children with no strings attached.

But seriously, if they had sung Diddle Diddle dumpling, my son John, anybody would have cried. They were just so darn cute. And they were smart. By the time these kids were five they would have begun to read and write in two languages.

The Peales were obviously pleased, but a little stiff with us. We invited the four of them, the Peales and the Gordons, out to our boat for dinner. The Gordons accepted, but the Peales preferred to go to their hotel.

Arthur and Pam Gordon took the sampan out to our boat and climbed up the ladder, good sports that they were. We cooked a dinner for them. We ate out on the aft deck by lantern light. They loved the boat.

"Ah, Norman's probably not too pissed, you know, but Ruth is. She's got her ideas of what's proper, and Norman just agrees. He probably wouldn't care that much. But you guys have done such a splendid job; she ought to be ashamed of herself for being so judgmental…" Arthur Gordon said.

"It does make us uncomfortable," Gordon admitted. "We've given it everything we have."

Arthur Gordon smiled and shook his head.

"Ah, just ignore it. They'll get over it. Dr. Peale's a practical fellow. He'll go with whatever works."

They had been good to us. We hoped the boat would not continue to be a sore point. Their disappointment did cast a pall over something basically joyous.

Maybe three years would be enough.

Then, one Saturday when Gordon and Ju Gwong were washing the windows of the wheelhouse lounge, Gordon leaned his hand against the wood. His hand went through the wall.

Dry rot.

The bane of boats. The hull had checked out solid, but the wheelhouse wall was going.

It was not a big deal. A carpenter would have to come and repair the damage, but it flipped a switch with Gordon.

We would have to sell the boat.

Perhaps, with all things considered, it would be wiser to move to one of the small apartments in Mei Foo Sun Chuen, where he could be closer to his work and we would not have the pressure of disapproval hovering over our heads.

We put our beloved boat on the market, and sold it to a man from Scotland with a Japanese wife and one small boy.

That was the short story. The long story was many months of people tramping through our boat, loving it, not buying it, listening to the stories of people who wanted it and were going to buy it if…

One bizarre story was of the man who would buy it if he came back alive. He had invented a gasoline additive that would cut emissions greatly, and the Swedish government was interested. The problem was that it would also greatly reduce the amount of gasoline needed to run a car, and the "petroleum people" had warned him not to put it on the market. He was on his way to a meeting in Europe. If he succeeded he would be rich; if he was unlucky, he might be killed. He would be back to buy the boat if he was still alive.

He never came back and we never knew if he had been killed or if he had just spun one more tale…

Gordon found an apartment on the seventh floor of a sixteen-story apartment building in Mei Foo Sun Chuen. Its total square footage was 450 square feet .

Four hundred and fifty square feet?

But we had lived on a boat. It did not seem small to us. It was cleverly laid out with a small entry, a tiny galley kitchen, a living-dining room, two bedrooms and a bath with a connecting hallway. One whole side of the main room was total windows, floor to ceiling. Seven stories up this induced a bit of vertigo, so we put up a large, see-through bamboo blind and covered the opposite side of the room in smoky grey mirrors. That gave the illusion of twice as much space (900 sq. ft.), and took away the feeling of being perched on the edge of a cliff.

The two bedrooms were enough, because Chris was the only one home. During her senior year at HKIS it was discovered that due to changing schools, De was only one credit short of graduation, and she had the mid-year option of beginning college for the February term, and graduating from HKIS retroactively.

Deidra and I were still struggling about smoking and other things that we could not agree on.

"De, I think it's time you and I parted company for a while. You are not listening to me, and I think you'd do better on your own. Go on and start college in February, and come back next summer when you've got the wind out of your ears."

She was accepted at Hope College, Gordon's Alma Mater, for the February term.

She was excited.

We saw her off at Kai Tak Airport.

She had turned 18 at Christmas.

Ready or not, she was off. The irrepressible Deidra was on her own.

Between the boat sale and the remodeling of the Mei Foo Sun Chuen apartment, we rented a horrid place halfway up the peak. It was the worst place we ever lived. If, God forbid, we had to go back in the kitchen at night after the lights had been turned out, and flipped them back on, hundreds of roaches had their late-night stroll interrupted—a swarm of awful brown things with dark hairy legs.

It was also there that I mailed the last re-writes to Frances Lindley, and totally depleted that day, went into the bathroom and fainted, coming to in a pool of blood.

The phone was ringing. My mom, who wrote regularly but never once had called, was on the line from the States.

"Are you all right?" she asked anxiously.

"Mom!"

"I was just sitting here and I suddenly had this strong feeling that you were in danger. Are you all right?"

I told her I was bleeding.

"Where's Gordon?"

"At work."

"Get a taxi and go to the hospital emergency room."

"I don't know if I'm bleeding enough."

"Go. Get a cab. Get to the hospital!"

At some visceral level, we were still connected. I went down and sat on the curb until a cab came by, and went to Matilda Hospital.

The doctor called Gordon.

I had a tumor the size of a four month's pregnancy. My body was trying to throw it off. I was hemorrhaging.

I woke up after the surgery with Gordon and Chris leaning over me, love on their faces.

I had a hysterectomy.

Oh, well, I was getting rid of my unneeded parts and pieces.

Ready to hit the road again and go on.

Thank goodness I had four kids.

When I left the hospital, Gordon had moved us into the new apartment in Mei Foo Sun Cheun. It was really quite charming. We had a round white table with a big red glass half-globe lamp over it (two, counting the one in the mirrors), a sofa in black plush that pulled out to make two single beds, our first real Persian rug, bunks in Chris' room, and a bedroom for us—lovely, but so tiny we had to stand on the bed to open the closet doors.

And work was just down the elevator and across the mall.

The Peales came back that spring, and greatly approved of our new, more respectable, quarters. They saw the student body, now five hundred strong, all dressed in their red blazers and navy jumpers, reciting the Lord's Prayer in Chinese .

Things were in order.

Maggie Tam continued to fascinate them. She was a middle-aged Chinese woman. She had a family still in China, and she had the kind of class that appealed to Mrs. Peale. She was a committed Anglican with a real passion for teaching the children to have a positive outlook on life. She was not one of those heavy mission types who sat on one's face like a wet frog.

She met their approval. We were glad.

They met us in a little café that was part of the Mei Foo shopping mall, for coffee.

Doctor Peale was interested in the book at Harper and Row, coming out in the summer.

"Good publishing house, Harper and Row," he said approvingly. "I wish you all the best luck."

Mrs. Peale eyed me keenly.

"Exactly what is this book about?" she asked carefully.

"My experiences growing up in Kentucky, in a mission that became a cult and turned dangerous…" I began.

I could see her eyes narrowing.

"I hope you will remember who your employers are, and do no harm to religious work," she said.

I knew what she meant. Remember which side your bread is buttered on.

We did not discuss it further.

With the book safely in New York, I began to dig out my oil paints. How long had it been since I'd painted? Years? Probably not since the portrait of Gina and the other pieces I had sold to the Klays in Orange City.

I wanted to paint differently, not so much realism, some sort of art that would be interpretive, but not abstract.

Photos…

Photos of Chinese children on a beach.

Of women, talking.

Of people in markets.

But not like that, not exactly.

Take a photo and strip it down to its essential form—lines with flat areas of color: two women sitting under a tree, talking, all red and black and white; boys digging in sand at the beach, gold black and white; a market where the fruits were circles, surrounded by white lines. My imagination had grown.

Paintings that were small, powerful and jewel-like.

The first reviews of the book were wonderful. Newspapers all over the United States were giving it raves. I was compared to Willa Cather and Faulkner. It was sent to thirteen movie companies.

We waited for the all-important *New York Times* review slated for the last weekend in July.

The window on 53rd Street was filled with the book, which the marketing department called *The Self Anointed*. I hated the title. It sounded like some sort of self abuse. I was overruled.

We were waiting for the 21-gun salute, as Frances Lindley called it. Then came the letter...

"So sorry. The *New York Times* strike. The day your review was slated, the *New York Times* began its strike. No one knows how long it will last. They will not be able to work retroactively.

A group of authors, including me, had just been dumped in the cracks.

Damn!
All that work—all those dreams!
What was going on?
Frances Lindley sent me a letter from Paramount, from Barry Diller, saying that their group had stayed up most of one night trying to decide whether to make a major American movie out of my story. They decided America was not ready for it.

And there was religious opposition to what I had written. Powerful people wanted it banned. I had touched their core...contributions.

From so far behind the rest of the world, I had leaped too far ahead. In 1978, America was not ready for it.

The kids came back that summer—all six of us in 450 square feet. After living on the boat, it was remarkably peaceful. The girls took a trip to southern China, to the area on the Yangtze River where the peaks and rocks look too magical to be true, and had a ball. They ate so much that no one else on the tour wanted to share a table with them. They sweated so much they came home pounds lighter. They had a new motto:

"The family that sweats together, sticks together."

They enjoyed poking around in all the shops in Mei Foo—fabrics, jewelry, wonderful little jade pieces.

Of course, no one had any spare money, but they had fun.

Gordon had been eyeing a jade horse from China, a beautiful light grey-green classic horse from northern China. Day after day he passed it on his way to the school. The man in the shop explained each part of the horse to him, detailing its fine lines.

The advance from the book had not been large, but it was sizeable to us. For Gordon's birthday, I used the whole advance to buy him the jade horse. He was thrilled. In the twelve-year cycle of the Chinese calendar, he and Chris were both born in the year of the horse. Someday, when Gordon and I were finished with the horse, it would go to Chris.

I felt like I would die of disappointment that summer, but I did not, of course. I painted. That had been a refuge from a broken heart when I was growing up, and it rescued me now. Someday I would get back to painting. To hell with those editors and their publishing houses. I hated doing things that I had no control over.

And, my heart was not truly broken. It had just been kicked in the teeth. I still had Gordon and my four wonderful kids. They were what deeply mattered.

When the Peales came back that winter to visit the school, we had made up our minds. The kindergarten was going well. Maggie Tam was totally in control, even thinking of reaching out to start another branch of Guideposts, and upping the enrollment to one thousand in the next year. The Hong Kong government was giving the school highest marks.

Gordon decided he had done the job he was asked to do. In the spring of 1979, we would leave Hong Kong.

The Peales invited us to their room at the Mandarin Hotel. They were all effusive praise.

Gordon thanked them for the opportunities they had given us, and told them of our plans, in light of the three-year term they had previously mentioned.

Mrs. Peale looked shocked.

"Oh, but you're surely not thinking of leaving, are you?"

"I thought that was the plan," Gordon said calmly.

"Oh, but the school is doing so well. You've been so successful. Surely we can forget the unfortunate events under which we issued those terms."

"No, I think that having established the school, it is really better for it to be run under Chinese leadership."

Doctor Peale shook his head and looked at his wife.

"Well..." he said, as though he did not know what to say. "Well, uh, we'll surely try to find something for you in New York, maybe at Marble Collegiate..."

He was a kindly man.

The problem was that they simply did not know what made us tick. Maybe we didn't know ourselves, but we knew when it was missing. And it was missing.

We were walking down the corridor of the Mandarin Hotel when Gordon asked me, "What would you think of working for them in New York?"

I don't remember exactly what I said, but it meant no.

We were on the countdown for leaving Hong Kong—this time for good. Gordon and Mike took a trip to mainland China that winter. China had finally opened to Americans, and the border no longer seemed so formidable. In April I went with a tour group. It was strange to finally be welcomed into a country that had been forbidden to us for so long. The world was opening up, and we were opening with it.

We went to Stanley Village and said our goodbyes. Our house on the corner had been remodeled as a French restaurant…on a Chinese street. We walked through the rooms, amazed that we had once considered limiting our life to this small structure. Now it was an integral part of what we had experienced, and we would forever keep it in our hearts as a part of the whole.

In February the Peales contacted a man from the American Bible Society in New York to tell them of our availability. Layton Holmgren came to Hong Kong and interviewed us. It was a secure feeling to know there would be a job waiting for us in New York, at least as a starting point.

Gordon went to the Ocean Terminal and had suits tailored. He would have an executive position, and needed to dress the part.

We said goodbye to this city that had been such a part of our lives for twenty years.

As the plane lifted off from Kai Tak Airport there was a sense of finished business, of having completed all that we could learn from this situation, unless we decided to stay on and become completely Chinese.

And that was not possible. We were Americans.

The apartment on Riverside Drive was a long narrow brownstone on 79th Street, with windows facing the street and rooms burrowing back into the building. The ground floor had a backyard garden, but on the third floor we had only back windows.

Settling into the city as residents was a first-time experience. Gordon would work on 59th Street, Chris would go to Collegiate Boys School, and I would be close to the publishing world.

This time we did not bring furniture from Michigan. We went to Macy's and bought a large sofa-bed which had to be hauled up three floors of narrow stairs. Fortunately, the delivery men were cursing in Italian, which we did not understand.

Gordon had a spacious corner office and a free parking space. He had smartly tailored suits, and well-shined shoes, and an apprehensive look on his face. The people at ABS welcomed him, and gave him a job thirteen other people had been hired for…and failed.

Surely he could do it!

The job was to replace a woman who was retiring, and did not really want to retire. She was hiring people and proving that she could not be replaced.

The salary was good.

Gordon tried being creative, as he had been in Hong Kong. Creative did not work.

At six months he told the staff that he admired their organization, but did not feel he was the person for the post.

They persuaded him to stay for six months more. He did so, quietly arranging for admission to Columbia University Teachers College in the fall.

The job ended, and with it went the salary.

Gone was the Riverside Drive apartment. We would be living in married student quarters at Teachers College.

When in doubt, go back to school.

Gordon's plan was to start a program for a Masters in ESL, thinking that in the future he might be qualified to work in New York's Chinatown, perhaps in a program geared toward Chinese immigrants.

We moved into Columbia's married student housing. It was a small, one-bedroom, one bath apartment between Broadway and Columbus with a tiny kitchen, a fold-out couch living room, and a table made in Romania that could fold up when not in use. In the one bedroom we put two bunks for the kids to use when they came from school. They would need a place to come for the summer. We would sleep on the couch in the living room.

In that apartment, we were not concerned with décor. It was pure survival. We were like cliff-dwellers living in a cave on the side of a mountain.

But just being in New York City was wonderful. Hong Kong and New York were both big cities, and we had become big city people. Busses...subways...even walking the whole length of Broadway from Columbia to 53rd Street where Harper and Row had their new offices was no problem. We loved it.

Our kids were city kids, and would do well.

They came to New York for the summer, piled into the bunks and took it all in stride. Deidra found a job at the Elaine Powers exercise studio. Marita hired on as a waitress in a restaurant on Broadway. Mike bluffed his way into a job as a chef on Amsterdam. Gordon took two teaching jobs at City College. I submitted a new manuscript to Harper and Row, and we all got ready for Gordon's fall program.

I went to talk to Frances Lindley. This was easier than all the mail exchanges, although she warned me that out-of-town authors get more attention than those living in the city.

"I'm sorry about what happened to your Kentucky book," she apologized. "Welcome to the vicissitudes of writing and publishing. You can't take it personally. It's only the writers who persevere who ever make it. You've been incredibly lucky so far, but you've got to keep on working."

"Do you think I should?"

She leaned back and appraised me through the smoke of her constant cigarette.

"You have a strong talent," she said, "but you're a bit spoiled. Now, this new manuscript you've submitted, of your life on the boat, it's just a bit too… precious…"

That appraising look again.

"You've set a high bar for yourself in writing the Kentucky story. Never mind what happened with the *New York Times*; that's a damn good story. Keep on writing at that level and someday you might be a great writer."

"But what's wrong with the boat story?" I asked, puzzled.

She gave me that weary look, as though there was not enough energy in the whole world to tell me what the problem was.

"Dig," she said. "Probe. Show us, don't tell us. And stop being so damn self-righteous."

Wham.

I went back to the Colombia apartment and looked at the writing. Okay. I could make it tougher, dirty it up a bit, maybe play up that scene with Lee. I could start the first chapter in the middle of the typhoon and the horrible stench of the shrimp paste drying on the boats…

The more I tried to write it, the worse it got. I submitted the first two chapters again, and we had another meeting.

I noticed she was not well. She looked thin and grey, and coughed constantly.

"I'm going to be under intense medical treatment the next few months," she said. "Why don't you lay this aside and we'll work on it later?"

Then she told me that she had lung cancer. It was serious.

I took the two chapters I had re-written for her and dumped them down the chute to the garbage. I kept my original work and laid it aside. Later. I could not write to suit someone else…someone so sick.

Summer settled over New York City, almost as hot and humid as Hong Kong.

The kids had acquired boyfriends and girlfriends at college. Life was getting more complex. Mike had met a girl in Iowa who was from New York City. Her parents were Jewish, and they wanted Mike to come and live with them for the summer.

What could we say?

Deidra had met a boy in Michigan from Long Island. They dated that summer...until she stood on a street corner waiting for him one time too many, and she decided to dump him when they got back to school.

Marita had met a professor who was dating her. Did they allow this at schools?

They were all over eighteen now, and had to make their own choices. We hoped they could live with the choices they made.

Chris was in Collegiate Boys School. No uniforms this time, just ties and blazers. He had tested in at a good level for his age in everything but math. The math at HKIS was a year behind Collegiate School.

The headmaster at the school was dubious about this.

"Give him the extra work," I said. "He can do it."

And he did. Chris worked long hours of make-up math. He asked us not to get a TV, as it would distract him. That worked out fine, as we could not afford it anyhow. He caught up with his classmates and began to make friends. He loved the school. Fortunately, Dr. Peale had pulled some strings and Chris' tuition was paid...a good thing with so little money coming in.

Where were we going?

Nobody knew, but we kept going.

College fees were coming up. We scraped our savings.

"You'll all have to work," Gordon said, "and try to get as many grants and scholarships as you can. Only take out loans if there's no other way."

De was mugged that summer. Two punks tried to take her watch. She told them it was hers and she was not going to give it to them. What right did they have to take something she had worked for?

Fortunately, they were just kids, and she scared them off. They could have been a few years older and had a knife or gun. We told her next time to give them the watch.

Marita met Woody Allen in the restaurant where she worked. She was so breathless she forgot to take his order.

We saw her coming home late at night, sitting on the bunk and counting her tips, and vowed never to under-tip again...

How we got through that summer I'll never know, but somehow we did. By the time school opened in the fall, Gordon was well into his program.

Deidra went back to Hope and the twins to Grinnell, and Chris was enjoying Collegiate.

It was at Collegiate School that I met Fran Wigotsky. She worked for Children's Television in New York City, and wanted to read the Kentucky story Harper's had published.

"Oh, this should be a movie!" she said after reading it. "I can picture this whole story so clearly!"

I told her about Paramount's response.

"Why don't you write the script yourself?" she suggested.

"I haven't the foggiest idea how to write a film script."

"I have a few scripts you can read that have been produced on TV," she offered. "Would you like to see them?"

I would.

It didn't look too difficult.

So, I began to write a film script of the Kentucky story. I worked on it all fall and winter, fueled with black coffee and hamburger.

That winter in New York City, in that cramped little apartment, should have been miserable, but it was not. We were all busy and happy. Gordon and I were 46 and 49, close, and very much in love, feeling young and strong, and full of hope that something good would happen. Chris was bringing friends home from school to play Dungeons and Dragons. He was one of the top students in his class. I baked brownies for his friends, who seemed not to notice our sparse quarters, or at least they were too polite to say anything. I was writing the script, not knowing what I would ever do with it.

I got the manuscript of *Festival* (the Stanley Village story) back from Harpers, and sent it on to Zondervans in Michigan. They had done books for us, and said yes, they would publish it. They were delighted.

Maybe New York wasn't everything. There was a whole world out there in the Midwest.

And, in spite of the Methodists, *Faces of God* had done better than expected. Groups at retreats were reading it—it was being studied all over the U.S. They wanted me to come and speak to them, to break through the complex walls of theology and see the Creative Power in the faces of the everyday people in their lives. I took every chance I had to go out and talk, excited about sharing the ideas, and hoping to earn a little money. Sometimes all I came home with was a gift of jewelry or a ceramic pot made by someone in the church. I tried to be thankful, but it was better when I could contribute a little money to the family struggle.

I went to Florida and spoke at an RCA meeting at the Fontaine Bleu, and flew to California to speak to a group on board the Queen Elizabeth, anchored in LA.

The book was finding its way, but I was not famous. Was that good or bad? It was what it was. Not everyone could accept the idea that ordinary people were the faces of God. It was too close, too threatening...too much to deal with. Keep God in heaven where he belonged. Having him loose in the world, in people, was too messy.

I was waiting at a bus stop downtown Manhattan one day when I noticed a man watching me.

"I like your hat," he smiled.

"Oh thanks," I said, in that way strangers speak to each other in a big city. "Would you like to try it on?"

It was a little purple felt fedora—anybody would look good in it.

We laughed and began chatting. He asked me what I was doing in New York, and I said writing.

"Writing what?"

"Right now I'm working on a film script."

"Ah hah!"

He was a package producer—someone who chose a book and did it as a package of a paperback and a movie-for general distribution.

He wanted to see my script.

I got Fran Wigotsky to check him out. He was a graduate of a film school, and a licensed film producer.

I was delighted!

He read my script, then called me.

"Oh my God," he said. "I'm almost through this thing. It has everything! It will make a wonderful movie!"

I thought I had died and gone to heaven.

Fran had cautioned me not to let the script go without drawing up a legal contract. Harold Rand wanted me to go with him to his lawyer's office and sign a contract. Fran had also warned me not to sign without a limited timeframe and option money...at least thirty thousand.

Harold Rand said he could not come up with that kind of money on short notice. Things were shaky in the entertainment industry right then, so that hung in the breezes.

It was the summer of 1981. Gordon was finishing his Masters in ESL. He went to the offices of the RCA on Riverside Drive and made a proposal. He would love to start an immigrant program in Chinatown, New York, teaching English and establishing a center for young Chinese immigrants, helping them find their way in a new country and culture. Having had a mirror-image experience in Hong Kong, he felt he would be unusually qualified.

The people at 475 were interested. It sounded like a great idea. Yes, they had heard about the Kung Lee School and Guideposts Kindergarten in

Hong Kong. Fine pieces of work, but such programs needed to be funded years in advance, and there was no funding for such a program. Not now...

Sorry...

Gordon was graduating in June. We had three kids in college. He was working three jobs. We had no insurance. Where would we turn?

John Fanslow, director of the ESL program at Columbia Teacher's College, suggested Gordon go to the teacher's fair at Cobo Hall in Detroit. Schools were there from the U.S. and around the world, selecting and hiring teachers.

It was at least something. It couldn't hurt.

I was in the Columbia student apartment when the call came from Gordon. He was in Detroit.

"I just had a couple of interviews," he said. "One was from a school in North Carolina...nice people, but it only pays thirteen thousand a year."

"We couldn't make it."

"I know. The other interview I had was with a guy from Saudi Arabia. He told me about a special program that Aramco Oil Company has this year. They're looking for people turning fifty, professionals, who want a second career. They're sending a hundred American families over this summer. The pay is two or three times what I'd earn here, plus free medical care, housing, travel, and no taxes."

"Where did you say this was?"

"Saudi Arabia."

I felt the little American town fading away...farther than ever...even the little neighborhood in New York City that I had begun to think might have taken its place...

"But we just got back in the U.S.!"

"I know."

"And we don't know anything about that part of the world."

"I know."

There was a pregnant silence.

"I guess that's a good reason to go, isn't it?" I said quietly.

He chuckled.

"That sounds like something you'd say," he said. "Shall we go for it?"

"Go for it," I said.

And I knew we were off and running again.

He came back from Detroit, excited. He had signed a contract to go to Dhahran, Saudi Arabia, to work in the Professional English Language Center of Aramco Oil Company. It had been the Columbia Master's Degree in

ESL, as well as the Masters in Education Administration that had qualified him for the job. It was a perfect fit.

They would even fly our children back and forth to Saudi Arabia, as needed, until they were married.

There was only one problem. They did not want American teenagers. Even the children who attended Aramco schools were sent out of the country after 9th grade. They must go to boarding schools or stay with their relatives in the States. Aramco would pay, but American teens were persona non grata in Saudi Arabia.

Chris could go with us for the summer, but in the fall he would have to leave, either to a boarding school or to stay with a relative in the States and go to school there.

Gordon called his sister Lila in San Francisco. She and her husband Ken immediately offered their home.

"We're happy with our three girls," Lila said, "but we've never had a boy. Chris would be ever so welcome to come and live with us and go to high school here."

It was decided. Chris would go to high school in San Francisco.

Everything happened quickly. Before July 15, we would need to pack something called an e-box, containing everything we would use in the first six weeks, and send it on. We were to report to Houston, Texas for a week of orientation training, then we would fly on to Dhahran, Saudi Arabia.

With one hundred American families—men, women, kids, cats, but no dogs. Dogs were considered unclean.

We flew to Houston by way of Michigan. Chris had recently adopted a black cat named Nicholas, and Nicholas had to go with us. We promised Chris we would take good care of his cat.

Mom and Dad were used to our erratic lifestyle by now, but we still all sat around the big kitchen table—so American—and discussed our move.

Dad was happy we had a job that would pay well. He did not offer to send furniture with us.

Mom was happy that Chris would be with Lila. Their son, Bill, was the other wanderer in the family. He was now an ambassador in Africa, and his children had attended boarding schools like all the other Foreign Service families.

"I'm not too sure about that sometimes," Mom worried. "I think those kids might get awfully lonesome. Lila will take good care of Chris."

No matter how good the arrangement was, I felt an ache in the pit of my stomach. Chris had been so close to us, so involved in our lives. And he was still small. Were we letting him down at an important stage of his life?

But we were all so brave, even Chris.

"This will be the first time I've ever gone to a public school," he reminded us. "I think I'll feel like a real American."

A real American, born in China…and at not quite fifteen, and we were leaving him behind to go to Saudi Arabia.

We flew to Houston.

The orientation program was intense. Women were strictly the property of their husbands in Saudi Arabia. Some women might find work, but they were considered "casuals," and had no rights or benefits. They must be covered at all times if they went to the towns 'off camp.' We were not required to wear veils. On camp there would be no shorts or tight-fitting garments. Hair must be covered if we went to shop in the local markets.

Alcohol was forbidden. Pork was forbidden, and could only be purchased at a special store for infidels.

If a woman broke the law, her husband would go to jail.

And most important of all, we were never, ever, to mention the name of God. Any mention of our faith, in any sense, was strictly forbidden.

It was the first time in our lives we would be taking a job strictly for the money. If we had ever wished that our paycheck would not be tied to our beliefs, this was it.

In a way, it was a relief. What we believed would have to be lived, not spoken.

We were being hired strictly for money—money to stabilize our lives and educate our children.

Money.

It felt so clean.

SECTION FIVE

1981-1990

CHAPTER FIFTEEN

July, 1981

THE NIGHT WE LANDED IN Saudi Arabia it was pitch black and stiflingly hot. We collected our luggage, plus the cat cage, and worked our way through the long immigration lines to the passenger exit. We were met by a representative of Gordon's department and driven to our quarters.

After a short ride through the darkness, we pulled into North Camp, a temporary housing site hastily put up to accommodate the large influx of new employees.

We had been promised family housing, enough space for six when we were all together, and we were eager to see what our new house would be.

We stopped in front of what looked like a large structure, perhaps fifty feet across. It was well lighted and looked welcoming, certainly larger than the cramped quarters in New York. This would be great!

Then we stepped inside, and were confronted by a wall eleven feet from the entry. It was a house trailer.

Not exactly what we had bargained for.

"Only short time," the driver assured us. "Maybe next year you'll be on Main Camp."

We went in and dumped our suitcases. Chris let the cat out of his carry cage. We looked around—four tiny bedrooms, two baths. a central room with a couch and two chairs, a kitchen and a huge bar. Why such a huge bar in a country where alcohol was forbidden?

The air conditioner was cranked up high so the temperature was cool, but the color scheme was definitely hot. Orange, brown, yellow- brown and yellow stripes, brown and orange plaids, dark brown shag rug, heavy brown and orange and yellow flowered drapes.

I started stripping the place down with my eyes.

216

Gordon saw me looking.

"Don't worry about it tonight," he said. "We'll think about it tomorrow. We have to get some sleep first."

"I tried to give Nicholas some water and he won't drink it," Chris said. "That's funny. He even drank out of the toilet in New York."

Well, this was not New York, and if the rest of us had to get used to that fact, Nicholas the cat would, too.

We awoke the next morning with gritty eyes and mouths. Our faces were covered with fine sand. There had been a dust storm in the night, and the dust had found its way through invisible cracks in the trailer. We curled up under the brown, yellow and orange printed spread and stared up at the heavy canopy over the bed. Everything was covered with dust.

We looked at each other.

Oh my God. What had we done?

"It's only a year, if we don't decide to stay," Gordon said.

"I'm not living with these colors for a year. I'm ripping these drapes down and recovering the couch. We have to find a place to buy some cooler light fabrics. I'll go nuts…"

"Patience, patience…" Gordon said. "We have to go down and hand in our passports at the admin building first, and then we'll see if there's a place to buy some fabric."

Luckily, we had a sewing machine in our e-box. They had been delivered, and ours sat outside behind the trailer.

We stood under a huge black rock called a jebel and waited for the bus to come to take us to Main Camp. The sun was just coming up over the flat-line horizon of the desert, a huge, round red globe casting a pink glow over the sand. Sand…sand…sand everywhere… Sand and rocks and trailers, and double-wides.

The bus came—a Greyhound—an American Greyhound bus appearing with a big round desert sun and sand around it.

Was this real?

This was as real as it was going to get.

Main Camp was a different world altogether. Once through the guarded gates the sand gave way to paved streets and lush landscaping. Flowers bloomed in almost unreal profusion. In the center of the camp, the administration buildings were multi-storied. There was a PX-like commissary, a post office, a dining hall, a bank, and leading off in every direction the streets of a smallish town. There was a school, a golf course, and a swimming pool. The golf course had browns, not greens. Sand, of course.

It was a replica of an American town with a slightly military edge. Five thousand people playing American in the middle of the Saudi Desert.

We turned in our passports to the Saudi government and went to the bank to open an account. Employee # 192132. All transactions must be done in cash (riyals), as credit cards were not in use.

The first bus we caught out of camp was to Al Khobar, the closest local town. The town itself was a sprawling village with hotels and street markets—the spicy smell of roasting meat, fabric stalls, gold for sale everywhere.

But the fabric stalls interested me more than the gold. I needed some cool off-white muslin.

We found a little stall and bought 25 yards of white fabric, plus a few cool accent pieces..

"This will get us started," I said. "We can get more if we need it."

Back in North Camp we began to tear the trailer apart. Down came the hot heavy drapes, rolled in a (respectful) ball and stored in a spare bedroom. I sewed up light airy curtains. Next I sewed a cover for the dark plaid couch, and made a few cool-colored throw pillows in blues and greens. The dark heavy canopy came off the bed. We even took the canopy apart and stored it. We rolled up the garish spread. We would find something cooler.

By the end of the week we had every piece of orange, brown and yellow striped, plaid, polka dot and floral fabric out of sight, and we felt cool.

But Nicholas still refused to drink the water. We looked at the pamphlet lying on the kitchen sink that suggested: "If you are pregnant or planning to become pregnant, you may prefer to drink bottled water. This is desalinated sea water, not normally harmful to healthy persons."

I didn't think Nicholas the cat was pregnant, but he knew something we didn't. We had to disguise the water, mixed in his food, or he would die.

But what the heck... We had survived things much worse than this. We decided to take a deep breath and make the best of it.

Besides, we were being paid well.

We had not come here to enjoy the scenery. We needed money. We would buck up and be grateful for a job.

We began to look enviously at people in the doublewides. They were the aristocracy of North Camp. If only we had a doublewide! But they were reserved for newcomers with higher grade codes, engineers and drillers, and pipeline men. Teachers were considered lower grade code people. We would have to wait.

But Gordon kept hounding the housing office.

The people next door, Brad and Kathy, came and knocked on our trailer door. They wanted to be sure we knew what the score was about wine, and were eager to share their recipes with us.

"You can get everything you need at the commissary," Kathy said. "We get un-pasteurized grape juice from Austria, and the rest is just sugar, tea, yeast—it's easy to make. You need two five-gallon glass jugs (sold as water jugs), and some hose and airlocks…"

"But we thought it was forbidden!"

"Only officially. Americans can drink as long as you don't share it with Saudis. Never do that. You could get deported."

It was like the religion and the pork—rules within rules. Yes, but no. Just don't shout and wave it about. These were the rules of a country and a culture that did not want to change. Well, they were picking up the bill. They could call the shots.

And we really didn't care. We rarely drank wine anyhow.

Gordon reported for work at the Professional English Language Center (PELC), a low-slung building of classrooms and a central office. The young men he would teach had been to the U.S., attended colleges and universities to obtain a degree, and had returned to Saudi Arabia with the promise of a job. But for many of the men, the educational experience in America had not resulted in fluency in English. Most of the young men could speak fairly well, but their reading and writing scores fell far behind. Gordon could sympathize with them. He had learned to speak Chinese, but learning to read and write in an unrelated language was much more difficult. Even the speaking for some of the men was sub-standard. Saudi students tended to clump together in universities in the U.S. and speak Arabic. Given the difference in the two cultures, one could understand why. Even socializing in college had its dangers. Saudi men could have girlfriends in America, but bringing home a Western wife was a dangerous proposition for everyone involved. Few Western women could live under the restraints imposed on Saudi women, and the men's mothers resented them.

But the students were pleasant young fellows, and Gordon began to enjoy teaching them. The men were eager to learn, as they were tested every six weeks and pay increments were tied to test scores.

Chris had only six weeks to be with us before he had to fly out to California for his first public school experience. Gordon was settled in his classroom routine, so I spent as much time as I could with Chris before he had to leave.

Chris was the baby of the family, seven years behind everyone else. He had always been with us, sharing in everything we did. He had never been any problem, just one of the gang. We had never treated him like a child...would never have thought of disciplining him. If a situation arose that needed discussion, we discussed it, and decided how to handle it. The idea of reprimanding him, or ever raising my hand to him, had never even crossed my mind. We respected and loved each other.

Now Chris, not yet fifteen and not quite as tall as his mother, was going to be on his own. He was bright, and insightful, and inquisitive, tender-hearted and small for his age. With his Dutch-boy haircut he still had the look of a child. His voice had not yet changed.

Was I ready to let him go?

Would he be hurt by this?

We sat around the swimming pool those few weeks, or went shopping in Khobar, and talked.

"Don't worry about me, Mom. I'll be okay, and I'll be back at Christmas. The time will go fast."

Staying together, through everything, had always been important in our lives. Were we losing our values for a paycheck?

"Chris, you study hard, and do the very best you can. We'll work hard here in Saudi Arabia so when you're ready for college you can go anywhere you want to, anywhere you are accepted. We'll back you up. And if we all work together, all the other kids can graduate without any debts, too. Think of Saudi Arabia as our big family effort to give all you kids a good, debt-free education."

"I'll do my very best, Mom, and don't you worry about me," he said bravely.

I promised I wouldn't.

The last week in August, Chris and I flew to New York and on to San Francisco. Gordon was already teaching, so this was the only way we could do it.

I left him in San Francisco with Gordon's sister Lila. She and her husband, Ken, a radiologist, had broken out of the Michigan family group years before and settled in Burlingame, a section of San Francisco. Having raised three girls, they were delighted to have a boy around the house.

I left him there.

Hoping that he did not feel abandoned.

My Chris.

As it turned out, we did not have to stay in North Camp long. A family that had been housed off-camp in Khobar was terrified of living in a local town without the protection of camp. We were given the opportunity to trade our North Camp trailer for an apartment in Khobar—a place called the Bin Juma building on King Abdul Aziz Avenue.

We were delighted!

We loved the idea of living in a local town, taking in all the sights, smells, sounds and adventures of a Saudi environment. It was like shades of Stanley Village.

So we switched. The other family got our redecorated trailer, and we got an apartment in the Bin Juma on the third floor.

The apartment was roomy. Two bedrooms, living/dining/kitchen, and a glorious deep, Mediterranean blue bathroom with a bidet(!) There was a long hallway leading to the bedrooms and bath, and a long balcony over the street.

We could rent furniture from the company at ridiculously low prices. We had not even brought any furniture along, preferring to keep anything we treasured in Mom and Dad De Pree's attic and claim it when we returned.

We had only planned to stay for a year, although now that had risen to a two-year minimum. Gordon had found out that one-year people would be taxed as though they had earned the money in the U.S. Not good.

Oh well…

Two years would pass quickly.

We awoke that first morning in the Bin Juma building to the sound of the local prayer call floating out over the dark morning air.

"Allah il Allah…"

Now we were really in Saudi Arabia.

Chris' room was very empty.

I walked past it at night with a slight pain in my heart. Had we done the right thing?

Nicholas the cat missed Chris, too. He insisted on sleeping in our bed. He did not want to sleep at the foot of the bed, of course, like a decent cat. He wanted to sleep between our pillows with one paw on each of us. We were hanging off the opposite sides of the double bed with the cat taking up the middle.

We had promised Chris to take good care of his cat, but this was too much. The cat had to go. We closed our door at night so he could not commandeer our bed.

He was highly insulted. He spent the first few nights racing down the long hallway and throwing himself at the door.

Finally, he gave up and slept in the hallway.

We were all a little uncertain.

One thing resolved itself. There was a letter from Harold Rand, the package producer in New York. That fall, one third of the entertainment industry in New York had gone belly up, and he was one of them. Bankrupt. There would be no film.

It was all right. Time to move ahead. That story would be hard to film anyhow. What if it had been pushed one way or another, and ended up X-rated?

I finally gave it up.

For the time being...

The good news was that the kids were coming for Christmas. Of course, Christmas in Saudi Arabia would be limited, with no Christmas trees (especially off camp), and no ornaments. But we would be together, and that was what counted.

Mike did not get his passport ready on time, but Chris and the girls would be with us. We picked them up at the Dhahran Airport, so happy to see them! Chris had finally started growing. I could see that his pants were too short, and he was trying to lower his voice.

We had collected extra Egyptian galabeyas for the girls to wear in Khobar—long off-white cotton gowns made by farmers' wives in Egypt, with colorful embroidered panels in front. Boys did not need to wear robes, but just for fun we had a white thobe and red checkered headdress with a black band for Chris. We were in style.

It certainly would be a different Christmas!

Gordon's students were interested to hear that his family was coming to Saudi for the holidays. A big chuffy student named Abdul Jabbar wanted to take us to his village of Hofuf for a real Saudi experience.

We, being used to village experiences, were eager to go.

He came to the Bin Juma early that morning, ready to give our family an adventure. We all loaded into his dusty car and he headed out of town, driving like the proverbial bat out of hell, ignoring traffic signs, cutting across lanes, driving much too fast. We glanced at the speedometer, but it was hard to convert kilometers to miles—maybe better not to know. Along with his wild driving, he kept up a lively line of chatter.

"First, we will stop at my friend's house on the way. He's a very interesting person. He just got married the second time. No, he didn't get divorced...this is his second wife."

"How old is he?" Gordon asked.

"Oh, he's just my age. We don't usually have two women when we are so young. We wait until the first one starts wearing out, but this friend (he swerved around a car—we were hanging on), he wanted to marry a girl and she said to wait a year and she would let him know. He waited a year and didn't hear from her, so he married someone else. And then, he was just married to her when the first girl showed up and said she had decided to marry him.

"He was outside his house, working, when this second girl showed up. He said to her, 'Look, I already got married. But I'll tell you what. You go in the house and ask my wife if she minds, and if she doesn't mind, I'll marry you, too.' So she went in and asked the wife, and she said no, she didn't mind; there would just be an extra person to share the work. So he married them both, and now they are both pregnant, and about to have babies at the same time."

"That can't be very peaceful..."Gordon said.

"Oh no! They all get along fine!" he said.

We drove down a narrow street and stopped at the house.

"Maybe they will invite us in for tea," he said, going to the door.

Abdul Jabbar was only in the house for a few minutes when he came hurrying out.

"No tea," he apologized. "They're having a big fight in there."

"The two women?"

"No, both women are mad at him!"

I breathed a sigh of relief. Maybe Saudis weren't as different as they thought they were.

We drove on toward Hofuf.

"We may get very lucky today," Abdul Jabbar said. "I think there may be a beheading, and we may be able to watch it."

We all glanced at each other, wondering what we were getting into.

"A beheading?" Gordon finally asked.

"Yes, it's an adultery case, made more complicated by a murder—quite a famous case, actually. The murder is easy. You take a life, your life is taken. You no longer have the right to live. But the adultery is harder to prove..."

"Why is that?"

"You must have two witnesses. They have to say they saw the woman committing adultery."

"Just the woman?"

"Yes, of course. It is always the woman's fault. She should stop the man."

Marita, Deidra and I were sitting in the back seat, Saudi style. The men were all in front.

"Can you imagine that?" Dede whispered.

"What, getting beheaded?" Marita whispered back.

"No, being stupid enough to commit adultery in front of two witnesses!" she whispered.

Maybe that was the safeguard.

This law was more complex than it sounded.

We arrived at the Hofuf Market and began walking down the street. Gordon and I looked at each other. How could we get out of this? We did not have our own car and could not leave. We were trapped.

It was noontime.

Abdul Jabbar suggested we stop at a local restaurant, a famous eating place. I hoped the owners would not make the women sit at a different table. Maybe they would be more liberal with Americans, since no Saudi women were in our group. Sometimes women were forced to eat in another room. Abdul Jabbar was in rare form.

"My treat!" he beamed, proud of his use of English. "Let's have a good lunch!"

We were still wondering what to do about getting out of the beheading when Abdul Jabbar started ordering. Fresh fruit, roasted goat, baba ganoush (eggplant), kibbe, hummus, dish after dish, stuffed sheep gut sausages...

"Enjoy!" he beamed as we began sampling the food. It was really quite good, but how could we eat when something so terrible was taking place out on the street? It was Friday, and the act would be done in front of the mosque to discourage others from committing similar crimes. In the name of Allah, the Merciful and the Just.

When we went to the cash register to pay, Abdul Jabbar clasped his forehead and apologized.

"So sorry," he said, "I forgot to take my wallet. Can you pay the bill and I pay you back later?"

So Gordon paid for the feast and never expected to be paid back later.

Out on the street the crowd was disappointed. The beheading was cancelled. No witnesses had appeared. No one seemed surprised, only slightly disappointed.

Relieved, we headed for Dhahran.

To say the least, it was an unusual Christmas.

The kids had gone back to their various schools. The house felt empty. Gordon was at work. What would I do?

As before in my life, I turned to art. Painting. I still had a few Hong Kong photos, and the Saudi markets were fascinating; women selling jewelry, baskets, pottery. Be sure to keep the women covered.

We took a trip across to Bahrain and photographed doorways, a wind tower, and Arabian Dhows (boats) in the water and on the shore. I did charcoal sketches, oil paints, even a few acrylics.

Every year Aramco had a huge art fair in Dhahran. I would enter the art show—my first ever.

I did, and sold every piece I had in the show. Would I ever become a working artist again?

Maybe.

Not now.

Having looked over the financial situation and the number of kids we had in school, Gordon began to worry. We were thinking about the amount of time we would actually stay in Saudi Arabia.

"We can't even scratch the surface staying here two years," he said. "We'll have to be here at least five years just to cover all the college costs."

"And we want to build a house when we go back." I added.

"That too. I don't think I can do it all on my own."

He left a silence.

"Why don't you go down to the admin building and see if you can get a job? I hear they're hiring casuals."

"But I've just started painting, and we'll be getting some book royalties."

"That won't be enough."

"You think I should get a job?"

"You could try."

"But I've never worked in an office in my life. I wouldn't have the foggiest idea what to do."

I stopped making excuses. I was 48 years old, brown and slim, and healthy. I had a big head of curly hair and a good smile.

I washed my hair, fluffed it out, put on my Macy's off-white linen suit from my speaking days, and a pair of heels, and walked into the admin building to sell myself.

I ended up with a job, one grade code higher than Gordon's.

We had a good laugh.

Of course, I was only a casual. I had no rights. I did not even officially exist. But I was hired as a writer for Government Affairs, a part of the company that did information liaison while the Saudi government was buying back its oil from the American owners.

In the 1930s, American explorers opened up the oil fields in Saudi, paying the king a royalty for all oil discovered. In the 1980s, the Saudi government wanted more than that. Over the years the balance had tipped in favor of the Saudis, and now they wanted to own the company the Americans had founded. They wanted their oil back, with Americans only remaining to train the new Saudi management and serve as advisors when the deal was finished. All physical and legal assets would belong to the Saudis, for untold billions.

Gordon was training future Saudi leaders in English.

I would be a part of the office force that answered letters of inquiry from the Saudi government, and researched to give them the answers and information they wanted.

It was an exciting time to work for Aramco, and I sensed it.

But I was terrified.

I had never worked in an office. This office would have Americans, Pakistanis, Jordanians, Saudis, and Palestinians. I would write letters to be translated into Arabic by the translation department, mostly Egyptians.

I was scared spitless.

I had never used an electric typewriter. For all the books I had written, it was always my trusty Royal portable manual typewriter.

Now I had a cubicle with an electric typewriter in it. I touched it and it jumped. I was petrified.

I had never even made coffee in an electric coffee pot.

I had a lot to learn.

And the politics...oh—my—God.

Bob Norberg. The American in charge of our division of Government Affairs, clued me in...somewhat.

"I read your book, the one about Kentucky," he smiled. "You're quite a writer. We're honored to have you join us. Do you play bridge?"

"No," I said, "I don't know the first thing about it."

I felt my worth go down a notch.

The other women in the group were avid bridge players, a little New Orleans French babe, and a tall red-haired woman who barely disguised her disapproval of me.

We had a meeting once a week to chart the progress of the group. I got my first assignment of seven or eight requests from the government to be researched and answered. In order to look up old documents we had to go

226

to a room where the microfiche was stored, and use the machine to call up the material.

Another process to be learned.

I wrote my documents and came to the next meeting with all of them finished and sent to translation. When my turn came around in the circle to report what I had done, there was a stunned silence.

Then somebody laughed.

"You did all your work in one week?" Bob asked incredulously.

More laughter. What was the joke?

"Slow down," Bob said. "If you work that fast you'll cause our department to get a spending cut. They'll expect us all…"

The rest of the sentence was lost in laughter.

I had tried too hard. I would slow down.

Should I learn to play bridge?

Weekends were crazy. Friday was the holy day, so Thursdays were like Saturdays. On Thursdays we were off, so we took the Aramco bus up to Ras Tanura to swim in the Arabian Gulf. It had a beautiful sandy beach with shells like Hong Kong. We were back to the sea again.

We walked the beach, limiting ourselves to just one shell a weekend. We were getting too many.

On Fridays (which were like Sundays) we sometimes went to church. Worship was forbidden to have any official sanction, but like the whiskey, pork and Bibles allowed the infidels, it was tolerated. We had the choice of an Anglican group, a loose-goose Protestant group, or the Catholics. Things widely divergent in the West were all thrown together here in the infidel category. It was the first time in our lives we had ever been classified as unbelievers. The Catholics had a Philippino singing group that was to die for, so sometimes we attended mass just to hear the music.

But in the afternoons we wrote letters, one to each of the kids, one to Gordon's parents, and one to my mom. It was a full-time Friday job, a holy obligation.

My mom was so pleased about the Kentucky book. She wrote that it helped her understand her life better than she had when she was living it.

Maybe we could understand each other better because of writing the story. I hoped so.

Then on Saturday we went back to work. Saturday, Sunday, Monday, Tuesday, Wednesday—work. Thursday and Friday—the weekend. It made sense if you could forget it used to be different.

The family was growing up, with or without us. Marita and Mike had graduated from Grinnell College in 1980, the year before we left New York. We had gone to Iowa to watch them get their diplomas with 'De Pree One' and 'De Pree Two' pinned on the back of their gowns.

Now Marita was a grad student in art, and had met the love of her life, Pete, a graduate of the Iowa Writer's Workshop and headed toward teaching literature in an eastern prep school like his father and brothers—a real blue-blood.

We met Pete that summer, 1982, in a motel in Iowa, where we all immediately jumped into the pool on a hot Iowa day. Pete must have thought it was the De Pree son-in-law test to see him stripped to his trunks before we gave him our approval.

Mike had gone on to law school. He had dropped the New York Jewish family and had found an Iowa girlfriend. She was even from a Dutch family—Dutch, and French-Hugenot, too yet.

In June of 1982. Chris finished his sophomore year of high school in San Francisco and flew back to Saudi Arabia by himself. When we met him at the Dhahran Airport I hardly recognized him. He had shot up six inches. He no longer looked like a child. He was becoming a young man. His voice had changed, and there was a self-confident look in his eyes. Bless him, he had survived. Maybe it had been good for him to be on his own.

That summer the three of us headed back to the U.S. by way of Hong Kong, where we bought Chris his first computer. He was doing well in school, but convinced us he needed this new tool. It was the thing of the future.

Everything that summer called for money.
What if we had stayed in New York?
There was no time to look back.

The summer of 1982 we stayed at a cottage on Lake Michigan for the month of company vacation.

Deidra was between boyfriends, was finishing up at Hope College, and thinking of going on to study journalism.

Mike was in law school. His undergraduate degree was in philosophy. It was hard to get a job as a philosopher.

Money.

We would need lots of it to get all the kids established. Our kids had experienced wonderful things overseas, but unless we equipped them to live life in the U.S., we would cripple them.

Money.

Thank God, for once in our lives, we had it. Not much, compared to other oil patch families, but enough for us.

Zondervan's had published the *'Festival'* book about Stanley Village, and it was doing well. That would help a bit...

But there was no way we could even think about going back to the U.S., even after five years. The new package available to employees was work for ten years, retire at sixty, healthcare for life, a pension, and savings matched by the company. It was too good to pass up.

By 1984, Chris would be in college.

We could not afford to quit.

We had to do ten years.

The good part of all this was that we were beginning to enjoy Saudi Arabia. It no longer seemed a terrible necessity. It was a golden opportunity, and we were grateful. Even the church authorities in Iowa to whom we were responsible agreed that we were a practical Christian presence in the Middle East, in the best traditions of the Reformed Church.

The summer we were all at the lake cottage, 1982, Marita was into wedding plans. She picked out a dress pattern and I cut it out of ivory satin, and sewed it far enough to see that it fit her. We went downtown in Holland, Michigan to buy packets of tiny pearl beads to sew on the train and bodice. I would take it back to Saudi Arabia to do the handwork and bring it back for the wedding in August of 1983.

"Don't fit it too tight," Marita begged. "I won't dare eat a bite all year!"

Like most brides-to-be, Marita was careful about her weight. She had grown into a beautiful young woman, blue-eyed and blond, with an abundant head of hair. Self-confidant and talented, she and Pete (whose real name was Arthur Shorey Follansbee) would make a splendid couple.

Back to Saudi Arabia for another year of work at PELC and Government Affairs...

The summer months were too hot to go anywhere other than the Arabian Gulf to swim, but as the fall temperatures cooled down to below a hundred degrees, we began to think of a camping trip to the Rub Al Khali, the southern part of the Arabian Peninsula known as the Empty Quarter.

There was no question of us going on our own, but having been at Aramco for over a year, we had met many other families whose whole life had been lived on camp. They, or their parents, had been among the original Americans working the oil patch. They were almost more Arab than American.

Kate and Criff Crawford were of this group. Kate had grown up in Iran, the daughter of Presbyterian missionaries. She and Criff had studied Arabic in Beirut, at the famous 'spy school'. He was a geologist, high up in the company structure. They lived in the executive section of 'Dhahran Hills'. Even the Aramco oil camp had its real-estate pecking order. We were honored that they had befriended us.

Criff, being a geologist, had a huge GMC vehicle, perfect for finding his way around the desert.

They included us in a weekend trip they were planning in the Rub Al Khali. We were delighted.

Proper preparation must be made. We had to sign up at Government Affairs, give the whole trip plan, and the date we would return. The understanding was that if we did not return that day, an expedition would set out in the desert to find us. No one could survive in the Rub Al Khali more than three days without food and water.

And, cardinal rule number one: never go with only one vehicle. At least two or three vans needed to go. One vehicle, stalled, could mean death.

Of course, that seldom happened…

We packed a tent, sleeping bags, water, food, cans of extra gasoline, sand boards in case we got stuck in deep sand, and were off. We had three vehicles, one of which would peel off after a day leaving two: the Crawfords and another family they knew well.

We drove south through hills of brown sand and the occasional oasis. The father south we traveled, the more scarce human habitation became, until all we saw was one camel caravan: white camels, white against the whitening sands, with biblical robes and head gear, looking almost Christmas pageant pristine.

Then we plunged into the desert proper, with no human or animal life in sight.

The sands stretched out before us and above us, huge mountains of totally white sand undulating like deep snow banks. The sky above was a vibrant turquoise blue, and then the mountains of white merged into dunes of rich raspberry red, ethereal, huge, awe-inspiring.

Was this the way the world looked before the advent of human life?

Sky…sand…silence.

We camped that night on the side of a pure white mountain, setting up our tents and building a fire. The golden globe of a moon rose above the white splendor of the dunes. The stars were huge, filling the sky with a powerful radiance. It was night, but it was not dark. It was luminescent.

230

We cooked our meat over the open fire, sparks flying up to meet the stars. Kate brought out large cups of home-made wine, and we settled into a cozy state of content, chatting around the campfire.

In our tent, we opened up our sleeping bags to make one big bed, and fell asleep in a state of mind we had never experienced. Where were we? Was this the world we had known?

Then the sunrise, the sun huge over the peaks and valleys of the dunes—red, fiery, shedding a rosy glow over the white sand.

One other couple around the campfire that morning was the DeWaards—Jack and Kathy DeWaard. DeWaard. Dutch too yet, from Grand Rapids, Michigan.

There was no way to escape it. We were still on planet Earth.

That morning we packed up our gear and took off over the trackless desert. There were no roads. We traveled by the compass on Criff's GMC. Today we would be in the most fantastic dunes of all.

It was breathtaking.
We climbed a white mountain and began to descend.
We were flying, not driving.
The wheels barely seemed to touch the ground.
White. Cloudlike. This was pure ecstasy!
Surely we had wings!
Flying over dunes…
Leaping the chasm from one dune to another.
Air bourn…

Suddenly, at the height of the euphoria, there was a crack—a clunk. The motor died.

We stared at each other.
What had happened?
The driver of the other vehicle pulled up beside us.
Trouble.
They hauled out a heavy chain and connected the two vehicles. Subdued, we were pulled behind the head car.
We realized our AC had gone out. The last time we looked, it had been 115 degrees.
It was hot…so hot.
We pulled into a low place between dunes where there was a sliver of shade and set up the tents.
We had no phones, not until we reached the nearest town.

The men looked under the hood. Then they pulled out a pan under the motor. It was filled with transmission fluid. It had leaked out.

We stared at each other glumly, planning what to do next, when a little bird alighted on the pan of transmission fluid.

A bird? We had not seen a bird in two days!

The bird tried to take a drink and a bath in the shiny fluid. The men chased it off.

Our van was hitched to the other vehicle and we slowly moved along through the desert. The men estimated that we were at least two hundred miles from Dhahran, deep in the desert.

Suddenly, the dunes did not look so magnificent; they looked sinister.

We traveled toward camp, windows open, dust covering us. Hot. Frustrated. Nature was not only splendid, it was also terrifying, all powerful in its force. Totally uncaring if we lived or died. We had ventured into the world of the silent desert and it had the power over us.

Hot…dusty…frightened. Jerked ahead by the chain.

"Don't worry," Criff assured us, "just hang on. We'll make it."

Hours. Hours. We traveled through the night. We could not risk more time in the desert.

Finally we reached a small town. We could call in to camp. They had just decided to send out a group to search for us.

But we were safe.

Thank God, or Allah, or whoever was on duty out there.

We were safe.

The housing office notified us that a place was available on camp. There was a row of single houses with walled-in courtyards along the edge of camp central, just short of 'The Hills'.

We had enjoyed living in Al Khobar. It had been beautiful to walk along the streets at night, to smell the wonderful fragrance of the shwarma stalls, to peer through the gates and catch a glimpse of family life going on in the courtyards.

But living on camp would be better. We had been going to the commissary after work to buy groceries and carry bags back on the bus. We had also begun to study Arabic. It would be easier to live on Main Camp.

Moving was no problem. We left the pieces we had rented in the Khobar flat, picked up our clothes and dishes, and rented other pieces of necessary furniture on camp. Beds, a couch, chairs, a table… We were portable.

The house, on what was ingloriously called 'the alley,' was a modest stucco structure. A gate led into a front walled garden. The house itself was one story with a living/dining room, kitchen, two bedrooms and a bath. Behind the house was a patch of grass and a big air conditioner on a concrete pad.

There was an extra room off the kitchen known as the AC room. Since the AC was outside, this must be the famous room where the wine was made.

We settled in and decided the front walled-in courtyard needed water, reflecting water. Over in one corner we built a 12x15 shallow reflecting pool with a circulating fountain pump. Two palm trees on either side of the pool provided a shady place to hang a hammock. It felt cool and inviting, the perfect place to relax after a day at our jobs.

The kids flew back to Saudi that Christmas. Marita would be getting married the next summer, and wanted to come as many times as she could before that date.

Mike finally got his passport in order and joined the rest of the family.

Gordon's students were interested again in seeing his family, especially a family with two pretty girls.

Our kids went to PELC to observe their dad's teaching. Gordon, usually a calm quiet person (no blowbag), amazed them when he was in front of a classroom.

"You should see him, Mom!" Dede said. "He keeps those guys hopping! He's a riot!"

A student from Qatif named Ali-al-awali invited us to his house for dinner.

Abdul Jabbar was a Suni.

Ali-al-awali was a Shia.

It might be interesting to see the difference.

"My mother wants to meet your family," Ali invited. "She's a school teacher; teaches in a girls school in Qatif."

We figured if she was a teacher she might be more relaxed and open-minded than some Saudi women.

Ali drove us to his home in Qatif. The house sat in the middle of a large, totally enclosed courtyard with high walls. No one could look inside.

His mother was a smiling, dark-eyed woman, unveiled and with no abaya. She was dressed in a modest long skirt and blouse. She welcomed us into her home. We went in and sat on formal chairs in the living room.

We could see the preparations for a meal going on in the kitchen. In the dining room, a large tablecloth was spread out on the floor. The beginnings of a dinner were already set out on it: fruit, vegetables, a basket of flat bread…

De poked me and motioned.

"Are we going to eat sitting on the floor?" she whispered.

"Looks like it," I muttered.

Ali's father and brothers were entertaining us while the mother worked in the kitchen.

"My mother doesn't usually eat with us if there are strange men in the house," Ali explained. "But today she is going to, since there are other women here. Otherwise, all of you other women would have to eat in the kitchen with her."

"If she prefers," I offered.

"No, she will eat with us today."

This woman was a teacher, and she was trying to adapt.

We sat for quite a while. I needed to use the bathroom. I went to the hallway room, a small hamam (toilet), basically a hole in the floor. Marita and Dede squeezed in with me.

The girls bravely used the Middle-eastern squat john, suppressing giggles.

"Where's the toilet paper?" De asked.

"You use the hose. I guess that's where the idea for the bidet started…"

There was a rap on the door.

Ali was standing there, looking bug-eyed.

"Excuse me," he said, "but my mother is very upset because there is more than one female in the hamam—this is against our customs."

"What?" I began. What the heck did she think we were doing…?

"Sorry," I reined in my indignation, and we all reassembled on the stiff living room chairs.

Eventually, we assembled around the tablecloth on the floor. The food was blessed in the name of Allah the Merciful and the Just, and we began to eat. Gordon was left-handed, and he had been warned to sit on his left hand so he would not be tempted to eat with it. He had to make do with his right, not too easy when we were not eating with forks. The rice and meat had to be rolled into small balls and popped into the mouth.

The food was delicious. Saudi food always was. Deidra especially loved the sausages, and ate several of them before she realized they were sheep intestines stuffed with goodness knows what.

It didn't bother me. People in Kentucky used to stuff pig intestines with pork sausage. It was all relative…

234

All protein.

Be tolerant.

After dinner we sat back in the hard living room chairs, conversing with Ali and his brothers, and their father. They wanted to know about our travels. About living in China. Where all had we been? Had we been to Russia? To England? To Greece?

Then the real question.

Had we been to Israel?

Not realizing the importance of the question, Mike said yes, we had visited Israel, and he began telling how much we had enjoyed it.

The room suddenly froze.

"You… You went to Israel?" Ali asked.

"We did!"

We still did not get it.

"Israel is our enemy," Ali's father said darkly. "Any friend of Israel is not our friend."

Ali's mother came in from the kitchen. She had a bowl of rosewater in her hands. We were asked to dip our fingers in the rosewater and given towels. Then the father brought out a lighted censor of incense to shake around the room, cleansing the air.

The party was definitely over.

We were friends of Israel.

As we left, I wondered what this woman taught the girls in her classroom.

Bless her; I knew how she felt. Radicalism was the same unreasoned blindness the world over, no matter what the name of the religion.

As a part of our new life on camp we needed to learn to use our 'air conditioning room'. On Aramco Camp, having people over for dinner without wine was not acceptable.

Alcohol had never been an important part of our lives…and it was officially forbidden in Saudi Arabia. What was the big deal? Forbidden fruit? Or was it simply a part of the oil patch culture?

After all, they had been granted three inalienable rights: whiskey, pork and bibles, and they intended to take advantage of them.

We collected our friends' wine recipes. Red wine and white wine. We bought two big five-gallon glass jugs in Al-Khobar, plus rubber hoses and a gadget called an air lock. Juice at the commissary (unpasteurized—we needed that bacteria!), yeast, strong tea and lots of sugar.

Once the mixture in the first jug started "perking," we knew the process was taking. It bubbled for a month, burping out the air lock until there was no more action, and a heavy layer of sludge settled at the bottom of the jar. That was the time to siphon the wine out into the second jar and throw away the sludge. The second jar had to set for a month and then it was ready to drink, or be bottled up with your own label on it.

Wine tasting parties were held in 'Dhahran Hills,' complete with fancy cheeses and first, second and third prizes.

We never won first prize, but we did improve as time went by. The first bottle of red wine we gave away did not fare so well. The guy who opened it ended up with a red splotch on his kitchen ceiling that looked like a murder had been committed.

That Spring, after work, I sat on the couch and sewed pearl beads on Marita's wedding dress. It was certainly a labor of love. A beautiful cream satin studded with hundreds of pearls, fitted at the waist and falling in gores to the train. We would have to pack it carefully to take on the plane in the summer.

And that Spring...
We had a miracle in Saudi Arabia. A Spring rain! The desert could go years without rain, and billions of tiny seeds incubated in the sand. But one good rain and the desert bloomed in such a profusion of wild flowers that it was totally magical.

We drove up toward Ras Tanura with the Crawfords and the DeWaards to witness this phenomenon—thousands of acres of tiny desert flowers that would drop new seeds...and wait patiently for the next rain. No one knew when.

We simply stared at them—the flowers. No way to capture them, or make it happen again. Nature at its most beautiful and most ephemeral.

It seemed everybody in our immediate family was getting married. It was an eighteen-month epidemic, just like their births.

Deidra flew to Saudi Arabia that spring, asking advice.

"Mom, what would you think if I decided to marry my best friend?"

"I'd think that was a good idea, if you really, really love him."

"Are you and Dad best friends?"

I thought for a moment. Would I define him as a friend only?

"He's definitely is my best friend. That's what a marriage comes down to in the end—a friend that you can totally trust and give yourself to in ever way, and never be afraid."

She was quiet, waiting for more.

"And, somebody who gives you goose bumps," I added.

We were out in the courtyard, sharing the hammock over the pool.

"Mom, I live in this group of kids. We share a house, and I've been dating a few guys. There's this one guy named Rob. He's been dating girls at school, but it seems like after we go out we always get together and talk about our dates—sometimes laughing about them—and now we're dating each other. Is it crazy to fall in love with your best friend?"

De was a graduate student at Columbia School of Journalism in Columbia, Missouri. She and Rob were in the same class.

It seemed that wedding number two was on the horizon.

But first we had to do number one.

We congregated in Michigan, flying in from everywhere. Chris had come from California to visit with his grandparents in Zeeland until we arrived from Saudi.

When we were all assembled we rented a cottage at Lake Michigan. Grandma De Pree had not been well, and we wanted a base of operations that would not involve Gordon's parents' house.

Marita chose the chapel at Western Seminary where Gordon had studied theology. I was surprised, because Marita was the one who always claimed she didn't have a religious bone in her body, but she chose the seminary. One of Gordon's friends would officiate. We arranged for a dinner reception at Point West on Lake Michigan.

Then Dede came from Missouri...sick. She was running a high fever. She was to be the maid of honor. Her dress was ready. I had a new dress.

We took Deidra to the doctor. She had a ruptured appendix and peritonitis had set in. She was very sick.

The day Marita and Pete got married, De was not there with her. She was in the hospital in Holland with seventy-two hours to determine if she would live or die.

Grandma De Pree sat with Deidra during the wedding. I did not know whether to rejoice with Marita or cry with Deidra.

I felt numb...

Marita's dress was beautiful.

She was beautiful—a young woman in the bloom of her life. Her tall, slender, blond groom, Pete, and all his family came from Massachusetts. All my Chicago relatives came up from the windy city. Gordon's family was all there from Michigan. My mom was there with her new husband from Florida.

It was a beautiful seven-minute ceremony. We were all aware that Deidra might not live. The minister was brief.

Such a mixture of joy and sorrow...

But Marita and Pete were properly married, and Deidra lived. She had extensive surgery which we hoped would take care of everything. Thank goodness we all lived through that horribly wonderful week.

Marita had her Master's Degree in fine art. She had a handsome blue-blood New England private school teacher husband. She was ready to begin her life. Pete had a job in Ashburnham, Massachusetts. Our first baby was a woman on her own!

Deidra rested at Mom and Dad De Pree's when she came home from the hospital. I stayed with her until she was well enough to go back to school.

She was serious about Rob.

Wedding number two was in the works.

But Deidra would not need a white wedding dress made for her.

"I want to get married in a red silk cheongsam, like a Chinese bride," she said, "and have a Chinese feast. I'm a Hong Kong baby."

We would deal with that later. Deidra still had a year before she graduated from journalism school.

While De was recuperating, Gordon and Chris were busy. They looked at Lake Michigan for a place we might buy to settle in when we came back to the U.S. to stay. Would a place on the lake be fun?

They were all terribly expensive, and Lake Michigan was having serious erosion problems. The beaches were washing away.

Did we want to live on water?

While we were living at Columbia University in New York City, the popular place to go for a weekend was North Carolina. Water property. Gordon and Chris took a flight south to look around.

Downtown Wilmington?

No...

Bald Head Island?

Kiowa?

Gordon and Chris came back to Michigan. Maybe someday we would explore these areas, but for now, Chris needed to finish high school. Then college...

Oh Lordy, these babies seemed so simple when we were having them, one by one (or two by two), but what a lot of work it took to help them grow up! And the cost!

But whatever it cost, we were committed to help them get launched into good lives.

Thank goodness for Saudi Arabia.

The whole incredible thing had rested on a single telephone call, and a simple yes or no.

I could have said NO and been safe.

Luckily, I said yes, and opened a whole new world of possibilities.

The power of yes, like a billion flower seeds in the sand, waiting for a rain to make them bloom.

The incredible power of yes.

We took the flight, by now routine, back to Saudi Arabia.

PELC was building new quarters.

Government Affairs was undergoing changes. With the deal between the Saudi Government and the American oil interests coming closer to completion, the department needed fewer workers like me.

My job would end.

Darn! I should have learned to play bridge!

But through fellow workers in the office I was recommended to the Aramco school system. They needed a publicist, a person who could write a bi-monthly newspaper for Aramco schools. The current person was leaving.

Bob Gaw, the superintendent of all Aramco schools on the East Coast of Saudi Arabia, interviewed me. He was curt.

"I don't even know if you can type," he said. "I'll give you the job on a temporary basis. Prove to me that you can do it, and it's yours."

All my life I have loved a challenge. For starters, I gave him a copy of my Kentucky book.

"You can check out my writing," I told him.

The woman who had been doing the job was packing. She had two weeks to train me. Part of the training was to learn to use a Wang Word Processor, the forerunner of the modern computer. I had just finally stopped jumping when I touched my electric typewriter, and now I had to learn to use this monster.

The job involved travel inside Saudi Arabia. I had to go to Dharan Airport, meet a photographer, board a 28-seat Folker plane with a pilot, and fly to the three other Aramco schools on the East Coast of Saudi Arabia: Ras Tanura, Abquaiq, and Udhaliyah. Dhahran, of course, was the main school where I worked. Each edition of the paper focused on a curriculum subject being taught, and how it was applied in the various schools, with news and photos from all the branches. The paper had to be written and laid out with photos, camera ready to be printed in Dammam.

The purpose of the newspaper was to convince parents that they were not ruining their children's lives by sending them to Aramco's schools in the desert.

I was glad I was not going to get paid for lying. The schools were fantastic!

I submitted the first draft with suitable photos. Bob Gaw read it. He came storming out of his office. I thought I was fired.

"Damn!" he said, "where did you learn to write like that?"

"I'm a writer," I said calmly. "Did you read the book I gave you?"

"I-uh-no. I haven't had time yet, but I will now."

"Do I have the job?"

"Of course you do!" he blustered." I never doubted it!"

He could have fooled me.

Bob never wasted time on compliments, but we came to respect each other. When he read the Kentucky story, he laughed and cried. He loved it. That accomplished two things. It made me glad I was working for him, and gave me hope that someday, somehow, something would still happen to the book.

I would not use the title they had given it in New York. I would give it a new name and a new start. It would be called *90 Brothers and Sisters*.

Barring all else, someday the copyright would come back to me.

Valentine's Day, February 14, 1984.

We were fast asleep in our house on the alley, two o'clock in the morning. The phone rang with that awful sound a phone has in the dead of night. Bruce, Gordon's older brother, was on the line.

"Gord," he said, "you better get a flight and come home. Mom's in Zeeland Hospital. She's had a heart attack and might not make it. Come right away…"

Gordon flew all the way to Michigan hoping he could get there while Mom was still alive, still conscious. Gordon had always been close to his mom.

He arrived in Michigan too late. She was already gone.

Lila flew in from San Francisco.

The family assembled to say goodbye to a strong and great woman.

So quickly taken.

So not there.

Dad De Pree seemed so small.

He needed to be reassured that he would see Mom again, in heaven…

Gordon flew back to Saudi Arabia, to his men in the classes, and to the prayer calls that rang over Camp, five times a day.

"God is Great."

He would never answer another phone call in the middle of the night for the rest of his life.

Mike was married in June at a tennis club in Chicago. Jamie, his Dutch girlfriend from college, was an artist—a long-haired potter and a guitarist. Our families gathered for an outdoor ceremony, conducted by Gordon, with readings Mike had chosen from *Faces of God* , which would prove to be ironic in hindsight...

I am a woman face of God

I am a Man face of God.

Mike had just graduated from law school in Iowa, passed his bar exams, and was getting married all in one week. He was ready to begin his life. He broke out in cold sores from all the stress, which we all told him, repeatedly, we did not notice at all.

Mike. Big warmhearted Mike.

Definitely his own person.

Not the slightest shadow of anybody else.

We wished them the best and gave them our love.

And last, but definitely not least, that December, on New Year's Eve, Deidra and Rob were married on the top floor of the Tiger Hotel in Columbia, Missouri. Deidra wore her red silk cheongsam with a high collar and a slit leg, and Gordon read a passage from Arthur Gordon's (*Guideposts*) *A Touch of Wonder*. Everyone was in tears, including the bride. Deidra had come so close to death, and now she and Rob could celebrate life.

Chinese Double Happiness characters were hanging everywhere, and we had a great Chinese feast for our Hong Kong girl.

They had all married within eighteen months, just like they were born.

Chris was seven years younger. We would have a break.

CHAPTER SIXTEEN

BACK ACROSS WORLDS...BACK THROUGH Amsterdam to Dhahran. Sometimes the 13-hour flight left one feeling rootless, almost soul-less.

Flying through worlds, boarding a plane in one century, getting off a plane in a culture that seemed centuries behind. The Hegira calendar had started in 622. That was point zero, so by 1984, what year was it?

Who knew? Who cared?

It was back to work... On a Saturday that was like a Monday morning.

Every year in June a new class of ninth graders graduated from Aramco schools. It was a big prom-like affair, almost like graduation from high school. But these students had three more years to go. Those three years could not be spent in Saudi Arabia. These fifteen-year-olds must leave the kingdom and study at boarding schools or stay with relatives to finish their education.

For some families this was the breaking point. They left and went back to the U.S. For other families, especially the old oil-patch hands, it was par for the course. They had done it, and their kids could do it.

We had done it.

We knew how much it hurt.

For the May issue of *School News* I wrote a cover piece called "Long Distance Parenting," and examined the whole issue from many angles. The response to this article was so positive that Bob Gaw asked if I would consider writing a guidebook, a kind of manual for families going through this traumatic experience.

Yes, I would like to do that.

It turned out to be a 100-page project, a hands-on workbook for parents and children to use in the eighth grade, the year before they must leave home.

The book was not abstract theory. It was written out of experience, carved out of our own journey. We hoped it would help other parents.

Chris would graduate from high school in June.

We had walked this path.

The little place on the alley was getting crowded. We were collecting rugs. It was impossible to go to Khobar without visiting the rug shops. Such beautiful things, and such good prices!

One day Gordon found a rug, a beautiful piece, at an unbelievable price. A charming young man from Afghanistan sat on the rug, and they visited for over an hour. Gordon heard the young man's whole history, the history of his parents, his brothers and sisters, and his whole country. Almost as an afterthought, he bought the rug.

When he brought it home and unrolled it, there was a surprise, a nice round hole, right where the young man had been sitting.

Gordon took it back, and the man very thoughtfully introduced him to a friend who mended such holes, very nicely, at a good price.

It really was a beautiful rug.

Perfect?

No.

Down the alley a few houses there was a slightly larger place. It was available. We carried our things down the alley and settled in.

A friend who had taught at PELC and was now in administration, since all female instructors had been let go (too tempting for the students), came to visit and loved one of the rugs we had brought from China. She traded it for a Kuwaiti wedding chest, a lovely, dark wood studded with brass in beautiful patterns.

We had a real keeper chest.

And a Bedouin carved door that took up half of our living room (a keeper?)...and a hand weaving from Southern Iraq, with a garden of Eden motif, bought from a blind man at a bazaar in Hofuf.

We were accumulating treasures.

Nothing that could be simply bought.

These treasures were mined.

Ever since my first job at Aramco I had been aware of the shadowy nature of employment for women. Casuals, we were called, and we did not really exist. We were the accessories to our husbands. Every time the price of a barrel of oil dropped, jobs were cut, and the women were the first to go. The most fragile jobs of all were those not tied directly to the production of oil. Dependent-related positions were the first to be terminated. My job, as much as it contributed to the peace of mind of parents on camp, was not going to get oil out of the ground.

Gordon's job would be secure. He was training the next generation of Saudi executives to communicate with the rest of the world. He was teacher and part-time administrator at PELC. His tenure would last the ten years.

But what if my job ended...what would I do?
Five more years...
I had turned fifty in this godforsaken desert.
Where was my life going?
You only pass this way once, woman.
What will you make of it?
Drinking home-made wine and playing cards,
And taking the ever-available valium?
What will you be when this is over?

I tried not to think about it too much as we flew back to the States in June. Chris was graduating from high school in Burlingame, California, and we were excited to witness the great day. We knew he had done well. His SAT scores were very high. He was a straight A student. How much love and how many quiet tears had gone into the accomplishment of this day!

We stayed with Lila in San Francisco. Chris had been there for three years, and for him it was a second home. Ken and Lila had been good to him, and he had not caused them any trouble. It had worked.

There was an air of secrecy in Lila's house the day of the graduation. What was it? Chris at seventeen was a tall, slender young man, with well chiseled features and a mop of curly dark hair (no more Dutch-boy look). He was self-assured, a son anyone would be proud of.

We sat in the auditorium that day, ready for the graduation ceremony. The speakers were on the platform.

Was that Chris up there?

And then we knew.

Christopher Gordon De Pree, who had barely come up to my eyes when I left him here three years ago, was graduating valedictorian of his class of 500!

In Burlingame High School.

He would be the speaker.

I watched his face, squeezing Gordon's hand. Gordon was looking at him, squeezing my hand.

Oh my God...

Chris was speaking calmly. I didn't even hear what he was saying, I was so stunned.

There was the roar of a waterfall in my ears, the rush of the life force...like the night he was born.

I was crying quietly.

Gordon reached over and wiped the tears away with his fingers, then wiped his own.

Chris had done it.

Chris had been accepted at quite a few schools, among them Stanford, Princeton and Duke. Stanford and Princeton had both offered him one year scholarships, with possible extensions for a high level of work, but the best offer came from Duke in North Carolina. They offered him a four-year, Red Carpet place as a Duke Scholar.

Duke?

Most of his classmates were going to Stanford or other California colleges.

Princeton?

We had promised we would send him to the school of his choice if he studied hard those three years and got high grades.

He really wanted to go to Stanford.

He really should go to Duke.

His classmates had, by and large, never heard of Duke. They thought it was a small private college out there in the wilds east of California, and that Chris was choosing to go there because of family finances.

What?

Decisions.

Promises.

Bruce was on the phone, Gordon's big brother.

"Gord..." said the accountant.

Lila withheld her opinion.

Chris decided, reluctantly, to go to Duke.

It was a difficult decision when we had promised him 'whatever.'

Gordon checked at Stanford. The place at Stanford had already been given to another student.

So it was Duke.

A Red Carpet, four-year Duke scholarship.

Was he disappointed?

Perhaps.

We hoped not.

We spent a month in the States getting him settled in. He was lucky. The other three had been shipped to college or dropped off at an airport and left to survive.

But Chris was our last crack at parenting. We were older and not so nonchalant. We bought him a used car in Michigan and drove down through the Smoky Mountains to Durham, North Carolina, to get him settled in for the fall term.

"Are you okay going to Duke?" I asked him.

He was quiet for a few moments, then he said, "I used to think the whole world was open to me, that the sky was the limit and all the choices were mine. But now I've had to make one choice, and all the others are gone. The world seems so much smaller…"

I wished I could help. Should we have let him go where he wanted to? Would this hurt him? Would it have been fair to all the other kids who had also worked so hard?

I knew what was bugging him, and it tore my heart in half to feel that we had gone back on a promise, but somehow, this had happened. We had to deal with it.

"Chris, think of it this way. Choices always limit us. That's what growing up is about. You've said yes to this part of your path, and you never know where it will lead. This is a wonderful opportunity. Take it and make the most of it. You'll rise to the top. You always do…"

We furnished a room for him and left him the car, and flew back to Saudi Arabia.

It was like the beautiful rug with the little hole in it. I hoped it could be mended.

But we believed in Chris. He would be all right.

That fall we made our last move on the Alley. A corner house with a large garden and a pool deep enough to cool off in came on the available list. It was a really souped-up place, almost to the point of being overdone. Our taste had always been simple. This place was not simple. Textured metallic wallpapers, ornate light fixtures, deep rugs. Dark. So much dark brown it felt like the inside of a cave.

But it had that pool in the front yard, and a beautiful garden. The garden was no trouble. They were always taken care of by Pakistanis or Indians—small, thin dark men who stood around squirting water from hoses. They were the watering system, much cheaper than automatic sprinklers.

The pool was not really a swimming pool. It was a round deep hole that looked like an oasis. It was even surrounded by trees, a cool refreshing pool deep enough to climb into and feel relaxed after a long hot day—the kind of pool one would dream of deep in the desert.

Perhaps my dark memories of that house were colored by what happened while we were living there…

I was deeply involved in working for *School News*. Every two months the paper came out and people actually looked forward to finding them in their mailboxes on camp. I flew to Abquaiq, to Ras Tanura, and down to the southern camp of Udhiliyah. We explored the ways math was being taught, and science. So far the job was holding up. Bob Gaw was delighted. And I was having fun.

That week I had to go to the dentist. The dental care at Aramco was unbelievable, at a fraction of the cost in the States. I needed a large bridge implant that would have cost me a fortune in New York.

On Wednesday afternoon I had been at the dentist for hours. My face was frozen stiff. I was walking home along a main street that was all but deserted. People were at work.

Suddenly a figure appeared close beside me. He was a heavy-set young Saudi in a white thobe and red-checked ghutra headdress.

"Excuse me," he said politely, "could you tell me how to get to the cafeteria?"

I was still groggy from the sedative, but even in that state I could tell there was something off about this guy. Not quite all there.

"Take this street," I pointed. "It's down about two blocks."

"Will you take me there?" he asked.

"No, you can find it on your own easily. Just down that way…"

I turned and began to walk toward the corner house.

I heard the sluff-sluff of loose sandals coming behind me. Good thing this wasn't New York or I'd be alarmed. Saudi Arabia was such a safe place, so little crime…probably because of their methods of dealing with it…

Suddenly a heavy body came hurtling toward me. He jumped on my back and stuck his hand on my bottom.

A huge rush of rage and fear and indignation sent the adrenalin flying. I instinctively bunched up my body and sent him catapulting over my head and onto the sidewalk. He scrambled to his feet and ran down a small alleyway to the right.

Damn. What should I do?

I looked down the street. No one was in sight. I couldn't go to our house. What if he followed me? What if he had a knife?

I started running toward the school, to the office where I worked. They would take care of me.

I stepped inside.

"I've been attacked," I said, and collapsed into a chair.

They were all over me and called the local police—The Aramco Guards.

I spent the rest of the afternoon cruising around in a cop car trying to spot the attacker. The cops were kind, but their attitude left a bit to be desired.

"Did you in any way provoke this man?"

"No, not at all!"

"What were you wearing?"

"A long skirt and dark stockings."

"Did you have your hair covered? You have a lot of hair."

"We don't cover our hair on camp."

They were trying to blame me!

"Do you know this man?"

"Are you kidding? I never saw him before."

They glanced at each other.

"Do you want us to be with you when you tell your husband?"

What in the world were they inferring?

"No, thank you, I'll explain it to him myself."

These guys were from Texas. Not Saudis. I could hardly tell the difference.

"I'll tell you what," I said, trying to be calm. "This guy is mentally disturbed. I don't think he's normal."

They laughed. Wink-wink-nudge.

"Oh, he's normal," they said.

What?

The attacker had picked a bad alley to run down. It was behind the house of the chairman of the board, the big honcho in Dhahran, and was armed with multiple security cameras. The next day when he approached another person and asked the way to the cafeteria, they were all ready for him.

He was taken into custody.

I had to go to the police station and make a statement.

That night we were called to come to the station just outside camp. I needed to identify the assailant.

We went to an outdoor area where a group of men stood in an open-sided shed. One light bulb hung overhead. They were all dressed in identical thobes and ghutras. The red-checkered cloths sent a shadow over their faces.

I had been warned by a friend who still worked at Government Affairs that nine of the ten men were cops. I had to find the right one. They would know.

I could not see their faces.

"I can't choose. This is too important for me to guess. I can't see…"

Then it was over…I thought.

The next night we had to go to the police station again. Ten men were sitting on the floor of a room. There was no glass for me to stand behind, no protection. I had to walk into the room, face the men and point one out.

I walked up to him and stood in front of him.

"You know what you did," I said.

Then we left.

They put him in jail until he could go before a judge. The judge discovered that the man had just been released from a mental hospital, and was wandering around Aramco Camp because he was visiting his brother. He was taken back to the mental facility, not jail.

I wondered if the rest of those goons should have gone with him.

Not long after that we moved out of the dark brown house. There was a place up on Apple Avenue, just above the school, half a block from work.

It would be our house for the remaining years in Aramco, a two-story stucco place with a lot of light. Living/dining room, large kitchen (with two ovens!), half-bath, and upstairs a bedroom and bath for us, bed and bath for Chris, and a spare room looking out over the garden that became my studio.

My studio!

Even Nicholas the cat liked it. Every time we had moved he became a bit more moody. Cats hate to move, and he let us know it. But Nicholas settled in on Apple Avenue.

We all did.

CHAPTER SEVENTEEN

THE LONG FORESEEN SHAKE-UP happened. The office force at Aramco schools was being cut. *School News* was being suspended. My job was over.

I could go into a secretarial pool at the administration building, or...

I chose or.

I had been thinking about it for quite some time. I needed to get back to being an artist, but not just any kind of an artist. I needed to learn a whole new world of skills.

While working at Government Affairs, researching those old reels of microfiche, I had seen them; past issues of *Aramco World*, the full-color company magazine printed in Amsterdam. Tucked into those issues were beautiful examples of Islamic art, jewel-toned paintings of a kind totally different from the Greek and Roman inspired art of the Western world. They were fascinating, especially the paintings done in Tabriz and Shiraz from 1400-1600, illustrations of the poetic works of names like Nizami andFirdausi—poets and painters of a world I had never heard of.

I could no longer access the microfiche reels. Where could I find them?

Were there teachers for this kind of art?

No.

Saudis were basket weavers and wool weavers, and potters. They had never been interested in any type of painting, especially not the representation of human figures. Since the 622 Islamic prohibitions against idolatry, only calligraphy and geometric mosaics had been used in decoration.

There were no teachers.

I would have to do my own research, hoping I was not breaking some cultural or religious taboo.

The libraries were the source. The Dhahran library was a treasure trove. The Ras Tanura library had other volumes. Even Abquaiq had a few. There were shelves of books. How did I know which ones would be the best? Most authentic?

The old Englishman who had died in the Stanley Village house came back to haunt me. His writings about Chinese creeds and customs treated the people of Stanley Village as though they were creatures in a Petri dish. I wanted to avoid that distant kind of analysis. How could I access the spirit of these ancient paintings?

A stack of books.

I piled them up next to the bed in the Apple Avenue house.

Every night before I went to sleep, I looked at the pictures, not reading the words. I was a child, looking at picture books on a pre-literate level, soaking in the colors and shapes, the elements of design like a child who does not yet know how to read. I did not want to be told, through someone else's cultural screen, what these shapes and colors represented...what their value was.

For three months I was a child looking at picture books.

Slowly, I knew.

I understood them on that pre-literate level, a very deep intuitive level.

I was ready to read the verbal explanations.

The first few books I read fell far short. Colonial observations viewed through Anglicized screens of Greek and Roman art, viewpoints that classified these pieces as not-bad decorative art, but lacking any knowledge of shadow or perspective.

I rejected those comments.

They were not evaluating this art for itself, but through the screen of their own cultural bias.

I read and rejected.

No. No.

Then one day I found it. A big wrist-breaker of a book written by a Greek in French. It had been translated into English and published in London, and found its way to the Saudi Desert. It was beautifully illustrated, and evaluated this art on its own merits, explaining what I had felt wordlessly.

One section of thirty pages on "The Art of the Book" was direct, simple, profound. Yes! This was it! This was what I had sensed.

But the material was so new. I read the words, knowing they were the real words, but there was no place in my head to comprehend them.

I read them over.

Once, yes, but...

Twice, yes okay, but...

I read them three times, and began to say yes! Yes! Yes! I get it. Oh yes, these are the words I need to know!

These artists were not ignorant of shadow and perspective. They knew about Greek and Roman art, and had rejected them as being too imitative of life, too disrespectful of God the creator. Life was not to be imitated. It was to be celebrated, from a respectful distance.

The first rule of this art was, don't make it look exactly like it is. The second was, this is an illustration...the viewer has to know what you are illustrating.

Okay, so don't make it like it is, but leave no doubt in the viewer's mind what you are drawing. Those were the main guidelines.

The others followed.

Color is an element of design. It need have no relationship to the color an object actually is.

No distortion of human or animal figures.

No nudity.

No shadows cast.

No disappearing lines of perspective.

Deal with a two-dimensional surface on which figures and objects are of equal size from top to bottom. Arrange for design, not reality.

Trees...rocks...invented.

Flowers, always blooming.

The specifications went on, eleven major ideas. They described what this painting was, not what it lacked.

I was grateful.

Yes, this was it!

Yes, yes! Yes!

The little studio up over the garden was set up. Al-Khobar had an office supply place on King Abdul Aziz Avenue close to where we had lived in the Bin Juma building. I stocked up on oils and brushes, a good drawing table from Italy, and got a work space organized.

Now, with this new style, what should I paint?

A marketplace...a souk?

How could I collect images without being able to use a camera? I would have to sketch, memorize. Avoid taking pictures of women unless they were veiled or totally covered.

Maybe I should start with charcoal drawings to get the juices rolling. We traveled to Bahrain, which was a little more liberal and allowed photos. A collection of carefully chosen shots turned into a portfolio of ten charcoal drawings of carved doors, a wind tower, a spice market, a basket seller, boats by a shore...

I began to see the beautiful designs of life in the Middle East as I never had before. Why did their art need to conform to Western art? I wanted to absorb this part of the world for what it was, to be enlarged by it, to celebrate it.

As the collection of charcoal sketches grew, I began to wonder if it would be possible to make black and white prints to sell at Aramco's art fairs.

Quietly, I began to lay out a five-year plan to maximize the time I had left in Saudi Arabia. As I looked back over the past five years, I had unknowingly been preparing for this moment all along. The microfiche at Government Affairs, the printing experience at Aramco schools ...

The printing!

While working those two and a half years in Bob Gaw's office, I had come to know Antony Cruz, a small wiry fellow from Velore, India. He had been trained as an artist, but came to Saudi Arabia as a printer, and like all of us, to earn money. Antony and I had become good friends, working together on *School News*.

I contacted him.

"If I make charcoal drawings of Saudi Arabia, can you help me produce black and white prints in quantity?"

He shook his head from side to side, that uniquely Indian gesture.

"No problem, De Pree," he smiled.

At the next art fair I had a variety of ten designs taken from Bahrain and Saudi Arabia: carved doorways, Arabian dhows... They sold wonderfully well at ten riyals apiece. I had my foot in the door. These things were just my ads.

With enough experience in black and white design, I turned to color. I would do a group of full-color paintings, not quickly, but very carefully designed according to the specifications of Persian poetry illustrations, the 1400 to 1600 Persian works, observing all the color and design laws.

I would observe all these NO rules. Usually artists in the West operated by disregarding rules, by proclaiming their total freedom, but here there were definite restrictions.

Could I exploit restrictions, use them as an opposing force to create energy?

It would be interesting to try.

We took an Aramco bus trip to Hofuf with a group of other Aramcons on a weekend. I was armed with a miniscule camera, a notebook and pencils. I dressed carefully in an Egyptian galabeya, a full long robe with convenient big pockets.

The Thursday market was bustling with customers. The street front shops had rice and spices, lentils and shoes. Inside were tailors of robes, incense burners, prayer rugs, blacksmiths, and women, carefully veiled, selling bright fabrics. At the very back there was a man selling date-flavored flat breads baked on the inside of his charcoal heated clay furnace—wonderfully fragrant.

I tried using the little camera and was immediately apprehended. I had figured as much, so, as plan B, I asked politely if I could make quick sketches. After much chatting back and forth with other market people, I was given permission to sketch…if I did not sketch women.

Between a bit of dodging and a little subterfuge, with a lot of smiling, I left Hofuf Souk with enough drawing ideas to begin the first painting.

On a canvas propped up on the Italian drawing table, I carefully laid out the design.

Geometric. Flat surfaces. Straight up and down, market places stacked like open-sided boxes. Geometric arches across the bottom. The top filled with a minarette and a stylized tree. Women in abayas, selling their huge wool balls while tending their children. Prayer rugs with the pattern pointing toward Mecca. It all fit together and began to look very Middle Eastern.

I worked in seclusion in the second-story studio, creating in fear and wonder, feeling that I was entering some secret and sacred cave of another culture—excited and exhilarated, and a bit frightened. What if I had violated some sacred code? What if I would be punished? What if I had my right hand cut off, the penalty for stealing? Was I stealing, or celebrating?

I needed to show Antony Cruz.

He climbed the stairs to our second floor and looked at the painting for a long silent moment.

"Oh, De Pree," he said finally, "this is a beautiful Indian painting."

"It's not Indian, Antony, it's Persian."

"Oh no, you know the Persian artists came to India when Akbar the Great was ruler, and taught our Indian artists to combine Hindu art with Persian to make the Moghul. This is like Mughal art. It's a perfect painting. You must make color prints of this."

"How, Antony?"

"You leave that up to me. I'm a printer," he smiled, wagging his head.

Antony brought a Pakistani photographer friend. They set the completed painting up against the stucco wall outside the house, in full sun, and took photos.

They sent the film to Thailand to develop and make into four color separations, the size we needed for a big print. There would be a yellow plate, a blue, a red and a black. When these separations returned in the mail, Antony took them to a one-color-at-a-time press in Dammam, four plates of microdots to be superimposed over each other, letting the ink dry in between coats.

I held my breath...

Then one day Antony came with a helper and they delivered a large heavy bundle of prints wrapped in brown paper. It was so hot outside that the brown paper was wet with sweat. They laid them on the couch in the Apple Avenue house. I waited until Antony was gone to look.

Then I opened them.

I gasped. Amazed...relieved.

"Oh my God, they're beautiful!" I whispered.

There they were, in full jewel colors.

Bazaar Fantasy. The Hofuf Souk.

My first Saudi Arabian Persian print.

Word got out around camp. People were curious. I took the prints to the Fall art fair. People were excited. An American had never done this before.

I sold the prints as fast as I could make change, almost selling out that first day—well over a hundred that first afternoon.

It was a real piece of Saudi tradition, in the color and style of the Middle East.

No one was angry.

I had kept inside the rules, and it was working. This was the way I would spend the remaining years in the Middle East.

I would have a treasure trove of knowledge to take back to America when we left.

We had never been under any illusion that Saudi Arabia was home. It was an unusual opportunity we had been given to expand our horizons and get ourselves financially stable, but someday we would leave it and go...

Where?

We needed to plan ahead.

Neither one of us wanted to go back to the places where we had grown up. Those roots had come up a long time ago. Life had changed us too much. We needed to find neutral ground where we could build new paths and create a stable life together, a place where we could gather our growing family together for times of sharing.

But where?

Somewhere near water? The ocean? A lake? Somewhere in the mountains? We would keep on searching. At the heart of the search was that old threadbare dream of a quiet town...a quiet street, with...oh my gosh! By now it would be cars, parked in the driveway, and soon the bikes would belong to their kids. Things were changing, but the dream was still there.

Chris was completing his first year in college. We drove to Durham, North Carolina during our summer vacation to pick him up and check how he was doing at Duke.

Apparently, very well. He had, as usual, worked hard and been an A student. He had decided on his major: physics.

"I want something that will really challenge me," he said. "I don't want to slide through college on the easy stuff."

He went to the office to pick up final grades while we were visiting. All A's, except for one. He had taken a senior level class, just to test himself. He looked at the grade, puzzled.

"What's a C?" he asked. "Is that for credit, or..."

"It's a C," we told him, laughing. "Some people do get them, you know. You probably jumped in over your head."

That broke the magic spell.

While we were in North Carolina we decided to check out future housing possibilities. Gordon and Chris had been to Bald Head Island while I was taking care of Deidra after Marita's wedding. They wanted to show it to me.

We took the South Port Ferry out to the island, as there were no bridges. We checked in at the real estate office and had someone show us around.

The island was charming—real seascapes, sand, tropical trees, the whole ambiance had the kind of dreamlike quality that made one wonder where one had been to miss this...

We looked at oceanfront property, and inland wooded areas. Would this be a good place for the family to gather when we returned to the U.S.? Our family would love the beaches. They had grown up like little sea-creatures in the South China Sea.

Was this the place?

We bought a modest lot in the thickly wooded area, in easy walking distance from the beach. The developer recommended a builder, and we set the process in motion.

We would be gone for a year, and hopefully come back next summer to a completed house.

Chris flew back to Saudi Arabia with us for the rest of the summer. It was pure delight to wake up in the morning and see him there, a tall wonderful young man who had weathered so much and come through apparently unscathed.

"Do you like Duke now?" I asked him one morning.

"I do. I have an advisor who's been very helpful..."

"Any girlfriends?"

"No, not yet. I hang out with a bunch of friends...no one special yet. Maybe I've been working too hard. Maybe next year I'll try to relax a bit and have a little more fun; maybe do some cartooning."

I knew it. That 'C' had done it. He had become a common mortal.

We took Chris along when we drove to Qatif to visit the Date Farm of a ninety-year-old Saudi. He still ran his own business out in the fields every day. We had permission from him to come and see his layout, and to take photos and sketches to plan a new piece of Persian art.

He came out to meet us, striding along easy and sun-browned, his white thobe and checkered ghutra worn with a jaunty air.

We toured his fields. His tall palm trees were loaded with clusters of dates. It was picking season, and Egyptian workers climbed the trees, tossing down heavy clumps of fruit to the gatherers on the ground. Deep irrigation channels circled their way through the trees. Goats and chickens roamed about.

Buyers came to look over the dates. Ali entertained them with cups of coffee, sitting on a rug under a lime tree. The whole place had the look of an enterprise that could have happened hundreds of years ago. Nothing had changed.

We asked him about his famous age. Was it true?

"Ninety," he said, holding up nine fingers.

"How do you stay so young?" we asked him.

"Amshi!" he said, walking his fingers like the yellow pages ad. "Walk. Every day, walk!"

"Is that all?"

"No drinking," he said, grinning.

Then he showed us a special vat he had where he brewed a thick sweet kind of date liquor.

"For mothers," he said. "After the baby is born...for getting strength back."

Was that the only use the date liquor was put to? We were careful not to ask.

That day we gathered all the elements of a new design. Tall rugged date trees with waving fronds, nimble men with bare feet, their bodies slung from the trees in rope braces, irrigation ditches winding through the trees, buyers sitting under the tree on a woven carpet, goats and chickens, and the date grower himself, at home in his trees.

It would make a great new piece.

That summer I worked on Date Harvest, following all the rules of design and color. Antony Cruz put it through the photo and printing process, and we had a new print ready for fall.

It was not as much of a shock to people as the first one had been, but it sold very well. People even came to our house on Apple Avenue to buy copies.

A frame shop in Khobar, Inma Gallery, asked if they could handle my work—wholesale.

The people at the American Consulate in Dhahran asked if I would do a black and white print for their place.

The consul general's wife told the ambassador's wife in Riyadh about my work, and they requested a show and lecture for sometime in the future.

Things were catching on. This was the 'or' that I had chosen.

It was exciting and deeply satisfying.

The night I had stepped off the plane the first time in Saudi Arabia, I thought I had died and gone to a cultural hell.

How little we know what we are doing at any given time, and what impact it will have on the future.

Chapter Eighteen

WE WENT BACK TO BALD Head Island the next summer and had a family get-together. The twins, married nine months apart, now both had babies—Marita's Adrian and Mike's Chelsea. We were grandparents.

The house was beautiful, but a bit short of our expectations. We realized that it was not wise to have a place built without being there. We had paid full price and a whole section of the house was missing.

But we still enjoyed the island that summer. My mom came. Her husband had just died and she was feeling alone. It was good to have four generations under one roof—almost Chinese.

We delighted in the waves and the sand, took long walks on the beach, swam and sunned and shared the cooking of meals, but there was something missing. It was not a town where people were at home; it was a vacation resort. It felt like a summer camp. The collection of people who formed the core group were not people with whom we had much in common. They were gracious well-to-do Southerners, much more wealthy than we would ever be. 'Whiskey-palians' who played croquet seriously. They put on something called a 'White Party' that left us wondering what it was all about. What if you were not white? Would you still be invited to the party?

Then we had a horrible hurricane. The wind and waves pounded the island and washed away much of the beach. Trees twisted and fell. The ferry service was cut off and we could not even leave. We crowded, wet and chilled, in our island house until the storm was over. When we finally made it to the mainland, our car was standing in two feet of water in the parking lot.

We all, mutually, decided that it had been fun, but it was over.

We would sell the house and start over. Someday we would find just the right place to gather.

Back to Saudi Arabia...back to the peaceful little house on Apple Avenue and the studio overlooking the garden.

The prints were doing well, selling at all the different Aramco camps where the art fairs were held, and at Inma Gallery in Khobar.

But there should be one more at least—something to do with the sea and the Arabian dhows, and the fishermen.

Where was the best place to photograph boats?

We asked Criff Crawford.

"Jubail," he said, " but it's a little tricky right now. That's very close to the Saudi Arabian-Kuwaiti border, and any photography of boats right now might raise suspicion of sabotage."

"Sabotage?"

"The whole Iraq-Kuwait dispute over oil rights affects the oil people in Saudi, so we'll have to get permission from Government Affairs."

It was as complex as going to the Rub-al-khali, but in a political sense, not a life-threatening sense.

We caravanned up the highway to Jubail, the Crawfords, the DeWaards, the Gaws and the De Prees. We were packed to the gills with food, water, gas, tents, and the obligatory home-made wine. We would camp along the Arabian Gulf, quite close to the Kuwaiti border.

"Don't be surprised if we're questioned by border guards," Criff warned. "In fact, I'd better go up to the guard post and tell them we're here so they don't accidentally discover us and tell us to leave."

We set up camp that evening with the Gulf water washing up close to our campsite. The moon came up round and huge over the sea...so luminous in the total absence of any other light than our campfire... Silver folds rolling with the motion of the water, gentle, molten, creeping in and slipping out...

There was a feeling in the air that night of things about to change. The DeWaards were getting ready to leave. The Gaws were wondering how long to stay. We were getting 'short,' and the Crawfords had been in Saudi Arabia for so long that they, too, were thinking of purchasing land or housing somewhere in the Western part of the United States for their future.

We quietly watched the sea, shimmering in the moonlight, and smelled the smoke of our beach fire roasting meat. We sipped Kate's wine, her special brew actually made of grapes trodden by foot in a tub.

Where would we go after this?

We awoke the next morning to the aroma of Jack's special coffee, and looked out over a sandy expanse.

Where was the sea? It had been right up on us when we fell asleep. Now it had receded so far out with the tide that it had almost disappeared.

"Strong moon gravitation," Criff explained. "There's a huge area of mudflats this morning. We can walk out hundreds of feet and explore the ocean floor."

I was getting anxious about the photos to be taken. What if we got arrested before I had a chance to get the boat shots?

"We can go shoot pictures this morning," Criff promised. "The tide won't start coming in until later this afternoon."

We drove to the industrial town of Jubail. It was more an oil pumping station than a residential town like Dhahran or Ras Tanura. One had the feeling of pipes and tanks...of oil happening.

The seaport was an important part of Jubail. A long pier stretched out into the water, and in the central area it was lined with small boats and fishing dhows. The dhows had an eerie resemblance to the fishing junks of Hong Kong, much the same ancient structure, still being used to procure food from the sea.

The waterfront was carefully guarded. Our camera was questioned. Why were we taking pictures? Who were we?

We showed our Aramco Id.

"What is your purpose?" the guard asked.

"I'm an artist. I'm doing a series of paintings depicting Saudi traditions, and I need to document the structure of boats used in fishing."

The guard looked doubtful. Criff threw in a few words of Arabic.

"Only if I can go with you and watch what you are photographing," the guard said cautiously.

"I assure you, I'm harmless."

The guard allowed us to photograph the hulls of the dhows, the cabin superstructure, small boats, fishermen at work with their nets...all that we needed to construct a seafaring painting along Persian art lines.

Luckily, we got what we needed.

It was after noon when we arrived back at our campsite. The tide had turned and was coming back in. We hurried out to get a look at the ocean floor before it disappeared under the waves.

There were big pools of water in the sand where sea creatures had been temporarily stranded, large squid, fish, others creatures we had never seen, waiting in the small pools until the sea returned to bring them their freedom in the great kingdom of water.

The sand patterns where the water had been were like the wind patterns on the dunes in the Rub-al-khali. Wind, water, sand, the great universal patterns of life, so rich and so unmindful of political lines and wars over oil...beautiful, beautiful world, so majestic in its unified power, so much more enduring than the lives of any of us.

We suddenly noticed that the tide was coming in fast. The sand we were standing on was becoming an island, surrounded by bigger incoming waves. We hurried to shore, not wanting to be washed out to sea.

Back on Dhahran camp I developed the shots taken in Jubail. They were superb. There were the dhows, their wooden structures clear and concise. The faces of the fishermen were varied and full of character. The little boats...the sea creatures found in the adjoining fish market...everything I needed to make a work authentic as well as well designed. Design from authentic information. It was the perfect 'know what you are illustrating, but don't make it just like it is' situation.

But waves. How does one depict waves if they are not to be like they are?

I drew a series of squares and within each square did a designed wave, crest and trough, repeated over and over, wave, crest, trough, contained in squares. It created the rhythm of the sea. I constructed one area above the sea with birds, one area on the sea with waves and boats and men, and one section below the surface, with schools of fish swimming in patterns.

It was the sea, in Persian art.

Fishermen and the Sea.

Now we were into the marketing, and to my surprise, I had started a business in Saudi Arabia. No tax. No accounting. Someone handed me riyals, and I handed them art. It was a business done out of my jeans pocket. I was earning roughly as much as I had when employed by the company.

And as a bonus, I had learned a new set of skills to take back to the United States with me.

Did I suffer in Saudi Arabia?

Not on your life.

It was a gift.

Ten years in the unwrapping.

In 1988, Chris graduated from Duke. We were there, proud parents. He had completed his undergraduate work in physics and now faced the question—What kind of physics? nuclear physics or astro-physics?

He did not want to be part of any weapons program, so he chose astrophysics. That meant grad school.

But Chris and his girlfriend, Julia, were getting serious. The question of marriage had to be decided. They were both through college. Was this the time?

Chris was in Saudi Arabia the summer they decided to get married. We took him to the gold store in Al-Khobar to get a diamond for Julia.

They were married in Cleveland, her home town, in her parents' church. The reception was at the University Club, with friends from the Cleveland Symphony Orchestra providing the dance music. Our whole family was there, toasting and feasting and dancing. It was a beautiful party...

But...was there a bit of reserve? A slight air of sadness? Did I imagine that?

When we kissed them goodbye, and they were going on their honeymoon, I felt it. They looked so beautiful together, the quintessential bride and groom—she, tall and blond, and he, dark and handsome...

"You two will have a beautiful life together," I said, hugging them.

"I hope so..." Julia answered.

Something about the way she said it struck fear in my heart. Did she really love him? I thought of the day Chris and I gathered shells on the beach, and hoped that this, his chosen woman, would love him as much as the woman who bore him.

On a summer trip to the States, right after the Bald Head Island venture, we had visited with Aramco friends, the Hahns. They had bought an old house in Raleigh's historic Oakwood District, and encouraged us to do the same. It was a good investment, and we were still in search of a home.

We purchased an 1895 'Pullen House' in Oakwood, a two-story brick house in good external and structural condition, but sadly divided inside into three tacky apartments. It would take radical remodeling when we returned to the U.S., but for the time being would remain a rental. Our friend, Nancy Hahn, offered to be the 'landlady,' and collect rents until we returned.

Two of the apartments were available, so, anticipating our return, Chris and Julia decided to live there for a year while Chris taught at a private high school. Deidra and Rob, still searching for what they wanted in life, decided to join them. So, for the 1988-1989 year, the Pullen House was inhabited by the De Prees before we ever lived there.

They enjoyed the old musty place, the crazy room divisions, the make-do bathrooms, and the backyard...grilling in the backyard oven an open fire, anticipating our return.

'Short' was the term. The word, like many other things on Aramco Camp, had military origins. Gordon had been 'short' when he was coming back from Korea. Now we were getting 'short' in the Middle East.

Even Nicholas the cat was getting short. The water finally got to him and his kidneys failed. He had been right all along. Fortunately, ours held up. We gave him a decent burial in the backyard at Apple Avenue.

That summer we took a trip back to the States, knowing that it might be our last leisurely vacation from Saudi Arabia. The question of where we would settle could no longer be delayed.

Did we really want to live in Raleigh, or had we acted too quickly?

We stopped by in Raleigh to check things out. It was hot—hot and sticky like Hong Kong. I walked across a parking lot and my shoes stuck to the tar.

Just before we left Saudi Arabia we had been invited to a friend's house for dinner. During the conversation around the dinner table we talked to a woman from Blowing Rock, North Carolina.

"If you're looking for a beautiful place to settle, you should check out the North Carolina Mountains," she suggested. "Start out at Blowing Rock, and explore the area. You might like it."

We drove from Raleigh, up through Chapel Hill and on up to the mountains. As we climbed higher that July day, the air cooled. We were going through a place called Deep Gap, four hours from Raleigh, when we opened the car windows and smelled the air. It was cool, fresh. The wind was blowing, and suddenly there were hail balls—in July!

I stuck my hand out, welcoming the cool.

"I don't know what this is," I called, "but I want it!"

We drove to Blowing Rock.

Yes, but no.

We checked out Boone.

If one worked at the university, it could be good. But for us, no.

Then the real estate agent, just short of dumping us, suggested a new frontier, a place called West Jefferson. It was a very small town, a used-to-be railroad town of around 1,000, but the center of a county with a population of around 25,000, all out in the country and tucked into back roads. Interesting demographics.

We drove down the hill on Highway 221 into West Jefferson. Before and above us loomed a huge, dark blue mountain. The whole scene was straight up and down, with houses and fields and trees tucked into the patterned hillsides. I would not even have to bend reality to paint Persian art here!

"You know…" I said slowly, "I think I could live here."

We drove into town. It was not much. Half boarded up. Quiet.

We let the real estate agent lead us through cow pastures and over a barely visible dirt road, thinking to never do it again. We stopped in a field where a log cabin was being built, a very little cabin built out of huge old logs.

We went inside and looked. It was clever, with a big fieldstone fireplace, log walls, an open kitchen, and a stairway leading up to the second bedroom and bath upstairs under the beamed ceiling. Bed and bath downstairs.

Then we stepped out onto the back porch and saw it, a wide mountain stream, gathered into a pool and escaping over a shallow waterfall, just big enough to create creek music within feet of the cabin.

We looked at each other.

It was a boat moment.

That creek…

"Thank you very much," we told the realtor. "We'll think about it."

We did think about it…all night in a motel in Boone.

We left the next morning to visit De and Rob, who had moved back to Missouri, and while there, telephoned the real estate agent asking him to send a contract to an address in New York City where we would be staying overnight. We would sign the contract there and mail it back to North Carolina before we flew out of the country.

We had bought a log cabin in the North Carolina Mountains, and a creek.

We thought we would be back in a year to live there…

We took the long route back to Saudi Arabia, sensing that this would be our last time to travel through Europe on company leave. We booked a riverboat trip from Amsterdam, up the Rhine River to Basil, Switzerland.

Lazy, wonderful days on the boat, going ashore to catch a glimpse into our Germanic/Dutch roots. If our ancestors had not been the adventurers they were, this might have been where we would have lived out our lives, eating German black bread and Dutch cheese. But this area had been the soil on which all the battles of the Reformation had taken place, the split between Catholic and Protestant, the further divisions into Lutheran, Dutch Reformed, and a myriad of divergent groups. These were restless, searching people, not unlike ourselves.

What was the meaning of it all, this insatiable search for a genuine consciousness of the Creative Power? Would it ever lead to a spirit in which we could all learn from one another what the true essence of this mystery signified—or would religious rivalries continue to create violence?

We stayed at a small hotel in Basil, and then flew back to Saudi Arabia, ready to settle in for our last year.

There was an undercurrent on Camp when we returned to Dhahran. Iraq was in the news. Saddam Hussein was saber rattling. Disputes over oil, who was stealing who's oil. Saudi Arabia would remain neutral, not wanting to get involved.

On August 5, 1990, we were on the beach at Ras Tanura enjoying a long leisurely swim, just days after we had returned to Saudi Arabia. We saw a friend come walking toward us, waving.

"Have you heard?" he called.

"Heard what?"

"Saddam Hussein has marched on Kuwait. There's a war!"

"A war? Not in Saudi Arabia!"

"We'll be involved. Refugees are starting to come over the border. America will probably be involved. The oil."

"But it belongs to the Saudis now."

"Yeah, well tell it to the judge. How are they going to protect it? The Saudis aren't fighters..."

We hastily picked up our belongings and caught a bus back to Dhahran. The busses were Saudi now. Greyhound had lost the contract to a local company.

Desert Shield was announced in a few days. We were at war. Heavy-bellied planes flew low over our house, heading for the military air field. The king had not yet given the go-ahead for American troops to land. These were only precautionary measures.

Things happened rapidly.

Gordon checked in at the admin building. Our status—we were just short of our ten years, but because he would turn 60 in September, and we had been here over nine years, we were eligible to retire with full pension and benefits on September 26.

This year!

In less than two months!

The family were all watching events on CNN. We had never had TV in Saudi Arabia, but we heard the war was being depicted on American TV as big-time breaking news. The kids were all writing, begging us to come back.

Secretly, we would have liked to stay, to see what would happen. Maybe we could ride out on tanks and bring ice to the soldiers in the desert, but the kids had other ideas.

"What good will it do you to earn a few more paychecks if you get killed?" Marita wrote.

She was always the one to clarify the situation.

So we put in for our leaving date and arranged for the packers to come and crate up our goods. This time we did have treasures we wanted to take back to the U.S., mostly our rug collection. The rugs from Iran were contraband, since the tensions with that country, but they could go back as household items.

There was only one problem with leaving so soon. The American Embassy in Riyadh had heard about my work with Persian art, and had asked me to come as a speaker and presenter for an American Women's Association meeting—a date I had confirmed before leaving for the U.S. summer vacation. It would take place just twelve days before we left the country, but I had to honor the commitment. Besides, it was a wonderful opportunity, and I did not want to miss it.

I was in Riyadh that day, having lunch with the ambassador and his wife, only the ambassador was not with us. He was in a meeting with Arnold Schwartzkopf and Colin Powell at the palace of the king, convincing his highness that America must send troops on the ground to Saudi Arabia to protect the oil fields.

We had our meeting at the embassy with a huge crowd of American expat women. They listened politely, and then swarmed into the area where embassy workers had laid out the prints, the three colored prints of Saudi Arabia. They were women with a lot of money and not much to spend it on, and they bought prints like they were going out of style. The embassy women handled the sales. I chatted with people and signed artwork.

The women had to board busses to get back to their compounds, as none of them were allowed to drive. It all came and went so fast—

We were in a war.

I was selling art.

We were leaving the country.

Life would change for all of us.

Back in Dhahran the packers had come and were boxing us up. The usual procedures—an e-box with our goods to arrive almost as soon as we did, and the rest of the shipment to follow. Into the e-box we slipped our three most priceless possessions, the three original oil paintings of Bazaar

Fantasy, Date Harvest, and Fishermen and the Sea, representing years of research and work.

We were leaving. So many people were leaving. Gordon had offered to stay a while and teach so the school would not be understaffed, but his papers got lost on someone's desk in the general confusion. We were packed and had our tickets to fly before they got back to him.

Yes, would he stay?

No. We had one foot on the plane.

The trip back.

We had always fantasized about our last flight out of Saudi Arabia. We had always traveled coach, or at most been upgraded to business class, but this last flight would be a celebration. We would go first class all the way!

But that is not exactly what happened. We flew out on a Jordanian Airlines plane with armed guards standing in the aisles. No gourmet meals...subsistence until we reach Amman...slogging it to New York. Dragging in like refugees.

By that weekend we were back in North Carolina. The little cabin on the creek that we had planned to see a year later was our landing pad.

The whole Saudi Arabian venture was over.

Our e-box arrived and we took the three oil paintings out, and hung them on our log cabin walls, on nails.

We bought a bed and a table and a small couch, and laid down a few Persian rugs, and began a whole new chapter of our lives. We had a big open stone fireplace and a creek tumbling over a waterfall, and a whole new life ahead of us.

At the Burgess Furniture Company where we bought our bed, Bob Burgess looked at us curiously.

"Where you all from?" he asked.

"I'm from Michigan; my wife's from Kentucky," Gordon said.

He looked us over.

"Well, we'll take her," he said, "but you're a Yankee. We'll give you six months."

SECTION SIX

1990-2013

CHAPTER NINETEEN

COMING BACK TO THE APPALACHIAN Mountains had a feeling of rightness about it—almost inevitability. I had been here before...

But the North Carolina Mountains were taller and bluer, and kinder. The rivers seemed cleaner, the sky wider.

It was as though the world itself had undergone a cleaning process, and now I could reach out to the beauty around me without the dark screen of pain and confusion of my younger years.

There was so much that was familiar. I knew the songs, the attitudes, the little 'in' jokes. If someone started a song, I knew it—all four parts and all four verses.

In many ways, I was back home.

But in other aspects this was like being newborn. We did not know a soul. We had no connections. In other parts of the world that did not matter, but here it did. We looked like everybody else, but were we?

Who, with all this scrambled identity and the acceptance of all things—who were we? What did we have to give this community? What did we want from it?

Many years before, the two of us had met in a log cabin in Kentucky. The magic of that meeting never left us.

The sudden presence of each other.

That flash of recognition of the other person.

Powerful, breathtaking...

We had never forgotten that moment. I had been nineteen and Gordon twenty-two. The power of that meeting had sustained us through years of wild adventures, always there, the underlying source, the motivation, the fire.

Now we were 57 and 60.

We had children and grandchildren. Did we still have that same fire, that same sense of magic and wonder that had taken us across continents and into cultures? Could we find that same sense of astonishment here in this small mountain community in America?

Yes, yes, but...

The fire was still there, but we would need to learn how to reshape it. These were not Chinese or Arabs. They were Americans.

In fact, given time, could this mountain village possibly be the little American town we had always dreamed of, the quintessential place we had been heading toward all our lives?

Our love affair with the mountains was at first less than mutual. The town of West Jefferson had been there since the early nineteen hundreds, and had arisen out of a community of Scotch-Irish who had lived there since the seventeen hundreds, even before the territory was called America. It had seen the Revolutionary War, the Civil War, and World Wars I and II. Its family names were engraved in the soil. Outsiders had come and gone. We were just two more outsiders.

We looked the town over. Jefferson Avenue ran like a long spine down the middle. One cross street called Main created a center where the town hall sat. Along the stretch of Jefferson Avenue, small shops spread their wares. Some shops were shuttered.

There were pawn shops, antique shops, a few dress shops and a gun shop. A drugstore. A restaurant...

There was a train station, now deserted, and a hotel, empty. The town had once centered around the train coming up to the mountains to bring tourists anxious for the cool mountain air, but the train had stopped in the mid-seventies. It was, in some ways, a town that had lost one identity and not yet found another—a place waiting to happen again.

The one identity that remained strong was embodied in the churches. There was a big red brick Baptist church, a red brick Methodist church, and a grey stone Presbyterian church with classic arches. Like most southern towns, the social structures were grouped around which church one belonged to. People who did not go to church basically did not belong.

Having been Presbyterian (by default) most of our lives, one Sunday morning we wandered in and sat down in a pew.

The atmosphere of the church was quiet. The walls were plain. The windows were simple panes of frosted glass, with one stained glass window at the back of the church. The minister was intelligent. No one offered to convert us. In fact, no one even noticed us.

We worshipped quietly and left. They were a busy group, all saying hello to the people they said hello to every week.

If we wanted to belong, we had some work to do.

Those first weeks we wandered about the quiet little town, wondering why we had come...and then we looked up at the big blue mountain and knew there was no reason. We had come because we were drawn, on a deep visceral level that we had learned to trust. Like falling in love with each other, we had fallen in love with this mountain community, and time would show us what that meant.

Our goods arrived from Saudi Arabia. Fortunately, we had not sent much, just important things. There was minimal storage place in the cabin. We rolled up the extra rugs and put them under the bed. There were closets built up under the eaves in the top bedroom where we stored other items. It was like living on a boat. Every inch counted.

Included in the shipment were boxes of prints from Saudi Arabia. What would we ever do with those here? People bought things that were familiar, not scenes from other countries and cultures.

We would have to adapt the art to scenes more appropriate to the mountains.

We unpacked.

Pillows made from the weaving done in southern Iraq.

The cushions of a majalis, big bed-sized couch cushions, so Middle Eastern.

Were we nostalgic for that godforsaken desert?

Not really—that was past. But there were people who came to mind, people we would never forget.

Mary Norton—a friend in Government Affairs who had been interested in what we were developing in Persian Art. She was a long-term Aramcon of the old school and had retired before we left. She might be interested to see how we had developed the ideas. We had her address.

We sorted out three eight by ten miniatures of the major Saudi paintings and sent them to her in Texas with a note, and our phone number.

A week later there was a call from Mary Norton. She was excited about the prints, and had sent them on to Washington D.C. to a friend working in the Saudi Embassy.

"You'll never believe what happened," she told us. "The very day the prints arrived and my friend was opening them, someone was looking over his shoulder. She turned out to be the emissary of Princess Haifa, the wife of Prince Bandar. The girl asked if she could show the prints to her boss."

"You're kidding!"

"Not a bit! And Princess Haifa is interested in knowing if the originals of these prints are still available."

"Yes, we still have them."

"You'll probably be hearing from her."

"But what if she wants to buy them? I have no idea what to charge!"

"Don't give them away," Mary advised. "You must remember, those paintings are the result of years of research and work."

"I don't have a clue. You'll have to advise me."

"I'll think it over and be in touch."

I hung up the phone. I looked around the cabin. This world we had now chosen, this simple quiet way of life… It was so far from the world of money and power we had left in Saudi Arabia. The paintings…how could I evaluate them, hanging on a nail in a cabin on a creek in the mountains?

I waited.

Mary would be in touch.

We needed to start doing art that would connect us with where we were, not where we had been.

The scene that had taken my breath away when we first drove into town…that was the place to start.

We reconstructed the moment, drove down 221, and stopped. This was it. The mighty mountain, patterned tree fields, houses, barns, horses and cows, fences… I photographed and sketched parts of the composition, and then took them home to begin designing the first Blue Ridge Persian art piece.

I drew and designed,

I inked the design, following the rules.

Then I began painting.

Yes, the ideas were transferable. The art was perfect for this terrain!

But the cabin was dark. The windows were small. The lights were dim. It was nice and cozy for a night by the fire with a glass of wine, but not exactly studio light. I took the painting outside, and was shocked. The colors that had looked rich and jewel-like in the darkness looked like they had been bleached to pastels in the daylight.

Yikes.

I looked out at the back porch perched over the creek.

"Could we enclose those three walls in glass windows, like big sliding doors, so we'd have plenty of light and could still walk down to the creek?" I asked.

That was all Gordon needed: a project. I was absorbed with the art, but he was getting restless. He needed to create a niche for himself, needed to form a new identity.

He went downtown in West Jefferson, asked questions, and ended up with the Pollards, the glass people. They built forms, enclosed the spaces with big doors of glass, and viola! We had a beautifully lighted working studio, only paces from the creek and the waterfall.

Mountain Patchquilt.

It began to take shape. Quilts were a popular art form in the mountains. Women worked in groups and singly to produce many patterns of quilts. Could I take patterns of trees, houses, fences, horses and cows, and make them into a design reminiscent of a quilt?

It would connect, and art was all about connections. If it did not speak the language of the community, no one would hear.

Mountain Patchquilt was finished.

It was Persian.

It was North Carolina Mountain. Would people accustomed to photographic reality accept this unknown approach?

Should I make a print? Where was Antony Cruz when I needed him? He had done it all. I knew nothing about making prints.

Like Gordon and the glass people, I searched for (and found) an art printer. Hall Printing Company in High Point, North Carolina, a huge lithograph company that made prints for artists across the whole United States.

Their representative, Cliff Snyder, met us at a McDonalds near the Greensboro Airport, and we signed a contract. He took our original and our first print was on the way.

Art fairs had been our way of selling prints in Saudi Arabia, so we began to search for activities of this type in our area. They would not begin until the next summer, but we needed to apply.

One of the biggest fairs in our area was right in the town of West Jefferson, on the 4th of July weekend. In honor of the local Christmas tree growers, a huge business, the fair was called 'Christmas in July,' and was held in the center of town on Jefferson Avenue each year. The street was closed to traffic, and vendors came from all over the state. There was food, music, crafts, art, and rides for the kids. It was a big deal, and I looked forward to being a part of it with my prints, both the Saudi pieces and the new Mountain Patchquilt print, which included a Christmas tree field, and should be just right.

Our whole family was coming for Christmas, the actual December Christmas. It would be a real squeeze—there were thirteen of us now—in around one thousand square feet. Marita and Pete had Adriaan and a new baby, Emma. Mike and Jayme had Chelsea. De and Rob, and Chris and Julia, did not have children yet. We would need lots of sleeping bags. Gordon had put bunks in the guest bedroom, and the pull-out majlis couch in the studio would help, but thirteen around the table! It would be like Chinese New Year in the Jeng's rice shop in Stanley. What a celebration!

Just as we were getting in the Christmas spirit in early December, we got a call from Gordon's brother Bruce that Dad De Pree was dying. We should come immediately.

Dad was 95 and had been lost ever since Gordon's mom had died.

We drove all the way to Holland, Michigan and straight to the hospital, but he had already passed away. Good Dad, who had worked so hard to bring up his family, and always been so generous...was no more.

He was laid to rest next to Mom De Pree in the cemetery where Gordon and the neighborhood kids used to play funeral, and Gordon had preached from the tombstones.

From now on we would put flowers on their graves every Memorial Day and remember their good lives.

Each of us wondered how we would be remembered when the time came. Love. Family. Giving. What else mattered?

Life, so long in the living, and then so suddenly finished.

But Life itself goes on. The family all came to the little cabin for Christmas, finding their way from Massachusetts, Missouri, Iowa and Chapel Hill, North Carolina. Mike was practicing law, Marita and Pete were involved in private school life, De and Rob had journalism jobs, and Chris was in Chapel Hill working toward a PhD in Radio Astronomy, Astro-Physics. Julia was getting a doctorate in French Literature.

Life flows on—joy and heartbreak, birth and death, and always the healing power of love. Hopefully, we would all find our way.

Getting ready for the fairs of the coming summer, I did another Persian Mountain design of Buck Mountain Road. When Cliff Snyder delivered the second batch of prints, I wondered where we would store them. The bedroom was full. We were sleeping beside stacks of boxes. These things were expensive. We had better be good marketers!

We began getting replies from the fairs. Out of seventeen shows applied for, sixteen gave a yes. I had only one no. It was from 'Christmas in July,' in West Jefferson, the town we had chosen to be our home. Our art, being 'strange and foreign,' was not acceptable.

What a kick in the teeth!

First I was hurt, and then I was mad. This damned little hick town. I was painting historic art, world famous art. Who did they think they were?

And then I felt puzzled.

We had made quite a few friends in town—had even started going to the Presbyterian Church regularly. The farm I had painted belonged to one of the pillars of the church, and she had bought one. Why were we turned down?

It was definitely a one-sided love affair.

We did the other sixteen fairs that year, taking our show on the road in a pickup truck with a covered bed. We had wooden racks built for displaying prints. Our big white canvas tent was festooned with Middle Eastern weavings. We won 'Best of Show' in Blowing Rock (with the original of Bazaar Fantasy). People were fascinated with the Persian Art—all except in West Jefferson.

What kind of a town had we picked to call home? Could we survive here?

We began to wonder if we had been hasty in our choice. Should we try a larger city, a place that had more exposure to different streams of thought? We still owned the property in Raleigh, and actually, we needed to decide what to do with it.

Should we take charge of the Pullen House on Elm Street, close it to the renters and renovate it, bringing it back to its original 1895 splendor? We could have a townhouse and a mountain house…

Gordon loved the idea. He was itching to fix up that grand old house.

Just when we decided we might make the move, leave everything in the mountain house and live in the historic house in Raleigh while we renovated it, there was a letter from Princess Haifa's emissary.

The princess had decided to buy all three originals. We should deliver them to an address in Washington D.C. Could we please state the price? A check would be waiting for us.

Oh my God.

The princess was buying.

What better validation of the Persian work could there be?

We called Mary Norton. She gave us a price.. The deal was concluded. We would deliver the pieces.

So there, West Jefferson!

Gordon was feeling a little strange. He had pressure in his chest. I thought he might be getting anxious to get started on the Raleigh renovation job. He went to a local mountain doctor who suggested he see a cardiologist in Raleigh. He might be having trouble getting enough oxygen in his heart.

We would check it out, as soon as we had time.

I looked at the three oil paintings hanging on the grey log walls of the cabin. They were suddenly worth thousands of dollars. I was almost afraid of them, as though they had taken on a life of their own.

We bought yards of wine-colored velvet fabric and I sewed covers for them, velvet envelopes to enclose each one for the long trip up to Washington D.C. in our pickup truck.

It was raining the day we drove to D.C. We were afraid the truck bed might leak.

We rang the doorbell at the given address, and a polite young Saudi woman came to the door. She was certainly not covered in an abaya. Short skirt and boots, low-cut top and long straight hair—the picture of fashion.

We stayed there that night and left the next morning, leaving the paintings leaning on the hallway wall.

"Princess Haifa wants to put your work in the new cultural museum she is building in Riyadh," the emissary explained. "You'll be getting the check in the mail from our office. Let me be sure we have your Raleigh address."

Almost stunned at what had happened, we drove past the White House that rainy morning, and waved to George and Barbara Bush.

Then back to Raleigh for the big renovation job.

Gordon remembered he needed to check in with the cardiologist. He would do it and get it over with.

They did a stress test, and sent him to the hospital for a catherization.. He was put straight into a room and prepared for surgery.

He needed a triple bypass.

I could not believe it…

Not that heart! The heart that had beat so strongly all these years—the heart that belonged to me! How could they take it out of his body and sew new veins onto it, like mending a sock? They had no right to do this—there was some mistake!

But it was true. Right in the middle of this big house renovation, Gordon needed heart surgery.

Not knowing who to call, I panicked and called Joyce Bell, my old buddy from Hong Kong. She always knew what to do. Bless her heart, she got in her Cadillac Coup Deville and came barrelling down from Philadelphia. She was there for us. The four kids all came straggling into Raleigh, looking like we felt—in shock. Joyce mothered all of us. She bought food for us and fed us in our torn-apart, second floor apartment covered in dust.

We would never forget it.

Gordon was all right.

He came to the big old house and rested in bed for exactly five days. Then he got up and walked around the block. They were making a film around the corner, and he wanted to catch a glimpse of Lauren Bacall, who was starring in it.

Gordon wrote lists of things to do. He could cross off the heart surgery. That was done.

Tear down the false partitions.

Restore regular room shapes and sizes.

Decide on paint colors.

Re-do plumbing and electrical wiring.

The renovation went on, and that was the end of the heart problem. He never missed a beat.

The check came from Princess Haifa for the art. I handed it over to Gordon without even opening it. We would need it for the renovation.

It would be well invested.

After months of work, the house on Elm Street was finished. Outside, the old red bricks had been power washed. The fenestrations had to be guarded by the Historical Society, then repainted with their historical colors. The landscaping was finished with an herb garden behind the house, graced with a white bird bath. We left the old camellia bushes, which must have been there for decades. In the backyard there were fig trees and a big pecan tree.

Inside, a curved stairway arose out of the central hallway, climbing to the floor above. On the main floor, the living room on the left was painted a deep suede green with a fireplace and creamy white trims. To the right of the central hall the dining room was a deep warm 'Raleigh Tavern Red,' with warm white shutters and a sparkling chandelier.

The kitchen had been given a gathering-room feel, with warm white walls, open beams, a working wood fireplace, and hand-crafted pine cabinets topped with marble from Saudi Arabia (Italian). There was a bar with colorful pendant lights and a wooden chop block.

A country English table completed the look.

All the bedrooms were in warm whites, with quilts and rugs, taking the house back to its post-Victorian era. We furnished the rooms with pieces of antique Stickley furniture.

There was a piano in the living room.

At Christmas the house was stunning. Lighted candles were in every window. An eleven-foot Christmas tree stood in the dining room, covered with 95 crocheted white angels to remember Dad De Pree. The table was set with bone China from Belks—the first china we had ever bought.

It was on the Raleigh Oakwood Christmas Tour of Homes. All the kids came to help us celebrate in the new house. Joyce and Steve even drove down and did a video of the whole place.

Then we got the bills for the taxes and insurance. We were still paying off the last of the college loans for four kids…

We could not afford to keep the big beautiful old house.

So…we sold it.

I really did not care.

Old is lovely, but one can never get all the cockroaches out of 100-year-old houses. They seem to be in the woodwork, as though it were their ancestral right. Someday, we would build just the right place and it would be new.

Contemporary.

Daring.

Dashing.

We moved further downtown, across from an artist's co-op named Artspace. It was a city-sponsored large gallery made over from an old Ford dealership, where many artists worked.

I had applied, and had been juried in, because of the Persian art. Getting in was not easy, and many people were juried out. Maybe being different was helpful in a larger city.

I was in, but by the skin of my teeth. All that was available was a small place on the third floor. We fixed it up, and I began to work in Raleigh.

We began to wonder where we were going. All of this seemed so random. Perhaps we should sell the cabin in the mountains. Even if we decided to go back to West Jefferson to live, we would need more space. The boxes of prints were beginning to take over. We could let it go and buy a piece of land farther on down the same beloved creek, and build a bigger cabin.

But while we were living in Raleigh, I wanted to use the Persian art to connect with the surroundings there. I designed a 'City Market Square' piece depicting the downtown cluster around the old market. I made prints. Then I began to eye the old capitol building. With its strong Greek Revival architecture it would make a perfect Persian piece. Statuary and pools, people, stone and brick work, fountains and paths, luxurious dogwoods and azaleas—it would be exquisite.

The group of artists working at Artspace were a motley crew, as artists tend to be. They were everybody from everywhere, atheists and Anglicans, lesbians and gays, health-food nuts and sports fans, portrait painters and abstractionists. Even the ACLU came around sniffing for a cause. It was a very creative group of weavers, sculptors, glass blowers, pulled print people, and painters. For me, art had always been painting. It was a real education to see the varieties in which the artistic impulse could be expressed.

The most interesting series of events that transpired while we were in Raleigh all centered around the painting of the old capitol building...

I was down on the grounds of the old capitol building one day, sketching, wondering how I could capture the attention of the people who worked there. Actually, the "sketch" was a carefully designed piece of work drawn on vellum with charcoal. I was checking the placement of details, since it would need to be architecturally correct.

Practicing a bit of deceit, I decided to go in to the information desk and asked if I could sharpen my pencil.

Just as I was standing there, someone came up behind me and said, "What have we here? That's a different view of the capitol. I'd like to see it when you finish it. Will it be a black and white sketch?

"No, an oil painting."

"Ah hah!"

He gave me his name and phone number on a card. Mr. Townsend, the manager of the capitol building.

Almost two months later, when the piece was nearly finished, I invited him to my studio for a look. He was fascinated.

"I'll have to get my capitol foundation committee to take a look at this," he said. "We've been thinking of a fundraiser for the old capitol. We could use this as a print...posters, T-shirts, note cards... I can see many uses for this design as a fundraiser."

I had to have people come and take a look. A procession of people came up to my little crow's nest studio at Artspace.

Then I got a taste of Raleigh politics. There was a meeting at which it would be decided. I was supposed to watch for a certain signal from someone to tell if I was "on," or if I should silently leave and forget it.

A big woman in a purple pantsuit called the project an 'unsubstantiated business loan.'

A shaker and mover in the North Carolina state government said if they wanted to take on the project he would see to the funding.

And that was the way it happened.

He 'borrowed' the Duke mansion in Charlotte for an evening and invited all his big money friends for a party. The painting would be on display and a dinner served. Contributions would be made. If the amount was enough to cover an edition of this painting as a fine art print, we would go ahead. All sales would go for the renovation and preservation of the historic capitol.

That was some evening. Gordon had taken me to the Belks in Raleigh and I bought a smashing black outfit. I had a big head of curly hair, and heels, and I was as nervous as a cat.

The painting was set up on an easel in the living room of the Duke mansion. One whole side of the room was glass, and the drapes were open. Just at six o'clock, when the group was to come through, the painting was in the bright sunlight. It was blasted with light and the colors were thrown off. Not good.

I did not dare to mention pulling the huge drapes.

There was a large tall man standing beside me, chatting.

"Would you do me a favor?" I asked desperately.

"Surely," he smiled.

"Would you stand right here so your shadow falls on the painting and shade it while the people go through?"

"I'd be happy to."

The man was as good as his word. He stood, perfectly shading the artwork from the glare of the sun, until the last person had gone through the line. The colors looked deep and jewel-toned.

I held out my hand to him and smiled.

"I'm sorry," I said. "I was so worried I didn't even ask your name."

"I'm John Belk," he said.

My jaw dropped.

"THE John Belk?" I asked.

"I guess so," he laughed. "I've been asked to do a lot of things before, but never to shade a painting with my body!"

We laughed. His family had the biggest chain of department stores in the whole South.

They collected more money than they needed that night.

The prints would be made. And on the 4th of July that summer, they held a SPIRIT OF THE CAPITOL day. People were lined up around the block to get signed posters and prints.

I was so impressed I ended up giving the original painting to the State of North Carolina, and it still hangs behind the information desk in the capitol, right where it started. At Christmas, when the Christmas tree is set up in that spot, it hangs in the governor's office.

I was satisfied.

I had "done" Raleigh.

By that Christmas there was a battle over whether Artspace should put up a donated forty-foot Christmas tree or not. The Jewish artists (who were they? I never could tell) said it was an infringement on their rights to put up a Christmas tree in a public gallery.

I had just come from ten years in a country where we were not allowed to celebrate Christmas. This was America where we were supposed to respect each other's rights. This was too much.

I told Gordon about it.

"Have you had enough of big city life?" he asked, giving me that grin.

I looked at him.

"Meaning what?"

"Would you like to go back up to the mountains where they grow the trees, and build another cabin further on down the same creek?"

I thought about it for a very short time, maybe ten seconds.

"You know," I said, "I think I would."

In 1994 we moved back to West Jefferson. The town had not changed much, but we had. Having weighed the options, we decided that we wanted to live in the mountains we loved…and we would not expect the mountain community to appreciate us. We would appreciate them!

We moved into cabin number two on the same creek. It had new log construction (no more wasps and beetles), a shake roof, fireplace, and a front porch that ran all along the creek about ten feet from the stream. There were a minimum of rooms, including a studio, and an enormous amount of charm. It had open kitchen shelves showing the dishes, and a red, half-circle pendant light over the table. Everything was small, but convenient.

We took another look at the downtown of West Jefferson;

The art center!

How had we missed that before?

An old stone building under a huge tree had been the library, now it was the Ashe County Art Center. Artists from all over the county belonged. Art shows were held there, changing every six weeks.

We joined. Count us in.

The library. How had we missed that?

We got library cards.

And a post office box.

And the church.

The grey stone church with the elegant arches and the intelligent pastor- by the name of Kermit. It just happened to be Presbyterian, and since

282

the Presbyterians seemed to have followed us all the days of our life, we joined.

The choir—great music!

I joined.

We joined and joined until we were well laced through the structures of the town. They could not move without bumping into us.

We were in!

There was a small music shop downtown called "The Luthery," with a young family of parents and five beautiful children.

I did a series of small portraits with each of the children playing an antique Celtic instrument. They hung in the art center.

But the biggest tie-in to the town came when I decided to take on the very beast that had bitten me and made us leave: Christmas in July.

I would do a Persian art piece of the festival and see what happened.

We went downtown and I sketched the old storefronts. Then when the festival itself happened that summer, I took dozens of photos—people in their stalls, tents, musical groups, the balloon seller, the ice cream shop—the whole ambience of the show, and arranged it into an authentic Persian art piece.

Word got out.

The newspaper came and photographed it while I was working. A frame shop owner came and looked. The Chamber of Commerce had to check it out. By the time there was a full page article in the *Jefferson Post*, the chamber of commerce and the frame shop all wanted a stake in the printing, so we shared the cost three ways, dividing the posters and numbered prints. The chamber wanted mostly posters. There was a heated battle about who released them as ads first. One of the partners threatened to sue me because the other party snuck their ad in first.

In short… We were connected!

At Christmas in July they sold scores of posters, and I got the 'job' of designing the festival T-shirts (for the next five years—always for free). They made the profit, but I got the fun of being vitally involved.

By 1995, we had outgrown cabin number two on the creek, and Gordon was designing cabin number three, a truly large place. It was farther on down the same stream with plenty of painting space and storage for prints.

From the front, lighted up at night, it looked like a hotel. The steps reached all the way from the creek to the lower deck, then led to a big front porch that wrapped all around the front and side of the house—with a porch swing. Inside, a true great room had an arched fireplace at one end, a roomy kitchen with a huge mahogany bar and pendant lights, a dining room, and a stairway leading up to the balcony off the bedrooms. The ceiling of the great room rose up two stories to the beamed roof, and the three bedrooms and two baths came off the balcony. It was truly a splendid design, and everyone loved it.

Chris called from Chapel Hill. He was finishing up his work there and then would be moving to Socorro, New Mexico, to do his practical work at the VLA where the giant disks were pointed at the sky, taking in readings from space.

And they were going to have a baby!

A star would be born!

Claire was actually born in New Mexico, at the same Presbyterian hospital where Marita and Michael had made their twin entrance thirty-seven years before. What an improbable coincidence!

We flew out to see the new baby—a solemn little big-eyed owl like her father had been, and so very beautiful

They seemed happy, but Julia was under enormous stress. Was the baby too much?

Chris was doing brilliantly, but we left feeling a little worried…

The year 1996 rolled around.

What could be more typical of Ashe County and the whole mountain landscape than the Christmas tree farms!? I would do a big tree painting, using two different farms so no one would claim exclusive ownership.

Rick Herman lived across from us. He had a crew of tree harvesters—Mexicans. They used tree bailers. Rick would help us get pictures.

I was busy painting the tree farm when Linda Burchette came out to see me. She was the main reporter for the *Jefferson Post*.

The big article, and the pictures, started a landslide of interest. I was painting what truly touched the life of Ashe County, and they responded—

Persian or not, they loved it, because it was about them.

The print business picked up, but we had basically nowhere to sell except in frame shops here and there.

One day we were walking around downtown West Jefferson, wishing we were busier. Many shops were empty. Some were wonderful, two-story brick and steel structures with space above for an apartment.

"What would you think," Gordon asked that day, "of buying a building down here and having our own gallery with an apartment upstairs?"

I didn't know. I loved the cabin. The kids all loved the cabin. But...

"It's a good idea, "I agreed, "but not just yet. We need to have more to sell than just a few prints. We would need a lot of originals to get started as a real gallery."

"Keep working," he grinned, "and think about it."

We had lived so many places, and knew so many people, but there were certain friends we never forgot. One of these was Ruth McDowell, a wonderful woman in Pawling, New York, who was from New York City, and lived in an apple orchard outside Pawling, up on Quaker Hill. She loved apples, cats, and people, in that order.

We kept in touch with her and had written to her on one of the Mountain/Persian cards we had made in connection with the prints. She, in turn, took the card to a good friend of hers from the city, Paul Rudin, who had at one time been the head of the American Sculptors Association, and in his spare time had taught Persian art at the Metropolitan Museum in New York City. When he saw the card I had made from the Buck Mountain Road painting, he wanted to meet me.

We drove to Pawling that summer to stay with Ruth, and she took us to see Paul Rudin, who was a wonderful old man with shinning blue eyes.

He talked to me about Persian art, and how excited he was that I was developing an American art based on Persian principles.

"I was a young art student in New York City in the thirties," he told us, "and a man came to my door selling a book of Persian art—the works of Nizami—and those splendid illustrations. I didn't even have enough money to buy food to eat, but I bought that book from him, and it became the textbook I used in later years to teach Persian art at the Metropolitan."

"Do you still have that book?" I asked.

"I do," he motioned to his wife. "Can you show it to her?"

I took the book with reverence, paging through the illustrations. I had seen these same paintings in the libraries in Saudi Arabia.

"I used to fall asleep looking at these every night," I said, telling him how I had learned to understand them.

"This is so important," he said, laying his hand on my head as I sat beside his chair. "I want you to promise me never to stop doing what you are doing. We have needed an American artist to understand these and incorporate them into our Western art—promise me."

I promised, feeling as if he had blessed me, or knighted me...

Paul Rudin was not well, and the next year I got a letter from his wife saying that he had died.

I told her what a wonderful influence he'd had on me, and asked her if there were any way I could see his book again or, if possible, if I could buy it, unless he had left it to someone...

"You can't buy it," she said, "but he did leave it to someone. He left it to you."

I started to cry. I really didn't even know the man, but he had reached out to me on such a deep level that I felt we were related.

I received the precious book in the mail a few weeks later.

I put it on my shelf, a treasure and a legacy.

Gordon was helpful with the art in any way that I needed him, but I began to feel that he needed a deep interest of his own. He had been forced to retire at 60, because of Aramco policy, but he still had so much energy, and so much talent.

Houses—the man loved houses. He loved designing them, buying the materials to build them, and getting a crew of men together to construct them. He was not a carpenter—never could drive a nail straight, but he loved the process, the joy of seeing a pile of lumber grow into a structure, the grand sweep of light across a room. He loved this like I loved to paint.

And I never objected. If I could paint, I never minded where we lived. We were a good pair .It was fortunate that we had married each other. We would probably have driven anybody else nuts.

There was one more piece of property along the same creek, and Gordon began to negotiate for it—not large, not expensive, but with a good mountain view.

We would build a small 'guest house,' on the property, and...

"And what?"

"I've been thinking," Gordon said, "about that idea of a gallery downtown."

"Yes?"

"If we found a really structurally sound building on Jefferson Avenue, we could live in the guest house while we renovate the shop."

"Hey, wait a minute. We don't even have the guest house yet!"

"Okay, so this is the order. Sell this big cabin to free up the money. When we have the guest house built, move into it temporarily while we renovate the building downtown."

"But we don't even have a building downtown yet!"

"Let's go looking."

We walked the length of Jefferson Avenue, the street that ran through the town like a backbone. Some things were poorly constructed, saggy wood structures that were not worth renovating. But right in the heart of town, clustered around Jefferson and Main, there seemed to be some consistency in the buildings. They were all constructed of steel beams and solid brick masonry. Each was 25 feet wide (or multiples of 25) and 75 feet deep. Most had a full second story.

There was a 'For Sale' sign in the window of one of these, temporarily being used as an ice cream shop. The upstairs rooms were being rented.

We went in and sat at one of the small tables, and ordered a dish of ice cream. The place was manned by a couple of teenagers. The manager was not there.

The floor was covered with black and white plastic tiles. Was there old wood underneath? The place had possibilities. It still had the original storefront.

We took the realtor's number from the window and called her.

The big cabin sold fairly quickly.

The guest house was completed. We moved in and the big commercial piece of property was under contract. We could own the whole structure for fifty thousand dollars. At one time in our lives (like when we bought the boat), fifty thousand dollars had seemed impossible, but now it was almost chump change. We had learned how to take a small amount of money, invest, leverage one property against another, and be more agile in the world of (very small) finance.

We took over the Jefferson Avenue building in early 1998, for a huge renovation. The renovation would cost more than twice as much as the building itself.

First the upstairs. Rooms full of trash, rats nests, pigeon droppings (the skylight was broken and birds were nesting in the trash). It needed a complete shoveling out. We hired a big dumpster in the alley behind the shop and a crew of men to completely empty the place. Partitions, out. Windows, out. Tear out the ceiling, everything except the beautiful wooden floors.

Jeff Grubb, a fellow who had worked with us on other projects, worked on the upstairs all winter and into the spring. It turned into a stunning, three-bedroom, two-bath apartment with a sky-lighted great room, a fireplace, big bar kitchen with the signature pendant lights, and the original wood floor. It was a city loft-apartment, seventy-five feet deep, and a visual joy. No one could believe the transformation.

Then we tore into the downstairs. People were curious. They peered into the "black hole" where we were prying plastic tiles off the floor with a straight-edged hoe and a blow torch.

"What you doing in there?"

"We're making a gallery!"

"A gallery in this town? There's no galleries in this town."

"Of course. That's why we're making one!"

"Well, good luck," several people said, as though we'd need it.

But we had done much crazier things. We had lived on a boat in a typhoon shelter, and camped in the Rub-al-Khali. Starting the first gallery on the main street of a mountain town did not seem dangerous at all.

While the renovation was going on, I was steadily painting. We needed a whole new show of authentic Persian art when the new gallery opened. The prints would not be enough. We needed originals to validate the stock.

The series, six in all, were not large, but they were rich. Painted with tiny brushes, designed to be authentic, surrounded by gold. They were jewel colors, using all the magic of Persian poetry illustrations to depict familiar scenes and activities in the Blue Ridge Mountains.

On December 5, 1998, De Pree Studio and Gallery opened on Jefferson Avenue, West Jefferson, North Carolina. It was a great day for us, and for the town. The curiosity had been building up, and we had a grand opening with food and drink, and a full display of prints and originals. A sound system played classical music, and a corner water fountain bubbled into a pool. The ceiling track lights spotted on the art and made each piece something important.

Ashe County, composed of its original families and many 'transplants' from all over the U.S., turned out in force.

We were off and running.

De Pree Studio and Gallery became the center of our lives.

At first there was much speculation on the street about whether a gallery could make it in West Jefferson. But there are few secrets in a small town, and the man who had refused to let us show our work in the Christmas in July show was now a vice president of the bank. He knew we were doing fine and came in to sheepishly apologize.

The area was full of artists. The mountains seemed to draw them as it had drawn us. The countryside was dotted with little studios on side roads. These were the people who belonged to the arts council.

One by one, artists came and talked to us.

"How did you do it? they asked. "Did you get a government grant?"

"Heck no," I joked. "You'd die while you waited. Just do it! Buy, beg, borrow or steal money to get started, and just do it!"

Real estate prices began to go up.

There was new excitement in the town.

In three years, thirteen galleries opened on the street.

It was becoming an "art destination."

Across the street from our gallery, a frame shop opened. The Dancing Pig was run by Barbara Farmer and her husband Joe. They became the extension of our gallery, or we of theirs. They framed everything for us, and we practically wore a path across the street. It was a perfect arrangement.

Barbara was actually a nurse, and a cancer survivor, and an excellent photographer. We went on photo shoots together, catching fall, winter and spring shots to be designed into paintings.

They came over every work morning to have coffee—our gallery was set up with a kitchen and we kept fresh coffee all day for customers. The water fountain, the music, the strong green plants, the coffee, it was all there under the spotlights.

The six Persians were made into prints, framed, on the wall, in the bins. We did a series of music boxes with a tile on top of the six Persian illustrations. The Christmas tree painting became prints, and a local weaving company made it into colorful throws.

The economy was thriving, and so were we. The dreaded millennium came and went, and we went out dancing until midnight. The town was growing and prospering, and more shops opened. Real estate prices had doubled and then tripled, and we were still multiplying.

We had 29 Persian designs in print. We began to print them on canvas.

Then suddenly, the huge lithograph presses across the country started to slow down. The United States was awash in paper prints, and they were losing value. Digital printing was taking over. Artists no longer needed to pay five thousand at once and be stuck with huge storage problems. One could start with digital photography and order as many pieces as required at a time, at a much higher cost per piece.

The big presses slowed to a whisper and then a halt. They closed. Everywhere.

A new product called a Giclee (French for ink jet) took over.

We began to produce giclees. (gi-klays)

Somewhere along the line, we had 65 designs in print. We were selling so many originals I never even recorded the names of people who bought them. Not smart.

We were successful, in a very small puddle. But who ever heard of West Jefferson?

During this time, Gordon built a little cabin out in the Todd area, just a get-away to get out of town when we needed some fresh air. The downtown was getting more prosperous, but it was still hanging onto some of the old customs, like cruising.

On the main drag of town, every Saturday night, the cruisers came out in force, just like an episode out of *Happy Days*. Horns honking, kids driving up and down the street, all the intrigue of a mating ritual on wheels. At first we were amused by the whole process, but when it went on until two in the morning, or someone was going at it in the alley under our bedroom window, we became a bit less amused. But no one wanted to outlaw it, even though some drugs and underage prostitution began to be a part of the mix. It was just like in Pawling. Everyone did it.

"Lordy, I met my husband cruising," was a common sentiment. "It's just kids."

We loved our chosen town, but we had no illusions it was heaven on earth.

While I kept busy in the gallery, and Gordon kept the books and paid the taxes, his mind (as ever) was searching for land and building ideas.

One day he came in with a building book of novel home ideas. It was a series of boxes stacked on top of each other. Three stories would be three 30 x 30 ft. cubes, stacked, with a long stairway connecting them. At the rear there would be three wide balconies, one on each level, to overlook something grand.

"Interesting, " I said, "but where would you build it?"

He had the answer.

"Out in the Glendale Springs area there's a woman with thirteen acres to sell," he said. "I went out to look the other day. It looks like a beautiful piece of land, mostly wooded, with big trees and a grand view of the mountains."

The grand view. Have boxes with balcony, need a grand view to justify all those balconies.

I went out to look, carefully stepping over fallen logs and watching out for snakes. It was a beautiful piece of property—maybe later.

West Jefferson was hopping, catching its second wind. Reporters came from other areas to see what our 'secret' was. Small towns were dying all over the South—ours was coming back to life. What were we doing?

The answer was simple. The artists were doing it. With the new spirit downtown, new restaurants were moving in. Real estate was rising. With the restaurants came a push for wine licenses—the county, a real source of moonshine liquor since prohibition, was officially dry. People began to crusade for wine. The arts council, under the leadership of Jane Lonon, was pulling us all together. The second Friday every month during the warm weather was designated Gallery Crawl night.

In 2003, the chamber of commerce met in a new restaurant on Jefferson Avenue. Someone called the gallery that afternoon and asked me if we planned to attend. I thanked them for reminding me, as I had forgotten. Life was so busy.

We went that night, and I was listening rather sleepily to the speaker, when suddenly I realized our name, De Pree, were being called.

De Pree Studio and Gallery was being given the Ashe County Small Business of the Year award. There was a little brown wooden plaque with a brass plate: 2003-De Pree.

We had done it.

We were a part of the community.

This town, this little American town, had become ours, because we had become theirs. It was not exactly as quiet as I had dreamed about, and the kids were all too old to park their bikes in our driveway, but we loved this town, and it was finally loving us back.

We had started the gallery when I was 65 (like my friend Colonel Sanders starting his Kentucky Fried Chicken business), and thought nothing of it. But now I was turning 70 and Gordon was 73. We were working 54 hours, six days a week. I was completely exhausted. I began to get chest pains.

I went to Duke Hospital for a checkup, stress test, CAT scan, the works. After all the tests a doctor talked to me.

"Physically, you have the heart of an athlete," he said, "but are you under a lot of stress?"

"I am."

"What are you going to do about it?"

I thought for a moment.

"Sell my business," I decided.

"Stress can kill you," he warned me.

I had never put it in words before, but I knew the gallery had to pass on to someone else…in the near future. Perhaps we had done our part by getting the street off to a new start.

We sold the Todd cabin to a group of six lawyers from Raleigh, totally decorated, because they knew six lawyers' wives could never agree on how to decorate it. So that freed up funds for the 13 acres. Gordon tried to get the owner of the land down ten thousand, but she was so offended she took it off the market. When he went back to negotiate, she had raised the price ten thousand. He paid it.

These mountain women were tough.

Gordon and a crew of men built "The Villa," the house of the thirty-foot squares. It was plain-looking from the front, but fit in beautifully with the woods around it. The first floor was see-through from the front to the back, looking out of the first balcony into the mountains. The second floor was the great room, kitchen and a fireplace, again with the big back balcony. The third was the master suite and guest quarters. All the back walls were solid glass with eight-foot sliding doors leading out onto the balconies with glorious views of the mountains for miles.

We were living in that house when we sold the gallery.

I was working one day in the little painting nook off the main gallery when a middle-aged man came in. He looked around.

"Nice place you have here."

"Thank you."

"You do a good business?"

"We sure do…"

"Would you sell it?"

We had not advertised. I would not put a 'for sale' sign in the window. It seemed embarrassing, and I was afraid it would hurt the business.

I took a deep breath, my heart starting to pound. Steady now.

"I might…if the price is right."

He laughed.

"Yeah, anything's for sale if the price is right, right?"

I tried to ignore the way he said it.

He wanted to see our books, our sales records. We gave a price. We negotiated. He bought it, with the whole print business. I would keep the originals. He asked me to sign a statement that I would not start a similar business on the same street.

Horace and his wife, Kathy, took over the gallery, and it was finished for us. It all happened so fast.

They moved into the apartment.

The signs would be changed to Flowers Gallery.

The people would change, but the gallery would go on. All the prints we had so carefully made would still be available to the people of Ashe County.

I was relieved.

I needed a year off.

We had found the town of our dreams, but not the perfect house. We kept trying. What, really, did we want? Did we intend to go on building house after house, building and selling? Gordon was enjoying the process. Like a master painter or symphony conductor, he reveled in the creation of each house, taking great pains with each detail, creating a thing of beauty, but he was just as happy to pass it on to someone else as to keep it. He was about creation, not possession.

But someday…would he find the one he wanted to keep?

I was painting. I did not really care. I, too, could love them and leave them, just as happy to fix up and decorate the next place. We always sold to friends, so we never made much money.

We took out a building loan against "The Villa" and began to build "The Lodge," an all-on-one floor house on the 13-acre property, closer to the road. The three-story place was great for people who did not mind climbing stairs, but if we were thinking long term, did we want to be living in a house with our bedroom on the third floor?

So, The Lodge was low and flat, four bedrooms, four baths, with the usual great room, fireplace and kitchen. This one had a dining room with a table for twelve, good for entertaining, and an extra place for sleeping down in the lower area. It was big enough for everyone to come home all at once and sleep under one roof. Maybe we should keep this one. It had a big front porch with a swing overlooking the fields, and a small oriental garden on the side entrance, and a huge studio where I could hang all the originals from the former gallery.

That house was the scene of many of my best paintings. Free from the daily work of waiting on customers and running a store, I bought large wonderful canvases. And based on the color vibrations and design elements of Persian art, I began to morph into post-modern contemporary art, Matisse-like canvases that were the antithesis of the tiny careful Persian paintings, yet drawing knowledge of design from them.

It was a glorious year.

I donated two large canvases to the new Ashe County Courthouse rotunda, and began to dream of doing a large piece of art for the Presbyterian Church, a twelve-foot mural that looked like a stained glass window up over the altar of the church. It began to haunt me…

In the year 2005 we celebrated our fiftieth wedding anniversary. We had been running around the world together for fifty years…and we finally had a house big enough for all the family to come and share the occasion with us.

Marita organized it. We were to do absolutely nothing. They set up tables in the yard with outdoor torches. Mike would be the grill chef. Deidra was in charge of getting 1950's music. Chris and Julia would provide the beverages. Julia was a wine expert. At the last moment there was a knock on the door and two of my sisters from Kentucky, Maxine and Ruth, showed up. It was a great occasion!

Then, somehow, the party started going off track. Julia, who had been having trouble with drinking, got terribly dunk, making a scene. It was a crisis moment... the culmination of years of hurt and disappointment.

Six months later they were divorced. We were all relieved. If a marriage was destructive, it should be ended. I had seen my mother suffer for twenty-five years in a terrible marriage, and would never recommend it. Chris had tried his best for sixteen years, and it was going from bad to worse. He deserved better. He had two beautiful daughters to raise, Claire and Madeleine, and they deserved better.

Mike's marriage of twenty years had also ended, and he was happily remarried to Loren, a doctor, whose three children Noah, Abby and Carlyn were a welcome addition. Our family stuck together, supporting each other in doing what we needed to do in order to survive.

We were not worried about appearances. We were not perfect. We were a part of present-day America where alcoholism and gender identity were realities. We would go on. Marriage was only sacred when everyone was honest.

Living in Glendale Springs we became aware of Joannie Bell. She and her husband, Michael, had owned and operated a gift shop just off the Blue Ridge Parkway for many years, starting right after college. She was from the D.C. area, and he from California. They had met in college. He was a professional musician, and Joannie was an excellent painter.

Joannie and I came to know each other at the arts council, serving together on the gallery committee.

After a year of working at home, I began to wonder if there was some less stressful way to work downtown—maybe share a gallery with one other artist, and in a rental situation, without the duties of ownership.

We began to look.

Downtown, a 25x75 foot florist shop had just closed. It had a 'for rent' sign in the window. It was right on the corner of the two principal streets, Jefferson and Main. Location...location...

Joanie and I began talking. Would she like to form a partnership with me, sharing equal costs and time in a rented gallery?

She decided she would. Joannie had a degree in fine art from Oberlin, but had not painted in oils for years.

We called the realtor and rented the space.

It needed total renovation. Even though we did not own it, we decided to get it in shape to become a professional looking gallery. We hired Jeff Grub, the fellow who had built so many of our houses, to tear out all the unnecessary walls, and shape it into a gallery. It would have umbered–white walls, blacked out ceiling, track lighting. The big purple carpet had to go, and two by four stringers were nailed into the cement slab. Over these, eleven-inch shelving boards were nailed and finished. As a crowning touch, a classical pillared dais was built in the middle of the long space, dividing it and making a focal point. And of course, there would be music.

The year 2005 saw the opening of the Originals Only Gallery, with Bell and De Pree as the artists. Bracketed by the now blooming "Arts District" of West Jefferson, we were a vital operation.

In a way, I missed having the prints, but it was a good clean professional feeling to have only originals in the gallery. The prints were still being sold down the street.

The "transplant" segment of Ashe County was growing. Word was spreading about this little mountain town and the surrounding area, about the music, and drama, and art. The demographics were changing, and a more sophisticated clientele was being established, people who had been everywhere and had a wider knowledge of world art.

But there were still a lot of the old mountain die-hards who wondered what all the fuss was about.

We had just finished the renovation and had a substantial show hanging on the walls. I had brought all the new large canvases from the lodge. They were spaced and lighted and titled...with prices.

A man walked in one morning and looked at the polished wood floor, the Persian carpets, and the paintings under the lights.

"Nice place you got here," he said. "What you-all going to sell?"

"This is it," I told him.

He looked around. He couldn't see anything. He walked out.

But many people came and looked...and bought.

It was good.

I kept thinking about the painting at the church. I knew it would be a huge undertaking, and that it would be pro bono. But what could the subject possibly be? Church-like paintings of Old testament characters or religious scenes of New Testament themes did not seem exactly right, yet it would need to be something deeply spiritual, something, that if hung in the front of the church, would inspire worship at a visceral level.

Kermit Dancy, the "intelligent minister," had retired after many years, and we had an interim pastor. He taught a class, and somehow his presentation of the story of Jacob's Ladder, with angels ascending and descending, the dream of the scoundrel Jacob who tricked his father and was running away from a brother who wanted to kill him for cheating him—this story struck me at a gut level, so earthy. But how could it be translated into a painting that could inspire worship?

One night, asleep in the lodge, it came to me.

The children of the church.

They could be the angels on the ladder, from newborn babies to eighth graders. They would see themselves portrayed as angels.

I awoke and sat up, covering my eyes.

"Oh God, no!" I said out loud, "that would be too much work!"

Gordon turned over and looked at me.

"What did you say?" he asked.

"I was just dreaming," I told him.

But the image persisted.

Being, by this time, a proper Presbyterian, I presented the idea to the session. They would have to be in total agreement or I would not even begin. The artwork would be enough of a job. I did not want to have any political opposition.

The idea passed, with some reservations. What if they, at some future point, wanted to change the church, and would be inhibited by a large mural?

Good idea. I assured them that the mural would be painted on five-foot by six-foot canvases totally moveable. I did not paint walls.

Jackie and Gail Blackburn, long-standing members, offered to buy the canvases.

The parents of the church made appointments for their kids to come and be photographed.

Ray and Lynn Updike offered their professional photography equipment and services to capture the young models just as I needed them.

Gordon had a structure built to serve as a ladder.

The kids posed in white robes and carried candles.

The ladder did not work. All we saw were kids' backsides, and I was afraid the candles would catch someone's robe on fire, so we scrapped that. How could we make kids in choir robes look like angels?

I saw that too, when I was sleeping. A Persian design, done in squares...jewel-colored glass in the background. A cadence, with each child's praying hands in front of him or her, letting the robe sleeves drop and rise to form a wing pattern.

It worked. Ray photographed all the kids, one by one, with their eyes slightly raised, hands tented.

I began drawing the master design on the five by six-foot panels, too big for an easel, propped against the studio walls.

Measure.

Draw.

Design. Ink. Sponge. It took weeks before I was even ready to begin applying paint. The new pastor had come by then, and three of his children were in the painting.

"Now, remember," he told the parents, "Lenore is using your kids as models for this work, but they probably won't look just like you kids…"

I told him that he was nuts. I had twenty-six mothers and grandmothers hanging over my head, and if these angels did not look like their Johnny and Mary, I would be dead meat.

In fear and trembling, I drew the kids. The fourteen-year-olds as acolytes, lighting the candles at the bottom of the painting, were first.

They looked exactly like those kids.

Whew. Angel acolytes of Jake and Taylor.

And the babies at the top, just tumbling out of heaven's light, looked like Sammy and Sarah, and Nathan and Colin and Adeline…

Their mothers would know them anywhere.

Thank goodness. There was no wiggle room for pretense here.

These angels were real.

When the two paintings were fitted into a frame and hung, almost eight months later, both newspapers in town ran full-page, front-page, color shots of them, and every kid in the painting felt very important.

People sat in church, looking up at the angels, seeing their children. Someday these kids would grow up and come back to the church, and remember that they had been angels.

The day the painting was dedicated, our beloved music director Jim Anderson had the choir sing "Surely the presence of the Lord is in this place, and this is the gate of heaven…"

I stood with them, but I could hardly sing.

I could hardly breathe.

I could hear that waterfall, long ago, thundering over the rocks and plunging into the chasm below…

This was what we had sought.

This was what we had lived.

A faith where the Creative Power

Shone from the faces of children.

CHAPTER TWENTY

THERE WAS STILL ONE ELEMENT of our lives that we needed to deal with—our Dutch background. Were we simply going to be absorbed into this seductive mountain art community without a backward glance, or did we owe our ancestors one more visit to the land of our origins?

My mother was the last of our living parents. She had been in a Chicago rest home for quite a few years. We drove up to see her at least once every six months and called her once a week. She had reverted to her Dutch roots, never venturing into the dangerous South again. She was still Christian Reformed, which was Dutch reformed taken to the highest power.

During one of our visits to Chicago, we began to hear of the wonderful transformation that was taking place downtown. Old areas were being cleared. New high-rises were springing up. A whole new art area was growing up in a place called River North. I began to have ideas about Chicago that had nothing to do with ancestry... or did it? My grandfather, the mythical grandfather that I had never seen, had studied at the Art Institute of Chicago. We had dated in Chicago and had memories of cherished spots along the lake where we had explored our love. We were married in a church on Michigan Avenue that was now in an all African-American area: Roseland.

Chicago.

Chicago?

Just as we were getting so well established in the mountains ?

We were still mulling it over when a call came from the Rest Haven office. My mother was seriously ill and was going to the hospital. She called before she went.

"Hey, Mom! I hope you'll be feeling better. We're coming up to see you soon."

Her voice was clouded.

"I'm not getting better," she said darkly.

"Sure you will. You always pull through."

She said something like. "...ninety-two."

The nurse took the phone.

"Your mom doesn't feel like talking," she said.

"Well, okay. You give me a call if you think I should come."

The next morning the nurse called.

"How's Mom?" I asked.

"She's had a change of status."

"Meaning what?"

"She has passed away."

"What do you mean, passed away? You said you would call...!"

"Your mother...sorry. She's passed."

I put the phone down, tears blinding my eyes. She was so afraid of dying alone, and I had not been there. I hated that. I wished I could have been holding her hand. We could have had one final fight about heaven. I smiled ruefully through my tears.

Well, Mom, for whatever it's worth, that's where you are now. I hope it's what you expected.

The funeral service in Chicago was nothing I ever want to remember. The minister ignored my poor mom lying there in a casket made up to look like Zsa Zsa Gabor, and concentrated on the souls of the living, which were perilously in mortal danger of Hell. So ugly. I felt tears sliding down my face, not because she had died, but because her life had been so sad, so restricted and tormented by this kind of thinking...never free to simply be a child of God, because she had been born and had a right to be here as a child of the Universe. I knew she thought I had brought my children up wrong. I had taught them the power of love, not fear.

Love...the great creative power of love...

So long, Mom. If you meet my dad, tell him I forgive him, but he's probably in the wrong place...

All such symbols of our culture.

All such unknowns.

The mysteries of life and death...

While we were attending the funeral we saw Aunt Clara, a woman who had worked for my father in Kentucky caring for a dormitory of small boys.

She had escaped, to "follow the world, the flesh and the Devil," and marry a Dutchman from Chicago, and have nine children. The youngest of those children, Carla, was at the funeral with her mother.

We asked her about the amazing changes in Downtown Chicago.

"Hey," she said, "we live right downtown. If you ever want to come and take a look around, you can stay with us and do some exploring."

All of our kids had attended the funeral.

We went out afterward and had a Chinese meal to heal our souls.

A few months later we were back in Chicago staying with Carla. On her way to work, she let us off at the northern-most tip of Michigan Avenue downtown.

We walked along the famous street, hand-in-hand like two star-struck lovers, fifty years later, and were blown away by it. The stores of the Magic Mile, the beautiful gardens on the median, the soaring skyscrapers, the galleries, the Chicago River, the Art Institute—so much beauty. The lake and the beach...

"My God, where have we been all our lives?" I said to Gordon over the noise of the traffic.

He squeezed my hand, remembering.

Marshall Fields had now become Macys.

Carsons...I bought my wedding nightgown there.

The elevated trains. The familiar clink of them.

The parks, so magnificent and green.

McCormick Square...people eating outdoors and enjoying life to the fullest.

The *Chicago Daily Tribune*... This was where I came from. This was full circle.

And then the slow, insidious and completely crazy idea...

Did we want to live here?

All the way back to North Carolina we talked about it. Were we fully committed to life in the mountains, or should we sell everything, come to Chicago, and find a place downtown...and consider that the logical end to our journey? Was this possibly the place we had been waiting to return to all our lives?

The people in West Jefferson could not believe we were thinking about leaving. We had burrowed deep into the heart of the town. They almost felt betrayed.

Deidra had been on the internet, looking over the galleries in River North. She was excited about the possibilities.

"Hey, Mom, if you and Dad move to Chicago, Rob and I might do the same thing. Rob is working for Oracle, and could telecommute. We could find a place and be there when you come. We'd have a blast!"

Did that turn the tide, or was I dreaming of hitting the Chicago Art market, maybe getting some national recognition ? Would it be possible to have an exhibit in one of the big galleries on Michigan Avenue? Should I look into studying at the Art Institute?

Whatever caused it, we found ourselves caught up in the excitement of going to Chicago.

The people at the church were stunned. They had finally taken us into their hearts and now we were leaving.

"You'll be back, won't you?" they asked.

But we did not know. We would go to Chicago with an open mind, ready to stay there if it worked out. We wanted to be unencumbered by property. We wanted to be free to buy something in Chicago.

We sold the lodge and moved temporarily into a smaller cabin Gordon had built. He had built a total of four houses on the thirteen acres. It was named, aptly, De Pree Circle.

We sold them all, and all the furniture, only keeping our treasures.

The day we drove to Chicago, to see property on Michigan Avenue that we had viewed on-line, all I could think of was Burl Ives singing about the rooster who;

went to the city of his own choice,
to cultivate his tenor voice…
 His voice was good, they all agreed,
for advertising chicken feed.

It was not a very pleasant thought, and I pushed it down.

Then I felt like Jonah running away from Nineveh and getting swallowed by the great whale, although that didn't exactly compute. I wasn't running away from Nineveh—I was running toward it, full force. I wanted what I was doing in art to be discovered and recognized. I wanted to carry out the promise to Paul Rudin and take the ideas forward. I did not care that I was seventy-three years old and unknown in a fiercely competitive market. I was wonder woman, and able to do whatever I set out to do. I was strong and healthy, and could easily pass for twenty years younger if I kept my mouth shut…of course, that might be my problem. I'd probably be bragging about my age and shoot myself in the foot.

We contacted the real estate agent Carla had suggested, and looked at the property, the one we had seen on line on Michigan Avenue and 16th Street. It struck us as right.

We signed the contract in a Jewish deli on State Street.

A month later we were there. The place had been repainted in our absence. The truck came from North Carolina and we moved in.

This was easy. Our rugs and colorful paintings looked great in the apartment. Our books. The bookshelves we had made, painted black. We went to Room and Board and bought black leather sofas, spare and lean and contemporary, a big reconstituted quartz white table and black leather chairs, a buffet, and a desk. We had the lights changed to be like our other houses—the gallery look. We had the realtor's dream of granite counter-tops, stainless steel appliances, and a fireplace. It looked superb. We felt like we had lived in Chicago all our lives. We put our big golden Chinese screen up over the fireplace and it shone like the second coming. It had never looked so beautiful.

We joined the Art Institute, the Chicago Library, and the 4th Street Presbyterian Church on Michigan Avenue. We were Chicagoans…and to top it off, De and Rob came to join us. They could come over for dinner, or meet us at Starbucks for a cup of coffee.

I started photographing scenes. Streets, restaurants, people on the beach, people eating, skating, the architecture—all the glory of busy city life. I painted all morning, every morning, and explored all afternoon, walking a minimum of five miles a day. I got in shape.

Gordon took a job in Chinatown teaching ESL, just a few blocks from where we lived. Renewing his Chinese.

This was great.

Then I began hitting the galleries. I was appalled at what I saw: a great conservative backlog of worship for European art, mostly of the dead and long dead artists. On the other hand, great globs of paintings signifying nothing. Displays of old shoes and chicken wire. Paintings to match people's ancestral furniture. There was no middle ground, the Post-modern contemporary art that had stirred me. Matisse had been burned in effigy outside the Art Institute years ago, and the ashes still hung in the air.

I inquired at the Art Institute what they had in the way of Persian poetry art, and they had never heard of it. They had nothing. But I persisted. The biggest gallery on Michigan Avenue liked my work, and promised me a show, but the economy was beginning to slide. The back room was stacked with paintings promised a show. I would have to wait my turn. They had not been selling well. The economy…

And then we discovered that, in our usual haste, we had not been aware of Chicago's geography, and had bought about four blocks too far south. Those last four blocks made it dangerous to walk home at night.

So we put it back on the market and it sold quickly, by the same person who had found it for us.

We discovered a place right next to the Field Museum and bought it straight from the owner over a glass of wine in a restaurant.

Carla, Aunt Clara's daughter who had become an investment broker, could not imagine how we could make decisions and carry them out so quickly, and apparently without losing our shirt. She had lived in the same house for years, and could not believe how we wheeled and dealed.

The place by the museum was truly beautiful, overlooking Grant Park and close to the lake. All around us huge, new apartment high-rises were going up. We were in the heart of the excitement, near the stores, the lake, the Art Institute. As family members visited us, we proudly took them to the Art Institute on our family passes, acting like we owned the place.

Chris came to Chicago to visit us for Saint Patrick's Day and saw Chicago at its wildest. The river was colored green, and the busses were jammed. Claire and Madeline clung onto us, caught up in the crowds. I wondered how often we would see them, living in Chicago. It was terribly far to drive from Atlanta, where Chris worked, and airfare for three was expensive.

Chris wanted to see us and talk, because important events were taking place in his life. He had met Sheryl, a Georgia woman his age whose daughter Matilda was in the same school that Clare and Madeleine attended. Sheryl had been through a divorce as well, and the two of them had much in common. Most of all, they had come to care for each other deeply. For the first time in his life, Chris had found real love. They would be married in Atlanta, and combine their four children,, including her son Dylan, into one family.

We were so pleased, and could not wait to meet her.

There were problems living so far from family, but Chicago never ceased to seduce us.

Walking out of the Chicago Public Library one day with a full backpack of books, I heard an electrifying sound, ocean waves of music flowing along the street.

"What is that?" I asked a stranger.

"It's the jazz festival down by the Marshall School of Law."

I almost ran toward the sound. Rich harmony, wonderful rhythm— Chicago Jazz. I listened and bought a handful of CDs...and became a total addict.

When Marita and Pete visited us, we took them to the House of Blues on the Chicago River, with tickets to the Sunday morning 'Praise the Lord and Pass the Biscuits' brunch. I wanted to hop on the platform and sing with them. The 4th Presbyterian Church had only professional musicians in the choir; I missed singing. The church in West Jefferson…well…you couldn't have everything.

I was painting some of the best art of my life. People were fascinated by it, but said it looked more like something you would see in New York. It was not Chicago art. It did not match their furniture. The places where it would have looked good had interior decorators whose idea of art ran to hammered aluminum and blue neon tubes.

It was too illustrative for some people, too interpretive for others.

One day an artist visited our apartment and told me not to be discouraged; he had tried to get into a Chicago gallery for forty years, and was still trying.

When he left, I closed the door very deliberately and firmly.

I realized that if I had to try for 40 years, I would be at least 115 years old.

That night I could not sleep. I wrestled with my dark angel until morning, and lost. I was in the wrong place at the wrong time in my life. I did not have the time or money to waste on Chicago, when there was a place like North Carolina where people loved us and appreciated what we did. I was being foolish.

And housing prices were in jeopardy. The economy was threatening to collapse. If we were lucky, we would get out without losing a lot of money.

We told De and Rob, who said that was fine. They would be heading back to San Francisco soon after we were leaving. It had been fun.

We e-mailed a place called Jefferson Landing, a housing community in Ashe County, North Carolina, and asked the sales office what they had available. We'd had enough of being out in the woods. Being in Chicago had sharpened our sense of design, and we had decided to come in out of the cold and be a little more civilized. Wandering through the Merchandise Mart in Chicago and seeing all the newest in designs, we had a little better sense of how we wanted the house of our dreams to look.

After eighteen months, in the summer of 2008, we packed up our goods in a moving truck and headed back to North Carolina. A place was waiting for us at Jefferson Landing, a gated community of about 250 homes. Just beyond Jefferson, NC, it was on the New River with wonderful walking trails, a clubhouse and a golf course. Neither of us were golfers, but we had learned to be avid walkers in Chicago.

We bought a condo and figured we would live in it until we got the lay of the land, and then we would build our own place. Not a house, this time, but a home.

Ashe County took us back. The first day we went back to our church we were welcomed like the prodigal son—with rejoicing. Of course there were a few elder brother types who thought we should pay for what we had done.

"Why did you leave?" they asked.

We told them we had some unfinished business up that way we needed to settle.

We rejoined almost everything we had un-joined, plus the Jefferson Landing Club. I found my old choir robe, number 10, on the rack downstairs, and had to beg to get it back again. Marlene, another alto, had been using it. Jane Lonon took us back into the arts council, and even asked if I would be interested in teaching Persian art in the new art school being started in Ashe County.

And, best of all, Joannie and Michael Bell asked if we would like to come back to Originals Only Gallery as partners again. We said yes, and took the gallery for three days a week. It was just enough.

Then one day when we were walking at Jefferson Landing, we took a path around the pool and stood on a charming oriental-looking white bridge. Below it a sparkling stream climbed over the rocks and fell into the pool. Mallard ducks floated in the water, graceful and free, and above it the mountain, the ever-present Jefferson Mountain, reflected in the water. Country cottages circled around the large pond...

Except for one spot by the bridge. It was empty. We walked over and looked at the lot. There were markers. It was for sale.

We bought it. We began to build, not another house, but a home.

The home we built is a house of the spirit. It is filled with morning light and joy. At its highest peak, the ceiling reaches up twenty-four feet with a Palladian window. All of the ceilings dance and rise and plunge, following the trusses. There is not a predictable ceiling in the place.

The warm white umber walls catch a rainbow of light. The floors are wood. Everything is black and white, accentuated with reds and greens, golds and rich blues, with large leafed architectural plants. It is a poem, with a Buddha head and a golden screen from China, rugs from the Middle East, and furniture from Chicago.

The art is big and bold—colorful country and city designs. The back is all glass, reaching out to the creek.

The kitchen has espresso cabinets and a long white bar with pendant lights the color of candles lighted.

Above the cabinets, two country dancers caper on either side of abstract Michigan Avenue tulips.

There are words in our kitchen carved out of wood, suspended and casting their own shadows.

Hope.

Joy.

Dream.

Believe.

And under them, a Chinese Kitchen God, painted by Mike, who still loves Hong Kong.

They all came here for Gordon's 80th and our 55th. We picked blackberries down by the river and baked pies.

Chris had remarried in 2007 to his little Georgia peach, Sheryl. It was a joy to watch them glowing in each other's light. Mike and Lauren seemed like they had always been together... so right. Marita and Pete had been married for over twenty five years, and Deidra and Rob were not far behind.

Now in 2013, three of our granddaughters have married- and their husbands are a part of our lives. We are a loving family who stick together and live bravely in an uncertain world.

Our house is not large in physical space. We have just enough room, nothing left over, and nothing crowded.

Three bedrooms. Two baths. A cozy great room with a fireplace, an entry with the golden Chinese screen, and a studio. There is a large open back deck facing the creek where we live happily in the summer, with a big red umbrella over the table signaling celebration.

Only 1,650 feet of pure joy.

After all these years and houses, after the long journey from who we were to who we have become, we have finally come to where we are.

We have come home.

And there is love.

CPSIA information can be obtained at www.ICGtesting.com
Printed in the USA
LVOW10s2058020913

350498LV00002B/4/P

9 781457 522